Harry Brett is a pseudonym for Henry Sutton, whose novels have been translated into many languages. He received the Arts Council Writers' Award in 2002 and has judged numerous literary prizes, including the John Llewellyn Rhys Prize and the Theakstons Old Peculier Crime Novel of the Year. He has been the literary editor of *Esquire* magazine and the books editor of the *Daily Mirror*. Currently he teaches Creative Writing at the University of East Anglia, where he is a senior lecturer and the director of the new Creative Writing MA in Crime Fiction. He lives in Norwich with his family.

You can discover more about the author at www.henrysutton.co.uk

Twitter @hesutton

RED HOT FRONT

Tatiana Goodwin has finally begun to piece her life back together after the events of the past year. Having taken over her late husband Rich's empire, Tatty has put together a massive deal to capitalise on his dodgy deeds — and hopefully extricate herself from a life of crime she'd been unwillingly drawn into. But following a suspicious fire in the firm's new HQ, and a number of unexplained deaths in the town, it soon becomes clear that there's more than one person who's after the Goodwin family assets. With her daughter in a rocky relationship and her teenage son Zach beginning to follow in the footsteps of his gangster father, everything is getting a little too close to home for Tatty's liking . . .

Books by Harry Brett
Published by Ulverscroft:

TIME TO WIN

HARRY BRETT

◆

RED HOT FRONT

Complete and Unabridged

CHARNWOOD
Leicester

First published in Great Britain in 2018 by
Corsair
An imprint of Little, Brown Book Group
London

First Charnwood Edition
published 2018
by arrangement with
Little, Brown Book Group
An Hachette UK Company
London

A catalogue record for this book is available
from the British Library.

ISBN 978–1–4448–3924–1

Published by
F. A. Thorpe (Publishing)
Anstey, Leicestershire
Set by Words & Graphics Ltd.
Anstey, Leicestershire
Printed and bound in Great Britain by
T. J. International Ltd., Padstow, Cornwall

This book is printed on acid-free paper

To Holly, Thomas and Stella

Wind was coming in waves. Not gusts. Up over the beach it pounded. Whining and rattling on through the rotten struts of the ravaged roller coaster. The second drop was the steepest, the beams looking like they'd knock your head off if you didn't duck.

Because the wind was a northeasterly it then slanted across acres of wasteland, where once stood a go-kart track, so he'd heard, and later an oil supply ship depot. Now razed, the contaminated ground was waiting for the super casino. It had been some wait already. Boom.

The wind was as wet and raw as the North Sea. June for you, in this part of the world. Picking up strength over land, it shot across South Beach Parade before funnelling through the potholed streets of boarded-up pubs, the odd, dismal line of small terraced houses and endless semi-industrial buildings. There were a few Victorian warehouses and smokehouses still standing, including his mother's — theirs.

'Forget it,' Zach said aloud, shaking his head in the storm, the storm of ages, not sure what that meant, what was happening to time. But there was no one to hear him anyway. No one was in sight. He scanned the road, the nearby buildings, the wind watering his eyes. Shadows creeping out from the dying night. 'Waster,' he shouted. He'd been left out on his tod, high and dry. 'High, high.' Not funny.

Even less of a joke was the fact that his car was at the other end of town — as if he'd have been able to drive. His head was buzzing. His stomach churning on empty.

Unclenching the fingers of his right hand, he reached into the front pocket of his jeans for his phone. He wanted not the time but the way out of here, even though part of his brain must have known exactly where he was. They were his streets, his history, how it was passed on from generation to generation. Nevertheless, his internal GPS was not as acute as it should have been. Bollocks. His eyes were too watery to read the screen.

He shifted across the street, took shelter against a tall, cold building. The brick was damp and flaky. He thought of wet chalk, his first school, pissing on his chair. Being dragged to the toilets in front of the whole class. But it wasn't chalk, it was brick, whatever brick was made of. Clay? Sand and clay? He could feel it rubbing onto his jacket. A car swept along South Beach Parade, the beam from its headlights illuminating the side street for a few seconds, making him realise how few streetlamps were working in this part of town. Were they searching for him? The bag of gear? The Candy Cane. He liked that riff, not that he'd come up with the name, yet another for roughly the same chemical compound. It was all in the marketing, the image.

Back in darkness he pushed off from the wall, braced himself for the wind. Wind like he'd never felt before. Hurricane force. He couldn't spend the rest of the night here. There had to be an all-night caff somewhere, for the supply vessel operators, the power station workers, the hookers. The hookers serving the seamen, and warehouse operators, the few leisure industry employees, the gangsters, all night, all day.

There was a twenty-four-hour caff, over on South Denes Road, a short way on from the old Goodwin Enterprises offices, he remembered. The town that never slept — his dad's lame line. It couldn't be far, just across the spit, which was made of sand, not chalk. Piss on sand and it washed away. Geography at school. Maybe he'd learned something, when he wasn't being dragged to the toilets.

He set off with his back to the wind, suddenly having more than a clue as to where he was. His head clearing with every step, his heartbeat calming. There were still not enough streetlamps. Few working security lights. Too much gear in his system. The dawn was struggling hard to make its mark.

His footsteps were being drowned out by the wind, but he was sure he could hear others. Someone gaining on him. His friends. Friends? Another big fucking joke. He'd kill them. He'd lost the Candy Cane, hundreds of tabs of MDMA, but he still had some bump. Bumpty bump. Boom, boom. They'd be circling, waiting to pounce. They were always up for it, man. Desperados. He knew how to control himself, that he had to keep his wits about him. Look who he was, master of these mean streets. It was a family thing, wasn't it, Master Goodwin? Yes, sir. Smack in the head.

He'd begun jogging, on the excuse of a pavement, beside a long chain-link fence. Chain-link fencing everywhere, like he was in a massive prison. He stepped up the pace. Running, it was a song he liked, but the tune wasn't coming. However, South Denes Road was opening up nicely ahead, and the further from the sea he went, the quieter the wind became. He could almost smell the river, the diesel, the decades of decay. That was another of his dead dad's phrases, *the decades of decay*, always said with a smirk.

Zach stopped by the corner of Suffling Road and South Denes Road. Glanced back towards the dark streets — some sort of barrier between him and the wild North Sea. He found he was reaching out, his hands held forward. An orange glow had appeared like magic. It was rising, flickering above the mass of buildings. The sun?

'The sun has got its hat on, it's coming out to play. Hip, hip hooray.' Was he at nursery school now? He couldn't remember whether he'd gone to nursery school, or not. His mum must have looked after him at some point, when he was young. His mum and an au pair, one of the endless. She'd never have been able to cope on her own — not then.

It wasn't the sun. He was looking back up Suffling Road, the rambling roofline. The orange glow was higher, and brighter, already. Was that a thickening cloud of smoke set against the first whispers of dawn?

Something was on fire. Zach smacked his head. Bingo, dingo. A warehouse. A smokehouse. The Smokehouse. Desperado.

1

'They could have told me earlier,' Tatty shouted into the ether. She was on Haven Bridge, the sun skimming the Yare below. The river was being whipped up into a flurry by the wind. Yet the sky couldn't have been brighter, her mood darker.

'The authorities round here?' Frank said, his voice coming through the car's sound system. 'On a Sunday?'

Zach had finally fixed the Bluetooth link-up for her after she'd been caught on the phone while driving for the second time in two months. The traffic cop, Yarmouth's one and only, let her off the first time, recognising her, though not the second time. He'd pay for that one day.

'You know the score,' Frank was saying.

'Don't give me that monkeys again. Where were they?'

'You don't know how much damage has been done. It might not be so bad. We'll need to get inside. There's a cordon. They're not letting anyone near for now. The roof might collapse, what's left of it — so they're saying.'

'Why did they call you first, Frank?' She was still stuck on the bridge, the lights taking a millennium. Everything taking a millennium today.

'You checked your phone?'

'I can't, I'm driving. Hands free.' She said it almost proudly, but it had always seemed such a stupid expression. Her hands weren't free, they were on the wheel. She wished they were round someone's neck.

'You didn't answer when I first rang at — what was it, six a.m.?' Frank said. 'Maybe you were asleep. Couldn't be woken. Happy as Larry in La La Land.'

'What're you talking about? Something like this? Course I'd get up.' Though she knew it was a strong possibility that she'd been out for the count — sleeping, not like Larry the lamb, but a baby. 'Who's there?' The lights changed, Tatty accelerated, hanging right, past what was Barclays and the Star Hotel, still boarded up. There were few other vehicles, no pedestrians. The quay was a slew of sparkling granite cobbles, though bare of a living thing.

'The fire service, en masse. Some uniform. No bigwigs that I can see. Took them a while to check the building was clear of people.'

'Of course it's clear of people. It's an office block, on a Sunday morning.'

'Even so.' He cleared his throat, or perhaps it was a gust of wind that she could hear. 'Tatty, you're not thinking straight. How do these things start?'

'Round here? Yeah — see your point,' she said, a new dawn dawning. 'I'm a couple of minutes away.' She ended the call by firmly pressing a button on the steering wheel. The very week they were to move offices. She couldn't believe it.

As South Quay turned into Southgates Road, and then swiftly into South Denes Road, Tatty thought of Nathan Taylor. Silly, needy, Nathan,

2

who'd nevertheless done a good job converting the old property first into a series of live/work spaces, which were always going to be more live than work — it was a council tax thing — then a state-of-the-art office complex. Not that Goodwin Enterprises had too many official employees. It was the statement that mattered, the fact that Tatty wanted a break from the past. Looks counted. Plus, she needed to spend some cash quick. Make it look like that anyway.

She swung across the road sharply, taking Suffling Road north. The sun was not creeping over the horizon but blasting straight at the windscreen, low and hard and with more than a hint that summer was around the corner, even here. She slowed well before Fenner Road, lowering the driver's window. She could smell the smoke, the ash, her ruined ambition, on the steady breeze.

Frank had said that he was parked up on the corner of South Beach Parade and Salmon Road, and that Salmon Road was blocked off. The Smokehouse stretched along Fenner Road to Salmon Road. It didn't appear that they'd blocked off Fenner Road, not this end.

It wasn't until she turned into the side street that she could see her building. The façade appeared intact, though squinting through the Merc's huge windscreen she discerned the soot around the upper windows, the glass gone from a number of frames, too. What she could see of the roof was not encouraging. Only yesterday there had been a fine, long, low-pitched roof with a row of stubby, wooden-slatted chimneys — the former smokehouse vents. Nathan was insistent that these should be restored, even if they were technically redundant. Like him, Tatty couldn't help thinking of her one-time lover.

The nearest chimney stacks were still there, but further away they were gone. The far end of the roof appeared to have collapsed. A mess of charred beams were poking up into the ridiculously blue sky, like the burnt bones of a giant animal, a dinosaur.

Sighing heavily, though determined not to feel her age, Tatty edged the car further down the narrow road. There were a couple of extended fire service ladders, but no one on them. The fire was out, that was clear. Her spirits quickly rose. Maybe the damage wasn't too severe. Hadn't Frank suggested as much? Maybe the fire service had got there in good time. A bit of roof to repair, no sweat.

Nathan's loft apartment had been on the top floor. It was where she used to fuck him. He thought he'd installed himself in her property, in her life, for good. She'd taken some pleasure in kicking him out, telling him that it was to be the new Goodwin Enterprises offices after all, not some fancy live/work space for arty types. Everything was up for grabs following Rich's death, he had to understand that. Where his bed had been was now her desk.

A fireman, in all his dirty padded clothing and huge helmet firmly strapped to his head, appeared from nowhere and was ambling towards her, holding up his right hand. She stopped the car and he came over to her window.

4

'You need to back up,' he said. 'There's no access this way. The situation is not under control. The building might collapse. We can't take any risks.'

'Are you reading this from a fucking manual?' Tatty said.

'I'm doing my job. No need to speak to me like that, lady.'

Lady? He was in his late thirties, Tatty reckoned. Heavily built, but part of that might have been the clothes. Tanned, clean shaven. Startling blue eyes. Surprisingly soft-voiced. Men in uniforms were not normally her thing, but there was something very attractive about him. Sort of vulnerable as well. The gentle-minded but tough outdoors type. She shouldn't have spoken to him like that. He'd help save her property.

'It's my building,' she said.

'Oh, right.' He was squinting at her. 'You still need to back up.'

'Heaven's sake,' Tatty said, pulling the key fob from the console, grabbing her bag and opening her door. Climbing out, she straightened her mac, tried to wipe some hair from her face, and smiled broadly at her handsome hero. 'Make sure nothing happens to my car, will you?' She handed him the keys, swerved around him and headed towards a massive insurance claim at the least. Nothing would give her more pleasure than to rip off an insurance company.

She didn't wait for the fireman to catch her up. She'd got dressed in a hurry and under the mac she was wearing her favourite cashmere

5

V-neck, with nothing but her bra under that, her jeans and trainers. The wind, smelling more and more burnt and toxic, was funnelling down the street, getting inside her mac, her clothes. She strode on until she reached the beginning of her building. This near corner was undamaged, even by the smoke.

By the time she'd reached the main entrance she wanted more signs of damage. She knew that could be arranged, even if the inspectors were quick off the mark. They were always corruptible, given the right incentives. Everyone was.

It seemed the fire service had had no problem opening the main steel doors, behind which were a pair of secondary, twenty-first-century glass doors, leading to the unlit lobby. Fortunately, or not, these had not been smashed either and were sitting open and gleaming as if Goodwin Enterprises' new HQ was ready for business.

The old offices, back on Fish Wharf, South Denes Road, were called Goodwin House. She'd decided to stick with the Smokehouse tag for the new digs. Had had it etched onto those very glass doors. She wasn't going to ditch the name Goodwin for the business, however, and revert to her maiden name, not a chance. Using Smokehouse was enough of a sign, she felt. Another way of moving on from her husband's death, signalling she was in charge, that it was a bright new chapter. Except now look what had happened to her plans — already.

'Tatty.'

Her first name was shouted loud and clear. She looked away from the entrance and the few

6

firemen milling about. There was a special constable doing not a lot as well. No one had stopped her from walking this way, getting this near. She wondered whether the man with the clear blue eyes was still minding her car. She wasn't going to look over her shoulder. She tried to shake some more hair from her own eyes while looking straight on.

At the other end of Fenner Road, waiting obediently by a fluttering taped cordon, was Frank, his big bald head picking up the crisp, early morning rays.

Did he want her to waive him through? 'Frank, what you doing standing over there?' she said approaching. 'Lost your bottle?' She could see his Range Rover slung on other side of Salmon Road.

'I'm not wearing the right shoes,' he said.

Tatty looked down at his shiny brown loafers — they could have been slippers. At her own trainers, which were soaked and filthy from walking only a few metres. She glanced back at the street, caught the puddles of oily water, dollops of deflating foam. 'I've seen you wading through mud thigh-deep,' she said.

'Besides, a couple of the guys, firemen, moonlight for me at the club — door stuff, mainly. I didn't want to get in their way. Thought I'd wait for you here. Should have known you'd have come the other way.'

'What's that meant to mean?' The wind seemed to be dying by the minute, but her hair was still in her face.

'You keep people on their toes, Tatiana

7

Goodwin. It's a good thing.'

She smiled. 'Mess, isn't it?' They were still either side of the tape. She wasn't going to climb over.

Frank exhaled. 'Whoever did it, didn't do a very good job. It looks worse than it is, I reckon.'

'So you said.'

'You know what the authorities are like. They'll make a meal out of anything. The roof's not looking too good, though — not from here. But that building isn't going to collapse. Do you see any damage on the ground floor?'

'Could be at the back,' Tatty said.

'The building is thinner than it's taller. Don't think fire works that way. The blaze was started higher up, I bet you. What did they do that for?'

'Maybe it was the electrics,' Tatty said, still trying to get more hair from her face, wondering whether she should have a trim, as she'd been planning. Not at all sure she wanted it to be the electrics — even if that might have made an insurance claim easier. She was spoiling for a fight, she realised. The spring had been too calm, fortunate, easy. Maybe she'd been waiting for something like this to happen.

'Be good if we decided what we wanted out of this before they come up with their bureaucratic bullshit,' Frank said. 'The minute local CID realises who owns the building, the investigators will be all over it.'

'You think they don't know already? Besides, you and I know how easy it is to get around those sorts of officials,' Tatty said. 'Still, the fire service must have got here pretty quick.' She

8

glanced over her shoulder. 'Do you know how it was reported?'

'Not yet,' said Frank.

'What about our files, our equipment? My office was on the top floor, Frank.'

'You think we're going to miss them?' he said. 'We should never have moved them over. Be a bloody good job if they've been destroyed. I always said the cleaner the move the better.'

'And that wouldn't have looked suspicious? To HMRC? A business with no paperwork, no records? We're not shutting the enterprise down and starting again, not as far as they're concerned.'

'We might be able to now.'

She could sense a large, dark cloud sailing across the back of her brain. 'Why am I thinking that someone was in my new office, snooping around, before they set fire to the place?'

'Because you're smart,' Frank said, nodding, but as if she wasn't particularly smart. 'We need to get in there, see if we can work out if anything might be missing. Soon as.'

'Whoever did this,' Tatty said, pulling the belt on her mac tighter, 'doesn't know how we work.'

'What do you mean?'

'That we're going to be stupid enough to leave the wrong sort of paper trail.'

Frank looked at her as if she still wasn't the brightest button in the box. 'Maybe it wasn't a work thing.'

'What's that supposed to mean?'

'That it was personal.'

'What's the difference, in our world?' Tatty

9

caught Frank's eye, a smile beginning to creep across his large mouth. 'It's a slight, Frank, however you look at it.'

'A slight?' Frank said. 'Biggest disrespect I've seen in a while.' He climbed over the tape. 'Let's see if we can get anywhere with this lot. We can't stand around on the sidelines all morning. It's your building.'

'Yes,' said Tatty, 'it is my building. Which of those firemen are in your pocket?' One of them in particular, she hoped.

2

When Sam rounded the corner of Yallop Avenue, turned left onto Marine Parade, the sparkling sea opening out straight ahead like a fat wedge of hope, she knew she'd made the right call. Pulling into the driveway, she felt her spirits soaring, even though her stomach was doing something else entirely.

It wasn't until she'd climbed out of her neat BMW I Series, and was standing on still, solid ground that the wave of nausea lifted and she realised that her car was the only vehicle outside her mum's home. There was the double garage, but now her dad wasn't around to shout at them, no one ever bothered to leave their cars tidied away in there. Her mum was the worst parker in the world, always leaving her Merc at some stupid angle as close to the front door as possible, so it was virtually impossible for another vehicle to fit on the forecourt. Not Zach's over-sized, over-priced Range Rover Sport anyway.

She still couldn't believe her little brother had persuaded their mum to part with that sort of cash. OK, it was in their dad's will, the money was to be Zach's when he was twenty-one. But he had a couple of years to go.

The wind coming off the sea was sharp and strong, but the air smelt good, and walking over to the front door she felt almost normal.

11

However, the second she started to think about what she'd come here to do, her legs went to jelly. She all but lunged for the door for support, then leant against it while she rooted around for her keys. There was so much crap in her bag, the keys were not immediately forthcoming. Where was everyone?

She pressed the bell, long and hard, hearing faintly its silly ding dong. It made no difference how hard you pressed the buzzer. That ding dong wasn't going to get any louder. She thumped the wood. The nausea was back. No one was home.

Clutching her stomach, she crouched, dropping her opened bag to the ground. Eyeing her phone in the mess, she had a sudden urge to call Michael. Feeling dizzy, her mind swirled around what time it would be in Amsterdam. It was nearly ten thirty here. She'd left London at eight. Drove like a maniac. There'd been little traffic. Eleven thirty in the morning was a more than acceptable time to call your boyfriend, even if he was away on a business trip. He was always on business trips.

Why the fuck hadn't he called her? Knowing what he now knew? She looked up from the ground, at the stupidly blue sky, some gulls flitting about as if they didn't have a care in the world, except where their next meal was coming from. She wanted her mum. She wasn't looking forward to telling her mum, but she wanted to be with her, at home. And she couldn't even get inside.

She retrieved her phone. Stood, feeling even

more dizzy. She rang Michael. It went straight to voicemail. 'It's me. Where are you?' She didn't know why she said this. She knew exactly where he was, the Hotel Ambassade, on Herengracht: a collection of ten canal houses full of art and antiques. It was near the Rijksmuseum, not that he'd be going there to check out the Vermeers. She knew everything about it, despite never having been there. It was where he said he always stayed. She'd seen it endlessly on TripAdvisor, working out whether it was such a good deal. Except he wasn't answering. His phone wasn't even ringing.

The wave of nausea suddenly went. She dug in her bag with more vigour. Found the keys. Where was Zach? She unlocked and opened the door. She wasn't exactly expecting him to be here. But she hoped he might turn up sometime soon. Sort of felt it would be easier breaking the news to her mum if Zach was around. She'd get inside, have a pee, make a drink, text him.

The stark wide hall was dim and chilly. It was always dim and chilly. She dumped her bag in the middle, rushed to the downstairs loo. Texted Zach while she was peeing. *Where are you? I'm in Gorleston, at home. Have news!!! Sis x.*

No reply came. She washed her hands and wandered through to the kitchen, suddenly feeling a fool for having driven all the way here, first thing on a Sunday morning, without warning anyone. Even Michael didn't know where she was. What if she'd crashed, doing ninety-five on the M11? She tried his number again. This time it rang, and rang, then went to

13

voicemail. 'Fuck you,' she said, aloud, though not directly into the phone.

She walked over to the great gleaming lump of machinery that was the coffee maker, but she didn't feel like a coffee. She hadn't for weeks. Tea held no attraction any more either. She had a glass of water instead. Thought she might go upstairs to lie down. A wave of not nausea but tiredness hit her, like jet lag. Heading for the stairs, this thing that had been bothering her tumbled into clear thought.

Not even halfway up the stairs and she was trying Michael's number again. This time it rang and rang, and rang out. It was a UK ringtone. He couldn't have been in Amsterdam, at the Hotel Ambassade, with its careful chintz. He was in the UK. But he wasn't meant to be back until Tuesday, at the earliest. He had an important meeting on Monday, which was why he was there now — so he could catch up with some relatives beforehand. He never normally had enough time to see his family when he went over. Besides, he had something to tell his mum and dad, his sisters. Would she ever meet them?

3

Tatty sat down in the hard, plush chair, waved to George over by the bar. The old man began tottering towards them. Tatty looked at Frank, perched even more uncomfortably on an equally stupid chair. 'He's not getting any younger, is he?'

Frank shook his great head. 'His heart's in the right place.'

'What about his mind?'

Frank exhaled. 'He's safe.'

'What are you having?' Tatty asked.

'Coffee?'

'I could do with a drink,' Tatty said. The old casino was empty. It wasn't yet noon.

'Good morning, Mrs Goodwin, Mr Adams,' George croaked, stooping by their table. 'I heard about the fire. I'm sorry.'

'Get me a Bloody Mary, will you?' Tatty couldn't remember the last time she'd had such a drink. It must have been years ago. She rarely deviated from champagne and white wine.

'I'll have a coffee,' Frank said.

George set off for the bar, his limp more pronounced than ever. Tatty turned once again to Frank. 'No club sandwich?'

'Even if I was hungry, I wouldn't,' Frank said. 'I've got to lose two stone by the summer.'

'Technically in a couple of weeks, then?'

'You think we'll have a summer this year?'

15

'Forget the weather, you'll have one if you want one.'

'Are you still going to Ibiza?'

'After this?' The damage was largely limited to the top floor and one end of the roof. Her office was effectively destroyed. She was no expert in such matters, though it looked pretty obvious to her and Frank that the fire had started in there. A tangle of burnt electrical wires wound around what was left of the desk. So yes, there could have been an electrical fault, something shorting. She didn't even know who the electrical contractors were. That had been Nathan's responsibility.

'Maybe it's not such a bad idea if you do spend some time in Ibiza this summer. Get away, stay safe,' Frank said.

She knew the fire was no accident, as did Frank. It was a warning, from a clever arsonist. Or a crap one who'd been unable to get the fire ripping. And if it wasn't started deliberately it was still someone's fucking mistake. Ibiza without Rich? She couldn't imagine the peace. No one to berate the gardener, the pool guy, the cleaners, the locals. Might get lonely. Would depend who else was around, she reckoned. Which of the kids she could persuade. There'd be a new vibe, that was for sure. 'You know what, I might do that,' she said, 'once I've nailed the bastard who torched my office. You said you were going to fix me up with some shooting lessons. When can I start?'

'You've still got that piece?'

'Of course I have. I keep it under my pillow.'

She didn't. But she hadn't got rid of it. It was well hidden, not least from Zach.

'You want me to get someone to sit outside your house for now? If they've gone for the office, what's to stop them setting fire to your home?' Frank leaned forward, lowered his voice, 'And doing a more thorough job. Unless they knew exactly what they were doing.'

'So the inspectors will blame the wiring? Look no further?' She tilted her head back, glanced up at the ceiling, as if for inspiration. There were a couple of tiresome chandeliers. She refocused on Frank. 'I'm now worrying that the insurance isn't up to speed. Sian's patch, but you know what that girl's like. She's getting worse. All talk, very little action.'

'Not what I've heard — round the back of her dad's caravans. When she was young anyway.' Frank laughed.

'She's hardly old now,' Tatty said.

'Look, don't worry. There're plenty of ways of making sure the paperwork stacks up. It's what's happening out there, on the street, that we need to keep on top of.'

'We're not, though, are we?' she said, knowing that the street was Frank's domain. She was meant to be the brains.

George brought their drinks over, taking another age to bend down and place the tray on the table. He left the drinks on the tray and the tray on the table, turned and began the long, slow journey back to the bar. Tatty thought that at least she still had a body to go with her brains. A half decent set of pins as well.

17

'Where's Nathan nowadays?' said Frank.

'Good question. Last I heard he was renting an apartment in Gorleston, on Riverside Road. Some new block.' She knew exactly where he was.

'Good views from there. You want me to pay him a visit?'

'No, I can handle Nathan. I don't want one of your mates parking up on Marine Parade for now either. Let's pretend it was an electrical fault. No fuss.'

'Shall we see what the investigators have to say, at least?'

'They know more than us?' She peered over towards the nearest window. The sky was still a brilliant clear blue. The skies over Ibiza were never so crisp, weighed down by the heat and the expectation. No one ever thought it was really going to be warm, let alone hot, in Yarmouth. She swallowed a large mouthful of well-seasoned Bloody Mary. Surprises happened here nevertheless. Now she was in charge it made even more sense for her to stick around.

Was she in charge?

Frank finished his coffee. He consumed food and drink with an urgent passion. She didn't think he'd stay on the diet for long. To drop two stone? He wasn't so overweight. Besides, she needed him to be big and strong. 'I guess I should get over to Goodwin House, see what we have to do to get the old offices back up and running for Monday morning. I'm not going to let this hold us up. Michael Jansen and his team are due in Yarmouth the middle of the week. We

18

need to make the old gaff look smart and functioning for them at least. Have you noticed how Michael dresses?'

'I've checked out his shoes.'

Tatty was hoping Sam would be able to come down with Michael; certainly in time for next weekend. Get Michael to stay too. Be good to get to know her fella better, see how he treated her daughter up close. 'We're lucky no one's taken up the lease.'

'Even if they had, we could have got them to think again.' Frank was wiping his mouth on the sleeve of his jacket. 'It's shaken you, this fire, hasn't it?'

How was she meant to reply to that? 'I've had an easy ride, for these last few months, I guess,' she said. 'And with the Dutch deal suddenly imminent, yeah, you could say it's all been blowing my way.'

'Blowing all right,' said Frank, shaking his head. 'Too good to be true.'

'Pessimist.'

'Realist,' said Frank. 'You're still a newbie.'

'Not to the town.'

'But the business.' Frank stood. 'Do you want me to come with you to Goodwin House?'

'No,' said Tatty. 'That building and me? You know we have issues. I thought I'd all but said goodbye — good riddance more. Seems as if I'll need to make peace with it for a few more months — bloody hell. And then, you know what? If ever a building needed torching . . . We should have thought of that already.'

'Lucky we didn't. Goodwin Enterprises would

be temporarily homeless.'

'It's only front, Frank.' She smiled. She had a good smile, everyone had always said so.

'Matters, when you're after two hundred mill,' he said. 'We all know that. You sure you don't want me to check out the old premises with you?'

'With your green fingers? No — something tells me you want to be somewhere else this afternoon.' She couldn't rely on Frank all the time, whether she happened to be carrying the Smith & Wesson or not.

'A day like this, in June? Yeah, you're right.'

'How's it coming on?'

'Pop round and have a look. You're always welcome.'

Tatty had been to Frank's house precisely once, to watch a video of her husband being killed. He'd served her a cup of tea, in a fine china cup on a saucer. The outside of his property might have shown some contemporary flair, particularly the shingle forecourt dotted with rare wetland plants, so he'd proudly described. Gardening being Frank's passion. But the inside of his house seemed like it had been lifted straight from an old black-and-white sitcom. She wondered whether Frank slipped into a housecoat to do the cleaning. There were plenty of things about him that didn't stack up comfortably.

'I'll get it,' Tatty said, watching Frank fish for his wallet. 'You only had a coffee.'

Tatty reached for her bag, retrieved her purse, found a £10 note. Put it on the table. Stood herself. The old casino never presented her with a bill. She'd leave denominations of £10 notes, depending on the rounds of drinks, the food. It was all her money in the end. Like most of the cash in Yarmouth. However, she had been thinking for some time that Frank might not be getting all that he deserved. There'd been the odd comment about gardening equipment, that a new car might not go amiss. Tatty had been surprised at how little Rich had left for Frank in his will. She'd been surprised at how little was in the will, full-fucking-stop. Rich had been very clever when it came to making out his and the business's net worth. He'd perhaps been a bit too clever when it came to hiding cash. She was still not on top of all the assets. Hoped the full picture was a little rosier. Otherwise, she'd have to be a damn sight cleverer than he'd been. But she was.

They pushed through the heavy doors onto the top steps of what was once a fine entranceway to a grand Regency building. Tatty had thought she'd turn the building into a boutique hotel, once the super casino got underway. Another project originally earmarked for Nathan.

She looked south, half expecting to see, above the low ramshackle Yarmouth skyline, thick black smoke being whisked up into the wickedly blue sky. There was none. Only a sharp wind smelling of salt and vinegar, fried food. Immediately ahead was the Golden Mile. Sparse traffic was trundling by. A few pedestrians were milling about the beginning of Wellington Pier. The

Winter Gardens was slumped in the early summer promise, like a scruffy, malnourished polar bear having run out of icecap.

'Frank,' she called after the large man as he made for his big black vehicle, 'come by Goodwin House tomorrow, though, will you?' Tatty could hear her phone going. Her mind shifted to her other staff: Sian and Celine; the only legits she'd kept on. She'd have to contact her PA at least. Prepare Sian for tomorrow. Would she have heard about the fire? She hadn't rung. It was unclear what the fire service and the police were planning next, but she knew it would be a pain in the arse.

Frank stopped by his car. 'Yeah, first thing Monday morning, if you want,' he shouted.

His hours had become even more irregular. Was he beginning to take advantage? 'There's something I've been meaning to discuss with you.' She was thinking on the hoof.

'Can't wait,' he said. 'Hey, is that Zach's car?'

Tatty looked over towards the wide road, catching the back of a sleek Range Rover Sport disappearing fast up the Golden Mile. 'That kid,' she said, not convinced it was his new car, or Zach at the wheel, 'needs to buckle down.'

'Shame about the computer suite,' said Frank.

'At least most of that equipment hadn't arrived,' Tatty said. She'd been livid when it hadn't turned up on time. She was even more livid now there was nowhere smart and new to house it — just a burned-out shell of a floor in a historic building. They'd have to get it delivered to Goodwin House for the time being; installed in Simon's old office? Her doubts about the crooks it was coming from were growing. Not more people out to take her for a ride, surely.

'He can always help me with some weeding,' Frank chuckled, pulling the driver's door shut.

'Oh, he'd love that.' Her phone, deep within the fine soft folds of her Birkin — the second Birkin she'd ever owned, though only the first original, which she'd had to buy herself following Rich's death — seemed to have stopped going. Though it was hard to tell with a couple of gulls on steroids making a racket right behind her. She found her car fob, beeped her Merc unlocked, quickly strode over and ducked inside.

How come Zach had managed to get himself a swanky new car? His dad hadn't left him that much cash, and that he wasn't meant to get hold of until he was twenty-one. Because she was a bad mother, weak when it came to her youngest, that was why.

Her phone was now telling her that she had a number of missed calls from unknown numbers. There were also two voicemails. And there was a missed call from Sam. No voicemail from her, which was not so unusual. She stared at the screen for a moment too long then threw the phone onto the passenger seat, looked at her watch, as ever forgetting the time had been right there on the screen. Rich's old Rolex — which had never been a fake because he'd bought it for himself — said it was twenty to twelve. She'd eaten nothing today. Quite fancied returning to bed, wanting the day to begin again. She started the car, flicked it into reverse. Began gently easing backwards. Looked in the rear-view mirror. Looked over her shoulder. Slammed on the brakes. Some idiot had stopped right behind, blocking her from pulling out further.

A particular idiot. 'Shit,' she said. It was the white Hummer, the size of a bungalow. Gleaming front grille. Grinning twat behind the wheel. A vast sidekick next to him, giving Tatty a royal wave. The Hummer gang, as she'd come to think of them, trawled the streets of Yarmouth looking to intimidate. Frank had always thought they were pretty harmless, unprofessional, all show. They were getting bolder, she reckoned, coming after her.

She closed her eyes, breathed out. Opened her eyes. Stay calm, she said to herself, quickly looking over her shoulder. Frank was nowhere to be seen. She put the car into drive. Pressed hard on the accelerator, rode up onto the wide pavement, the undercarriage clanking loud and hard, and onto a chunk of communal verge. Half on the pavement and half on some attempt to fancy up the Golden Mile, Tatty got the powerful coupe to swerve around a couple of other parked cars, churning grass and soil as she went, and back down the kerb, with another almighty crunch. She powered the car straight out and on to the Golden Mile, heading the wrong way for Goodwin House.

Not looking behind her, she wondered, as she was quickly passing the Sea Life Centre, then Jaws Restaurant — no sign of life inside there, let alone a thrashing great white crashing through a shark cage — whether they'd been watching her all morning. She couldn't imagine they were normally up and running Sunday morning. Frank should have dealt with them months ago.

Frank? Why Frank? Because that was his job.

There'd been far too much leeway since she'd assumed control, she considered now. Everyone else seemed to be having a field day today apart from her. Sunday, 11 June, wasn't it? Why did that date ring a bell?

4

Frank pulled over by the Coastwatch tower. A couple of other cars were also parked up at the end of North Drive. The wind was still fresh, ripping across the dunes, rustling the gentle mounds of marram grass, and the heads of a few dog walkers. The odd mutt could be seen running wild, chasing gulls. Beyond the shore the wind turbines were rotating with intent, the sun catching the giant white blades.

He scanned the area more closely, once designated as of outstanding natural beauty; he didn't know when or why that accolade had been withdrawn, but the signs were gone. It still seemed beautiful enough to him. Rich had hated the wind turbines of course. Not because he thought they spoilt the view, and not because he'd been a nuclear man, but because Goodwin Enterprises had never managed to scam anything from that industry. The manufacture, supply and upkeep of them all going to other contractors.

A massive new wind farm was now in the offing — East Anglian One. A £2.5 billion project. It made the super casino plans look like peanuts, even if the Dutch involvement had doubled the potential investment, and ambition, to £200 million.

For a moment or two Frank wondered, and not for the first time, whether they were still on the right track. Who on earth would want to come to Great Yarmouth to blow what little money they had on blackjack, roulette, poker, slots? The country had changed since the Brexit vote. This part of the country even more so. Less money, more anger. Everyone's dreams were in tatters. The UK drifting further out into the Atlantic. Would the locals be willing to host boatloads of European gamblers, steaming across the North Sea from the continent?

Yeah, course they would. Rich had always made a packet out of corporate and council catastrophes. A national disaster offered up even greater avenues. Rich had shown them how to capitalise on deprivation. Besides, Michael Jansen had turned up, with a back pocket full of euros. The cheap pound and the prospect of highly restrictive EU gambling laws on the horizon were making Yarmouth as attractive as — as what? Shangri-La?

Grabbing his phone from the passenger seat, Frank opened the driver's door, having to push it against the wind. He climbed down and immediately headed for the shelter of the Coastwatch tower. Out of the wind, against the rough brick wall once painted bright orange, he tapped Zach's number, put the phone to his ear, heard a lot of squall and faintly Zach's phone ring, and then ring out to voicemail. It had been Zach, or Zach's car powering along the Golden Mile, Frank was certain. Sometimes the kids would race their vehicles up this end of the town, taking the dead end at speed — burning rubber in the early hours. Or bang in the middle of the day for that matter. They didn't care.

It didn't look like Zach had come this way this morning, nevertheless. There was no audience. No fresh tyre marks. Still, the boy needed to be reined in, Tatty was right. Besides, Frank didn't want him upsetting his mother now. He should have taken a firmer hand, weeks, months ago, knowing just what it was like not to have a father at that age.

He tried the number again, decided he'd leave a message this time. 'Zach, you young tosser, ring me straight back.' The boy had grown up being insulted by his father. Sometimes he listened if he was spoken to sharply enough. He didn't always read texts — anything. Like his dad, he was dyslexic, wary of the written word. But brilliant with software, systems, logic boards. As was often the way, apparently. Letters, numbers, neither meant much to Frank. The physical world was his domain, so he'd always thought anyway.

He pushed off from the faded orange wall, dotted with a few pathetic squiggles of graffiti, deploring women, foreigners, *faggots*, though instead of heading back to his car, he crossed the wide road, and walked over to the sweeping entrance to the North Beach Caravan Park. He hadn't been here for months. There'd been no need. He felt a creeping necessity to dust away the cobwebs. Check the facilities, that a few items were still tucked neatly away behind false panels.

A car was sitting by the reception lodge. An old Beamer, silver, 3 Series. Frank didn't recognise it. It was not Rolly Andrews', the park's owner and manager. He had a clapped-out Rolls, the colour of mustard. It was forever in the garage. Frank doubted anyone would be manning the reception anyway. The sun might have been out but summer had yet to begin.

Taking the path on his left, which swept around the lodge and into the park, he felt his phone go, the electronic trill suddenly loud and clear out of the wind. He pulled it from his jacket pocket, pleased Zach had seen sense so quick. But it wasn't Zach. For another couple of rings Frank contemplated not answering it. He had an idea he was being watched, too. Someone lurking in a static caravan, behind a tiny square of net curtain. 'Yeah?' he eventually said, slowing but continuing on the gravel path.

'Sorry about the Smokehouse, Frank,' Graham Sands said.

'How do you know about that?' Sands lived in Caister-on-Sea, last time Frank had paid him a visit. It was a good way beyond the racecourse, and the golf course. At the other end of town from the port and the old industrial quarter, it thought it was something, in a small-minded way.

'Lit up the sky like a beacon, Frank,' Sands was saying.

'Yeah? What time was that?'

'I don't sleep so well in my old age,' said Sands. 'Hell of a lot of responsibilities nowadays. I have to let the dog out — the animal's bladder is about as weak as mine. So there I was, standing in the back garden, watering the plants, thinking the sun's coming up awfully fast this morning.' He laughed. An old smoker's laugh.

The caravans on either side of the path appeared well shut up. Frank decided to let Sands ramble on, sorry for the man's plants. Obviously, there was going to be a point to the call, beyond commiserations. It wasn't as if the owner of Admiralty Steel usually rang him.

'Still, I've seen odder sights in the middle of the night.' The laugh this time was gravelly and thick with menace. 'So, I went back to bed. Got a call mid-morning from one of my associates. Tatiana Goodwin's new gaff, up in smoke, they told me — would you believe it? The thing is, Frank, before you lot go sticking your well-powdered noses in the wrong place, it was nothing to do with me, or my crew. Believe me, matey, I couldn't wait to get Goodwin Enterprises off my backyard. The shit that you people have carried on there.' He tutted now. It was no less menacing than the laugh. He was trying too hard.

'I'm a respectable man,' he continued. 'A pillar of the community.' He didn't bother laughing. 'What she was doing with that old smokehouse was good for the local business community. Posh renovation job. Nothing but good, Frank. That's how I saw it. But she shouldn't have cut corners. Dodgy contractors. The wrong suppliers. Always the way with the Goodwins.'

'Why are you ringing me?' Frank said. He was well into the park by now, heading towards Rich's old hideaway, otherwise known as the company caravan. Still no sign of a living soul, despite it being midday on a clear, bright Sunday in June. June the what? 'Fuck,' he said, stopping dead in the middle of the path.

'What was that?' Sands said. 'Take a tumble?'

'I was talking to myself,' Frank said.

'Are you going senile too?' The laugh was back.

'Anything else you want to tell me?' Frank asked. He couldn't believe he'd forgotten it was his birthday. Yes, he could. Old age getting to him, too? Last year it was easier to remember because Simon was around and, of all the fucking people, Simon had the same birthday. Rich made a small fuss — of Simon, not him.

'I wanted to let you know what's what. I know how you lot do business,' Sands prattled on.

'How we do business? I don't know what you're talking about.' Frank could see the caravan, its pale façade looking worse than ever. The tree nearby was in full, fluttering leaf. It was a common lime, not his favourite. It must have grown over the winter. But that didn't happen, and spring certainly hadn't come early. Yet a few too many branches were overhanging. The roof was covered in dirty moss and bird shit. So much for insisting on this quiet corner of the park.

Maybe it was time to get the old crate shifted to the front of the park, with the fine sea views. They could stick on a deck, like many of the others in the prime spots. Complete it with a white plastic balustrade. Make a tiny bit of rent. Fuck's sake. Something was steadily telling Frank that the caravan would continue to serve a worthwhile purpose, all but hidden at the back here. His garden might have to wait today. It could always wait. It was a long-term project, evolution.

'Frank? You still there?'

It seemed Graham Sands had something else to get off his chest. Frank pressed the end call button. Whatever it was he didn't want to hear it right now. He marched the rest of the way over to the caravan. Dug for his key ring, which had been weighing down his jacket pocket. Whizzed through the keys. Found the smallest. Inserted it into the lock, pulled the flimsy door open, climbed up: the steps creaking, the caravan trembling.

'Shit a fucking brick.' The smell was monstrous. Frank immediately leant back, craning for fresh air. He took a big gulp, stuck his head in again. Searched the dimness. Something must have died inside, a while ago.

Vermin weren't usually a problem. Despite the age of the caravan, the doors and windows fitted well, the seals were intact. Though thin and bouncy, the floor had always seemed solid, complete. The whole thing was metal and plastic. It wasn't meant to rot. It had often been left empty for months on end.

He edged inside, his eyes growing accustomed to the light, though not getting used to the smell for a second. He looked about the small kitchen and sitting area, the forward compartment of the caravan. He crouched down, studying the floor, all the shady corners. He returned his gaze to the counters, the sink, the cupboards above, and the panels further along, behind which were stashed emergency aids and provisions. All seemed bare, neat and secure. But the smell was not letting up.

He knew where it was coming from — behind the closed bedroom door. He looked at the narrow barrier, the thin plastic handle. Don't fucking tell me, his mind whirring, there's going to be a horse's head resting quietly on the pillow. Frank felt himself shaking his own great bald head. Sensed his heartbeat rise with anger. Only two other people knew enough about the caravan. One he would trust with his life, the other wouldn't have the guts to do anything so stupid. Even Tatty didn't know about it — though he supposed Rich, in his time, might have bedded a fair few women here.

Frank blasted through the door, without turning the handle. The tiny bedroom was even dimmer than the living space, the threadbare curtains having been pulled across the two small windows for the winter. The smell was almost insufferable. Frank thought he might puke. He would have puked, had he had anything in his stomach besides coffee to throw up. For the first time in his life he was pleased he was on a diet.

An old duvet was on the bed. It had been casually left. A couple of hard, single pillows were at stray angles at the head. No covers on anything. The lumps under the cover were beginning to trouble him.

With one hand over his nose and mouth, Frank reached for the nearest window and pulled on the curtain. Thick dusty light shot into the room. He began unscrewing the first security bolt, but gave up, as the smell and a swarm of flies from nowhere overwhelmed him. He rushed out of the room, and out of the caravan, sucking in the fresh air. He'd dealt with enough corpses. He should have been able to cope with the simple smell of death. But this was different. Besides, all the bodies he'd ever had to bury were fresh.

He looked at the sky, some wisps of high cloud beginning to shift across the vast emptiness. He didn't want to think how old he was, how long he'd been living and breathing on this planet, his own evolution. He wasn't sure he could even remember. He knew he'd have to go back in there, check the cupboards, under the bed. Under the duvet itself. The paths leading to the caravan were still deserted. The wind rustled the thick, sticky branches of the over-grown tree above him. His phone started to ring. He was not going to be put off.

He took another huge gulp of air, headed back inside, stooping unnecessarily, the phone ringing out. He opened the bedroom cupboard. The ping of an incoming message. Nothing in there, except an old white shirt hanging on a hook. Rich's? Looking around the bed he checked the floor, the corners. Another ping. He thought of the gun wrapped in a tea towel and hidden behind a panel above the sink in the living area. There would be no use for it this minute.

Finally he crouched down. It was a very old caravan. The bed was only half built-in, having two legs at the foot, like the dining table. There was space underneath for suitcases, shoes, holiday crap. The floor was some sort of lino. A shit brown colour. There was nothing under the bed, except greasy dust.

Standing, letting the dizziness pass, Frank at last grabbed hold of the end of the duvet, yanked it off the bed. 'Holy fuck,' he said, feeling his mouth turn into a tremendous scowl. On the middle of the bed was a lump of something, mottled greenish black and pale pink. It was moving. It wasn't moving, the maggots were moving. Stepping back, staring hard, he couldn't work out what the fuck it was. There seemed to be bits of shredding plastic around the lump, which had fallen onto the mattress. There was nothing anywhere that looked like hair. It wasn't a head, human or animal. A yellow stain was surrounding the mess. It looked damp, wet, gluey. What appeared to be half a label was still attached to a piece of plastic.

Holding his breath, squinting, as if the stench was getting into his eyes, making them water, Frank leaned forward. But the label, it was a label, was folded in on itself. He wasn't going to touch it with his bare fingers. He needed something to prod it with, and unfold it. He turned, left the room, went for the cutlery drawer, knowing there was no cutlery as such, but the odd plastic spoon, for tea, for pharmaceuticals, and some chopsticks that had come with the takeaways.

He found what he needed, went back to the bedroom, lunged for the label with a single chopstick. Flipped the half out, a crispy dead maggot coming with it. He swallowed bile, still not breathing. The label told him that he was looking at the remains of an uncooked Norfolk turkey crown. It might once have been frozen. It certainly hadn't wandered in here of its own accord, tucked itself up in bed.

Had someone tried to defrost the fucking thing, under the duvet? Having first slit the plastic to attract the flies, the rot?

The door to the caravan had been locked. None of the windows looked like they'd been tampered with. He couldn't quite make out the sell-by date. As if that would help.

5

Sam! Tatty's mind was a squall. What was Sam's BMW doing in the driveway? Her daughter was days early, wasn't she? Tatty brought her car to a standstill, for once making sure she was leaving Sam plenty of room. Her mind switching back for a second to the arseholes in the Hummer.

Unarmed, unaccompanied, she'd decided to leave Goodwin House until tomorrow, and head home, desperate to get out of Yarmouth. It was easier, she supposed, when Frank wasn't watching her, judging, looking for leadership, strength.

Grabbing her bag, a sense of joy finally beginning to surge through her, she climbed out and rushed towards the front door. Locating her keys, she grappled with the lock, opened the thick, solid door, shouted, breathlessly, 'Sam?'

No reply came. 'Sam, darling?' Tatty sniffed, wondered whether she could smell her daughter, her perfume — not that she was certain what she wore nowadays. She'd glammed up since she'd been with Michael. Or rather he'd glammed her up, polished and loaded as he was.

Tatty stepped through to the kitchen. Thought she could detect signs that someone other than herself or Zach had been in there today. An empty glass was on the counter, the faintest trace of lipstick on the rim. No sign of Sam's bag though. Leaving her own bag on the counter, though still in her mac, Tatty walked back out into the hall. 'Sam?' she shouted softly once more. 'Sam?'

'Hey, Mum.'

Tatty watched as her daughter walked slowly down the stairs. She was yawning, in bare feet. Yet dressed. Tatty waited until Sam reached the bottom before rushing over to her, arms open. 'Hello, sweetie,' she said, hugging Sam tight, taken aback as ever at how slight she was. She was an inch shorter as well. 'What a lovely surprise.'

'The sun was out,' Sam said. 'Thought we could have a walk by the sea. Maybe I miss this stupid part of the world more than I realise. Can you believe that?'

'Have you been lying down?' Her hair was ruffled. Her eyes a little bloodshot. Tatty hoped Sam might miss her more than she realised as well. 'Have you been crying?'

'No.' Sam turned away, started walking towards the kitchen. 'Where's Zach?' she asked.

'No idea. Yarmouth maybe. I might have seen him driving along the front an hour or so ago. That boy.'

'That car of his,' said Sam, pausing by the door to the kitchen.

'You've got a nice new one as well.'

'Mine's not going to fuck up the planet. Have you seen the real emissions figures for new Range Rovers? It's a disgrace. I need something to eat.'

'I don't know what's in the fridge,' said Tatty. 'You didn't give me any warning.'

'I'll go back to London then.'

Tatty caught Sam in the kitchen, by the counter. Touched her arm. 'What's up?'

'Nothing, I told you.'

'Everything all right with Michael? Where is he?'

'Yes, of course. What's up with you? Did you get dressed in a hurry?'

Tatty looked down at her clothes, the mac, what had been hurriedly chucked on under it. Her filthy, wet trainers. She grabbed the edge of the counter for support. Sighed. 'You won't believe what's happened. The Smokehouse has gone up in smoke.' It almost sounded too absurd. 'Up in smoke.' She had to repeat it.

'What?'

'Yeah, there's been a fire. A chunk of the top floor's destroyed. Some of the roof's collapsed. We weren't allowed to get too close to the damage. They have to assess everything, apparently — bloody officials. It's going to be a right pain in the arse.'

'Oh, Mum, I'm sorry. Weren't you moving in soon?'

'Soon? We'd already moved most of the files and furniture. We were meant to be up and running from tomorrow.' For a meeting with your boyfriend later in the week, she could have added.

'Tomorrow? Shit. No one was hurt?'

'Not yet,' Tatty mumbled, turning away. She wanted a coffee. No, another Bloody Mary. Food? She didn't know what she wanted. She walked over to the dining table and pulled out

39

one of the hard, metal chairs. Sat and stared at the neatly tended garden through the triple-glazed sheets of light-sensitive glass. She didn't get Frank's obsession. Was more than happy to pay people to attend to hers. To be honest, she struggled to see him out in his garden in Bradwell, pruning, pulling weeds. Some pastime. He was handy with a shovel, however, she'd give him that. The sun had gone in.

'What's that mean, Mum?'

'What?'

'Oh, forget it,' Sam said.

'Why are you here really, darling?' Tatty said. 'I can see you're upset about something. Don't tell me you've split up.' That would really make her day. Michael's £200 million up in smoke as well. Tatty was staring at her daughter, who was over by the kitchen island, but Sam still wouldn't look her in the eye. 'OK, I guess we both need cheering up,' Tatty said loudly, fearing Sam was about to rush out of the room. 'Let's go somewhere for lunch.'

Sam walked over to the table, pulled out a chair opposite Tatty, sat heavily. 'Bit late for lunch, isn't it?'

'Tea then.'

'I'm hungry, but I don't know what I want to eat. Tomatoes?'

'Tomatoes?' Tatty looked at Sam, looked beyond her, and out into the garden once more. There'd been a sandpit up against the back fence once. Rich thought it was absurd, with the beach being so near. But he'd never had to get the kids dressed, all three of them, get them out of the

40

house, over the main road, down a cliff path to the beach, in the wind and the drizzle. Besides, there'd never been much sand on the beach all those years ago.

'Oh my God.' Tatty looked back at Sam. Tomatoes? Another memory hitting her. 'You're pregnant.'

Sam lifted her head, finally looked her mother in the eye. Smiled shyly. 'Yeah, I guess so.'

'You've driven down to tell me.' Tatty got out of her chair, walked round the table, bent over Sam, put her arms around her. Kissed her on the cheek, top of her head, hair, everywhere — her hair smelling nice. 'That's wonderful news.' Tatty wasn't sure she sounded as enthusiastic as she should. 'Fantastic,' she added for effect.

Fantastic? It was and it wasn't of course. Sam was too young — not as young as she'd been, but that wasn't the point. 'How are you feeling?' Michael Jansen was some catch, no denying that. 'What's Michael say?' Tatty fancied him like mad. Any woman with any taste would. He was due in Yarmouth next week of course. Wednesday? With a team of advisers, associates, the £200 million getting ever closer. She'd been planning on showing off the new offices.

'Calm down, Mum.'

'I'm excited.' Tatty was walking round the dining table, she realised. Round and round. She was going to be a grandmother. Michael was now family. 'Have you told Zach?' She knew her kids told each other things way before they ever told her, while their dad had always been the last to know. If not kept firmly out of the loop.

41

'No, I haven't actually. I've been trying to get hold of him this morning. Have been for days.'

'Ben?'

'Not yet.'

'Have you seen him?' Tatty realised she hadn't been in contact with her eldest child for far too long. She needed his advice on a couple of things, not unconnected with the proposed Dutch deal. Currency was a question which kept cropping up. The fluctuating, precarious exchange rate. Who'd shoulder a sudden loss. But Ben was still keeping Yarmouth, the family business, at arm's length. He had to be won over sooner rather than later.

'No. I've been busy, too,' said Sam. 'Haven't been feeling great either.'

'Morning sickness?'

Sam nodded.

'Poor you, love. How many weeks, months? How pregnant are you? How long have you known?' Tatty was pacing again. Finally shrugged her mac off. Flung it on the back of an empty chair.

'I've known for a few weeks.'

'A few weeks? Thanks for telling me.' Tatty couldn't sit back down.

'You know how it is. Come on, Mum. I had to be sure — about a lot of things.'

'Of course.'

'I'm only like two months and a bit pregnant. It's still really early.'

'A Christmas baby.'

'I guess.'

Tatty was also trying to work out when Sam

42

could have got pregnant. How long she'd have been with Michael by then. Weeks at most, practically days. How could she have been so careless? 'This is such exciting news,' she said, glancing once more at the garden, thinking how quickly life went. But she remembered struggling with three small children, even when they'd had au pairs. Never any help from Rich. Would Michael be any better? Times had changed.

'You don't sound that excited, Mum.'

'It's quite a lot to take in, darling. And the day I've already had, with the fire and everything.' She forced a smile. Her lips felt dry. She had not put on any make-up when she'd rushed from the house earlier. 'Are you excited, more to the point? Happy?'

'I think so. OK, it wasn't quite planned.'

Tatty could feel herself smiling.

'But it wasn't unplanned. I didn't know I'd get pregnant so quick.'

What was that meant to mean? 'I never had any problem,' Tatty said.

'I wanted something to change, I guess. London was getting to me. It's so crowded, polluted. Maybe I was looking for a way out.'

And back here? Tatty didn't say it. 'And Michael? How's he about it?' she said instead. The more she thought, the harder it was to see Michael with a baby, young children. He was too smooth, too corporate, too male. But times really had changed, hadn't they?

'Yeah, fine.'

That was said fast. Tatty knew her daughter well enough. Was it just because she was not feeling great, the morning sickness? 'Where is he?' If he messed Sam around, he'd have her to deal with as well. But he couldn't mess her, them, around. He was family now, with a spare £200 million.

'He's in Amsterdam,' Sam said, rising slowly from her chair. 'Seeing his family. Telling them about the baby too.' Tatty watched her daughter smile, but it wasn't the most definitive smile she'd ever seen from her. 'And then he's got some meetings on Monday.' Sam swung her head towards the garden now.

With who exactly, Tatty was thinking. She didn't know anything like enough about where the money was coming from. Frank had been warning her, and Ben was no help. Another thing that had come out of nowhere. 'Then he's down here on Wednesday?' Tatty wondered whether she'd have to delay the meeting. She couldn't have him bring associates to Yarmouth. Everything had to look right. But that amount of money? It had to be secured as quickly as possible. No going back.

'I think so,' said Sam.

'Can you stay until then?'

'I'm meant to be at work on Monday.'

'Call in sick, darling — honestly. It's more than you deserve from that place — a few days off? You need to look after yourself, these early days of a pregnancy.' Tatty wished Sam would jack in the whole London thing once and for all. Their dad's death had certainly unsettled her more than her siblings. Perhaps this would seal it.

44

'I don't know. I'll see how I feel later.'

'What are we going to do about something to eat?' Tatty said. 'A treat?'

'Of tomatoes?'

'We'll find the best, sure,' Tatty said, shifting towards the door. 'I have an idea. Let me go and put some proper clothes on, then we'll go out.'

'Please, not the Pier View Hotel.'

'You think I'd go there? You know what, there're a couple of new places down by the old harbour. They've even done up the pavilion, on the lower esplanade, across the way.'

'The old shelter that used to stink of piss? Where Zach used to go with his mates to spliff up?'

'It's a lovely building, now it's been renovated. Right on the front. You can sit outside, on the promenade. They serve fresh fish, lobster even, wine, cocktails. You wouldn't believe it.'

'No,' said Sam, 'I wouldn't.'

'I'm telling you, it's all happening here.' Tatty realised she'd already embarked upon yet another PR drive to get Sam back. 'Gorleston's hotting up. With the beach we've now got.'

'When the sun's out maybe. Where's it gone? What's happened to the weather? It was lovely earlier.'

Tatty was by the door into the hall. Sam was still over by the dining table and the French doors. 'It's not so cold out,' said Tatty. 'Bit blowy though.'

'Who set fire to the Smokehouse?'

Tatty couldn't have Sam worrying about things like that, in her condition. 'I'm sure it was an accident, darling, an electrical fault. There was a lot of complicated wiring. It was a historic building.' Noise was coming from behind her. A key was being inserted into the front door, hurriedly, recognisably.

'Someone's going to pay for it, aren't they?'

Nathan's name immediately sprang to Tatty's mind, as she was looking over her shoulder. An easy target for sure — but so what. He had to be partly responsible, even if it were only for installing flammable materials. He hadn't badgered her in weeks, which meant he was up to something, with someone. She quickly extinguished the tiniest spark of jealousy, that might have momentarily lit a dark corner of her heart. The fireman's beautiful face flashed into her head.

Then the front door was pushed open, and Tatty knew exactly what was about to mess up Rich's beloved oak floor, vacuumed and polished twice a week by Nina the cleaner. Yep. Scuffed Converse, ripped, skinny jeans. Much of the rest of Zach's body was encased in a dark blue hoody. He had numerous pairs of fancy trainers, tight trousers with neat roll-ups that didn't have rips in them. At least one smart navy All Saints mac. Yet he currently preferred the feral look.

'Yo,' he said, beaming, but making no effort to remove the hood. 'The mother lode, here to greet me.'

'Where have you been?' Tatty said.

'Zach!' Sam shouted, rushing past Tatty, then stopping short of him. 'You smell weird.'

'Hey, give me a break, Sis. It's been a long night.'

46

'Naughty boy.'

Zach whistled. 'The town that never sleeps.'

'Where have you been?' Tatty repeated.

'At some mates'. Driving around.'

'Not in that state, I hope,' Tatty said. 'You do smell. What is it?'

Zach sniffed the sleeve of his hoody. 'Beats me.'

'You haven't been on the glue, have you?' Tatty said.

'Mum, for God's sake,' Sam said. 'People don't do that any more.'

'Wanna bet?' Tatty said.

'Skunk more like,' Sam said. 'Or some new synthetic variety. Spice? A legal high?'

'It's not legal. Hasn't been for years.'

'Whatever. That stuff is bad, Zach.'

'Bad drugs — we care about that in this household?' Zach said.

Tatty looked at her feet, her own dirty trainers. 'As you know, we're fighting hard to keep the wrong people off the streets.' It was a chemical smell all right. And he'd clearly been smoking again — nicotine at the very least.

Sam snorted. 'So we can exploit the vulnerable.'

'People make their own choices,' Tatty said. 'It's a free world.'

'Yeah, right,' Sam said. 'I thought we were now living in a fascist state.'

'What you doing here, Sis?' Zach asked.

'Surprise visit,' Sam said, brightening. 'I've been trying to get hold of you for days.'

'Are we going to stand around here all

47

afternoon?' Tatty said. 'We were going out for something to eat, Zach. You want to come?' She was feeling hemmed in. It was tough being a single parent, even of grown-up kids.

Zach looked down at his clothes, ran his hand through his dirty blond hair. 'Where're we going?'

'Mum says there's a new cafe down by the beach. In the old pavilion?'

'There?' said Zach dismissively.

'Take it or leave it,' said Tatty.

'What's wrong with it?' said Sam.

'There's nothing wrong with it, except the clientele.'

'What's that mean?'

'If you lived here, Sis, you'd know what I mean.'

'I'm going for a shower, get some clean clothes on, and then I'm heading out for something to eat, with whoever of my children want to accompany me,' said Tatty, moving towards the stairs. 'Oh, by the way, Zach, there was a fire at the Smokehouse early this morning. I don't suppose you happened to see or hear anything about it? My office is gone, destroyed, and a load of the top floor. Where your computer suite was going to be.'

Zach shook his head, for far too long. 'No way,' he eventually said. 'Fuck, Mum.'

'And your sister's got some news as well.'

'Yeah, Sis?'

'In my own time. Thanks, Mum.'

6

The day had turned to mush. The sky quickly blended into the flat grey sea metres from the shore. It looked like March, not June. Only a few brave souls were now out on the sand, exercising reluctant dogs. Wind was sliding over the water, on shore, bringing with it a strong hint of not the Netherlands but the Arctic. The Arctic Ocean did run into the North Sea, sort of, Tatty knew. And not so far away, she was thinking. 'We'll sit inside,' she said, pushing off from the railing and looking over her shoulder for Sam and Zach, only to see that they'd already gone inside.

She walked over to a long line of closed French doors, and the entrance, which was at the far end. This door was firmly shut too, seemingly held in place by a particularly strong door closer. It took some effort to get inside. But once inside it was warm and cheery, smelling of grilled fish and coffee. A light sprinkling of low-key drum and bass was coming from the speakers, the odd vocal pleasingly female — for a split second she thought of Ibiza, how she and Rich once went to Pacha, Rich paying for a VIP table.

Inside this cafe, a million miles from the Mediterranean, Sam and Zach had already found themselves a table, not exactly VIP, but side on to the view. She was pleased Zach had bothered to come too, despite worrying that he might bump into the wrong people. Who'd he in mind? Wasn't that a problem they all faced? The arseholes in the Hummer still stinging.

'Can you manage something to eat, Sam, now we're here?' Tatty said, taking her seat. Her back was to the room. She didn't like having her back to the room.

'Double helpings, Sis?' Zach said.

'Piss off,' said Sam.

He'd also changed out of his reeking clothes. For some stupid reason — because she was taking a couple of her kids out for a Sunday treat? — she'd put on a skirt. Too thin tights, too high shoes. Adding to her unease was the fact that Frank had been calling her, and she'd not been answering. This was family time. 'The fish is what you have here, Sam.'

'I don't know,' said Sam. 'You've got to be careful with things like fish.'

'Shellfish,' said Tatty. 'Fish is fine.'

'If it's fresh,' said Zach.

'You need something inside you,' Tatty said. She knew best, and she wasn't going to have Zach putting Sam off this new establishment, or for that matter Gorleston, her real home. Or Yarmouth, the land of golden opportunities.

'Mum,' said Zach, looking not at her but the specials, on a chalkboard above the counter — where specials seemed to live nowadays. 'I've just realised — you know what it is today?'

Tatty followed Zach's eyes, which were still on the chalkboard. They were even specials for the day and not the week, as the date was up there as well, in big, well-drawn white letters. There was grilled sole, local lobster, homemade rhubarb ice

50

cream. Everything was fresh and modern and more than welcome, Tatty thought, relaxing into her seat, the atmosphere.

'What?' she said, suddenly no longer so comfortable, because she had an idea of what he was going to say.

'It's Simon's birthday, isn't it?' Zach said.

She sighed. Willed her heartbeat to steady. Simon, Rich's bastard of a brother, and so-called business partner, who'd disappeared shortly after Rich's death. 'I don't know how on earth you've remembered that, Zach,' she said, as calmly as possible. The kids didn't know everything. She wasn't sure she did.

'It must have come up when I was doing some work for Dad and Frank.'

'Hacking?' said Sam.

Zach nodded proudly. 'DoBs can get you a long way. Come to think of it, someone else has the same birthday. It was like a big joke.' He exhaled, as if he'd taken a large toke of a spliff.

It had been years since Tatty had smoked weed. They were on coke when they went to Pacha, over 90 per cent pure or something. Maybe weed would help her relax.

'No, can't think who though,' Zach continued, shaking his head, 'the number of names and birthdays we were going through.'

'Simon,' said Sam, 'the bloody thought of him is making my stomach churn. Is there anything with tomatoes?' She lifted her head from the menu and turned to the board.

'A Bloody Mary?' said Tatty.

51

'Even I know that wouldn't be a good idea, Mum,' said Zach.

'A Virgin Mary?'

Zach laughed. 'Here?'

'Sorry,' said Tatty, 'wasn't thinking properly.' She looked away from her children and through the glass and out to sea. But it wasn't such a big world. It wasn't flat either.

'Where's he now?' said Sam.

'Simon? Still in America, maybe,' said Tatty. That's what Frank had always presumed.

'And Jess?' said Zach.

It was Tatty's turn to exhale, practising perhaps for when she had something proper to breathe out, rather than just spent air. Though who dealt with that in the locale? Who dealt with the synthetic stuff? Frank had always said the profits weren't big enough for them to get involved. That it was a cheap, smelly business, best left to knackered old hippies, and kids with chemistry GCSEs.

'Fuck yeah, and Jess?' said Sam, animated now. 'That was weird.'

Tatty's head was beginning to pound. Were they winding her up on purpose? In her silly little skirt and barely there tights she felt cold and hot at the same time. Where was Simon, on his fucking birthday? How old was he? Forty-nine? Jesus, no, he'd be fifty, today. He was three and a bit years younger than Rich. Except Rich wasn't getting any older. Nor was Simon's young wife Jess.

Tatty knew where Jess was. Her body at least. Simon had killed her, and for a reason Tatty could no longer quite remember, she and Frank had helped get rid of the body. Frank meanwhile had Simon tracked to the States, as far as Nevada, last autumn. The police back in the UK seemed spectacularly unconcerned — missing adults were not their concern. Jess, it transpired, was not very popular with her so-called friends or family either. No one was clamouring for news, justice. Tatty understood why.

'Jess, Mum?' Zach was prompting.

He knew, knew something. 'Beats me,' she said. 'Up north somewhere?'

'You said you'd never lie to us, Mum,' Zach persisted. 'You'd only ever be straight with us from now on. That that was how it was to work. Some ideal, from the mother lode. More bollocks.' He pushed his chair back.

'Why is nothing ever discussed in this family?' said Sam.

'It's a post-truth world,' said Zach, smirking.

Tatty looked out to sea once more. What a day. Why couldn't she be having a nice meal with her kids — with her daughter, who was pregnant, and her youngest son? It had to be some sort of special occasion. 'That's not true any more,' she said. 'We do discuss things, things that matter. But I'll tell you something — that someone told me shortly after your dad died.'

'Frank, don't tell me,' said Zach. 'The old wizard.'

'Can I get you anything? Drinks?' A waiter had popped up. A tall, skinny lad, clean-shaven, with a sharp haircut, and bad acne. Zach was looking away hard.

53

'Sam?' said Tatty. 'You ready?'

'Oh God, I don't know. A tomato juice, plain, please.'

'Zach?'

'Beer, lager,' he said, still looking away. 'Whatever's on tap, man.'

Tatty ordered a large glass of Sauvignon Blanc, from New Zealand. Small world maybe, but that had to be quite a long way away. She'd never been out of Europe, despite endless promises from Rich of Florida, the Caribbean, South Africa. He'd done his travelling, however — for work. She sent the young man off to get their drinks, told him they weren't quite ready to order food. She was immediately regretting this, however, because a large group of oldsters were fighting the door and tottering inside. Tatty hoped they weren't going to sit down, take an age to order, clog up the kitchen. More of them were still outside. Some having failed to dismount from their mobility scooters. Small, wiry-haired dogs were clustered around one of the scooters. One dog was dribbling diarrhoea onto the esplanade.

'Yeah?' said Sam. 'What were you going to tell us, Mum?'

'There are certain things that you are better off not knowing,' Tatty said, shaking her head in horror at what was happening outside. The dog finished, unnoticed by any scooter occupant. They weren't going to clear up the mess. Why would they? Their feet rarely touched the ground. 'Yobs,' Tatty muttered.

'Sorry, Mum?' Zach said.

'The people outside, love. They're letting their dogs mess up our esplanade.'

'I'll go out and have a word,' said Zach, rising from his chair. 'I could do with a fag anyway.'

'No,' said Tatty loudly, glancing at Sam, the discomfort on her face. 'It's not our job.' Yet none of the staff seemed to have noticed. Why would they? They were too busy doing what they should be doing — preparing proper food and drink, rejuvenating Gorleston.

'What's that meant to mean?' Sam asked.

'Let the people who run the place sort it out.'

'I thought we ran the place,' said Zach, smirking and moving towards the exit.

'No,' sighed Sam, looking at her mum. Looking pale. 'What this person told you after Dad died.'

'Frank,' said Zach, over his shoulder, stepping away, his right hand reaching into the pocket of his fresh hoodie — for his fags presumably, the stupid lighter his father bought him for his eighteenth.

'These things that we are better off not knowing,' said Sam. 'How does that make any sense? Keeping stuff from people, if that's the point. Lying, you mean?'

'It's not lying,' said Tatty. 'It's about not telling people things that could get them into trouble with the law. It's about not incriminating people. It's very easy to be an accessory to this or that, simply because someone tells you something.'

'I thought I was the lawyer here,' said Sam. 'I do know how it works — and there is such a thing as a cloak of privilege in any case. It's a very misinterpreted bit of defence practice.'

'Well, what would you advise me to do, knowing certain things?' said Tatty, running out of patience, peering through the Perspex, yet not being able to spot Zach, where he was supposedly smoking. Smoking what? She looked back at the sea, catching the top of the wreck, an old coalsteamer apparently, over a hundred years old, and a couple of hundred metres from shore. The tide had to be going out.

'How Jess was bumped off, you mean? Where she's buried?' said Sam.

A phone was going. Tatty smiled. Thank fucking God. Frank again no doubt. She opened her bag, began delving inside, only to realise it was not her phone, but Sam's. Sam was already tapping the screen of her own iPhone, putting the device to her ear, looking quizzical.

'Hello?' Sam said, tentatively, her beautiful pale face pulling in odd directions.

Tatty looked back out at the wreck, the black iron rising from the grey sea. It was too late now in any case, she was thinking. Since Rich had died she'd done nothing to be ashamed of. Far from it. The whole world was greedy and corrupt. She was simply carving out her niche, providing for her family, and others. In difficult times, as well. It just meant she had to work harder, be tougher still.

'Oh . . . I guess,' Sam was saying, without any enthusiasm. 'But you could have rung me sooner. It was a bit bloody weird. Unlike some people, I do like to be kept informed you know. You are meant to be my boyfriend.' She pulled her phone away from her head, stabbed at the screen. Dropped it onto the table. 'Sod him.'

'What's happened?'

'That was Michael, ringing from the hotel, in Amsterdam. He says he was mugged last night, making his way to the hotel. They took his phone, his laptop.'

'Poor man,' said Tatty. 'Mugged, at his age?'

'Yeah, I know. It took him long enough to get in touch. Said he didn't know my mobile number off by heart.'

'What about Facebook, Twitter, Instagram?' Tatty said proudly. 'What you kids are all into. Not that difficult to communicate nowadays, is it?'

Sam's face said piss off, mind your own business. 'His phone and his laptop were taken,' she said, verbally. 'He doesn't do social media. Thinks it's too revealing, too compromising. You can get into all sorts of trouble, in his world.'

There was still email, so-called clouds, but Tatty was not going to push it. 'Well, he's got hold of you now. I don't know your mobile number off by heart.'

'I should have rung his hotel. I nearly did. But, I don't know, I didn't want him thinking I was chasing him all over Europe. I can't stand this sort of worry, any worry.'

'It's your hormones, darling. Is he all right? Was he beaten up?'

'He sounded fine to me.'

'Did he go to the police?'

'I didn't ask. But I seriously doubt it.'

Michael had connections, naturally. Tatty

57

couldn't imagine he wouldn't be dealing with it somehow. But to get robbed, mugged? That was stupid. At least he'd finally rung Sam, given all that was at stake. Family and business — same old. 'He's getting a new phone, is he? I should talk to him. He needs to know about the fire. I don't want him hearing about it from anyone else. He knew you weren't being serious when you hung up on him, didn't he, darling? He is still coming here next week?'

Tatty's phone was going now. It was in her bag, which was still on her lap. She retrieved it, saw that it was Frank once more.

'You only care about your bloody business,' Sam said, rising from her chair.

Tatty pressed the red icon. 'Darling, I understand why you're upset. Try to calm down. I'm here for you, always will be. For the record, no, I don't only care about the bloody business. You're my primary concern — you, Zach and Ben.' Tatty was aware of Zach coming back into the cafe, making his way with his usual sulky jaunt to the table. 'And it's not my bloody business either. It's our business.'

'You won't see a dog shitting on our promenade again,' Zach said.

'What have you done?' The oldsters were now shuffling out of the cafe, considerably faster than they'd come in. Tatty could no longer see the mobility scooters outside.

'Trust me,' said Zach. 'Hey, what's up with you, Sis? Why are you crying?'

58

7

Night was taking a decade to roll in from the east. Time of the year, he supposed, a couple of weeks off the longest day. Frank had always wished he'd had a winter birthday — so he could spend more of it tucked up in bed, out for the count.

Red lights were barely visible atop the stilled wind turbines. The breeze had died. The sea was as flat as a sheet of steel, the sky heavy with dusk. It was as if the world hadn't just stopped turning, but was plummeting into a black hole. The beach was wide and empty. The end of the pier was deserted. Frank pushed himself off the railing, his back now to the sea, skirted the cheap plastic rides, shut up for the night, and made his way over the soft, weathered decking of Britannia Pier to the solidity of the pavement.

She hadn't come. She hadn't sent her messenger either. Silence from both Britt Hayes and Howie Jones, the most unlikely of couples: one a bent copper, the other a former hitman struggling with retirement. They would have known about the fire, though not the turkey. Frank needed counsel, friends. He scanned the street, the Golden Mile — looking left towards the old theatre, now a cinema chain, and right towards Joyland, and the ugly, windowless chunks of the Marina Leisure and Fitness centre. Somewhere a mile or so on was the smouldering roof of the Smokehouse. He glanced at his watch. It was nearing 9 p.m.

For a moment he contemplated walking to the Smokehouse. There'd be no one standing guard. He could let himself in. See if he'd missed anything earlier. Besides, a stiff walk, the exercise, would do him some good, given what little he'd achieved in his garden that afternoon. He was supposed to cover so many steps a day — ten thousand. It was rare that he achieved a third of the quota.

He kicked at the remains of a Toffee Crisp wrapper, curled into submission on the wide pavement. His foot, now encased in recently polished black leather evening shoes, made better contact with an empty can of Strongbow a step away. He was still seething. Not sure what was most riling — the fire or the turkey. His private space had been invaded, while the front of the organisation had been dissed.

Frank crossed the road. He could see his car a hundred metres further on, in an empty bay by the leisure centre. Since he'd been jumped by a couple of scum with a pistol in the dim alley that was Bermondsey Place, he'd taken to leaving his car out on the Golden Mile. Not that he hadn't been able to deal with them, or didn't now relish owning the Glock 19.

Entering the pedestrianised Regent Road, having turned away from his car, he thought once more that a change of vehicles was long overdue. Sam and Zach had fancy new motors. There'd been bugger all in Rich's will for him. Tatty had made him feel wanted, necessary

— nevertheless. A Lexus, he had been thinking. One of the hybrids. Seemed right. Do his bit for the planet, the next generation. He laughed out loud. Besides, the American, over here scouting for the US casino consortium last autumn, had driven a Lexus. He had style, and a beautiful smile. He was called Dennis. Frank still had his number. He would be some present all right.

Had the shutter not been down on Candy Kingdom, Frank might have popped in, bought a bag of sweets, sod the diet. As it was all the shutters were down on Regent Road. The black hole seemed to be creeping along the shopping precinct with him. Past a string of closed and unlit stores: Pownalls Fishing and Field Sports; and his favourite, Fashion Choice — as if; Frank began to hear the low trill of some high tempo dance. The music was not his decision, nor to his taste, but it was what was expected.

Sunday night, the club could always do with some extra custom, even if the business was his, the till receipts up for his own manipulation. He'd buy the boys a drink; whoever else was in there. Rich had always spent his way out of a sulk. Hadn't believed there was anything that money couldn't resolve.

Frank reached the door to the club, having walked the length of Regent Road without encountering another soul. There was no one on sentry duty either. Fuck were they? The bouncers were the real reason he had decided to stay up past his bedtime.

He looked again at the unguarded door, the blankness of it, where the sign used to glare above. They'd never bothered replacing the neon that spelt out *Adams* in electric blue and pink, once it was smashed. Everyone knew what sort of club it was, and if they didn't the graffiti on the surrounding walls would direct them. There was a small CCTV lens somewhere up there too, capturing the view up Regent Road towards the Golden Mile.

He pushed on the reinforced door, half expecting it to be locked, a private gathering going on inside, Terry up to his usual jinks. The music was only a little louder immediately outside — which could mean any number of things, some of which Frank didn't want to contemplate. However, the heavy barrier gave way easily enough and Frank stepped into a chilly fug, and a wall of tinny dance music, the bass seemingly being sucked elsewhere. He walked along the dismal corridor; half the spotlights out of working bulbs. The place needed a serious revamp, had for years. The thing was, it was never meant to be too popular with real punters. It was another washing machine after all.

Any revamp or building project gave you plenty of opportunities to whittle away large amounts of cash, of course. Except the club was technically his, not part of Goodwin Enterprises, and his cash flow hadn't exactly improved recently. Neither had the organisation's, since Rich's murder. Tatty appeared to be playing a longer game, with far bigger ambitions. She seemed happy enough to let a number of the operations run down as well. Cash wasn't what it was in any case. They were now living in an electronic world, and a place where goods, property and services were more readily swapped than bought. Brexit was only adding to the bartering — everyone desperate to avoid the prospect of new borders.

A wave of nostalgia swept through him as he pushed on the inner door, which led to the bar area at the back of the building. Strobes immediately began pulsating and the music exploded. Some people leapt towards him. 'Fuck's sake,' Frank shouted hopelessly.

Terry was leading the charge, was smiling stupidly right in Frank's face. 'Surprise,' he was mouthing.

'You're not fucking kidding,' said Frank, inaudibly. Terry's partner Scott was there too, holding back like normal, but waving frantically. A few other men were in the room, Frank could see as light flashed on their faces, their torsos.

'Turn the fucking music down,' Frank shouted, using his hands to indicate as much.

There wasn't a dedicated dance floor, but an area in front of the bar that served the purpose. Frank didn't dance, ever, but he was now standing in the prime spot, and by the looks of Scott and Terry, the others, some movement from him seemed required, expected. Thumbs were being held up. A skinny, bare-chested youth was clapping manically, another person was using his fingers to whistle, not that Frank could hear. The music wasn't being turned down.

Something caught Frank's eye — a tall beer glass standing alone on the bar, glinting under the strobes. Frank pushed through the small throng, swiped at the glass with the back of his right forearm. It wasn't empty. The lager and the glass went arcing over the counter, the glass coming to a crashing halt against the back wall of the bar. The damage could have been so much worse. Frank wished it had been. The volume was finally cut.

'Fuck's this about?' Frank said, looking back at Terry, who was now keeping his distance.

'All right, boss?' Terry said. 'Little celebration.'

'Little celebration? For what?'

Terry frowned. He was a soft, round man, with smooth, sweaty edges. Always looked like he wouldn't harm a flea. Frowning didn't suit him. Nor being scared. He was not a local. Frank decided not to punch him. He turned away, sought Scott for some explanation, but Terry's business and bed partner had scurried away, as was his way. The few other people had drifted to distant dark corners of Great Yarmouth's only gay club.

'Your birthday, boss,' Terry was saying behind Frank. 'Thought we'd put on a surprise.'

'Your office, Terry, now. We need a chat.' Frank looked about the dim space again, the lights switched to static, knowing they could easily have sat at one of the tables, the bar, and been left more than alone. But the music was rising in volume and Frank didn't want to watch anyone clean up the mess he'd made, even if the club was used to spilled drinks, smashed glass, violence.

'Sure, boss,' said Terry, leading the way.

They took a narrow, dark corridor to the left of the bar, passing the toilets, and hitting a matt-black door at the end. Terry tapped the old combination lock, and pushed the door open, flicking on the lights. Frank followed him into the crammed office, watched as Terry walked around behind the small, cheap desk, and sat heavily in the plastic chair. There was no leather in here. No real wood either.

Frank remained standing. 'What the fuck makes you think it's my birthday?'

'We thought you might show up this evening,' said Terry quickly. 'Caught you walking down Regent Road. Only had seconds to prepare.' Terry looked over to the computer screen, which was at an angle on the corner of the desk. 'We'd been taking it in turns to monitor the CCTV.' Terry smiled — a big round smile from a pumpkin of a face.

Frank shook his head. The things people did on Sunday nights in Yarmouth. 'You haven't answered my question. What makes you think it's my birthday?' In all the years he'd known Terry and Scott he'd never revealed such a thing. 'Why'd you think I'd come by the club in any case — on a Sunday night?'

'The fire,' said Terry quickly. 'Sorry, mate. Didn't want to ring you unnecessarily. Course I heard about it. It's all over town. But Malc's not in. Nor the other one, Shane. He's also in the service.'

Frank nodded. Shane had the most beautiful eyes. The colour of the sea in the Caribbean. He'd clocked him by the Smokehouse that

65

morning, in his full regalia. 'Who's on the door tonight then? No one around when I strolled in. I could have been a fucking Nazi.'

'It's Sunday, Frank. Yeah, maybe in July, August, high season, we might go back to manning the door. Too expensive off season. Besides, I'm building Scott up. Sending him to the gym.' Terry laughed, weakly.

'I thought I paid the wages,' said Frank. 'My orders.'

'You haven't been here for a while.'

That was true. Now Rich wasn't around, Frank supposed this part of his pension plan seemed less important. 'What exactly have you heard?' he didn't like to be fleeced, nevertheless. Terry would know better, wouldn't he?

'About the fire? I don't know what's been going on that end of town at night.' He shook his pumpkin head. 'Some of those warehouses have been holding parties, raves. A lot of kids off their heads. There's some mean gear on the street right now, Frank. Nasty, synthetic stuff.'

Terry's eyes were dark and deep set, like lead shot. Music was seeping down the corridor, through the cheap door, which Frank knew didn't meet fire regulations, and into the office. 'The Smokehouse was not an empty warehouse,' Frank said. 'Everyone knew who owned it, what it was to become.'

'Destroyed, is it?'

'No, it's not destroyed. But it's set things back. Upset Tatty. Some important people are due in town this coming week.'

Terry was nodding. 'I'll keep my ear to the

ground, Frank. You know me.'

'Course you fucking will. Anything you hear, anything at all, it comes straight my way.'

'You don't need to tell me that, Frank. We've been working together for long enough.'

'I need to speak to those bouncers, Terry. Malc, Shane — give me their numbers, will you?'

Terry pulled out his phone, began tapping away. Read Frank the numbers. Frank inputted. He already had Malc's he realised, but not Shane's. That was the one he wanted.

'Can I get you a drink, boss, seeing as — '

'Who told you it was my birthday?'

'Someone was in here yesterday, asking after you. Said he was an old friend. He got chatting to the barman — Ted was on. Seemed like he knew you pretty well. Good-looking man, by all accounts. I was in the office, so I missed him. Shame.'

'Where was Scott?'

'At the gym.'

Nose to the table, more like, Frank was thinking, snorting up someone else's profits. 'My birthday — who told you?'

'That bit's weird. According to Ted, the man said he had the same birthday as you. Was the same age. That it was going to be your fiftieth today. No offence, but Ted thought he looked a tad younger.'

Frank gave him a stare that was harder than a smack in the head, a knee to the groin.

'In any case,' Terry added quickly, 'the man thought he might catch you out on the town, seeing as it was Saturday night. Your birthday weekend.'

'My birthday weekend?' Frank roared. 'What's the world coming to?'

'He wanted to surprise you,' Terry's voice tailed off. 'That's all.'

'It's not my fucking fiftieth. Get Ted in here now.'

'He's not on tonight either, Frank. Sorry.'

'I said get Ted in here now.'

8

'What time do you get up?' said Sam, having pushed opened the door to Zach's room.

'Piss off,' said Zach eventually, not lifting his head from the covers.

The room smelt of skunk, dirty trainers. Something else Sam didn't want to contemplate. 'It's like — ten.' It wasn't. It had barely gone eight. But she'd been awake for hours, wondering whether she should go back to London. Waiting for Michael to call again. He still hadn't. Feeling sick, then not. Waiting for her mum to leave the house before she ventured out of her room. There was only so much love and attention from her mum she could take. Having been ignored for, like, the first twenty-four years of her life by her, Sam was still struggling to get used to it. She missed her dad, even though he'd been a wanker to everyone else.

She remained by the door, watching her younger brother not stir. Looked over her shoulder at the bright day pouring onto the landing. She wondered whether it would cloud over again, like it had yesterday. She stepped into Zach's sock. That's what his bedroom was, like all young men's bedrooms, a disgusting sock. She'd once read that description somewhere. Except Michael's bedroom, in his minimalist penthouse, a stone's throw from Tower Bridge, was not a sock. It was a graceful boot. A Crockett and Jones Chelsea boot, which was what he'd taken to wearing. She still wanted to kick him in the arse.

'What are you doing?' Zach's head was emerging now.

His hair needed a cut. Michael was exceptionally well groomed. She liked that. 'Waiting for you to get up.'

'Why?'

'What goes on in here? It stinks.' The curtains had only been half drawn and there was plenty of daylight.

'Give us a break, Sis. Jesus.'

'I want you to help me with something.' Zach's bedroom looked out onto the back garden, and the tops of the houses spreading into Gorleston suburbia — Buxton, Batley, Youell and Arnott Avenues. Beyond, though not visible from their house, was the crumbling 1960s concrete sprawl that was Cliff Park First, Middle and High Schools. They'd all been there at some point.

'What time is it?' More of Zach had emerged from the covers. He needed a shave as well as a haircut.

'I told you, ten or something.'

'What day is it?'

'For heaven's sake, Monday, you arsehole.'

'What are you doing here?'

'What do you mean?' She was by his desk, looking at a couple of shut and dusty laptops. One a Mac, one a Dell; a bird's nest of wires, plugs, adapters, shoved to the back.

'Why aren't you at work?'

'What time did you get in last night?' After they got back from the cafe, Sam had gone to lie down. Zach had disappeared out for the evening by the time she'd re-emerged, leaving her to watch crap on TV, while her mum tried to microwave them some ravioli — the spinach and ricotta variety. Cooking was not something that came naturally to the woman.

'Late, I guess.'

'I'm taking the day off. The week.'

'Steady on.'

'I am pregnant.'

'Yeah, course. Still trying to get my head around that.'

'How long's it going to take you?'

'You want me to help you with something?'

'Yeah.' She picked up the Dell. It weighed a ton. Dropped it back down. 'If it's not too much trouble.' She was coming to the conclusion that Zach shouldn't have delayed going to uni. She and Ben had thought it would be nice for their mum to have him around for the year, help her find her feet, feel safe. But no one seemed to know what he did all day, and night, except drive around Gorleston and Yarmouth in his fancy new motor, like the spoilt rich kid that he was.

'Then be nice,' he said.

'Sorry,' she said. 'Can I get you a coffee, or something?'

'You offering to bring me coffee in bed?'

'I'm being nice.'

'You up to it, your condition? Shouldn't you be lying down or something?'

71

'I wouldn't have offered if I wasn't. I'm not an invalid. You wait until you get someone pregnant, if you haven't already.'

'Whoa.'

'You still take sugar?' She wasn't sure she was up to going down to the kitchen, fiddling with the stupid coffee machine, the size of a Victorian steam engine. The smell of coffee was no longer pleasant.

'What do you want me to help you with?'

Sam stepped over, sat on the corner of Zach's bed. It was hard, like hers. She couldn't understand why the house was still so uncomfortable, so unhomely. 'Can you, like, find out where someone is electronically? You know, where they're ringing from?'

'On a mobile? Sure. Well the pigs can. They calibrate using phone masts and so on. It's simple.'

'But can you do that?'

'You're the lawyer, Sis.' He had sat further up in bed. He was bare-chested.

'What's that mean?' she said, thinking he couldn't have been to the gym in a while.

'No. I don't have access to that info.'

'And you can't get it? Hack into the right places?'

'Too many permutations. That would be some job. There are other, simpler ways. There's software you can put on someone's phone to keep track of them — there're even apps. Find My iPhone, etcetera. And if you have someone's phone it's not too difficult to see where they've been, through their history and stuff. Laptops are harder. Tracking people, vehicles, is a piece of piss now. There're gadgets all over the market: this thing called TrackR, minimum. What do you want to know?'

She didn't want to spell it out. 'So like if I had hold of someone's phone you could tell where they've been? I'm a corporate lawyer, Zach. Not a criminal defence barrister. Or a prosecutor.'

'If you had the password, or a way in.' He scratched his head, messing up his hair further.

It was beginning to mat. Dreads, Zach was cultivating dreads, she realised.

He yawned. 'Maybe you should start to specialise. Could help us.'

'Are you helping Mum, with the business? Not from what I hear.'

Zach was rubbing his eyes now, yawning some more. 'I'm here for her, when she needs me. You know what she's like. Still not letting us know the half of it. What am I meant to do? Hang around all day on the off-chance? Hey, Sis, do you think it's a good idea she's going into business with your fella, now you're carrying his child?'

'Carrying his child? Fucking hell, what century are you living in?' The nineteenth, she thought. Where the coffee machine had come from. What the fuck had been going on here these last few months? Wasn't her mum meant to be pulling the business into the twenty-first century?

'You don't know what he's up to right now, do you? You want me to track him down — suss out where he's been?'

Sam could feel the heat rising in her cheeks. 'Course I know where he is. He's in Amsterdam.'

Zach spluttered out some air, like he was choking. 'And we know what goes on there, don't we?'

What had she been thinking? 'He is Dutch.' A spasm shot through the middle of her, like a blade of period pain. She needed Zach on her side, her mum too, and Ben. This was her real home — whatever century it was in. Michael was welcome to be part of it. But it was their rules, not his. The pain subsided as suddenly as it had hit her. She stood, walked towards the door.

'I don't think it would be so easy to calibrate all that stuff, work out where someone is, if they're abroad. But you could try calling him. The ringtone's different. Simple enough.'

'I'm not that stupid. He was mugged, wasn't he. His phone, his laptop, nicked. Do you ever pay attention?'

'That was convenient.'

'And what does that mean?' But she knew.

'Are you getting me my coffee, Sis?'

'Get it yourself.' She walked out onto the landing and into a pool of sunlight. Paused, looked at her phone. Still no messages had arrived this morning. Hotels had phones, landlines, receptions. Besides, why hadn't he yet gone out and bought a new one? Why hadn't she tried to contact him, via reception, or whatever? Because she was scared of what she might be told? Her mother had never known where her father was. Why should she let Michael get away with it? The thing was, her mother had long

74

stopped caring, before her dad had died.

'Sis?' Zach was shouting.

She scrolled through her contacts. Found Ben's name. Tapped away. Put the phone to her ear, expecting it eventually to go to voicemail.

'Hi, Sam,' he said, after three or so rings. 'What's up?'

'I'm pregnant,' she said, walking towards her bedroom.

'Wow. Bloody wow. I wasn't expecting that. Michael's?'

'Of course it's Michael's.' She changed her mind, and headed downstairs.

'Well, congratulations, I guess. I'm the last to know, am I?'

'Yep,' she said, stepping onto the hard hall floor. She was in bare feet, and the wood was cold. She thought wood was better at retaining heat than stone. Not here. The house was always cold.

'Are you at work?'

'No, I'm in Gorleston, at home.'

'Where's Mum?'

'She's gone to Yarmouth. Shit's going on. There was a fire at the Smokehouse yesterday.'

'No way. No one's bothered to tell me about this either. Mum could have rung.'

'Maybe she tried. It's not easy getting hold of you.' Sam was in the kitchen now.

'What do you know about Michael's business?'

'How bad was the fire? Jesus.'

'Don't know. Mum doesn't seem to be making too much of a fuss.'

'She'll be planning something.'

'Michael's business — what's your angle?'

'Nada, really,' said Ben. 'Except, he's doing this deal with Mum. I'm keeping out of it.'

'He controls funds — is that right?'

'Capital, not hedge, as far as I'm aware,' said Ben. 'Less regulations, believe it or not.'

'Venture capital, yeah? With money from the Netherlands, and elsewhere in northern Europe?'

'Eastern Europe, I reckon. Who knows how much is above board. But it's not my nasty little world,' said Ben.

'Can't you make it?'

'Not you as well.'

'Yep.' She looked up as Zach walked into the kitchen.

'That Ben on the other end?' Zach said. 'Tell him to get his lazy arse down here.'

9

Morning rush hour meant Gorleston High Street was clogged rotten. Having no idea where everyone was going, or why, Tatty gave up, indicated right, waited another age for the funnel to go green, and the cars ahead to get with it.

Some time later she was heading down Baker Street, not humming the tune, passing My Plaice Fish and Chips, which always made her smile, until she was veering left by Solana Beauty and Hairdresser, the pink-and-lime-green-painted building neon in the morning brightness. Scrappy industrial units then led all the way to the river.

Riverside Road was teeming. A convoy of trucks was heading from the Gorleston basin upriver, shaking the very ground Tatty's Merc was idling on. Across the river more industrial units and larger warehouses, rusting silos and the huge outer harbour cranes, littered the horizon. She couldn't quite see Goodwin House, ripe for demolition like much of industrial Yarmouth, from here. Her staff would be awaiting orders. They'd have to wait a little longer.

She pulled out and almost immediately swung across the road and parked tight against the concrete flood barrier. She didn't care whether she was seen. She reached for her bag, heavy today, and climbed out, beeped the car locked, and walked back across Riverside Road to

Gorleston's newest residential development — three blocks of apartments, some with balconies, some not. The views weren't the development's best selling point, she reckoned.

Better was the fact that the ground floor was effectively on stilts, in case the Yare burst its banks. Between the thick, brick-lined columns was space for parking, all neatly marked out. That would appeal to Nathan, even if the colour of the bricks wouldn't. Tatty had no idea how he'd landed a flat here. She hadn't been aware he had contacts with the developer, or much cash. Yet he must have slimed his way into another property.

Her pulse quickened. His car was there this morning, the glaring white Audi, neatly parked. There were few other cars.

She crossed the parking space and entered the building by a side door. Wires were poking from the wall by the edge of the frame. They still hadn't secured the door electronically. The building was new, but not that new.

Nathan's apartment was on the top floor, facing east. She decided to take the stairs, the fire escape, rather than the lift, uncertain whether that had been plugged in. She practically ran up, her handbag banging against her side. Reaching his door, she paused, gathered her breath, would have retrieved the gun from her bag then and there had it not been for someone down the corridor exiting their apartment, even though they then hurried the other way. Late for work?

She pressed hard on his buzzer, letting go after

a few seconds. She returned her finger to the button, longer and harder this time. 'Nathan?' she shouted. She looked over her shoulder, up and down the thickly carpeted corridor — it was like a cheap, corporate hotel. Nathan hated carpet. 'I know you're in.'

Finally, there he was, opening the door a crack. Dishevelled grey hair, hazy hazel eyes. 'Tatty, what are you doing here?' he said, in a half whisper.

'You're not dressed,' she said. Through the tiny opening she could see he was wearing boxers and a T-shirt. Nothing else.

'I was in bed, asleep,' he said, still hanging onto the door.

'Have you not got any work to go to?' Tatty doubted it somehow. He quickly looked over his shoulder. Facing her again she realised he was anxious. 'Have you got someone in your bed?' she demanded.

'I got in late last night,' he said. 'I've been in Manchester. Big project on the go. I've been there for the last month. I'm only back here for a day or two to get some stuff.'

'You might need to stick around. Are you going to let me in?'

'Do you want to come back once I've had a shower, got dressed?'

'No I fucking don't, thanks. Nothing I haven't seen before.' He was still not opening the door any wider.

'You have got someone in there, haven't you?' Her foot was in the gap, so he couldn't slam the door shut. However, he had hold of it too, she realised, which was why she couldn't open it any further. She was stronger than him. More determined anyway. 'Open it, for God's sake.'

He gave in to the pressure Tatty was exerting, just as she heard someone say, 'Nat? Who's there?'

'Nat?' said Tatty dismissively, stepping inside. The accent was not local, nor British.

'It's a business colleague,' Nathan called behind him. 'No need to get up. We'll be in the kitchen.'

'Who is she?'

'It's not what you think.' Nathan turned quickly and stepped down the soft, dull hallway, pulling the bedroom door shut, then hanging onto the handle.

'You think I care?' Tatty said, brushing past him and on into the small living area. She'd never been here in daylight before. There was a tiny kitchen counter against the far wall, and two medium-sized windows at the front, with a dim view of the Yare and Yarmouth's industrial quarter. She was not impressed. She went up to the nearest window, peered out, squinted left. She couldn't see either Goodwin House or the Smokehouse. 'I don't care who you fuck Nathan.'

'It's not what you think,' he said again, shaking the fine grey hair from his eyes.

'Not much of a view,' she said. Her bastard of a brother-in-law had a place a little further upriver, perched atop Ferry Hill. That had the view, all the way to the sea. But Simon's swanky modernist box had been firmly shut up behind its shiny steel barriers for months, since he'd scarpered. Neither she nor Frank wished to be

80

caught disturbing the scene of Jess's murder.

'It's a temporary measure,' said Nathan, a little too close behind her.

He was still distraught that she'd deserted his bed, and kicked him out of his loft. Why wouldn't he be? She glanced down at her mac, tightly belted, the heels on her feet. Her Birkin hanging from her right hand, weighty. Maybe she'd been a bit rash. 'What time did you get in last night?'

'I said — late.'

'With your friend?' Tatty swung round, fed up of the view. Not overly impressed with the alternative. Though Nathan did have a good body, for a man his age.

He was nodding, meekly.

'Where's she from?'

'Manchester,' he said.

'Originally?'

'Manchester,' he repeated.

'There was a fire at the Smokehouse over the weekend. Early Sunday morning.'

'No,' said Nathan, stepping back. 'No way.' He sounded genuine. Even looked a touch shocked.

'It was started on the top floor. Part of the roof's gone. My office has been destroyed.'

'My loft, you mean,' said Nathan, a smile emerging on the lips more used to brushing across her bare skin.

'In your dreams.'

'Shit, I don't believe it. I'm sorry, Tat.' He stopped smiling. 'Weren't you about to move the office across. Get up and running.'

'Yeah. We were scheduled to be in from today,

81

as it happens.' She whistled, lightly.

'How did it start? *Was started?* What do you mean?'

'What do you think?'

'What do the fire service say?'

'They'll say whatever we want them to say.'

'For now — what are they saying for now?'

'Maybe electrical, Nathan. You sorted those contractors, didn't you?'

'Yes. All the contractors. But they are professional people, Tatty. Not cowboys. I've worked with some of them for years. All over the region. These people are highly skilled, the sorts of buildings we deal with. Heritage renovation is a demanding job. People don't get involved if they only want to make a few quid. These people are artisans.'

'Artisans, what's that mean in this town? Heaven's sake,' said Tatty.

'You don't think I'm somehow responsible, do you?' His smooth forehead was creasing up again.

'The thought never crossed my mind.' She flexed the muscles in her right arm. Men. They were all the same — dishonest, duplicitous philanders. Except Frank. But Frank was beginning to trouble her, though for different reasons.

'Tatty, you have to believe me, I love that building. I spent practically two years of my life renovating it.'

'You weren't too happy about being turfed out though, were you?'

He shrugged, in his fine cotton T-shirt. Grey of course, like his boxers. 'I love that building, and I loved you.'

Tatty looked away, back out of the small

82

windows to the narrow, neglected port. Rich might have benefitted from it being all but forgotten; the fact that rivals were few and far between. She wanted some spark, however. Some polish. Competition kept you on your toes, didn't it? Though try to make a statement, and look what happened. 'You know what you need to do, right?'

'No,' he said.

'Check out all of those contractors — I want to be certain here. Ask some questions. Ask some questions of yourself too.'

'I had nothing to do with it, Tatty. How many times?'

'Prove it then.' She couldn't hurt him, let alone shoot him, dressed like that. It would have been a waste of a good body. She sighed. She was never going to shoot him anyway. She was carrying the gun today for other reasons.

'Isn't that what the fire service is for?'

She laughed.

'I'm going back to Manchester in a couple of days.'

'No you're not.' She walked around him, out of the cramped little room, and Nathan's shrivelled world. He didn't move. He was never going to move. The moves were always all hers. Halfway along the hall she couldn't help herself, and grabbed at the bedroom door handle, pushed it open. There was a smell of cheap perfume, sex. It was so predictable, as was the startled face looking back at her. Young, high cheekbones, blonde-ish hair, tanned skin, slender, naked shoulders. She could have bothered to put on a T-shirt, a dressing gown, knowing another woman was in the flat.

'Fuck are you doing?' Nathan said behind her.

'Seeing how low you've slumped,' Tatty said. 'Don't wear him out,' she added, looking at the girl. 'He's an old man.'

Tatty didn't look at Nathan as she made her way to the front door, and quickly let herself out. The thing was, Nathan might have been her sort of age, but she knew he was a tiger in bed. He had an energy and appetite that defied his careful, monochrome looks.

Competition? Is that what she was after?

10

Frank pulled across South Denes Road, clocking Graham Sands' green Jag, arrogantly perched on the public pavement by the corner of the block that Admiralty Steel took up. Frank had thought he wouldn't have to be confronting that sham of a fabricator on a daily basis any more. As for Sands' call yesterday afternoon, and what was left unsaid — it was now worse than a bout of indigestion after a late-night curry from the Bombay Mix.

The day had darkened almost before it had begun, while the wind had shifted from the east, and was now heavily internal. Frank's Range Rover creaked up and onto the empty forecourt of Goodwin House, well out of any pedestrians' way. He had long stopped parking at the rear of the building. Couldn't stand the view from there, the proximity to the quay, and the fatal edge Rich's car had gone over. He got out, the hard soles of his derbys tapping onto the tarmac. Why wasn't Tatty here?

He found his old entry card in his wallet, pressed it against the bar. Waited for the door to click open. Pushed when the click didn't come. 'Fuck's sake,' he said, feeling eyes on his back. While a couple of lorries trundled past he tried the card and the door again. Nothing happened. Where were Sian and Celine? Had Tatty not informed them? It wasn't his job to round up the office staff, make them aware of the circumstances. He dealt with the street workers — in every sense.

He pulled his phone out of a pocket while more trucks blasted past. As the noise died down, another gentler but more disconcerting sound picked up. Hurried footsteps. Heavy breathing. He quickly looked over his shoulder to see a man rushing across the side road, and onto the Goodwin House forecourt.

'Frank,' the man said.

The sun was not in Frank's eyes. The sun was no longer in the sky. But Frank was squinting nevertheless, his brain trying to catch up with what he was seeing. What Terry had all but told him last night. The two and two he'd been too stubborn to put together. Here it was, bang in front of him. Frank should have retrieved the Glock from the stinking caravan when he had the chance. Should have warned Tatty last night that her brother-in-law was back. That they needed to come up with a new plan. There were times when business, this sort of business, took priority. He returned the phone to his pocket.

'Fuck you doing here?' Frank finally said. But it was a family issue for Tatty as well.

'That's a nice way to greet an old friend,' Simon said.

He'd cropped and lightened his hair, grown some stubble, was wearing shades, aviators, gold rim. Same tight leather jacket though, and black jeans. He looked ridiculous. He was holding out his hand. Frank looked beyond Simon to see if he was accompanied. No one else appeared to be in sight.

'Are you not going to shake my hand?'

Frank could have throttled him then and there, in cloudy daylight. 'Like I said, what the fuck are you doing here?'

'I just had a meeting with our old chum Graham Sands. Saw you turn up, thought I'd come right over and say hello.' He smiled, slyly.

'Bit early in the morning for a meeting with that slob, isn't it?'

'He's a very busy man,' Simon said. 'He's branching out like there's no tomorrow. Besides, did no one tell you that he's the new head of the council's regeneration committee — Rich's old post?'

Was that what Sands had been itching to tell him? That he had the ultimate say over who knew how many grants and planning permissions. That the shaping of Great Yarmouth for the next decade or so was in his control — on paper. Backhanders galore. The unlikely rise and rise of Admiralty Steel — but whenever there was a vacuum . . . 'Does Tatty know you're back?' Frank spat in Simon's face. Had he paid her a visit late last night, or earlier this morning? She would have told him if he had, surely.

Nevertheless Frank couldn't help thinking that Tatty had been outmanoeuvred by Sands, and probably Simon. She'd been too slow. Too concerned with the look of things. High tech this and that in such an old building. All manner of fancy finishes. But it was the wrong sort of statement for this part of the world, for this old crowd. Operating from the shithole that was Goodwin House had never bothered Rich.

'Not as far as I know, Frank,' Simon said. 'I wanted to speak to you first.'

'Why shouldn't I knock your fucking head off?' Frank had lost track of the weather. That he was standing outside Goodwin House, breeze coming from somewhere. He was boiling inside. He'd never been so fucking affronted, even if he'd always known that Simon would return one day, his tail between his legs, bullshit dribbling from his mouth.

Simon shrugged, removed his silly sunglasses. 'There are things I want you to understand. You've been around, Frank. You know how it works.'

'And Tatty doesn't?'

'She's a bird, Frank. Birds from her walk of life think differently.'

'Fuck off,' Frank said, turning. He'd kill him later, slowly. And enjoy it.

'Listen to me, for a second.'

Simon tapped Frank on the arm. Frank swiped Simon's arm away. Simon immediately held his hands up.

Not interested in the slightest whether Simon was trying to make peace — it would never happen — Frank found he was staring beyond Rich's brother again. Something in the periphery of his vision was disturbing him. 'I have a house, a phone,' Frank said, distracted. 'It's not that hard to get hold of me.' Was that movement over by the entrance to Admiralty Steel? 'You've been following me around town, haven't you, for the last day or two? Popping in here and there, telling more fucking lies.'

'I don't know about the lies, Frank. Look, I didn't want to rush straight round, hands up. I thought I'd get you used to the idea that I might be back, see what I could pick up while I was at it. Been staying in a nice hotel, the other side of the Yare from here. It's fully serviced, if you know what I mean. All my requirements are being met in the most obliging ways.'

'You dirty cunt.'

'See what I mean? It's easy enough to make the wrong conclusions, reach for a gun, Frank.'

'What the fuck are you talking about?'

'There's a lot I still have to explain, Frank. A lot you need to listen to as well.'

'You don't need to explain anything to me. I saw what you did to Rich, courtesy of some CCTV footage from your new best friend. What you and Jess did, and then we all know how you got rid of her, the poor cow.'

'Are you talking about the night Rich went over the edge?'

A man, two men, were standing in the dark opening of Admiralty Steel's massive front loading bay, a block on from the factory's reception. Frank knew they weren't standing there by accident. 'Did anyone ever tell you about loyalty, Simon? How it works? Whether you are the boss's brother or not? An organisation like ours?'

'That's the thing,' Simon said, 'times have moved on. What happened with Rich was unavoidable. Leadership of such operations is never a given. It has to be earned, then nurtured. I wouldn't pay too much attention to some

89

grainy old footage. Cameras are always getting the angles wrong, the lighting. You heard of Photoshop?'

'I even cleaned up after you, respecting the business, the new head,' Frank said. 'I should have fed you to the cops, if not the fishes.' Where was Tatty? She'd be driving up the road any second now.

'Jess paid the price,' said Simon, shaking his head, 'for her betrayal.'

'You haven't, for yours. You haven't paid a fucking thing.'

'Oh yes I have,' said Simon. He gestured up towards Goodwin House, the grainy windows picking up a flat sky. 'You think Tatty's the right person to control all this?'

'Why don't you ask her in person?'

'She can't even protect her new offices,' Simon said. 'I wanted to speak to you first, Frank. I know exactly why you're outside this dump, tail between your legs.'

'Yeah?' Frank asked.

'If you can't even protect an old smokehouse, how are you going to look after a super casino? Or any other investment that might come your way? The small amount of business that you've still got going?' Simon shook his head again. 'What I'm saying is, I'm concerned, very concerned, Frank, about the state of Goodwin Enterprises. Tatty can't even look after her kids — from what I hear.'

'Why are you really here?'

'I come offering the hand of friendship,' Simon said. 'And a hundred million dollars. I've been working hard in the States. The Prime Poker deal's back on. If you want it. Otherwise it's going elsewhere.'

'Bullshit,' said Frank. The Prime Poker deal was dead the moment Rich hit the water, last September, so Frank had always thought.

'Don't believe me. You never have. I'll be seeing you, Frank, very soon.' Simon stepped back, swivelled on his designer trainers and began crossing Barrack Road.

The two figures were still over by the Admiralty Steel loading bay, loitering by the crack in the ten-metre-high shutters. Get pulled inside there, Frank had a feeling, you'd never get out.

Simon couldn't bring that sort of money into town without Goodwin Enterprises' say so — not in the old days. So Simon was considering teaming up with Sands, the man who'd effectively framed him not so many months ago? Or was Sands using that footage, that intelligence, as currency? Was Sands really about to shift into the casino business? He wouldn't dare. Neither of them would. Frank drove the hard leather heel of his right shoe into the ground. Swore. There were no gulls nearby to startle, only his ego to shake, his very being, to the core.

He stared again at the locked entrance to Goodwin House, the empty shell of a building that once housed so many dreams, and more than few nightmares — for others at least. The trucks were still powering along South Denes Road, the outer harbour doing something to earn its keep this morning. Who exactly was

Simon offering the hand of friendship to? Him and Tatty? Or just him?

Frank felt for the fob. Beeped his car unlocked. Climbed in. Press-started the super-charged motor, the combustion catching in an instant. He still wanted a Lexus hybrid, an executive saloon, more than ever. He had a feeling that the American, anyone with an ounce of sophistication, would not be impressed by such an old and obvious display of power and guts — a black Range Rover for God's sake. He reversed, swung the vehicle round, bricked the accelerator, powered across South Denes Road, some wheel spin on tired tarmac before he was in the correct lane, heading north.

11

Tatty caught sight of Frank's Range Rover coming at her then roaring past, hugging South Quay, going the wrong way for Goodwin House. Frank normally stuck a little closer to the speed limit. Was weird when it came to obeying the laws of the land. It didn't appear anyone was chasing him. He was a big chap, in a big motor.

As had Rich been.

She glanced at her watch. Nathan had already taken up too much time this morning, reminding her of past mistakes. But that didn't mean he could sleep with whoever he wanted. She tapped the leather-covered steering wheel, whistled. Glanced down at the passenger seat, her Birkin sitting comfortably, menacingly. A day out on the dunes was long overdue. Frank had been promising her that, and some ammo. Six bullets only went so far. Zach had been mouthing off about getting a shotgun licence. Thought he could take up clay pigeon shooting, go on pheasant drives, with the local nobs. She asked Frank whether it was a good idea. He wondered whether she'd ever shot anyone in the chest with a twelve bore. 'Stick to small calibre,' he'd said, meaning it.

Where the fuck was Frank going in such a hurry?

Not so many seconds later she was slowing as Goodwin House loomed. It had always looked half-crocked, it appeared completely dead right now. She had to wait for more than one truck to pass before she could pull across South Denes. A weight in her stomach like a bowling ball as she did so. Nostalgia, and perhaps a trickle of fear, made her skirt the front of the building and drive round to the back car park. Sian's tiny, blood red VW Up! appeared more than downcast sitting there all on its own.

Tatty crawled past it, not coming to a stop until she was by the steel barrier, which sat some ten metres from the quay edge. Flat grey light was skimming the river. A supply vessel was heading out to sea, its huge helicopter deck hanging empty above the bridge. She'd like a super yacht with its own helicopter, one day. Cruise around the Balearics, like an oligarch.

She got out of the car into a clod of early English summer. She slammed the door shut, hooked her bag firmly on her arm, tightened her mac, strode towards the rear entrance. Her phone was trilling away somewhere in the folds of the soft suede. It had better be Frank — he must have seen her vehicle on South Quay. She reached the fire exit, put her shoulder to the door, gently back-heeled the bottom, and bingo. It sprung open. A trick she'd learned only recently, but had kept to herself. She'd also learned, and not so long ago, that the alarm on the door didn't work. Neither did the building's main burglar alarm. She doubted it had ever worked.

There'd been an alarm at the Smokehouse, however — state of the art, supposedly. No one

94

had said anything about that being set off. The fire service had not yet been in touch today, neither had the police, to update her. She was not impressed. How much effort were they putting into the investigation? How much effort did she want them to make?

What she did know was, she needed Sian to get the old office back up and running. Frank's place was out on the street, marshalling, digging, enforcing, while she had to keep up the calm, bright front. Michael would be here in days, hours. Would he and Sam be getting married?

Tatty hoped that Sian had brought Celine to work with her — more hands on deck. Sian sometimes gave her a lift, now she had a company car. Tatty had told Sian by text to meet her here first thing, and to pass the message onto Celine. Sian bossed Celine around, just as she bossed Sian around.

She quickly pulled the door shut after her, not wanting the weather to creep in as well. Hurrying up the stairs, she called Sian's name. There was no reply. 'Sian?' she said again, reaching the old first-floor reception area. 'Celine?' The shitty black leather reception chairs were sitting there hard and empty. As was the cheap reception desk that Sian used to perch at while attending to her make-up. The office plants had gone, into the drink, as had the computers, but some old telephones had been left, and a row of filing cabinets. Sitting on the top of one was a model of a wind turbine, a corporate gift to Rich she'd always supposed. Someone having a laugh. You could plug it in, generate a cooling breeze, as if that was ever needed.

'Sian? Celine?'

Sian's bag was not in sight. Neither was her jacket. Tatty headed back to the stairwell. The building had never been friendly, had always given her the creeps. She shot up to the next floor, where her office used to be. It had been Rich's office for considerably longer. He'd never made her welcome here. She didn't miss him. But perhaps being without a partner, a lover, was beginning to drag. She'd always been with someone, whether they were shouting and bullying her or not. Loneliness was new.

Across the hallway was where Simon had positioned himself. He'd wanted the view across the river, to his designer home. Tatty had presumed Goodwin House would be demolished sooner rather than later. As for Simon's concrete and steel box? She had once imagined living there. But her stretch of Gorleston was coming up. Moving was such a hassle. Besides, her place on Marine Parade was where the kids grew up. It was the family home, even if it didn't always feel like that.

Her office was empty, except for Rich's old desk, and his disgusting chair. She'd told Sian to make sure that went into the river as well. Couldn't believe they were still there, mocking her. She stepped up to the desk, shaking her head, thinking she'd seen something else she shouldn't have seen this morning. A shoe, a foot, still attached to some leg, curling awkwardly around the corner of the desk.

Clutching her bag, Tatty took another couple

96

of steps forward, quiet as a mouse. It was a male foot, a male leg, belonging to an old man. He was wearing filthy dark suit trousers and a thick navy jumper. Dirty white trainers. He must have been in his late sixties. Maybe older. A head of scruffy grey hair, some white stubble on what she could see of his face. He was lying on his side, practically bent double, as if he'd gone to sleep in some pain, and never woken up. She didn't think she recognised him.

He was very dead. Though he couldn't have been dead for too long. There was an oily, diesel smell in the still air. Maybe it was more chemical than that. There was a whiff of vomit too.

Tatty delved into her bag for some tissues. There were none. She got her phone instead. Tapped away. Put it to her ear.

'Frank?'

'Tatty.' At least he answered immediately. Was he still driving?

'Where the fuck are you?'

'At home.'

'Home? Weren't you going to meet me first thing at Goodwin House? I saw you heading the wrong way along the quay only a few moments ago.'

'I forgot something.'

'Not like you.' He had the brain of an elephant, it must have been about the same size as well. He never forgot anything. 'What? Your shoe polish?'

'I'll explain when I see you. I'm heading straight back. Be with you in ten. Where are you parked?'

'What?'

'Where are you parked, at Goodwin House?'

'At the back.'

'Good. If anyone comes to the door, rings the bell, don't let them in. Keep out of sight. I'm on my way.'

Tatty was crouching, trying to discern how the man had died. She couldn't see any blood. Any fatal marks. It didn't look like he'd been shot, or stabbed. His brown skin was very pale. He had not been a large man. 'Fuck happened when you were here earlier?'

'What do you mean?'

'Was Sian in? Celine?' Tatty straightened, looked towards the door. Too many people used to pad softly around this building. Except Rich, by all accounts. Stealth had not been his style.

'No. No sign of them. I was stuck outside. The front door was locked. My card didn't work. Couldn't get in. The building was empty.'

'I'm not sure it was,' Tatty said. 'Did you try the back?'

'No.'

An honest reply? 'Why not?' Frank would have thought nothing of barging through the fire door, breaking in.

'What, do you mean you're not sure the building was empty?'

'Just what I said.' Tatty was resting her behind against the desk now, knowing her fingerprints, DNA, would be all over the place — it was her damn office. Besides, the man wasn't going to suddenly get up and attack her. She had a strong sense there was no one else in the building, alive.

'My attention was diverted, put it that way,' Frank was saying, 'while I was out the front. Reminded me of what I'd left behind. Who was in the building? Is someone still there?' He sounded anxious. 'You all right Tatty? Safe? Armed?'

'Are you being straight with me Frank?'

'What's that supposed to mean, Tat?'

'We haven't been working together long, have we?' She didn't like him calling her Tat. Tatty was OK. She was coming back round to Tatiana. Why shouldn't everyone call her by her proper name? Tatiana Jurkovic. She was born in this country, but her father wasn't. His surname had haunted her at school — when she went. No, she was not going to revert to using that. No way. She was a Goodwin through and through.

'You know where my loyalties lie,' Frank was saying now. 'You need to know that now more than ever. Wait there. Stay away from the windows. I'm on my way.'

Tatty looked over her shoulder, noticing what appeared to be a small dark canvas bag half under the man's chest. What was Frank on about? Why shouldn't she be seen here, answer the door? It was her business, her building. 'Frank, there's a dead body in my office. Can you tell me how it got here? Frank?' But the connection had gone. He'd hung up.

She pushed herself off the desk, walked out of the room, across the hallway and back into Simon's old office. Much of the furniture was still in situ. But that was about it. What she and Sian hadn't gone through, she and Frank had.

They'd checked everything, even managed to break into his aged computer, with help from Zach, before that went off the quay. Simon, to give him some credit, had kept his side of things in order, seemingly on the level. His desk was now bare.

She stepped over to the window. It was brighter out. A break in the cloud was allowing the river to gleam. To her right she could see the edge of the Admiralty Steel plant. No one was standing by the water's edge smoking. She stood back from the window, turned. Her phone was still in her hand, her bag hanging heavily from the crook of her left arm. She scrolled through her contacts, found Sian's details. Pressed call.

As she thought it was about to go to voicemail, Sian answered. 'Tatty?' she said faintly.

'Where are you?' Tatty shouted.

'At home,' Sian warbled.

'What are you doing there? You were meant to meet me at Goodwin House, first thing. You and Celine.'

'I don't feel well,' she said, sounding like she'd been to a very bad acting school.

'Why didn't you ring me?'

'I was going to, Tatty.'

'You don't sound ill to me.'

'Migraine, it's just come on. I've got like a terrible headache.'

'Why's your car here, Sian?'

'It's not.'

'It is, Sian. Sitting out the back.'

'It can't be. Dad's got it. He borrowed it, for the weekend.'

'It's Monday.'

'Yeah, well, I'll be lucky if I get it back for days. You know what's he like.'

'No, I don't — never met him. It's a company car anyway. Did I say he could borrow it? Sian?'

'No, I guess not, but I didn't think it would matter.'

'What did he borrow it for?'

'He's my dad, I don't have to ask him everything.'

Was she now being petulant? 'Hasn't he got his own car?'

'It's broken. It's always broken, that stupid old Rolls-Royce.'

'Can't he walk? Take the bus?'

'He's used to driving around in a Rolls, you think he'd take the bus? Besides, he hasn't been too well recently.'

'Why's everyone ill all of a sudden?' Thoughts were coming to Tatty thick and fast.

'Time of the year?' said Sian. 'Summer colds?'

'How tall is your dad?'

'Why?'

'I'm wondering whether I might have seen him about town.'

'He hasn't been going out much. Bad chest.'

Tatty was shaking her head, looking towards the open door onto the hallway. 'I imagine he's not too big, is he?' Sian was tiny.

'You're not going to do anything to him, are you? He's an old man.'

'Where's Celine?'

'Is she not in?' Sian had put on her faint, croaky voice again, full of thick lies.

'No.'

'I honestly don't know.'

Tatty sighed, glanced at her watch. People only used the term honestly if they were being dishonest. 'Did someone tell you both not to come here today?'

'No, course not. Look, I'm sorry about the fire. Can it all be fixed?'

'We'll see. Don't go anywhere, Sian.'

'What do you mean?'

'Stay at home, will you?'

'I'm ill, Tatty, like I told you. I've got a migraine. I ain't going anywhere.'

Tatty ended the call, left Simon's office, went back into hers. Had another look at the body. She wasn't going to touch him, turn him over, so she could get a better look at his gob. She didn't think she needed to. She scanned the room. Frank would be there in a few minutes. She supposed she'd better wait for him. Apologise for questioning his loyalty. Now wasn't the time.

12

'Michael?' Slowly the blur of colours stabilised, while the pixels began to bleed into one another. Definition resumed, as too Michael's sharp, beautiful face.

'Bad connection, Sam, sorry.'

Michael was sitting in a cafe, but not one of those cafes, so he said, in Amsterdam, waiting for his meeting. It looked like Amsterdam to Sam. Though she supposed it could have been a hipster place in Shoreditch. She couldn't see any Dutch writing, or hear anyone speaking a foreign language. 'It might be this end,' she said. She was in her bedroom, where the Wi-Fi sometimes struggled to reach. She needed to stop being so suspicious. Her hormones, like her mum said, were playing havoc. Her stomach was hurting her today as well. The morning sickness was horrendous. It was as if it'd burrowed deep inside her, like a growth, or something, which she supposed it was.

'I need to be quick, anyway,' he said.

'At least you got a new laptop.' She tried to sound positive. 'Back in the land of the living. And you weren't hurt.'

'No,' he said.

But she was. 'So?'

'So?'

'How are they then?'

'Who?'

'Your family, you idiot. Who did you think I was talking about?'

'Are you all right, Sam?'

'Apart from being pregnant, you mean?'

'You know what I mean.'

His English was perfect, though every so often she caught an accent. 'I wish you were here.' His face collapsed, then came back together again, perfectly. There was some echo on the connection as well. He might have been jumped, his stuff nicked, but he hadn't been hurt. Not so much as scratched. That was more than clear.

'I'll be back in London tomorrow,' he said. 'Wednesday latest. Depends how this meeting goes. Whether I have to see anyone else. I hope there won't be a hiccup. But some other people are in town right now.'

'And here?' she said. 'When will you be in Yarmouth?'

'Oh yeah, I forgot. You're staying there, right?'

'It made sense. I don't feel great. I'd be useless at work right now.' I need my mum, she also didn't say — and my brothers.

'I'm due there later in the week. Meetings with Goodwin Enterprises.' He smiled.

'I know. Another reason why I'm sticking around.' She forced a smile now. 'You can fly direct to Norwich from Amsterdam,' she added, feeling her face fall. 'Why don't you come straight here?'

'That's true, I forgot. Maybe. Let's see how these meetings go. And what else might be going on in London, whether I have to be there first.'

He was never easy to pin down. But it wasn't

normal circumstances. 'Have you been in touch with my mum?' she asked. 'Like today? About the deal?' She wasn't going to mention the fire. That slight hiccup.

'Not since last week. She's all right, is she?'

'Yeah fine — I guess.'

'What's the weather like?'

The weather? Something was distracting him. 'Same as always,' she said, not meaning it, because it had been brighter than normal, more welcoming. Or perhaps she was simply pleased to be out of London. 'And your mum, your family? You did see them?'

'They're good people, Sam.'

'And?' She paused, ran her hand over her stomach, her knotted insides. 'What do they think — about us, the baby?' Why did she have to spell it out?

'Yeah, good,' he said, while his face collapsed again.

Sam peered away from the screen, while the airwaves tried to pull themselves together. 'What did they say?' she said loudly. 'What do they think?' Though she was not sure the connection was still strong enough for him to have heard her hurt.

There was little in her room to remind her of when she was a kid. Now she had to create a new room for her child. She couldn't stay here forever. She and Michael would have to buy a home. She couldn't live in his penthouse, by London Bridge. That wasn't the place to bring up kids. Sea air was what children needed. Simon's minimalist box would be the sort of thing that would appeal to Michael. Maybe they could take that over, seeing as it was sitting there empty. She knew her mum had considered it. But her needs were suddenly more pressing, weren't they?

'They're happy for us,' Michael was saying. 'Hey, I should probably be going.'

Someone moved across the space behind him. Someone else. Both girls. Pretty from what she could see as well. 'Michael, they must have said something more than that.'

'You'll meet them, soon,' he said. 'I'll take you to see them. They're good people. You'll love my sisters.'

'What's this bloody deal worth?'

'Which deal, baby?'

'With Mum, with Goodwin Enterprises, the casino investment? The capital you're putting in, and your cut?'

'It was two hundred million pounds — euros — same thing.' He momentarily looked away from the screen.

'I know that, you idiot. What's it worth to you, personally?'

'It's a big investment for my organisation.'

Organisation? He hadn't used that word before in relation to his work.

'But there are benefits for my backers in putting this sort of money in the UK quickly and quietly,' he continued. 'Nevertheless, they expect results, from such developments. We all do. But your mother and I, we speak the same language.'

'Double fucking Dutch,' Sam muttered. 'You didn't answer me, Michael,' she said. 'You, what

106

are you getting out of it?'

'It's business, Sam. It's what I do. There'll be a percentage or two. I'll benefit, for sure.'

'Is that right? Is that what I am?'

'I'm losing you, Sam.'

'Is that what I am,' she shouted at the screen, 'a bit of business? Part of the organisation? A percentage?' Why couldn't he talk to her straight? She was a corporate lawyer, not a fucking bimbo.

'Baby, we are like the confluence of two great rivers. Our union is being blessed by the gods.' He was not looking at her again, but over his shoulder. More people were moving around in the background. They were in T-shirts, casual summer gear. Was it hot in Amsterdam? Was it Amsterdam? Michael was in a suit, looking immaculate. 'We are at the most important point of our lives, baby — creating new life.'

He was wearing the wrong clothes to be talking such shit. Or maybe he wasn't. 'Will you Skype me later, after the meeting?' she said, exhausted. 'Any time? I don't feel great. My stomach hurts. I miss you.' What else could she say?

'Yeah.' He was still not wholly focused on the screen, on her. 'I'll get you later, for sure, baby. Stay resting. You're carrying an important package.' He smiled now.

She smiled back. Blew him a kiss. Though not all was forgotten, or forgiven. 'We're not good people, Michael — I want you to know that.' She wanted to threaten him, not warn him. Wasn't sure she got the tone right.

She clicked the red icon, heard the horrible

Skype swooping tinkle as his image disappeared. Flipped over her iPad, as if that would somehow erase the conversation. Swung her legs off the bed, stood, feeling dizzy and sick. She only just made it to the edge of her room, before she had to grab the doorframe for support.

Breathing hard, she opened the door. 'Zach?'

'Hey, Sis,' he said. He was hurrying down the corridor, in bare feet, jeans, bare chest, towards his room. He stopped, looked over his shoulder. 'Everything OK?'

'Were you listening into my call?'

'No, course I wasn't. Is everything all right? Michael back on track?'

'I'm pregnant, Zach.'

'How many times?'

'It's not something you can change your mind over. And for what it's worth, Michael is on track — if I get your drift. He wouldn't dare not be.' She looked down at her own bare feet, and baggy trackie bottoms, with their elasticated waist. What was going to happen in a few weeks' time? She would never let Michael see her like this as it was. She needed to get dressed. 'What are you doing now?'

'Mooching, man.'

'Do you want to take me for a spin in your new wagon?'

'Sure.'

'I need to get out of here, clear my head. Perhaps we can head into Yarmouth. Check out the fire damage. It's our future that business, isn't it? Maybe we can meet Mum for lunch.'

'There's something I need to tell you about

the fire,' Zach said, disappearing into his room.

'Yeah?'

'Let me pull on some gear first,' came his faint reply.

13

'Yeah, it's him,' said Frank. He pulled out a handkerchief from his jacket pocket, wiped his big brow.

He was practically dripping. Tatty was surprised he had a handkerchief on him. Couldn't see him laundering such things at home. Laundering anything except cash, but Frank had the strangest domestic life. She looked up and towards the bank of windows. The weather was not stable. It was now coming in from the west, which normally meant it would be warmer, and wetter. Yet rain seemed less certain than more sun these last few minutes.

She was weighing up the options, she realised. The practicalities of a trip out to Breydon Water. Frank appeared to be doing the same. She had no idea of the state of the tide. 'So?'

'It's one thing disposing of someone you've done in, but getting rid of a body that happens to be in your way?' he said. 'Fucking mess.'

'It wouldn't be the first time,' Tatty said, thinking of Jess.

'Sian?' he asked, clearly looking forward, not back.

'She's at home. Said she has a migraine.'

'Why did she say that?

'You mean, why didn't she come in? An excuse? You think someone told her not to? There's no sign of Celine either. It's Sian's job to

110

contact her. I'm not office dogs-body.'

'Sian would not be expecting to find her dad here,' Frank said, 'dead as a fucking dodo, however you look at it.'

'Poor thing,' said Tatty. 'She seemed to have got on with her dad. They were still talking, communicating, loving each other — parent and child. Now that's fucking rare.'

'He was using her, if you ask me,' Frank said.

'No mum about,' Tatty continued, 'she's going to be very upset. What do you think he died of?' They still hadn't moved him. Or the bag that he seemed to be lying on.

'Fright?' Frank laughed, sticking his foot out, and gently kicking Rolly Andrew's stiff, crooked leg. 'A situation has arisen, Tatty — why I rushed home.'

'Not this?'

'Him?' He now poked Andrews in the back with a smart, black, leather-soled derby. 'He's been here a while — twenty-four hours at least, I reckon. He'll start to stink soon. No, not him, not this.' Frank had opened his hands, was gesturing towards the desk. 'I had no idea he was in here. I didn't get inside the building. I'm talking about a real fucking problem.'

'Plenty worse than a dead body on your hands, I suppose,' Tatty said, trying to lighten the mood. Bracing herself.

'Simon's back.'

Her mind went blank, then her head exploded. 'You have got to be joking.' She stepped towards the office door. It wasn't a shit-storm, it was a hurricane of excrement. She swivelled, strode

111

back, fixed Frank with her meanest stare. Felt the skin on her face stretch and all but tear. This job was ageing her fast.

'I'm sorry, Tatty. He came out of the blue, skipped across the road looking like a right twat, when I was here earlier this morning, trying to get in the front entrance. He'd been having a breakfast meeting with Sands, so he said. What's this town coming to?'

Tatty felt the world stop and start spinning the wrong way. That shaky weather system up above was now firmly inside her head. Coming in from the east, the west? It was a solar storm. She couldn't stand around any longer guarding some old geezer who'd croaked in her former office, even if he was the father of one her few employees. 'What else did he have to say for himself?' She was pacing her old office again, visiting corners she'd never had to venture to before. 'How come he thought you wouldn't waste him then and there? Come to think of it, why the fuck didn't you?'

'Calm down, Tatty.'

'Where's he been all this time?'

'We'll get to the bottom of that. It was a brief conversation.'

'He's coming back to see us?'

'He's playing a game. Dangling a carrot.'

'Of course he's playing a game. That's all he's ever been doing. I'm disappointed in you, Frank. You just let him walk up to you in broad daylight? The man who killed Rich?'

'Calm down, will you?' he repeated.

'Don't you tell me to calm down, Frank. You

112

work for me, don't fucking forget it.' She lurched for the door, her bag swinging back into her side, reminding her that she had a gun, loaded with six bullets. Who was she kidding? She'd never have the nerve. She wasn't Rich. He was the real heartless bastard. How many people had he shot in his lifetime? Not enough, was her immediate thinking. He'd left too many loose ends. He had not been in control. Not towards the end.

'You said you were going to take me on a shooting lesson,' she said, finding that she had her right hand in her bag. It seemed to be rooting through all the war-paint, trying to get hold of the hard plastic handle of the Smith & Wesson snub. Who said men were more likely to resort to violence than women? She had so much to prove, not least to herself. 'How hard can it be to pull a fucking trigger?'

'Don't, Tatty,' Frank said, putting his hand on her arm.

He had a firm grip, was stopping her from pulling out the weapon, and carrying out a small atrocity, by blowing a tiny hole in a big head. 'My organisation, my rules,' Tatty said. But she knew the words were hollow. She was not in control. She couldn't even retrieve her weapon from her bag. She flinched, thinking Frank was about to strike her with his left hand. He didn't. He smacked the wall instead.

'You're smarter than this, Tatty. You need to calm down and think. We both need to think our way through this.' He let go of her arm, though didn't exactly step away. 'You've got responsibilities.'

'To you? Sian, the others?'

'To your family.'

'And you know all about that, don't you?' She tried, but she couldn't look at him, his massive, soft face and large sad eyes.

He flinched, like he'd caught hold of an overhead power cable.

'Sorry,' she said.

'It's a learning curve, right?'

'I was never a good student. I'm all over the place today.'

'Understandable.' Frank smiled.

'Sam's pregnant.'

'Even more understandable,' said Frank. 'Bloody hell, that is something.'

What would he know?

'This fella Michael's?'

Tatty nodded. She didn't want to talk more about it. The context was all wrong. 'Should we get out of here?' she said.

'He tried to make sure no one could get in while he was here.' Frank was looking back towards Tatty's desk, and dead Rolly Andrews.

It didn't seem Frank was too keen to pursue a parenting, or grand-parenting, discussion either. 'By jamming the front entrance?' Tatty said. She had to go down and let Frank in manually, finding the electrics removed from the front door, and wedges holding it shut on the inside as well. She'd come clean about her rear fire door trick, how she'd managed to get in. 'Unless someone attempted to trap him inside,' she said.

'Wrong way round,' said Frank. 'Besides, you couldn't trap Rolly inside any building.'

'He knew what he was doing then?'

'Before the caravan park, how do you think he earned his keep? He was a master at breaking and entering. The park was his retirement present to himself, a trickle of rent and all the easy pickings he could ever dream of. I thought he knew better than to diss us. What I want to know is what he was doing here.'

'We need to talk to Sian,' said Tatty, looking at her watch.

'We need to do something about this body as well.' Frank stepped towards it.

'We're not going to call the police then?'

'I've never called the police in my life,' Frank said.

'That's a lie,' Tatty said, embarrassed she'd even mentioned calling the police. 'What about your contact? That woman?'

'That's different.'

'Your rules, my rules, are we ever going to see eye to eye, Frank?'

'Give me a hand, will you?' Frank bent down, behind the desk.

Tatty couldn't quite see what he was doing. Was reluctant to get any closer. 'Breydon Water?'

'No, not this time. In broad daylight? There's somewhere a lot simpler.'

'Yeah?'

He was puffing a bit. 'Don't give me a hand then.'

She wasn't going to. 'Still doesn't seem quite right to me. It's not our problem.'

'That's where you're wrong,' Frank said, straightening. He was clutching the dark canvas bag that had been half stuck under the body, awkwardly using the sleeve of his jacket. 'This weighs enough.' He dropped it on the desk, with a thumping clatter. Opened it, also carefully using the sleeve of his jacket. He looked inside. 'Standard kit for smash and grab. Over the top for breaking and entering.'

He used his elbow to open the bag wider. 'I thought Rolly had a bit more nous. Ooh, what have we here — a large bag of homemade pills by the looks of it. MDMA, or some derivative, if I'm not mistaken. Pink and white. Yeah, I've heard about this. The kids call them Candy Cane. This lot must be worth a few bob. Since when had Rolly been dealing? I'll tell you what else is in here, Tat: a large tin of lighter fluid.' Frank stood back, letting the bag close in on itself. 'This makes even less sense.' He rubbed his chin.

'You think he was going to set fire to the old office as well? Popped his clogs before he could strike a match?' Tatty slowly walked closer, her mind moving quickly. It seemed incredible if that were the case. To have a heart attack, or a stroke, or whatever, an aneurysm, on the job. Her father had died from an aneurysm, so she'd heard, some years after the event. She had no idea where her mother was now, even if she was still alive. Or her sister.

Frank was behind the desk again. 'You old cunt,' he said, as he kicked the corpse in the back. There was a muffled thud. 'That's for the turkey.'

'That's for the what?'

116

'Another thing that's baffling me.'

'I don't like loose ends,' said Tatty, watching Frank step away, pull a face, shake his head.

'You think I do?'

'Neat and tidy, that's me,' she said, knowing it was a silly thing to say. Nevertheless, Frank's face was doing sillier things. The thing about Frank was, you could always tell when he was thinking hard. Not that you could tell what he was thinking.

He went back to the bag, opened it up, not bothering to use his sleeves. He took out the tin of lighter fluid. It was yellow. 'Jesus, this is old hat. Didn't know they still made this stuff. There're some great firelighters on the market — bio oil, odourless, all but untraceable. What a cheapskate. Probably had this at the back of some cupboard for a decade or two.'

He shook the tin. 'It feels full enough. If this was used in the Smokehouse, it could only have been a drop. Any more than that and the investigators wouldn't be able to claim overtime, that's for sure. But if you know what you are doing, you only need a drop. Rolly should have known.'

He put the tin back, grabbed the bag of pills, stuffed them in a jacket pocket. Then he pushed the canvas bag across the desk until it fell off, and onto Rolly Andrews. There was a faint squelch.

'Now what?' Tatty said, fighting the sudden smell of death. As much as she didn't want to get her hands, her clothes, dirty, she wasn't particularly happy being a witness, simply

117

standing there. Right now she knew that Frank was indispensable, that she'd have to do as she was told. Fortunately her phone started up.

'We have some options. Not many,' he said, cutting in above the ringtone. 'None particularly appealing. Then I'll take you out to the dunes for some shooting practice.'

'At last,' she said, her mood brightening, then almost as instantly sinking. She'd all but forgotten about Simon.

'You're going to have to give me a hand first, like it or not.'

She retrieved her phone. 'I have to take this, it's Sam.'

14

Zach looked at his phone. No messages. Bastards. How many hours had it been? Fucking days, man. He looked up, through the windscreen. Sun had come from nowhere and was pounding the flat surf. The sea was still an endless sheet of icy-looking steel. He couldn't remember the last time he'd even dipped a toe in it. 'Are you all right, Sam?' he called through the wide-open front passenger window.

Sam was on the pavement, retching, by a scruffy hedge. They were at the start of the Golden Mile, on a slip road off North Drive by the old theatre. He hadn't even been driving fast, as he'd negotiated the endless mini-roundabouts as they crossed Yarmouth. She'd told him to wait in the car. 'Sam?' he called again. She didn't so much as glance his way, was bent double, trying to look discreet. Bits of hedge must have been in her face.

He got out of the car, looked seawards. The roadway split an old bowling green, waiting for some seasonal care and attention, and a long block of public toilets. It was dead-ended by a cafe and the promenade. 'Hey?' he said putting his hand on her back. As he did so he felt her heave, but no puke came. There was no splattering on the pavement, only the squawking of gulls.

'It's like this,' she gasped, 'you want to be sick

but you can't. Sorry.'

'Shit, man, don't say sorry. It's the way of the world.'

'Yeah? What do you know? I'll be all right in a minute.'

Zach reached into the front pocket of his hoodie for his cigs. Sparked up, inhaling deeply. 'There's no hurry, Sis,' he said, exhaling. Breeze blew the smoke straight back into his face. He smoked some more, listening to Sam retching and gasping, the gulls overhead, the wind, and the sea, he realised, flopping faintly onto shore. It was like everyone was holding back today. Scared to touch, scared to speak. He was still weirded out from Saturday night. Didn't know how much he should say. But he couldn't keep it all to himself. It would backfire sooner or later. There'd be chatter.

He took a couple of hasty drags. Dropped the butt on the ground, trod on it hard. Removing his foot, he was pleased with the dark smudge he'd left on the pavement. Marking territory was what he used to do as a kid. He wanted to be a kid again, and ditch the responsibility.

He got his phone out again. Messaged Liam. *You owe me, big time. We need to meet, mate. Share the spoils.*

Almost instantly a reply pinged back. *Joke. Not.*

Sam was upright at last, wiping her mouth with the back of her hand.

Zach looked to where she'd been crouched. Still no result. 'You want to sit down, on a bench?' he said. 'Get some sea air. Or have a

120

drink or something? There's a cafe over there.' He was looking back towards the promenade, at a building with a red-and-white striped roof. He hadn't paid attention to that detail before. Must have seen it a thousand times.

He and some mates — including Liam, come to think of it — broke in there a couple of years ago. There was no money. Nothing worth taking. The most fun they'd had had been smashing the slush puppy machine, even though it'd been empty at the time.

'No, let's continue,' Sam said, making for the passenger door of his big baby.

'All righty.' That would be the place to sell Candy Cane, Zach was thinking. Could see the people on Friday and Saturday night queuing around the block. One for you, and one for you . . . as the cash and favours piled in. Just who was he? Willy Wonka?

Shaking his head, dislodging the thoughts from his still scrambled brain, Zach headed to the driver's door, climbed in. There was the usual minor thrill as he settled himself behind the wheel: the dash, the console, promising the world, and all at his fingertips. 'Who do you keep in touch with, Sam?' he said, starting her up — it was a her, a female Ranger Rover Sport, no doubting, with a LR-TDV6 3.0 litre under the bonnet. Two hundred and fifty-eight brake horse power; nought to sixty in a tad over seven seconds. 'From round here. It's like you never make any effort to see anyone when you're back.' Might she have heard something?

'There's a simple answer to that,' Sam said,

sounding better. 'Who do you see, more like? You live here.'

'It gets under your skin, doesn't it?' They were passing the old theatre on their right and more municipal buildings on their left, lazily stretching back from the promenade, like the toilets would never end. One big fucking toilet. But they did end, as another bowling green took over and for a moment or two the grey North Sea reared its evil head between more scruffy promenade structures — the old concrete rain shelters, where drunks and junkies came to rest, and those a little younger to finger-fuck. He loved it. He did, honestly.

North Drive curved round a fat chunk of pavement marking the beginning of Britannia Pier on their left, and the start of Regent Road, the long pedestrianised shopping street, on their right. Frank's club was down there too. Zach had no idea how that place had survived. How it had even got up and running. A gay club, in the centre of Yarmouth?

Of course he knew. Frank's head was armour-plated. 'Sis, you OK?' He glanced over, feeling his age, his responsibility. She was looking out of the side window.

'I'm trying to work out what you mean,' she said. 'What I feel about the place. Now, with everything. You see things afresh, I guess.'

'Yeah, course.' He thought he knew what she was getting at. Another generation on the way.

What traffic there was was moving freely, but Zach had slowed to mobility scooter pace. A couple of kids — hoods up, heads down, bulging trackie pockets — were loitering under the awning of the Beach Hotel. They weren't waiting to hail taxis for departing guests. They'd be selling crack, for sure, perhaps some flat. Bump and flat. Candy Cane he seriously hoped not — that was rare, his and Liam's franchise. 'I'm glad I didn't go to uni,' he said.

'You're a mummy's boy at heart, aren't you?'

He could have told her to fuck off, pushed her out of the car. But he was feeling sorry for her. 'Everything's here, Sis, if you know where to look.'

'Friends?' she asked. 'Mine all pissed off as soon as they could.'

'Mine weren't smart, like yours.'

'Don't know about that. Some of them were cute.'

'Are you joking? Not any more.'

'They're all still around then, are they?'

'Some of them.' They were a good way up the Golden Mile already, even though he was keeping the Sport crawling: past Leisureland, Magic City, some chip shops on their right, and the pirate crazy golf plot on their left. Zach drove slowly on, thinking of the amusements he and his mates had violated along the front, the amusement they'd had. He felt differently now, now he understood who owned and controlled what, where money could be made and made to disappear. 'None you can trust, though, Sis,' he said, putting his foot down.

'You still haven't told me,' Sam said, adjusting her position in the acres of well-padded leather, 'about the fire.' She whistled. 'We're nearly there.'

'Why don't we have a peek first?' he said. 'I'm still clearing my mind.'

'Oh, I'm on the edge of my seat.' She was continuing to shuffle uncomfortably.

'Do you want me to stop?' He couldn't have anyone puking in his car.

'No.' She did something with the seatbelt. 'How much did this car cost?'

'There's plenty of money swilling around. You only have to ask Mum for it.'

'And I didn't? That's what comes from being Mummy's boy, I guess.'

Again he resisted telling her to fuck right off, and tossing her out. Marginally. 'We've got to look after each other. Family's what matters.'

They were now passing the log flume, the roller coaster creeping into view. There were no pedestrians about this end of the Golden Mile. There wouldn't be for a number of weeks.

'Mum's nuts,' Sam said, obviously thinking something similar. 'As was Dad. This place will never take off.'

'Not what your boyfriend has in mind,' Zach said, as they hit the beginning of the land earmarked for the super casino — a long stretch of scrub bordered by the beach and the road. It had lain vacant for far too long, much of it behind a busted-up chain-link fence. They could have used it for a car park in the interim, except there would never have been enough cars to fill the space, even in high season. Too much effort for too little gain. Frank had been telling him about economy of scale, what to prioritise. He indicated, unnecessarily, before pulling across

South Beach Parade into Salmon Road. 'And he is the father of your child.' She'd been rude enough this morning.

'Look at it? How long will it take? How much money?' Sam said forcefully.

'A hundred, two hundred mill.'

'That's quite a difference already.'

'The Europeans, as you should know, are a lot keener than the Americans ever were. Gambling in the EU's about to be fucked by more regulations than you could imagine. Thank God we're leaving.'

'You don't mean that.'

'Helps our business.' He felt himself wink. 'Opportunities like this don't come around every day.'

'I do talk to Michael.'

'Yeah?'

'Even so, where are all the people going to suddenly come from? You know, people with cash to spend in a swanky casino complex, and not just those shoved here on probation, because there's nowhere else to put them. Or those unlucky enough to have crawled out of some container on the docks.'

'Oh man, the London liberal elite, how it talks. That's not our worry, for now. You need to spend more time here. Learn what's what.'

'We'll see.'

'Your boyfriend gets the potential.'

Sam sighed. 'I don't trust him.'

15

Zach pulled up by the corner of Salmon and Fenner Roads. 'See that?' Dirty red-and-white fire service tape was strung across the entrance to Salmon Road. The road was empty. There were no official-looking vehicles on the other side of the tape. There was no sign of anyone. Zach was pleased, and surprised.

'The roof, Sis.' He had thought it would be worse, an image of flames shooting into a blustery black sky coming to him, but that wasn't the point. 'You don't think there's competition for what we're trying to do? The sort of money we'll be dealing with?' He was pointing up, into the sky that was not black now. It was a mottled blue and grey. Had he imagined the flames? Losing the drugs? Saturday night?

'This is about competition, is it?' Sam said, getting out of the car. She paused in the middle of the road, looking skywards. 'Other crooks having a say, by striking a match? That didn't happen when Dad was alive.'

'You kidding?' said Zach.

'No one set fire to Goodwin House, did they? Do you think Mum's out of her depth?'

Zach was shaking his head. He honestly didn't know. If anyone had been making mistakes recently it was him. 'Do you think Michael's out of his depth?'

'I doubt it. Though I haven't told him

126

anything about the fire,' Sam said, distracted. 'Thought Mum could. It's her business.'

'Yeah, well that's the thing,' said Zach. He looked at his sister, her pale blue eyes, not like any sea round here, and stupidly fair skin. She was not wearing make-up today, and her hair appeared as if it hadn't been highlighted recently. It was mousey, mottled, dull — exactly as he was feeling. 'It's our business, isn't it? All this. That's what Dad wanted. He set us up. That's what Mum wants, to continue it, for us.'

'Yeah? Dad was something else. You think you are cut out for it? You and Mum?'

'Me? Yeah, no sweat. What do you think I've been doing all these years?'

'You're like nineteen.'

'I'm twenty — thanks for remembering.'

'You know what I mean.'

'What about you?'

'Life's got in the way, hasn't it? I'm going to be having a baby.'

'I thought it was the twenty-first century,' Zach said, proudly. 'Mothers do work, you know.'

She didn't tug his arm this time, but smacked him on the shoulder. 'Piss off.'

'You can't duck out anyway. Michael's bang in it.'

'We'll see.'

'You're going to sit back for the next twenty fucking years, or whatever, like Mum did?'

'I said, we'll see, Zach.' She paused, wiped some hair from her face. 'So, like, the fire was only on the top floor?' They'd climbed over the tape and were nearing the main entrance. The outer doors were firmly shut. 'Why's no one here?'

'Yarmouth for you.'

'I'm sick of hearing that, Zach. You're the one who loves this place so much.'

'Love and hate, no escape, it's in our blood.'

'The only thing that's in your blood is some nasty drug or other.'

'Oh, another low blow.' He faked a small faint. Picked himself up. Patted his brow.

'But true. What's the high of the moment?'

'Funny you should ask.'

'Yeah?'

'I said I had something to tell you about the fire.'

'You did. But you haven't said it.'

'It's complicated.' They had reached the entrance, the old industrial doors, neatly renovated. Sympathetically, was the expression his mother had used. Fuck's sake. Zach thumped one for the hell of it. There was barely a sound. Nothing budged. No one came. He didn't have a key. 'I was here on Saturday night.'

'What do you mean — in the building?'

'Not exactly.'

Sam also knocked on the door, with little energy. She then leant against it, bending forward. She began taking short hard breaths. 'Ooh, my stomach.'

'Sick?'

'I guess,' she said. 'Nothing will come up again though. I don't know, maybe it's something else, not morning sickness.' She looked at him, her

128

eyes were watering. 'How do I know how I'm meant to feel? I've never been pregnant before.'

'You could ask Mum. Should we go back to the car? I'll take you home.' Suddenly he wanted to get out of here. He hadn't thought it through.

'No. It won't make me feel any better. We're here now. You have to carry on, don't you?'

'Maybe you should see a doctor.'

'What do they know?'

'Mum's got a good one.'

'Isn't he private?'

'I guess.' He stepped back into the road, looked up. 'A few people have been having parties and stuff in some warehouses up this end of town.' He held his arms out, swivelled round, like he was a helicopter — Budgie, from the kid's book. How'd he remember that? 'There's a lot of vacant properties. Some amazing space.'

'Yeah?' Sam was still not standing straight. 'How many kids go to these things?'

'They're not like massive raves, yet. But the word's getting out. A couple of DJs from London have come to check it out. One stepped into a set. A guy who's played in Ibiza — Amnesia, Sankeys, DC10. They like the space here. The nostalgia.'

'The nostalgia?' Sam almost spat it out. 'Who's organising this? You?'

'Some.' He looked at his feet. 'These things, they spring up fast. Kids today. Got to keep on your toes.'

'Where's this leading? I'm not feeling great.'

'Sure you don't want to head back?'

She shook her head. Then focused on

something to Zach's right.

'OK, your call — ' He looked over his shoulder. 'Who's this wandering down our street?'

Two men had appeared at the Salmon Road end, some sort of damp daylight wavering around behind them. They'd stepped over the tape and were walking towards the entrance to the Smokehouse with some purpose. They were in suits, ties, no anoraks. One had a clipboard under his arm, the other had a stiff, black shoulder bag, the sort that looked as if it contained a laptop, of the vintage variety. Both were carrying white hard hats.

'Morning,' one of the men said loudly, the guy with the laptop pulling his shoulder out of joint. 'Are you who I want to see?'

'Depends what you're after, mate,' Zach said.

'A Ms Goodwin,' he said, looking at Sam.

Sam had gone from pale to green. Though it could have been the light reflecting off the cold steel doors. 'Me?' she said, weakly.

'If you're the owner of this building,' the man said.

'Who are you?' Zach said.

'Bill Collins,' he said, not holding out his free hand. 'I'm from the council. The Health and Safety executive.'

'And?' Zach said. He'd never seen or heard of Collins before.

'My colleague's from the Norfolk Fire and Rescue Service.'

'Alex Fields,' he stepped in to say, nodding, 'investigator.' This was added with relish.

Fields was a good decade or so younger than Collins. He had the clipboard in his hand now, the hard hat awkwardly under his other arm. The front sheet of paper on the clipboard seemed to be a form, with endless boxes. He caught Zach staring at it. 'You do realise this street has been roped off,' Fields said, sticking out his chest. He was new to suits, Zach reckoned.

'For safety reasons, and whatnot,' Collins added, not so confidently.

'You shouldn't be down here, without permission,' Fields said, getting into his stride.

'You wanted to see a Goodwin,' Zach said.

'I'd hoped to meet a Ms Tatiana Goodwin here,' Collins said, looking at his watch. 'About now. And the police.'

'We're standing in,' Zach said.

'She's our mother,' Sam said.

This annoyed Zach, he wasn't a kid. 'We work with her,' he said. 'It's a family business.'

Collins was pulling a mobile phone from his pocket. He checked the screen. Looked back up at Zach. 'No one's said anything to me about this.'

'No message?' said Fields.

'Nope,' said Collins. 'The police forensic service should be here too by now.'

A gull came swooping by, slowed, but decided not to settle. Zach was not going to call his mum. If she was held up it would be for a good reason. 'What is it you want?' he asked the departing gull.

'Access to the building would be a start,' said Fields. 'Who secured the site yesterday?' This was directed at Collins.

'Community Support?' said Collins, shaking his head.

'We need to get on with this,' Fields said. 'Can you two let us in then? You'll have to wait out here.'

'It's not going to be safe,' added Collins, tapping his hard hat.

'No,' said Zach, his mind once again up in the sky with the flames and the sounds, Saturday night moving in mysterious ways. Sankeys in Yarmouth. Right.

'We don't have the keys,' said Sam, looking at him. She didn't look happy. She looked confused, and ill. But she'd said the right thing this time.

Zach had never broken into the Smokehouse, though he doubted it would be too difficult, especially if he didn't have to worry about the alarm. However, that wasn't what he was going to do right now, not for these monkeys. 'Even if we did have the keys,' he said, annoyed, 'our insurers have instructed us not to allow anyone in the building. They need to assess the damage for themselves, without anything being disturbed, any possible contamination. The boss's orders.'

He paused, quickly looked to the busted roof, the shifty sky. 'To be honest,' he looked back down and straight at Fields, 'they don't trust you lot to do a thorough job. You're welcome to assess the damage from the outside.'

'Young man,' said Fields, 'this is a Fire and Rescue Service investigation. We go where we want. The police will be involved. The forensic scientists, the crime scene investigators. It's a highly complex process, involving many experts, doing what they're trained to do.'

'Who said anything about it being a crime?' Zach said.

'That's for us to determine,' said Fields. 'Any fire of this nature.'

'There're safety issues as well,' chipped in Collins. 'We can't have buildings standing here that pose a threat to the public.'

'Where're the damn police?' said Fields. 'I'm not standing here forever.'

'You're not based in Yarmouth, are you?' Zach said to Fields. Collins seemed to shrink back as he said it.

'No, mate,' Fields said. 'That's one pleasure I don't have.'

'Then you don't know how it works, do you? The pleasure's all ours.'

'Are you trying to be clever?'

'I don't need to be clever,' said Zach. 'I have other ways of being heard.'

'There is a legal issue here,' Sam said, quietly. 'Until a building is declared unfit, according to the Fire Services Act, 1983, then the council, or anyone else for that matter, has no jurisdiction over that property, except the owner. You can't walk in there, unless we allow you to. There are no indications that I can see,' she continued, 'that suggest this is a crime scene, which of course would change the situation.'

Fields looked at Collins. 'What's going on, mate? There's tape up.'

'That is not crime scene tape,' said Sam. 'No notices have been pasted on the entrance. The Fire Service only has command and jurisdiction over an active situation. The police then take over, if necessary. That doesn't appear to have happened here. Not that I can see.'

'Someone's not been very clever,' said Zach.

'You've got this all wrong,' said Fields, pulling out his mobile phone.

As he began tapping away at the screen, a car with a hefty engine not being pushed hard made its presence felt. Zach turned towards the other end of the street as his mother's Merc appeared. If there had been any tape that end it hadn't hindered her passage.

Fields did not put his phone to his ear. Tatty stopped metres away, leaving the long, low bonnet of her SL at a slant, some metres away. Zach wasn't sure whether she was trying to make a statement, or it was her usual crap parking. He watched his mother take her time climbing out, reach for her bag, hook it on her arm, slam the wide driver's door shut, pat down her mac, smile casually at the street, and walk over.

'Hello, darlings,' she said, aiming straight for Zach and Sam. 'How nice to see you both.'

Zach was glad she didn't say, 'surprised'.

'How are you feeling, Sam?' she said, putting her hand on the small of Sam's back.

'Not great,' said Sam. 'I'm all right at the minute.'

'And who have we got here?' She'd stepped back and was now looking at the two men.

'Tatiana Goodwin?' Collins said.

Zach watched his mother nod slowly. 'Mrs Goodwin, yes, that's me,' she said.

'Mrs Goodwin,' Collins said, hurriedly, his checks immediately taking on some colour, 'I'm from the Health and Safety executive.'

'I know exactly who you are,' Tatty said. 'Both of you. Sorry I'm late. You want to come in and have a poke around?'

'That's the usual way of doing things,' said Collins. 'Indeed, we'll have to ask you to wait outside.' He was tapping his hard hat again.

'We'll be accompanied by the police, forensics, as well,' said Fields.

'Yeah?' said Tatty. 'I don't see them.'

'They're on their way,' said Fields.

The gull was back, Zach couldn't help noticing. It was swooping low over his mother's car. Unless it was another gull. They were so fat around here, he couldn't understand how they managed to take off. Had no idea what they could eat. No one he knew ate anything particularly nourishing in Yarmouth. Except perhaps Candy Cane. A gull on MDMA? That would be something to witness.

Tatty was looking at her watch. 'I'll tell you what, because I'm short of time as well, and I want to do all I can to assist and speed up this investigation, I'll open up, let you two pop upstairs, while we wait in the lobby. I don't trust it not to rain.'

'Thank you,' said Collins. 'I appreciate that.'

'We'll still need to wait for the police,' said Fields. 'There're many elements to these investigations.' He was not remotely happy.

'You might have to wait some time,' said Tatty.

'What about our insurers, Mum?' Zach asked, hoping she'd get the drift.

'We're doing these two a favour, Zach. I'm sure when it comes to it, they'll return the gesture.' She smiled at him, at them all. Dug lightly in her bag, retrieved a bunch of keys. Went for the impenetrable steel double doors.

Pointing a key towards the first lock, Zach noticed his mum's hand wasn't steady. There was a smear of what had to be dried blood on the sleeve of her mac as well. Unless it was hot chocolate. Grouped around her, they were crowding out the daylight. The reclaimed steel continuing to distort colours in the sudden dimness.

His mum never drank hot chocolate.

16

'Britt Hayes, the very person. At last.' Frank removed his phone from his ear, swapped hands, scratched the side of his head, thinking it needed a shave, thinking also that he needed a new burner. He used to change them every fortnight. He'd been getting sloppy as well. He put the device against his other ear. He was hungry. Fat, fifty and hungry.

'I'm busy,' Hayes was saying.

'Course you are,' said Frank. He'd pulled over on the wide and empty Jellicoe Road, the other side of the bridge, by the entrance to the racecourse. The latest poster was advertising a race day on Wednesday. Frank hadn't been to see the gee-gees for donkeys.

'Besides, I'm not who I was any more. Didn't Howie tell you?'

'Haven't seen Howie in . . . ' he almost said donkeys, ' . . . months. Can't get hold of him.'

'That's what you want me for, is it?'

Frank felt himself smile, at the big creased picture of a bunch of horses — little jockeys sticking their tiny arses up into the purple air — taking a corner. Those horses were giving it some welly, leaning into the white fencing, on an unnaturally sunny day. The jockeys' arses were too skinny for his liking. He'd never humped a jockey. Had never thought about it until now. 'No,' he said. 'Something else for once.'

'For once?'

'Can we meet?'

'I told you, I'm not who I was any more. There's been some restructuring.'

'You've still got your job?'

'Oh yes, I've still got a job.'

'So what's changed?'

'I'm on secondment. We're all on secondment, my level. We now have to change roles every twelve months.'

'Why? To stop the wrong connections developing?' Frank said, thinking fast and sharp. He could have gone into the force. But he took the other route of course.

'That's not how they're putting it. It's to get fresh eyes on the big situations. Management bollocks. The roles are having to expand as well.'

'Your world.' Frank's eyes kept being drawn back to the horses, the jockeys. He was old and hungry, and sex-starved, he suddenly realised. Galloping horses. Rising sap. Spring. Or did he want more than a one-night stand? At his age, maybe it was time to settle down with someone. 'You're still in Wymondham, aren't you?'

'I'll be here until I die,' Hayes said.

'I hope not,' said Frank. 'So who's doing your old job?'

'Serious and Organised is now under the control, the temporary control I guess, of Kyle Neville.'

'Never heard of him.'

'He's from Suffolk, was with terrorism.'

'What have you got?'

'You're going to love this: domestic, sexual

138

violence and hate crimes.'

'They lump all that together, do they?'

'Cost-cutting,' Hayes said.

'I can see why Howie's been keeping his head down.'

Hayes laughed. 'This conversation has to end. This conversation should never have started.'

Frank wondered how far back she meant. 'Sure,' he said. 'I still need a favour.'

'You'll have to go elsewhere.'

'Don't hang up.'

'Frank, there's something else you should know. I'm also Assistant Chief Constable.'

'Big cheese — wow.' Frank realised he was not going to keep her on the line forever. 'There's something you should know — Simon Goodwin's back, and he's cosying up to Graham Sands.'

'Not my bag.'

'Sexual violence? Domestic abuse? Child abuse? Are you kidding me?'

'What was the favour you wanted from me?'

'I just told you. Oh, and when you next see your boyfriend, pass on a message will you? I'd like to sit down and have a turkey sandwich with him.' Frank ended the call before Hayes could, threw the mobile onto the passenger seat, flicked the Range Rover into gear, gave the jockeys one last glance, then powered due east. Howie would have no idea what he was talking about. *Turkey sandwich?* At least he hoped not. He needed to see the fucker.

The sea appeared, grey and cold and wet, before the slap of sand and dune warmed the vista up. He couldn't determine what the sun was doing, where the day was heading. The wind turbines, clogging the horizon, didn't appear to be moving. Though an unpleasant smell had now penetrated the cabin. Frank carefully slowed for the junction with North Drive. Eased the vehicle left and along the seafront for a couple of hundred metres. The Coastwatch tower was looking as lonely and redundant as ever. One or two figures were out walking dogs. Seabirds had more purpose about them.

He turned into the caravan park, swung the vehicle to the right of the lodge, past the silver Beamer, which was still sitting there. The track was more than wide enough, though cars weren't normally encouraged to go this way. This was for pedestrians, kiddies — OAPs more like. Not that any were about. More smell was seeping into the cabin. Frank had had it with rotting meat, and this vehicle, even if he wasn't hungry. The cure-all diet. He should write a book. Wondered whether morticians ever felt famished.

The Range Rover rolled slowly along the track. The track wound slowly through the park, past caravans that came in small, medium or large. The smaller were further from the sea. Frank did not spot a single living face as he drove on towards the company caravan, now stuck in the sticky shade of the massive lime. He turned the vehicle round on the wet ground, not caring what tracks were left. He reversed up so the boot was as close to the door as practical. He took another wide peek, doubting there'd be occupants in any of the adjacent caravans. Rolly Andrews had always kept this part of the park for special clients. That's what he'd been paid to do.

Who else had been paying him?

Livid, leaving the Glock safely tucked under the front passenger seat, Frank climbed out. The day had softened at this dead end of the park. He could hear birds, and once he was out in the open, smell vegetation, before other smells began to ruin the idyll. He looked about him once more. Walked to the back of the vehicle. His black Derbys were the only solid, sensible things anywhere near here that he could determine. He opened the boot. Stepped over to the caravan. Found the tiny key. Opened up, while trying to keep his nose in the opposite direction.

He'd left the remains of the turkey crown where he'd found it. It was a shame Rolly Andrews was dead, otherwise he might have forced him to take a few bites. He went back to the car, the opened boot. Zipped his jacket up. Took a deep breath. Leaned forward, grabbed hold of the body by the legs, pulled him towards the edge of the boot. Got him by the waist, lifted him out of the vehicle and straight into the caravan head first.

He was not so heavy for a little old man. It was easier without Tatty trying to help. They'd wiped the blood away from his mouth as well. That had made Tatty scream when he'd first tried to move the body. They hadn't been expecting a mouth full of congealing blood and vomit to trickle out. Which made Frank think Rolly had had some sort of haemorrhage, rather than a heart attack. It didn't look as if he'd been punched in the face.

141

He was becoming stiff fast. Frank thought of a battering ram. Using Rolly's head to batter down Graham Sands' fucking door, to begin with. The caravan was nothing like as stiff as Rolly's body, and was bending and shaking as Frank struggled to get the corpse through the kitchen and lounge area and into the disgusting bedroom. He all but threw it onto the bed, next to what was left of the turkey. The flies and maggots would have plenty to be pleased about, for a short while.

He wasn't going to bother positioning the body too carefully, trying to make it look like anything other than the last gasp of a silly old man. He backed out of the bedroom. Stepped over to the sink. His mind focused on what not to forget. He reached above, tapped the right panel. Lifted it away when it came clear. He'd already removed the gun. Now he took the thick plastic bag containing the emergency cash — sterling and euros — and Rich's fake identities. He didn't know why he'd kept these. Perhaps he should pass them on to Tatty, some sort of keepsake. Perhaps not.

He folded and rolled the bag as best he could. Stuffed it in the left inside chest pocket of his jacket. The other inside pocket had the large plastic bag of pills. It wasn't the tightest fitting jacket, the most fashionable thing in his wardrobe. He went back outside, wondering whether he was growing used to the smell. You could grow used to anything, couldn't you? Part of how the species survived.

Sweating badly, he reached into the cavernous boot once more. He dragged out the canvas bag, hefted it inside the caravan, took it through to the bedroom, dropped it on the floor. Felt the reverberations shoot through the soles of his feet and up his solid legs. His bones still tingling, he backed out of the bedroom once more. He had another good scan of the kitchen and lounge area before stepping the short way down and into the real world, pulling the door closed behind him. He was not going to lock it, even though he wouldn't be torching the caravan just yet.

'Frank?' A man stepped from behind the Range Rover. He was Frank's height, but not Frank's weight. His jacket, a dark puffa, fitted snugly. His black jeans encased muscular legs. His boots were Redwing. His hat was a navy baseball cap, no logo.

'Fuck you spring from?' Frank said, wiping his brow with his sleeve.

'I was in the area,' Howie said.

'Like fuck. How did you get here so quick?'

'I was, mate, walking. Baz? Baz?' Howie was shouting, looking to his left, his right, over his shoulder. 'We were out on the dunes. I saw you drive in.'

'Like fuck,' Frank said again. But Howie's dog came snuffling up, its great black and tan chops covered in frothy saliva. It bypassed Howie and went straight to Frank, leaning hard and hot against Frank's left tree-trunk. Frank's legs were not so muscular, as knotted and stumpy. Reluctantly Frank bent down, patted Baz on his bony head. He loved this dog.

'Odd day. The weather's all over the place,' Howie said.

'Odd day?' Frank said. 'You wouldn't believe what's been going on.'

'I did see you drive in,' Howie said. 'Honest. I also got a message from the missus, same time.' He smiled. 'Uncanny.'

'Say that again,' Frank said.

'She cares about you. We both do.'

'Yeah?' Frank whistled, shaking his head, a whole world of worry, but knowing it wasn't going to be going away anytime soon. 'I'm not sure we want to be seen hanging around here for long.'

'Are you telling me people have already pitched up for their summer hols?'

'Not in this part of the park.'

'Rolly's still doing his job then?'

'That's why we don't want to hang around.' Baz was now more interested in the door to the caravan than Frank's leg. The boxer was manically sniffing around the bottom of the frame.

'I take that as no then. Never trusted that man — you know what they say about gyppos?'

'You could get into trouble for a comment like that,' Frank interrupted, smiling. 'Isn't it what they call a race hate crime?'

'Wasn't there the offer of a turkey sandwich?' Howie looked away, through the chain-link fence and towards the racecourse — a vast stretch of fuzzy green dotted with dirty white railings. The concrete stand was out of sight from here. Howie looked back and down at Baz — the dog still desperate to get inside the caravan, making a racket about it as well. 'Has the meat gone off?'

'Where have you been for the last few weeks?'

'Keeping Britt sweet. Domestic chores.'

'So she doesn't lock you up?'

'Norfolk Constabulary — I don't like to see Britt so stretched. And just as she was getting the hang of the serious stuff. Pity.'

'Domestic abuse isn't serious?'

'You know what I mean.'

'Do you know this Kyle Neville character?'

'No.' Howie was shaking his head now. 'Britt says he's clean as a whistle.'

'He's come from terrorism — I suppose they vet them more thoroughly.'

'He's also in the territorial army.'

'Don't tell me we've got Dad's Army on our back.'

'Britt's still there, Frank.'

'Don't give her any wrong ideas,' Frank said. 'You and your dog.' But he couldn't smile at his own joke this time. It wasn't a joke. He wasn't a funny guy. What he should have said was, don't abuse her trust, or something. But Frank knew Howie wouldn't. He'd never met a couple like them. 'Do you want a lift?' He opened the driver's door of the Range Rover.

'You're not going to show me what's inside the caravan? Ask me in for that sandwich?'

'You wouldn't be able to restrain your dog.'

Frank climbed into his vehicle. Reached behind him, opened a rear passenger door.

'You're letting Baz in your car?' Howie shouted. He hadn't got in. Was looking at Frank quizzically.

'I love that dog,' Frank said. 'Only dog I do love.'

145

'There's always a first.'

'And a last,' said Frank.

'Up you get then, Baz — you lucky boy,' Howie said, directing the boxer onto the back seat. 'Look at all this luxury for you. Cream leather seats. Individual climate control.' Howie shut the rear door, and climbed into the passenger seat. Shut that door too with a thud. Sniffed. 'This car stinks, Frank.'

'I've been ferrying around the wrong sort of rubbish.'

'What state was he in?'

'Twenty-four hours, a bit more maybe.'

'Did you shoot him?'

'No I didn't.'

'Warm enough for you, Baz?' Howie was looking over his shoulder at Baz.

Frank could hear the dog panting and slobbering. He hated to think what he was doing to the seats. But he never sat in the back, and he had plans for the vehicle, like the caravan, in any case. Howie was not going to quiz him further, about the body or the smell of rotting meat, the promised turkey sandwich, though he knew he owed his friend an explanation. 'He was dead when we found him.' Frank pulled away from the caravan, checking in his rear-view mirror that the front door was properly closed. Howie hadn't put his seatbelt on.

'We?' Howie said, ignoring the gentle beeping, telling him to put his seatbelt on.

'Tatty found him. He was in Goodwin House, in her old office, behind the desk. With a standard bag of breaking and entering tools.

Arson gear as well.'

'Whoa — you reckon he set fire to the Smokehouse, then went over to Goodwin House?'

'Unless he was part of a team.'

'Possible.' Howie opened his window.

'Yeah, I know,' said Frank, 'that's what's worrying me.' He now opened his window. 'Been meaning to change this vehicle for a while.' They'd reached the main track, and were heading for the exit.

'Which was why you so kindly let Baz in. Should have guessed.' Howie paused. 'It's not totally empty, is it?'

Frank knew he was referring to the park. A man was washing the windows of a huge static to their left, sponge on a stick in one hand, smouldering fag in the other, while a couple of women, stooped with age, were chatting by the steps to another static; this one with some white plastic wraparound decking. Frank couldn't see how they'd ever climb up, clamber on board. He wouldn't forget the man, even though he had to be on the wrong side of fifty — skinny fellow, like he'd smoked the life out of himself.

'Rolly had a bag of pills on him — MDMA. This new Candy Cane stuff people are talking about, most likely.' Frank patted his chest pocket, indicating where the pills were now. 'Rolly wasn't a dealer.'

'Not that you knew.'

'He wasn't, Howie. At his age? It's not something you take up in your seventies.'

'Is that an ageist comment?'

'You're the PC one.'

Frank huffed. 'Right.'

'Maybe he stole them,' Howie said.

'On his way to set fire to Goodwin House?'

'You know what they're like — gyppos.'

'How does Britt put up with you?'

'That's one of the great mysteries, Frank.'

'Maybe he took a handful. Had a bad reaction.' Frank was thinking aloud. 'We found him by Tatty's desk. No injuries on him that we could see. There was some mess in his mouth, stuff that had come up.'

'You didn't think to leave him there? Get the hell out? Call the cops?'

'Me, call the cops?' He laughed, turned serious. 'There's too much going on this week. Big investors coming in. Couldn't have police getting in the way. And with this new guy in charge of Serious and Organised?'

'You didn't know that when you moved the body.'

Frank was slowing by the lodge. 'That's weird. The Beamer's gone. There was an old three series parked by the lodge when I drove in. Was there earlier as well. Rolly's Roller's at the menders, apparently.'

'I cut through the fence further down,' Howie said. 'I didn't walk this way.'

Frank stopped the car, turned to Howie, thinking back. 'Best that we deal with the body, you know that. Don't want to give anyone a chance to pin the wrong thing on us. Besides, we need to know who he was working for.'

'He's going to wake up and tell you? You can't

148

leave it in that caravan for long.'

'I'm fully aware of that, my friend. But it's not the only rotting thing in there. That caravan's fucked. Like this car. I'll torch the caravan later, and the car's for the drink. But there're going to be a few more bodies to dispose of soon, so it might make sense to hold fire for a little while.'

'Don't get too clever,' Howie said. 'Time catches everyone out.'

Frank navigated the condemned vehicle beyond the front of the lodge, turning left onto a track that led nowhere but a high wooden fence marking the lodge's immediate boundary. They were tight to the side of the one-storey building, with something approximating a corrugated roof immediately above them. The car port was not visible from the front of the lodge. Frank knew it had never been used much by Rolly Andrews, who preferred leaving his Roller out the front for all to see. 'I just need to pop in here, have a snoop,' he said, turning off the engine.

'It's not a game, Frank,' Howie said. 'Remember that.'

'You hungry?' Frank said. 'I'm on the lookout for some turkey crowns.'

'Norfolk Bronze?'

'I thought you'd have some idea.'

'Top of the range. The region's finest. No others worth considering.' Howie glanced over his shoulder, as did Frank. Baz had fallen asleep already. 'We've been out since early,' Howie said. 'He's getting old.'

'We're all getting old,' Frank said, climbing down, trying to stifle a groan. His right hip had been hurting of late. His right knee had been more painful. Could he even still get it up?

'A container was busted into a month or so back,' Howie said. 'Leftover stock from Christmas, apparently. The poultry was destined for some poor Third World country. Or maybe a landfill. They're all over the place, kitchens awash with salmonella. You wouldn't want to eat one.'

'Someone left one in my caravan. Must have been there a few weeks.'

'Shame Rolly's no longer got an appetite.'

17

'Mess in here, all right,' Howie said, sniffing.

He was over by something that resembled a single bed, pushed up against a far wall. The air was musty. Faint smells of distant summers, and decayed fabric. A chemical smell too.

They hadn't switched on any lights, but they could discern enough to see that the place had been turned over. The side door had been locked, however, when Frank had initially tried it. There was no broken glass, splintered wood, or obvious signs of a break-in. As it was, Howie had sprung the lock in two seconds flat. Perhaps that's how their immediate predecessors got in. Or maybe they'd had a key. Whichever, they'd been looking for something. 'He lived in here as well,' Frank said.

'You're not telling me,' said Howie. 'Beats a caravan, I guess. The wind coming off the sea. Though these storm surges every other week — not sure this would offer much protection. The weather, Frank, we're fucked. And we've only got ourselves to blame.'

'You're full of doom and gloom today,' Frank said, kicking a cardboard box out of his way. It was more solid than he'd been expecting. Felt like a lump of cement in there.

'I don't like trouble,' Howie said. 'Not manmade.'

'Rubbish.' The side door had led them into the

151

back of the lodge. Living quarters for a certain sort of man. Frank's mind flashed to his own pristine lounge.

The front of the lodge acted as the caravan park's reception. Frank had to step over a couple of overturned armchairs, some cushions and a heap of old newspapers and magazines. The bottom of one of the armchairs had been ripped apart, revealing nothing but cheap craftsmanship, shoddy materials. The door to the reception area was ajar. Frank pushed it open. A small flood of daylight met him coldly. He blinked. Blinked again. Nothing seemed out of place.

The counter was clear, a tad dusty. A row of shelves behind the counter displayed a few utility items for sale. Soap, washing-up liquid, clothes pegs, lighter fluid — the same yellow tin. All a time warp. A faded map of Yarmouth was on the dog-leg wall to the counter. Frank gave it a quick glance, noticing that the outer harbour was not present. Neither any hint of sand on Gorleston beach. The sea had gone white.

'Frank?' Howie called from the rear of the building. 'There's something here you might want to see, mate.'

Frank headed for the door, stopped mid-stride, swivelled back round. Beyond the counter, in the far corner of the reception, was a large freezer cabinet. He crossed the length of the short counter and out into the public area. He peered through the misty glass top. Pale dark shapes were about all he could see. Some darker and brighter colours the longer he looked. He pulled on the glass, the small lip by the partition, but it wouldn't slide open.

'Frank?' Howie called again from the other room.

He tried the glass panel once more, then noticed it was locked shut. A tiny brass padlock, towards the rear edge, was winking at him. Frank felt his pockets, the huge packet of pills, the roll of money and fake documents. He had nothing hard, heavy. The Glock was in the motor, with Baz. Couldn't understand why the freezer had remained padlocked, yet Rolly's living quarters had been given a thorough going over. Had they not ventured this way? For fear of being spotted through the large windows out front? Perhaps they'd found what they were looking for in the back.

'What have you got, Howie?' Frank shouted.

'How well did you know this guy?' Howie shouted back.

Frank looked at the shelves. Stepped over. Pulled off a packet of washing powder. Daz. Let it drop to the floor. Grabbed the tin of lighter fluid. It had to be the same vintage. He went back to the freezer, took a swipe at the lock with it. Nothing happened. He took another swipe. The lock was undamaged, but the lip of the glass panel was coming away. Another thwack and the lock and some plastic trim flew across the room.

'Frank?' Howie was by the door. 'What do you reckon?'

Frank couldn't work out what Howie was holding. Yes, he could. A black leather bag, with some gold buckles. 'It's a handbag.'

'Yeah, I know it's a handbag. Fake leather,

153

plastic metallic trim. Who do you reckon Rolly's been entertaining?'

'Not Tatty, that's for sure. Where was it?'

'Under his bed, with another twenty or so.' Howie started laughing.

'Old habits die hard,' Frank said, turning back to the freezer. It took some effort to slide the top open. The edges of the panel were stuck with frost and faint purple grime. There was a loud creaking sound, and finally he got it open enough to see that the inside was heaped with frosted lumps of what had to be turkey, turkey crowns. Yeah, same vintage as the one that had been left for him, judging by the labels.

Pushed to one side of the freezer were some opened cardboard boxes of ice creams. The few Cornettos did not look appetising, even though Frank was starving. Impossible to tell how long they'd been there, or the turkeys. Who'd buy a ripped-off turkey from a caravan park, summer or winter?

Frank still couldn't see Rolly leaving a lump of poultry in the company caravan, Rich dead and out of the way or not. He peered closer, brushed some frost off one of the labels. The best before date was March that year. 'They weren't here for the scoff,' Frank shouted. 'Or the fashion accessories.' He glanced behind his shoulder. Howie was not in sight.

'Hard to tell what they were looking for,' Howie shouted back. 'Whatever it was, seems like they've taken it.'

'That's the conclusion I'm coming to,' Frank said loudly, returning to the living quarters. 'Or they were disturbed.'

'Doubt it,' said Howie. He was in the living area, bent over the cardboard box. 'Something tells me that whoever was in here is not easily scared off.'

'Nothing's unturned in here.'

'I doubt it was very clean or tidy before.'

'No wonder he never asked me in for a cup of tea,' Frank said. He'd never seen so much clutter. Stuff pilfered from caravans and chalets. How'd he got away with it? 'His daughter always makes an effort. Neat little thing. Must get it from her mother.'

'The mother not around?'

'No,' said Frank. 'No idea what happened to her. Never thought to ask. Me and Tatty will be having a word with Sian later. Her car was out the back of Goodwin House this morning. She claims her dad had borrowed it for the weekend. His Roller's fucked again.'

'So whose is the three series you said was outside here earlier?' said Howie, straightening.

'You tell me.'

'Quite a few of them around.' Howie licked his finger, kicked the box at his feet. 'This is a box of lactose powder, gone damp.'

'You think Rolly had a sweet tooth?'

'Did he have teeth?'

Frank thought of the moment he and Tatty first tried to move the body and Rolly Andrews' mouth fell open. If he had false teeth, they didn't budge. Cemented in? Tatty was not at all happy about the fluid on her mac.

'The sort of operation that would use this

155

amount of filler,' said Howie, 'could be MDMA, in the powder form. More likely to be crack, or smack. Perhaps coke. There're more convincing agents than lactose. Cheapskate.'

'Cash and carry?' said Frank. 'Perhaps he could only get it in this quantity. Or maybe, out of the blue, he came across a box of this stuff, thought he might make fifty pence out of it.'

'Passing it off to who? He'd have known what it was for. Where would he come across it in any case? You know what, Frank, maybe he stole it from the wrong people — along with the stuff that really counted.'

'And have who knows after him,' Frank said, wistfully, looking towards the door Howie had broken through. 'Why was this door locked?' Frank began letting himself out of the lodge. 'Someone breaks in, trashes the place, then quietly departs, making sure the door was locked behind them?' Frank checked. 'It's a Chubb, not a Yale.'

'The main reception door?' said Howie. 'Did they get out that way?'

Frank was already retracing his steps, hurrying through to the front. He could see before he even got close that it was bolted from the inside at least, top and bottom. He could also see a man staring at him through the window, from the far side of the tarmacked drive. He casually looked away when he realised he'd been spotted by Frank. He was heading out of the park, towards the dunes. It was the same man who'd been washing windows. He was still smoking. A Jack Russell was trotting loyally after him.

There were busybodies everywhere. Snitches too. That man needed to mind his own business. Or there'd be a nasty accident.

18

'Darling, I'll pop back up in half an hour or so. I'll only be downstairs.' Tatty gently pulled the door closed as she left Sam's bedroom and stepped out onto the landing. Murky daylight was creeping across the soft carpet. Just one day of solid sun by this time of year, was it too much to ask for? And no damn easterly wind.

She looked at her watch, the gold glinting wastefully away. It was too late for lunch and too early for tea, even if she had been hungry. She was worried about Sam. She'd had morning sickness with Ben, but not, that she could remember, with the others. Besides, with Ben she'd been so bloody anxious about being pregnant, and with Rich's child, it was hardly surprising. She'd tricked him, she supposed. Said she was on the pill when she wasn't any longer. It was making her too bloated. Had no idea it would be possible to get pregnant, let alone so quick. Not after endless issues with STDs and the rest of it. She'd been punched in the stomach more than once, had drunk too much, smoked too much, sniffed glue because it was practically free. She wasn't the most rebellious of her girlfriends, they were all at it. There was nothing else to do on a council estate in the East Midlands in the 1980s. And then her mum moved them to Norwich, where it only got worse.

At the foot of the stairs, she turned on the spot, headed back past Sam's room, to her own bedroom. Rich had been such a big man. She remembered worrying about how on earth she was ever going to push out his baby, once she'd decided to keep it. She'd been tiny then. A size six. As it was she'd had Caesareans for all of them. At least her pelvic floor was not giving her any grief. Other things had begun to go on down there, however. Estrogen pills were what her doctor had suggested. Having weaned herself off all manner of other prescription drugs not so long ago, she was reluctant to begin another course of medication.

Her blouse was off before she'd made it into her room. She quickly stripped out of the rest of her clothes and headed into the en suite. She was convinced she could still smell death on her hands, her skin. Couldn't believe the man had been Sian's dad. She was livid Sian had lent him her car, which wasn't hers anyway. Sian wasn't telling them the whole truth, of that she was sure. But Tatty didn't think she knew her dad was dead. She'd have been more upset on the phone.

They should have quizzed Sian by now, face to face. Tatty would have, if she hadn't suddenly needed to keep an eye on her own daughter, drive her home from Yarmouth and tuck her up in bed. Zach had offered, but he shouldn't have dragged her out of the house in the first place. She didn't trust him to look after his sister properly. Besides, she needed him to stick around the Smokehouse, keep an eye on the clowns who appeared to have all the time and the pettiness in the world.

Let them think they were in control, at least until she'd decided what she wanted their reports to say.

The water was hot and invigorating and she stood there not enjoying the sensation while the steam built up, because thoughts of Simon were now seeping, cold and chilling, into her head, like she had a leak up there. Shuddering, she watched the suds disappear down the wide plughole, watched some more as clean water washed off her. She then stepped out of the shower, grabbing a large clean towel off the rack.

Her phone was going as she walked back into her bedroom. Stepping over to the bed, where she'd thrown it, she saw that the number was *Unknown*. She'd had enough unknowns for one day. She dabbed her hands on the towel some more, lunged for the device, swiped answer. 'Yes?'

'Tatty? It's Michael.'

'Oh, Michael, good afternoon.' She looked over to the French door, caught a wedge of sea.

'I've been ringing your office.'

'My assistant's off today. Family problems. Where are you?'

'Still in Amsterdam. Family problems too, Tatty.'

'What do you mean?'

'Change of partnership. We've had to bring in some new investors.'

'Slow down. What are you saying?'

'I thought it only right to inform you

160

immediately. These new partners, they have different expectations, demands.'

'Are you telling me that the finance was never in place?'

'It was in place, for sure. But there've been some amendments. These things happen. New players come on board. Others disappear.'

'What sort of operation is this you're running?' Tatty hissed. 'Call yourself a financier? You approached us, Michael. You came running.' The sea, straight out of the window, was no longer a flat grey. A wide band was sparkling. Some sun was getting through somewhere.

'It's an unstable world right now. Currencies are going up and down like there's no tomorrow, along with all manner of economic outlooks. These things have to be taken into consideration. You're lucky we're still in the frame.'

'Lucky? And you've just rung up to tell me this?'

'I've been trying you all day — when I could. I've been in and out of meetings. Plus, I've been having my own communication problems, if you haven't heard.'

'Should we even be having this conversation on the phone? Can't it wait until you're here?'

'I'm keeping you in the picture, that's all.'

'Which is what exactly?' The towel had slipped from under her arms. Tatty was standing completely naked in the middle of her bedroom, no blinds down.

'With a change of partnership comes a change of terms, naturally.'

'Naturally? I can see where you're heading

with this,' Tatty said. 'Forget it. We're not budging. Nothing's changed this end.'

'Not quite what I'm hearing.'

'Get here and we'll have a chat,' Tatty said.

'Fireside?' he laughed.

'What do you know?'

'A heads-up, Tatty — that's what you say, isn't it? I won't be coming on my own.'

'I didn't think you ever were. I was expecting a troop of overdressed, overpaid flunkies. Lawyers, accountants, PAs.'

'Think again. These new people, they don't negotiate. They don't wear suits either.'

'Why are you bringing them, then? You know exactly what's on offer.' She looked down at her bare feet. Her pale legs. Her tan needed topping up, urgently.

'A few charred remains? They expect more than that. They need to know that their money is secure.'

She laughed. How the fuck did he know about the fire? Had Sam said anything? She'd promised she hadn't. 'My word sticks, Michael,' she said as calmly as possible. She looked out of the salt-smeared glass again. What she'd do to spend the summer in Ibiza, lying by the pool. Or on a yacht cruising around the Med. Frank was right, she needed to get away. One day, when she'd properly earned it.

'And that's before dividends come into play,' Michael continued.

Who was putting on the bigger act here, Tatty wondered. 'Nothing happens in Yarmouth without my say-so.'

162

'I wish that were the case,' Michael said. 'They want operational control. They'll be putting a team in place. For the transition, it'll be me and a guy called Hans. I won't be there all the time. My office remains in the City. But Hans will relocate.'

'Hans?' She laughed again — you couldn't make it up. 'This is not how we do things. Hands fucking off.' Who'd he been talking to locally? Had he gone behind her back?

'Oh, and they're reducing their investment by a hundred mill.'

Now another thing. 'No they're not.' Goodwin Enterprises and the super casino project was back where it started. *A hundred mill?* She was still staring at the sea, the smoky horizon, the round world.

'You have no option. These new people, they mean business. They want something, they get it.'

'I can turn my back, go elsewhere. Do what the fuck I like. It's my project, my town.'

'No you can't, and no it's not. Look, Tatty, I'm just the messenger. I'm doing all I can to keep this thing from collapsing. To keep you all safe and secure.'

Just the messenger. Where had she heard that before? 'Yeah? Is that right?'

'I have a lot at stake here as well, if that's not clear to you.'

How dare he. 'Sam's not having an easy time of it, Michael. She's sick. She's in her bedroom, puking her guts out right now. Don't put her under any kind of pressure with this. You upset

163

her, you'll have me to answer to.' What had Sam got herself involved with? What had they all?

'I am aware that Sam's not feeling great. I'm sorry. But what can I do? I'm away on business. Bit of morning sickness — you'll take good care of her. She's in the best possible place. Times like this, a daughter needs her mother. My precious Sam.'

'Get on a fucking plane, Michael — on your own. But don't bother unless you've got the money in place. All of it. A hundred mill will not wash.' She wasn't going to lose that sort of face. He'd come running, open arms, with two hundred mill. That's what it was going to be. Double what Rich had hoped for — in his wildest dreams.

'Tatty,' his tone had changed, 'get real. The world's changing faster than any of us can keep up with.'

'Not here it isn't,' she said. 'It's going backwards.'

'Be grateful for anything,' he said, maybe not getting her drift.

He ended the call before she had a chance to. She quickly swiped through to Frank's latest number — which was under the name Rosemary, Rosemary Thyme. She'd been watching a run of *Rosemary & Thymes* on TV. Thought the gardening reference was appropriate. Nothing else was. She much preferred *Death in Paradise*.

Frank wasn't answering. She didn't leave a message. What could she say? She ran out of the room, along the landing, barged straight into

164

Sam's room. The room was dim and still. 'Sam?' The bedcovers were thrown back, leaving a vast empty space. 'Sam?'

'What's up?' Sam emerged in the doorway to her en suite. Hung onto the doorframe.

'I didn't know where you were,' Tatty said.

'Mum, you've got no clothes on. I was on the toilet.' She let go of the woodwork and shuffled back to bed.

Tatty was still clutching her phone. She looked down. Sam was quite right, she was naked. She had nothing to be ashamed of. 'I've had a difficult conversation with Michael,' she said.

'At least he fucking rang you,' Sam said.

'Everything will be all right, darling.'

'Why'd you rush into my bedroom then, naked?'

Tatty sighed. 'Men, darling. You can never trust them.'

'Great,' said Sam, pulling the duvet up to her chin.

'You didn't tell him about the fire, did you?'

'No — how many times?'

'Michael's business, his associates, his connections, does he talk much about them?'

'I always said to you, Mum, that I wanted to keep out of it. Your and Michael's business is your own concern. It's unfortunate I ever came across him.'

That was true, Tatty couldn't help thinking. Though hadn't he come across her — on purpose? It had to have all been planned. A man who was that careful with his appearance? 'Don't say that, darling. It'll all be fine.' She sat on

Sam's bed, reached over, brushed her daughter's hot cheek. Tatty was starting to get cold. She would like to have crawled under the duvet too. 'So you know, Michael made the first move with regards the business,' she said. 'He suggested it, knowing that the American deal had collapsed and that a very significant investment opportunity was up for grabs.'

'He didn't get any of this from me,' came Sam's curt, muffled reply. 'Can you, like, let me be alone, Mum — don't mean to be rude. I need to lie here and stop feeling sick.'

What was Tatty saying to her daughter? She'd encouraged Michael like there was no tomorrow. Was she prepared to use her children in the same way that Rich had used them? She was here to protect and provide for them, wasn't she? To care for them. She put her hand on Sam's forehead. 'You feel a bit hot, darling. Do you have a temperature?' They could all be so much stronger, safer, and richer, if they kept close, worked together.

'No, I don't think I have a temperature. This is the winter duvet. Leave me alone now, will you?'

This was not said unkindly, but Tatty still felt gutted. She stood, made for the door. 'I'll be here for the rest of the day in case you need me.' That was the least she could do. She wondered whether she should call the doctor.

19

Sun had appeared in the back garden. At some angle, it was cascading onto the tidy shrubs and odd bits of greenery. No one else had appeared, or been in touch. Tatty couldn't remember the last time she'd been stuck at home, looking after a sick child.

Maybe she'd get the whole garden paved. Do away with the plants altogether. The gardener cost enough. Would she have to start watching the pennies? Reviving old revenue streams seemed more fun. She should never have shut down the brothels, the live import business, and pinned so much on something more legitimate — at least from the outside. Her cut from the construction alone, would that ever have been enough? Manipulated the right way, yes. Yes, it bloody would. Even in this stupidly fast-changing world.

Zach was up to speed, wasn't he? But it was impossible to keep him tied down to a computer for more than five minutes. Where was Ben when she needed him? He was solid, reliable, if distant. He understood numbers. Though they needed Zach for the access, the law-breaking.

Standing, walking over to the sink, she knew she had to be smarter, quicker, tougher. Nevertheless, Yarmouth was an old-school place, wasn't it? For now.

Focus was the thing. She drank a glass of

water. Returned to her seat at the dinner table, but not to Sam's *Vogue*. Her phone was next to it. It hadn't rung for too long. What was keeping Frank now? Because she was here, playing mum, she'd told him to interrogate Sian. He'd known her for years. They must have had some sort of rapport.

The longer Tatty looked at her phone, urging it to ring, the longer it sat there remaining stubbornly silent. She was no good at hanging around at home, not any more. She'd spent far too long doing that. Decades.

When the phone did go it made her jump. But it wasn't Frank, or Zach. Or the police. Or the fire service. Or some silly council official with a half-baked notion of public duty. It was not an *Unknown* international call this time. It was a UK mobile, not that she or her phone recognised the number. But she knew who it'd be. Intuition. Mothers had it.

'Yes?' she answered.

'Tatty?'

She recognised the voice instantly. Out of the window the sun was still falling. The world was still spinning — she presumed. 'I'm listening.'

'Did Frank mention he'd seen me?'

'He said he'd seen a ghost. But I don't believe in ghosts. Dead man walking is the phrase, I think.'

Simon coughed, the way he used to. Coughed some more. 'I come bearing gifts,' he said, gravelly. 'Did he tell you that?'

'I would not have expected anything less — you dare to show your fucking face. But that

168

doesn't change a thing.' Frank hadn't spelled out to her exactly what Simon was offering. Why not? She looked down at *Vogue*, the July issue, a model wearing a bikini, huge white sunglasses, and a wafer-thin wrap, perhaps Hermes, hanging off her bony hips. No pens were on the dining table, otherwise she might have given the model a tattoo.

'Can we meet — to discuss business?'

'You have a very funny way of doing business, Simon.'

'At least hear what I have to say. From me, not Frank.'

What was he sowing? 'I thought I was doing that right now,' she said, staring at the *Vogue* cover. She'd been offered some modelling jobs, all those years ago. Not that they'd have wanted her wearing even the most translucent wrap, and definitely no bikini. Others would have been involved as well, men and girls. Amateur casts. She had just enough dignity, even then, to say no. She sold her body in other, less public ways.

'In person, Tatty. I want to meet. Today, this evening.'

'I'm busy.'

'Tomorrow?'

'Busy.' She wasn't sure where she'd put the tattoo. On the model's arm? Her shin? Her tummy? Her beautiful forehead? That was for Simon. He needed branding, before snuffing out for good.

'I might have mentioned to Frank, Tatty, that there's a lot of movement right now when it comes to the front, the redevelopment, and certain licences. People getting into position. Graham Sands? He knows how to get business done in this town. He's got the vote as well. There's not one committee or member on the council that would go against him. You seem to be having more than a few problems right now, if you don't mind me saying so. I wouldn't want you to miss out, because your attention was elsewhere.'

'How considerate of you.'

'Goodwin is my name too.'

'Your name begins with a c and ends with a t.' That's what she'd like to stick on his forehead, complete with the u and the n.

'Oh, Tatty — we live in a harsh enough world. Forgive and forget, sweetheart.'

She was going to end the call first, this time.

She stood, tapped some triple-glazing, catching the cheery weather — had a sudden craving for grilled lobster. A glass of champagne. In a fancy bistro, on a smart, bustling seafront, awash with top-notch restaurants, bars, cafes, ice cream parlours, games rooms, slots, arcades, and the glittering casino complex at the end of it all. Simon was right. They did live in a harsh world. Her mission was to brighten it up. The right sort of company would be nice occasionally too. A dinner companion, with looks and a firm body, who didn't inhale his food at the same time as a Montecristo. She and Nathan had never had the nerve to have dinner out. Since they could, she'd changed her mind about him of course. That fireman, with the startling blue eyes? She couldn't get him off her mind. However, she couldn't see him tucking into lobster. Steak perhaps. Her later on? She was way too old for him. Not that that would stop her trying if she set her heart on it.

What was she hungry for? Back on the dining table the cover of *Vogue* was making her feel worse by the second. No one real looked like that. She walked over to the kitchen island. There were a couple of cans of Heinz tomato soup on the top. Sam had asked her to pull over and get some on their way back from Yarmouth. She took a can, went over to the wall-mounted opener with it. Located a bowl, poured some soup. Stuck it in the microwave.

Toast, that's what else she had to make. Did they have bread? Marge? Did Sam still eat marge? She doubted it. The microwave pinged.

Something else did. Turning her back on the machine, she quickly walked out of the kitchen. Crossed the hall. Pushed straight into the study. What used to be Rich's study. Nina kept it clean and dust free. It was a small space. Dim and claustrophobic, however sunny it was outside. Slime-coloured carpet. Cigar smoke still in the air. But not Rich's sweaty, animal smell. That was gone forever. The same few books were on the shelves. Books he'd never read.

The desk, which she and Zach had had a good go at attacking in their various ways, remained, defiant. There was a dent in the back wall somewhere. On the chestnut-coloured veneer stood an old landline and desktop computer. Nina hadn't dusted the computer for a while — lazy cow. Tatty sat at the desk, in a chair that

171

was trying too hard to be anything but an office chair. The buttoned leather padded to bursting, though barely worn. Rich had never spent much time in here. He'd never been any good at sitting still, keeping focused on one thing at any one time. Like his son.

The top drawers were devoid of anything useful. Tatty needed a pen, a pad. A business plan. She wasn't going to set up shop temporarily in Goodwin House, she'd work from home. It was the twenty-first century. She'd be on hand to keep an eye on Sam, should she stick around during these crucial early weeks and months.

She switched on the computer. Zach had set her up with her own username and passcode, dragged her through some basics. Frank, nevertheless, was always warning her against leaving any incriminating electronical trails. 'Stick to the old-fashioned way,' he'd say. 'Pen and paper if you must. You don't want to start mucking about on an alien system. Leave the tame stuff to Sian, anyway. She's your bloody secretary.'

'Personal assistant,' Tatty would reply.

Sian. She logged on. Played around with the old mouse, the grimy keyboard. She eventually opened a new Word document. Wrote *Projects.* Deleted it. Wrote *Operations.* She could see them in her mind, those that still existed, those she'd wound down, the current casino business, and the one that was to come. She didn't need a Word doc, she needed a spreadsheet. She hunted around for the Excel tab. Once she'd opened that, she thought harder about the figures. The cash operations and those that went through the books. The way she was being taught by Amit Sharma, the accountant, to manipulate the facts. The tax implications of what they did then declare. The various grants and tax breaks and legal loopholes that she'd been informed of.

The offshore trading company and new investor vehicles they were setting up for the casino cash. The network of trusts that were then to umbrella the holding company. Sharma couldn't believe how Brexit was opening such avenues, while the EU, and the US — whatever the idiot in charge said to the contrary — were desperately trying to close them down.

'You're in a good place, at a good time,' he'd said during their last meeting.

Not what everyone was saying. Not if the casino deal collapsed, she thought. Not if certain men had their way. Would they have treated Rich any differently? Course they would. Yes, she could run the business from this tiny room, for a few weeks; have people running to and fro. She stood, pushing the chair back with her legs, but only if she knew what was what, who was who. And people did as they were told.

Walking back to the kitchen, it hit her. Loyalty was one thing, respect another. She was not respected. Because she hadn't yet had to prove herself. Because she'd tried to go along with the way things had been; to fit into their world. Or so they'd thought.

'Mum?' Sam was calling.

She was in the kitchen now. A middle-aged

woman in her kitchen, in the middle of a working day, tending to her daughter. Did she need to reheat the soup? 'Sam, I'm coming, sweetheart,' she shouted over her shoulder. She could do it all. Her terms, her time. Couldn't she? Or had she forgotten who she really was? First and foremost, a mother.

20

With the car stinking, and Frank feeling furious, he swung left at Suffling Road, having decided that he'd come at the building from the other way for once. Tatty always came at things from unexpected angles. Plus, he'd be able to drive right up to the entrance without flattening the tape.

He was being considerate. Thinking of Shane. Especially as the fireman had been more than illuminating on the blower. Frank couldn't wait to buy him a drink. Take him somewhere smart. Out of town. That place Rich used to take his birds — St Dunstan's? Where they had the spa treatments. Shane in a sauna, that'd be something, if his ticker could take it. Except he wasn't convinced Shane was gay. Besides, he needed to stick to men more his age, men of a certain sort of standing. Like Dennis the American.

First thing Frank saw, turning into Fenner Road, was Zach. Sitting on the kerb, smoking. His Sport was a short distance away. There were no other vehicles and no tape that Frank could see blocking the far end of the street in any case — sod that for being thoughtful. But some gulls were making the daylight flicker. Zach was doing his best to look like he didn't have a care in the world. He hadn't even glanced up.

Frank nosed his vehicle towards the kerb. Changed his line of attack. Aimed straight for

Zach. Stamped on the brake when he could have been no more than a hundred millimetres away. Everything in hundreds today, including his blood pressure. Zach still didn't look up. Frank cut the engine, climbed out, reached inside his jacket, got hold of the packet of pills, threw them at Zach. Got it just right and knocked the fag straight out of his hand.

'You don't need to play it cool with me, son,' Frank shouted.

'What the fuck?' Zach croaked, finally looking up, then searching for his cigarette. It was by his left trainer, in the filthy gutter, smouldering lamely. His heel stamped down on it, while his hand reached inside his hoodie pocket and came out with a packet of cigarettes, the brand blanked out, a photo of someone dying a horrible death visible. He lit another, taking too long over the first drag.

'It'll kill you, you know,' Frank said.

'That's a conspiracy, man. Anything that's enjoyable. Besides, what'd the government do without the tax revenue? Didn't you ever smoke, Frank? Every kid's got a right to have some fun while they're young. Have some fun, man. It's a short life anyway.' He laughed, coughed and laughed, and Frank got a bad whiff of Simon coming off Zach for the first time.

'Short all right, for some,' Frank said. 'You think I'm talking about your smoking? You think I care about that?' He did, but it wasn't where he wanted to go with this right now. 'The pills,' Frank said. 'What do you know about those?'

Zach looked down at his lap, where the bag

had landed, what he'd so far avoided acknowledging. 'How did you get hold of these?'

'Know what they are?'

'Course, Candy Cane. They're all over the place, man. Crazy hazy. This is some load.'

'Ever seen so many, in one bag? A bag like that?' What the fuck, Frank stepped over to Zach, bent his knees and lowered his arse onto the kerb. Adjusting himself awkwardly, running out of breath, and with some mild creaking of bones, which all took a while, he eventually caught Zach's eye. Smiled. 'Don't say it.'

'You're not that old, Frank.' Zach was clearly finding it hard not to laugh.

'All right, say it then.'

'Out of shape, maybe. On the heavy side.'

'Steady.'

'How old are you?'

'Thirty-two,' Frank said.

'You ever tried these, young man?' Zach said, winking and holding up the bag, using his fingers to prod the pills through the plastic. 'They're ace.'

Frank was shaking his head. 'Ace? You think I'd touch that shit? It can kill you.'

Zach laughed. 'Candy Cane? No one I know's copped it. But this is some load.'

'You said. How strong is it?'

'It's a modest buzz,' Zach said. 'Better than some. Not the sweetest I've ever had.'

'Wow, the connoisseur.'

'It's how it is.'

'What'd be a lethal dose, do you reckon? Four, five?'

'I've no idea. Ten?'

'What about dealing it? That can be lethal. Bad guys wanting their commission.'

'Bad guys? I thought we were the bad guys.' Zach laughed. 'This stuff, man? A few chemicals, mostly lactose? You're kidding.'

'You're smarter than that, Zach. You know your way around, don't you? You want me to give you a lesson in economics? Cornering a market, in a backwater?'

'Just a lecture will do.'

'Personally, Zach, I think it would be bloody hard work to make any real money from such stuff around here. Not so many kids like you, are there? Too many OAPs.'

'You said it,' said Zach.

'The bulk you'd have to shift to make a decent wage,' Frank continued without knocking his block off. 'You'd have to expand way across the region. But that doesn't mean others think the same. Plenty of idiots around, and they're always the ones with the most to prove, and the shortest tempers.'

'That's a big bag of pills right there,' said Zach. 'Ten K? If the price is right, there's always a market.'

'Ten K? I'll take your word for it. Who would the customers be, then? This amount, surely wholesale.'

'I'm not sure I'd disagree,' said Zach.

'The thing is, I've got age on my side, Zach. Some wisdom. That's why I'm still alive.' He looked across the road, at a brick wall, a row of barred-up windows. Filthy security glass behind.

It was a 1950s industrial building, which had been vacant for more than a couple of years. 'But not everyone ages gracefully.'

'What are you saying, Frank?'

'Young or old, idiots everywhere. Do you know anyone who drives a knackered, silver-coloured BMW, three series?' Frank was looking at Zach again intently, trying to catch his eye, trying to catch him out.

He shook his head, too slowly, and avoided glancing Frank's way. 'Nope,' he finally said.

Everyone lied, but not always so obviously. 'Do you know Sian's dad, Rolly Andrews?' Frank asked.

'Can't say I've ever had the pleasure.'

'You're kidding me. You've spent your whole life here.'

'OK, I might have seen him driving around. Not in a Beamer, though. He's got a Rolls, hasn't he? That stupid canary-yellow thing. Now that is one knackered vehicle.'

'How well do you know Sian?'

'Sian?' He shrugged. 'Yeah, a bit — she's cute, isn't she?'

'Have you ever been to her place?'

He looked away. 'I might have been there, once, twice.'

Not a total lie this time, Frank thought. He'd multiply Zach's once or twice by, say, ten. 'I liked the girl,' he said. 'She was always upbeat — you know what I mean? Big smile on her tiny face. Never thought she had a bad bone in her body. Like her dad. Always thought he knew how it all worked. Who not to cross. Fucking idiot.'

179

He looked up at the sky, where there was no heaven or hell. God was for people who couldn't see straight. Life wasn't so complicated, if you kept your eyes and ears open. Though that wasn't always easy.

'What's happened to her?' Zach's tone suggested he hadn't been seeing straight.

'That's what I want to know, Zach. That and why her dad had that bag of pills on him.'

'These?' Zach tossed the bag into the air, caught them too casually. Proceeded to weigh the bag in two hands, shaking his head. 'Rolly Andrews? How the fuck did he get hold of these?'

Frank exhaled, stretched his legs out. He was getting cramp. He hadn't sat on a kerb for a decade or two. 'What happens in that building, over there?' He nodded towards the vacant block, the gunged-up windows. Amazed there was no graffiti in sight.

'Nothing,' said Zach, 'by the looks of it. Another eyesore, waiting for demolition.'

'Or renovation,' said Frank. 'Renovation, rejuvenation — regeneration. Do you ever think about these concepts? Regeneration is big business right now. Heaps of even legal incentives. Your dad understood that. You could say it was his overriding mission.'

'And not making money for himself?'

'He wanted to transform this town, Zach. And he wasn't prepared to wait forever to do it. Councils, corporations, competition — rules galore. He was an impatient man. There're always ways to bend the rules.'

'You still lecturing?
'At night?'
'What?'
'What goes on in that building at night?'

Zach was shaking his head, looking hard at the oily tarmac.

'Think of it this way,' said Frank. 'This scene that's going on this end of town, in buildings like that one, maybe even in that one, mate. I'm trying to join some dots here, Zach. A friend of mine, in the fire service as it happens, was telling me only a few moments ago that Saturday night, Sunday morning, the place was awash. Pumping music. Kids off their heads.'

'Hardly,' muttered Zach.

'It was a windy night. You know the wind, wind like that, can be very disorientating. And if you're off your head already — smoke blowing about. Yeah, could be very confusing. But something was going on. Open your fucking eyes.' Frank reached out, grabbed the hood of Zach's hoodie, wound it in his hand, pulled tight. Not so tight that Zach would choke to death, but tight enough so Zach knew Frank meant business. 'Time for some straight talking, son.' He let go.

'Where's Sian? What's happened to Sian?' Zach said.

'Her car's parked at the back of Goodwin House. But she never made it into work today. She had a migraine, so she told your mum. You know, one of those ailments that crop up when it makes life easier. Now she's not in her pad either. I even checked under her bed.'

'Whoa — slow up. What was her car doing at Goodwin House?'

'Looks like her dad drove it there. He'd borrowed the car for the weekend — so she told your mum.' Frank glanced up and down the empty street. He wanted night to start falling, but they were approaching the longest day of the year of course. 'We found him in your mum's old office, dead as a fucking dodo.' He couldn't get the phrase out of his head. *Dead as a dodo*.

Zach was looking at Frank now all right, startled. 'Fuck was he doing there?'

'The equipment he'd brought with him? He was about to set fire to the place.'

'And someone did him in?'

'No.' Frank could have laughed now. He grunted instead. 'The stupid old sod had that bag of pills on him. Maybe he'd helped himself to one too many. Or maybe he died of natural causes, his heart beating hard with the excitement of taking on a job he knew he shouldn't. Damn inconvenient either way.'

'Fuck. Does Sian know? Where is Sian?'

'You tell me. I don't know whether she knows about her dad, or not. I seriously hope she hasn't gone far.'

Zach got out another cigarette. Lit it. His hands were shaking far too much for a twenty-year-old.

Frank watched the smoke disappear. Felt the hollow in the pit of his stomach. 'Can you put that thing out?'

'It's never bothered you before.'

'I've never been so bothered before.'

182

'Even when Dad died?'

'Simon's back, by the way.'

'Simon? My sodding uncle?' Zach took a large drag, flicked the cigarette across the road. Hurried to his feet. Started doing some boxing moves. Punching the damp, salty air.

He'd lost some of his muscle over the last few months, Frank thought. He used to be such a fit young man. He was all scrawn and street, in squashy trainers. He needed a decent haircut as well.

'Bet Mum's not too happy.'

'She's not the only one.'

'Where's he been?'

'Sit down, will you?'

Zach sat. 'What's he want now?'

'He's been in the States, all this time, so he says. Who cares where he's been. Fact he's back is the problem.' Frank exhaled, blowing out his cheeks, as if he'd been puffing on a cigar; the Montecristos that Rich loved, more than his family, so it had often seemed. 'You know what he wants. He wants the business.'

'Still a greedy cunt then.'

'He says he's got the Americans back on board, the Prime Poker people. Of more concern is his love-in with Graham Sands.'

'Fuck,' said Zach.

Frank shook his head. 'Yeah — Simon seems to have been cosying up to that fat turd.'

'This is getting too complicated for my young head.'

'Grow up quicker then.' Frank stretched his own legs and feet out again. It was never going to be a short sit down. He looked over his shoulder at the Smokehouse — another car crash. 'How did you get on with the fire investigators?'

'Mum left me here. She had to take Sam back. Sam's not feeling great.'

'So I heard. What did they say?'

'They nosed around for like fucking ever. The police turned up as well, but they weren't here for long. Sam gave the council guy some legal bollocks before she buggered off with Mum, about who was allowed in the building and who wasn't. There wasn't so much fire damage, at least not on the ground floor, if you ask me. Plenty of space to get the operation up and running, while the top floor's fixed, as far as I could tell.'

'Your mother would want it all spick and span from the off. Did they say how come the fire hadn't spread further?'

'They kept banging on about how quick the fire service got there. How it was all credit to them the damage wasn't worse.'

Shane had mentioned as much to Frank. But Shane had been no wiser about who alerted the service in the first place, who rang it in. 'Did they apologise for the water damage? That's no easy fix.'

'What d'you think?'

'You've got the keys?'

'No. They took them.'

'Oh, Zach, my son, that's why you were sitting on the pavement, sucking your thumb. Little, lost boy, turfed out of his own building.' Frank shook his head. And they used to own these officials. Pathetic. 'You didn't threaten them — with our lawyers at the very least?'

'Sam had gone home. Don't rub it in.'

'Make amends, then. Whose pills are they? How do you reckon Rolly Andrews got hold of them? And where the fuck is Sian?'

'I've no idea how he got hold of them. That is a mystery, man. No one's said anything about him dealing, manufacturing. I heard they were coming in from the continent, Amsterdam. That's all.'

'This end of town, late Saturday night, what was going on? You were here, weren't you?'

'Yeah, I was,' Zach said slowly, nodding solemnly. 'So what? I was with some mates. There was a happening a few streets away. In a building that's been used before.'

'A few streets away? You want to take me there?'

'No sweat. But there'll be nothing to see now. The equipment all gets taken away straight after.'

'Whose equipment is it? Who's running this shower?'

'People from London, mainly. I know them a bit. There's a Lithuanian guy as well.'

'There always is,' said Frank. 'Does he drive a Hummer too?'

'Not that I've seen. And my mate Liam, he's one of the locals involved. It's not my op, though.'

'Why the fuck not?'

'Other priorities.' Zach held up his hands. 'Not enough money in it?' He laughed, grabbing the bag of pills, which had been lying on the pavement. He ripped it open, stuck his nose in. Fished out a pill, held it up. The pink and white stripes showing little manufacturing panache from where Frank was. 'Sian was there Saturday,' Zach continued. 'Don't get what she sees in Liam. He's a wanker, man. She needs to watch him.'

'Where's this Liam hang out?'

'Up the coast, towards Caister. His family has some cash. Plush crib. He's never bothered to move out.'

'Like you then?'

'No, not like me at all. His dad's in the energy business. Renewables, wind farms.' Zach flicked the pill away. The wind helping to carry it out into the middle of the street. It had a soft landing.

Slowly Frank got to his feet. Shook his right leg. Dusted the backs of his trousers down. 'Anywhere else this Liam likes to hang out?'

'The usual — arcades and stuff. Not sure his parents are too happy with the direction his life's taking.'

'Do you think he's with Sian someplace?'

'Could be.' He shrugged his shoulders.

'And they're both in on this MDMA business?'

'The Candy Cane?'

'What else am I talking about?'

'Who said anything about them two dealing, making?'

'You didn't think her dad was up to it.'

'She's not either. It's not her. No way.'

'How come her dad got hold of the pills then? They just dropped into his lap, did they? I'm trying very hard, Zach, to make sense of all this.'

'Can't believe Simon's back.'

'Let's not change the subject right now.'

'ADHD, that's what they always said I had at school.'

Frank looked away, into the godless space. School was not a high point for him either. But he did remember that the earth rotated around the sun. He was still urging the darkness on, he realised. The natural order of things. He returned his gaze to Zach, who had remained perched on the kerb. The boy needed a damn good hiding. Frank wasn't the person to give it to him. That was a father's job, a mother's. 'I doubt Sian will take long to break,' he said, suddenly aware that Sian now had no mother or father. He wouldn't touch her. Knew it wouldn't be necessary.

'All right, so Liam likes a hit or two,' Zach said. 'He's not opposed to making a few quid out of it as well.'

Frank hadn't thought Zach would cough quite so quickly. 'Get up, Zach.' He nudged the boy in the back. Where was his resolve?

'Hey,' said Zach, 'leave it out.'

'Up. You can't sit there all evening.'

Zach got to his feet, still carrying the bag of pills. Frank snatched them from him, spilling a few. 'I'll hang onto these, thank you very much.' Not bothering to pick the loose ones up, he turned, began walking towards his motor.

'Where are you going?' Zach shouted after

him. 'Didn't you want to see where these parties happen?'

Frank opened the driver's door, looked back over the bonnet at Zach. 'I know exactly.' He nodded towards the building opposite. It was a good guess. 'Besides, you've got more urgent things to be getting on with.' Frank climbed in, shut the door, started the engine, reversed, manoeuvred the vehicle double quick so he was facing Salmon Road. Lowered the passenger window.

'Yeah?' said Zach, his voice dripping with worry.

'Find Sian for me, will you?'

'I'll give it a go, suppose,' he shrugged, trying to play it cool.

'Bring your mate Liam to see me, as well, will you?'

'What for?'

'Tell him I've got his merchandise. I wondered whether he'd like a business lesson while he was picking it up.'

'Where are you going?'

'There's something I should have done hours ago.' His mind filling with an image of a vast plate of fish and chips, mushy peas, a mound of ketchup. A side of bread and spread. A pint of lager. A view straight onto the Golden Mile. Amazonia across the way. A sprinkling of green, and then a hefty slice of cold grey North Sea.

As the car window was going up all on its own, the soft, automatic whirr, Frank had another thought. 'I'm presuming you didn't see anything of the fire, Saturday night, Sunday morning

188

— when you were up this end of town, off your head? Flames shooting into the sky, that sort of thing?' If Sands had fucking seen it from a couple of miles away.

'And I wouldn't have already told you, Mum, if I had?'

'I think you need some rest, son. Clear your head. Have an early night. You look knackered.'

'All right, Dad.'

21

Tatty woke with a start, but tried to conceal the fact. Slowly she reached under her pillow, despite knowing there was nothing there. The air pressure had changed. It was suddenly cooler, breezier, on the parts of her that were not under the duvet. Someone had opened her bedroom door. The gun was in the drawer of her bedside table.

'Mum?'

Tatty turned over, sitting up. 'Sam?' She reached for the light switch.

'I'm bleeding.'

Sam was by the open door, a large towel clutched to her stomach. Tatty flung away the covers, rushed over to her daughter. Led her gently into the room, helped her to sit on the bed. Sam remained perched on the side, practically doubled over. 'How much are you bleeding?' Tatty asked, unable to hide the concern.

'Like a heavy period. My stomach hurts. It feels all hard and loose, weird, like everything is about to drop out of me.' She was shivering.

Tatty sat beside her, put her hand on Sam's back. Her nightie was damp with sweat. 'We need to ring a doctor, an ambulance.'

'An ambulance?'

Tatty now had her arm around Sam and she hugged her softly and tightly. 'I'm sure everything will be fine. We just need to get you checked out.'

'I don't care,' said Sam. There was a sob in her throat this time.

'Don't say anything,' Tatty said, leaving Sam's side and going for her phone, which was on her bedside table. 'Stay still, lie down. It'll be OK, darling. Everything will be OK.'

'I can't lie down,' she sobbed. 'It hurts.'

Tatty had her phone, thought for a second about ringing her doctor. He'd probably be there quicker than the ambulance — he cost enough. Thought back to when her friend Susie had had a miscarriage, and how she'd tried to help. Susie had been off her head. Barely conscious of what was pooling on the settee. Tatty hadn't realised Susie was on smack then. Tatty tapped 999. Walked out of the bedroom while she was waiting to be connected. She didn't want Sam hearing her call for an ambulance.

Dull daylight was trickling onto the landing. She was staring hard at the carpet. Couldn't see any spots of blood, a trail from Sam's room. Her heart did something funny and unusual, and made its presence felt. Maybe it would be OK. A little bleeding. Not normal, for sure, but not necessarily fatal for the embryo. It would be the size of a pea. A he or a she. How she suddenly wanted that pea to grow and grow. She wanted to be a grandmother. She could put her life and soul into it. Perhaps she'd be a better grandmother than she ever was mother.

'Hello?' she said, at last.

'Please state which service you require.'

Time travel, she wanted to say. 'Ambulance,' she said.

She was put through and had to wait some more and then rushed the nature of the problem and their address and was told to sit with the patient, use plenty of towels for warmth and comfort. *Plenty of Towels?* Where do you think we live, John Lewis, she wanted to say, the White Company? Her mind a churning sea of rage, hope and terror.

She looked down the corridor. The door to Zach's room was shut. She quickly strode over, opened the door. 'Zach? I need you.' The smell hitting her suggested he'd had a late night full of weed and chemicals, and some physical activity, though not necessarily with a girl. 'Zach? Get up.'

But there was no stirring and she knew he wasn't under the twisted duvet. He wasn't that bony. 'Zach?' she said again pointlessly.

She ran back to her bedroom, through the lame dawn. Sam hadn't moved. Her daughter looked up at her, however, sort of smiled, some spirit there, then her beautiful face crumpled and her shoulders began to heave, and the tears came, along with great gasping sobs that pierced Tatty like hot skewers.

22

'Your phone's going again, bro,' Liam said.

'Yeah, I heard,' said Zach.

'It's disturbing my kip,' Liam said. 'Smash it.'

Zach wasn't sure he had heard it, but he could hear it now. Again? He opened his eyes, saw some light, a lot of blur. Smelt fresh cigarette smoke. The tail end of a skunk session hanging in the early morning air as well. It was catching in his throat and he hadn't even opened his mouth. He'd been part of the party. A party of two. Indulged, as they said. Only way to bring Liam round to the rational world, the inevitable. He was still being a jerk.

Zach was lying face down on the couch. He peeled his cheek off the leather, tried to raise his head. His phone was on the floor, trilling away. Yeah, he'd like to smash it. Do Liam, and himself, a favour. He didn't want to be disturbed. He didn't want to be a part of this any more.

Zach could only see Liam's feet, in their trainers. The pool table was blocking the rest of him from view. The distance between the couches was considerable. Liam's house had a triple garage. Above the garage was the games room. The games room had become Liam's bedroom, while the games played here were becoming more deadly by the day.

Feeling for his phone, Zach's fingers encountered a fag packet, papers, a plastic lighter, an overflowing ashtray, a glass, a glass his knuckles immediately knocked over. He shifted his head, body, opened his eyes properly now, his hand still trying to locate the device, which it did before any vodka could seep near.

Fortunately there was an oval rug next to the couch he was on, which Zach had always thought of, ridiculously, as an animal skin, a polar bear's. It was thick and hairy, and had once been cream. Zach remembered it from when it had been in Liam's parents' living room. It had probably cost a packet. Now it was a stained, dirty relic of Liam's sweet and innocent childhood. Zach shook his head, pleased to see the rug had soaked up the vodka miles away from his phone.

He reached for the device, seeing before the screen went blank that it had been his mother calling. There were four missed calls from her. 'Yada, yada,' he mumbled, shutting his eyes, rolling back onto the couch. 'I turned off voicemail,' he croaked, trying to ignore the fact that his mother was trying to get hold of him at this hour. 'People who leave messages only want to nag,' he mumbled.

Frank had advised him to do this some time ago. To keep changing his device as well. Go for a burner. Yeah, yeah, yeah. But he wasn't going to lose his contacts, have his contacts lose him, every week or so. There were mates, birds, business to attend to. His business away from the family business.

'Frank giving you no let-up?' Liam laughed. 'Big, bad Frank.' He laughed again. More of a whine. 'Who'd have thought people would run around after him. He's got the bulk, I'll give him that. But he's queer, man.'

'Piss off,' Zach said, trying to shut his eyes tighter. What was he meant to say? It's my mum, checking up on me? 'Homophobe. He'd beat your shiny white arse to a pulp, that's for sure.'

'No way's he getting anywhere near my arse.'

'You want to watch it. You don't know what he's capable of.'

'He's got my gear.'

'Your gear?' Zach couldn't believe Liam had started up where he'd left off in the early hours. Zach had no idea what time it was when they'd conked. But that skunk? Would knock anyone out. The wonders of the natural world.

He opened his eyes again. Daylight was zooming into the room, picking up the detritus. Liam's folks might have been on his case workwise, but they seemed to give their son plenty of slack when it came to amenities. Maybe they wanted to keep it cool at home, so they could latch an eye onto him once in a blue moon. Zach was dealing with a different world of priorities, when it came to his folks, his mum. Frank.

He swung his legs off the couch, sat up. Rubbed his shaggy mane. Looked at the rips in the knees of his jeans. Maybe he did need to smarten up, in every sense.

'Fuck, man,' groaned Liam. 'Time for a morning pick-me-up.'

Across the playpen Liam was building a spliff. 'You've got to be kidding,' Zach said. 'That stuff'll send you straight back to bye-byes.'

'No alternative,' Liam said. 'Now, if I had my pills . . . '

'Our pills,' corrected Zach.

'That's what we need for a sunny Sunday.'

'It's Tuesday,' said Zach, tilting his head towards the ceiling. 'And it doesn't look too sunny to me.' A dump of flat white light was sitting still and heavy on the row of large Velux windows, like a metre of snow.

'I gave them to you, man, for safekeeping, and what happens, they fall out of your fucking pocket.'

Zach thought they'd had the conversation. 'They didn't fall out of my pocket. They were removed from my pocket. Where were you lot anyway? You were meant to be watching my back.'

'You're a big boy now — swimming with the sharks.' Liam sparked up. Coughed. Laughed.

'Sian, man,' Zach said, 'what's she see in you? I'll never know.'

'She sees, my friend, the future.' He cackled, blew some smoke Zach's way, but it didn't even make it as far as the pool table. 'This is sweet.'

'Liam, you and I have an appointment this morning.'

'All in good time.'

'He's not happy,' Zach said.

'He should be,' said Liam. 'Those pills must be worth ten K.' Liam smoked some more.

'Ten K, in your dreams.' Zach was thinking back to the conversation with Frank.

'You sure you didn't give them to him? For safekeeping.'

'My business is my business.' He hadn't told Liam how Frank had got hold of them. He was keeping that card close to his chest, and until he had a better understanding himself of how Rolly Andrews might have got hold of them. Fuck those pills — they fucked you right up.

'Our business.'

'You know what happened, Liam.' God, he was tired. 'I was robbed. About the same time you lot ran off. That isn't suspicious?' The thing was, Zach wasn't at all certain he hadn't dropped them — when he was off his head, his limbs not obeying his own orders.

'And where's the gear now?' Liam said. 'With Uncle Frank. In the clear light of day this is still looking awfully fucking cloudy.'

'I didn't give them to him — how many times? He has mates, people who do things for him all over the place. Keep him informed.' Even as Zach said it he knew that that simply wasn't true. Tight ship wasn't the half of it. Like him, Frank had no idea how the pills could have ended up in Goodwin House, with a dead Rolly Andrews. Yet Zach knew he was partly responsible. He'd had them on him, and then he hadn't. Candy Cane — there was a sour taste in his mouth right now, for sure.

He owed some explanation to Frank — in the clear light of day. Yet did he really want to let Frank loose on Liam, let alone Sian? If needs must. 'He's not happy with this stuff flooding the market,' Zach said. 'Quantities turning up in unexpected places.'

'Because he thinks he runs the show?'

197

'It's not like that. There are far bigger things going on that he doesn't want scuppered. Where'd you get them? How much of this stuff is out there?' Zach's involvement so far had been minimal. Distributing at a few raves. Two in fact, including Saturday night — which he'd so spectacularly fucked up. However, he knew he should have been more involved before now — Frank implied as much. Shouldn't have kept any of this secret from Frank either. Frank watched his back for him, didn't he.

He wouldn't have been in this mess if he'd stuck to the family business. If he hadn't wanted to nick Sian off Liam. It was weird; see someone around for years on end, without so much as a fumble — all right, the odd finger — and it was only when you thought you'd lost them that you wanted them badly. He could see her mouth. Her tight little body.

'They come from across the Channel,' Liam was saying. 'That's all you need to know — with your connections? Big, bad Frank — I should never have got you involved.'

'You had no choice.' Zach felt some weight behind that statement. Had he forgotten that he was a Goodwin? With all the perks that came with it? He didn't like Liam dissing Frank either.

'They were in your possession. You lost them. Lucky you're still breathing.'

'Give it to me, baby.' He was smarter than his mate. Always had been at school. He could outmanoeuvre him. Maybe he wasn't so effective in the bird department, though. Liam had always been more successful there. Fuck knew why.

'Where'd Frank say he got it from again?' Liam asked.

'Back of a lorry.' Zach looked at his phone. Thought of his own mum. Couldn't piss her off as well as Frank. Then he really would be out on a limb, reliant on hopeless amateurs like Liam. What would he ever have to do to make her proud of him? 'You're going to have to start talking when you meet Frank,' Zach said. 'You might as well get it off your chest now. Your source?'

'My source?' said Liam. More smoke drifted Zach's way. 'HP.'

'Laugh a minute,' said Zach.

'Come on, mate,' said Liam, 'how the hell did you lose them?'

'We were all off our heads. Wouldn't surprise me if you nicked them off me. For a joke, yeah? Whatever.'

'They were ours, Zach. Why would I do that?'

'So you and Sian could have a long and sweaty night together.'

'That girl doesn't need any artificial stimulants.' He laughed a sly, croaky laugh. 'You were meant to sell them. I want my cash, my share.'

'I want *my* cash. We had a deal.'

'Don't look at me.'

'You know the source. You know where Sian is too, I bet. I'd like to ask her a few questions. Before Frank gets hold of her.'

'What's he want with her?'

'Same as he wants with you — the truth. At the very minimum, I'd suggest, a slice of the cake. His patch.'

'What were you doing mucking it up then? Going behind his back.'

Perhaps Liam wasn't so stupid. Perhaps he'd smartened up since he'd left school — like all of them. It was hard out on the street. 'He doesn't control me,' said Zach. 'He works for us.' The complete stupidity of his venture with Liam was only beginning to dawn on him. Out of his depth, that's what he was. Little lost boy.

'Don't make me laugh,' Liam said.

'Two things I need to know,' said Zach, standing, demanding respect, sense, intelligence — from himself. He took a couple of big breaths, waiting for the dizziness to ease, some competence to catch up with him. 'Where is Sian, man? And the gear — what you took from me, and the rest of the order — where the fuck does it come from? What's the big secret? Are we in this together, or not?'

'Sian's whereabouts is her concern. She's an adult. As for the gear, the rest of it, where it comes from? It pays not to be so fucking nosy. Made that clear, haven't I?'

'Speak to Frank.' Zach felt a chunk of himself fall off his shoulder. He almost looked to the floor to see what part. His ego?

'I thought he worked for you.'

Zach looked at his phone instead, brought the screen to life. Saw that it wasn't even seven in the morning. He couldn't remember the last time he'd been up so early. Would Frank be awake, eating Cheerios? Maybe he'd already be out in the garden, weeding. Zach could see it might have therapeutic benefits, if your head was spinning. Could they pay him a visit right now? Wasn't sure how much longer he could stick around Liam's crib. Besides, he knew he should ring his mum. Doubted it would be good news, but he was her boy, first and foremost.

'Oh, by the way, Sian's dad is dead,' he said, sensing time running away. 'Suspicious circumstances.' He lisped this.

'What? No way,' said Liam. 'Sian's said nothing. Holy fuck. What do mean, suspicious circumstances?'

'I don't think Sian knows. Unless she was with him when he croaked.' Zach thought that that might just have been possible. But then Liam would have probably been there too. His reaction didn't suggest such a thing. 'Was he caught up in all this?'

'What, Sian's dad?'

'Yeah, the pills, the Candy Cane.'

'He's like an old gyppo,' Liam said. 'Forget it.'

'Does Sian like it when you use that term?'

'Tramp then.'

'What's she see in you? He drives a Roller, man,' said Zach. 'He drove a Roller,' he corrected himself, while checking out Liam's face for any cracks. Across the airy room his skin appeared pale and lifeless. They'd both had a solid schooling of truancy and drug abuse. It was catching up on Liam, Zach thought, wondering whether he should start going back to the gym.

'When it wasn't at the menders,' Liam said.

'Not like your Beamer. Bet that's never conked.' Zach hadn't seen it outside when he drove up last night — Frank's mention of it sounding horn-like in his head yesterday evening. He presumed it was in the stable below, on a bed of straw, where Liam usually kept it. Should have checked then and there. Thought he'd ease it into the conversation, and then with the spliff, he'd forgotten until now. Another fuck-up.

'It's a very reliable piece of German engineering,' Liam said. 'Shit, Rolly Andrews is dead? Poor Sian. She loved him. Only relative she had.'

'Do you want to tell me where Sian is now? And what your car's been doing outside Rolly's lodge?' Zach had raised his voice. 'As a friend.'

'You don't think I'm involved in anything heavy? This is way beyond my pay grade.'

Maybe he'd have to summon Frank. Didn't think it was going to be easy getting Liam into the Sport, and driving over to Bradwell. Yet Zach still had an urge to get to the bottom of this before he called on Frank's services. He wanted to prove that he wasn't just a loser. Plus he wanted to do what he could for Sian as well. 'Your car, Liam, was seen outside the lodge.'

'Surely some mistake.' This was said in a silly Scottish accent. That Bond actor from decades ago, Zach thought.

'No joking,' said Zach.

'Nothing to do with me.' Liam's hands were outstretched, pleading innocence, or ignorance. The rest of the spliff was between his lips. It looked like it had gone out.

'What's that meant to mean?'

'Sian borrowed it. She said she had to move some stuff around.'

'When she was meant to be at work?'

'I thought it was to do with work. She like took it on Sunday. Weren't you like moving offices or something?'

'What was wrong with her car?'

'Too small? I don't know. Oh, yeah, now I remember, her dad had borrowed that one.'

'Where's it now?'

'Her car?'

'Your car. When did she bring it back?' Zach suddenly knew the answer.

Liam smiled at him. Removed the spliff from his mouth. 'This is dead, man. Time to build another.'

23

Tatty drained the last of the coffee from the disposable cup. Looked around for a bin. Stood up, went over to it. Saw that it was overflowing. There was no way she'd be able to squash the cup in. The coffee had been foul. She wished she hadn't bothered. It had been some trek to find an open cafeteria. Endless, brightly lit corridors, stinking of disinfectant, reminding her of the end of the world. It was far too clean. Give her a cosy grave in the mud anytime.

She'd only gone on a coffee hunt because she wasn't allowed in while they did the procedure. She looked at her watch. It only took five, ten minutes, they said, but they'd told her not to come back for an hour. She wasn't going to forget Sam's face as she left her.

There were not enough people to empty the bins, or their shift had yet to begin, she decided, going further afield in search of a waste receptacle. Hardly surprising given the numbers waiting around. Endless streams of anxious loved ones shuffling from here to eternity like zombies. But these zombies were eating. Comfort eating, she presumed — a habit she'd never succumbed to.

Support staff might have been in short supply at this time of the day, but the doctors and nurses were blessed with patience and compassion. Expertise as well. The James Paget, once they'd finally got Sam here, was pulling out all the stops. This might have been another NHS hospital on the brink, according to the local media, but the staff were performing miracles. If only she employed such characters. But these people wouldn't come to work for her, would they. They were good people, their hearts in the right place.

An image of the fireman with the blue eyes and smooth cheeks dropped into her mind like a gift from God. He was serving the community. Putting his life at risk. She doubted he was squeaky clean, nevertheless. He knew Frank, didn't he? She should ask Frank for his number. Get him to make an introduction at least. An 'accidental' meeting could be arranged, couldn't it? What was she thinking, and now of all times?

Tatty left the waiting area clutching the empty coffee cup, and began the relentless walk back to the EPU. More and more zombies were heading the other way. She couldn't keep to a straight line. It was like avoiding skittles. She couldn't stop thinking about life and death, whose decision it was, who was controlling it all. Why? How? Life was not fair. *Get over it*, came a voice from the past. She glanced from left to right, behind her, but Rich was not there. Though his bloated body had been in the James Paget some time ago. On a steel tray. His skin a bluey white.

Through the shuffling, ragged bodies, arms outstretched, she pushed on. Her mac tightly belted, her bag over the crook of her left arm, the stupid coffee cup in her right hand. Nearing another double door, that led closer to the EPU, she finally saw a blurry bin. She couldn't tell whether it was rammed or not, because of the tears filling her eyes, wetting her own cheeks. Who needed rescuing?

She was twenty-three when she'd had Sam. Sam was twenty-five, and not to be a mother this time. The steeliest part of Tatty's body, her head, her whole being, was telling her that this really was for the best. Michael Jansen would not have been an appropriate father, husband, son-in-law. The way he'd caved in to new backers? Dropping the price by a hundred mill? Threatening to bring someone here to oversee it all? You don't go back on such deals.

Sam was better off shot of him, they all were. If that was how it was going to play out. Who knew how love worked? Would Sam be able to think straight after this? What would it do to her confidence? Tatty wondered what had happened to Susie. She imagined, hoped, she was long dead, the heroin taking her effortlessly away, before some man raped her, smashed her face in and then strangled her to death.

There was space in the bin, acres of it, Tatty could finally see, now she was up close and the tears were drying. The cup fell into the mouth, landing without a sound. A big gaping hole. Tatty couldn't let Sam dwell on such a void.

Soon reaching another set of double doors, behind which she knew lay the nurses station for the EPU, Tatty delved into her bag for her phone. Saw that Zach still hadn't replied. Pausing, she thought about calling Frank. She'd have to call him soon enough, with everything that was going on. But she wasn't sure she'd be able to talk to him just yet. What did he know about such things?

She'd lost touch with her one and only female friend, Megan, following Rich's funeral and the airing of a few home truths. Megan not understanding Tatty's need to fill Rich's shoes, and take over the business. What a man's world she operated in. Like Sam too. Sam's workplace sounded a nightmare. She didn't think Sam had many female friends. It was in their genes, not to trust outsiders.

Tatty pushed through the doors, waved meekly at the nurse behind the low counter. Same nurse, same look of calm panic on her tight face. She was giving nothing else away.

Sam was going to be in the recovery room. They weren't even giving her a bed, as she was only having a local anaesthetic. She would be able to go home within the hour. The walking wounded. The longest queue Tatty had encountered that morning had been in the cafeteria.

Tatty supposed there were beds, wards, somewhere in this unit, but the recovery room was right by the station, for obvious purposes, she reckoned. She could see Sam through the glass panel in the door, something shifted in her chest, and she opened the door, smiling. Sam was standing — standing — by one of the windows across the room. There was no one else in there. Sam didn't turn as Tatty crossed the room, but kept looking out of the window, onto a splodge of grass, and a chunk of the car park, already full.

'Hey, darling,' Tatty said, gently putting her hand on the small of Sam's back. 'Should you be standing up?'

'The anaesthetic probably hasn't worn off,' she said. 'I don't feel a thing.'

'Still,' said Tatty. 'How's your head? You must feel a bit faint. Sick?' There were half a dozen municipal armchairs, coated in dirty orange vinyl, arranged around the room. Tatty was relieved no one else was in there. Didn't blame Sam for not sitting either.

'I had a local, Mum. No big deal.'

Sam was in her own clothes, every bit as tough as her dad had been. Tatty supposed she was expecting to see her in a hospital gown — in a hospital bed, hooked up to a drip, out for the count. Susie'd had other issues going on as well, she recalled. 'Can I get you a drink, a snack? Something sugary?' she said, quickly, trying to shove Susie from her mind. She should have bought something at the cafeteria for her. Stupid.

'Can we just go?'

'Now?' Tatty said, looking at her watch. They'd be home practically in time for breakfast. Brunch anyway. But it wasn't the weekend. She had so much work to do. She looked at her watch again, urging the hands to stop and start moving backwards. But then Sam would have had to go through the operation and all the pain and worry again.

'Yeah. I want to get out of here.'

'Sure,' said Tatty. 'Are you allowed?'

Sam gave Tatty a look that suggested that she

was not going to be taking anyone's advice apart from her own.

'OK,' said Tatty, wanting to hold her hands up. 'Is there not even a form to sign or anything?'

'I've done all that, waiting for you. I am an adult. Have been for some years.'

'They said you'd be an hour. That I couldn't come in with you.'

'Yeah, well — the wonders of modern medicine.' Sam's smile quickly collapsed. 'They gave me a load of bumf.' She pointed to a heap of flyers on the chair she was standing over. 'They said I should sit here for an hour, and then I'd be free to go. Fuck them.'

'They've been very kind, and efficient, Sam.'

'Efficient? Is that how you see it?'

'I'm sorry. You know what I meant.' Tatty looked away, through the nearest window and out onto the car park. People were parking on the pavements, the grass. Yet they were the only ones in the termination recovery room — or whatever it was officially known as. But that's what it was.

'Stop looking so glum,' Sam said, brightly. 'It's a relief. I didn't want his stupid baby anyway.'

She said it. 'Oh, Sam, don't talk like that. Come on then, let's get you home.' Tatty hooked her arm through Sam's. Led her slowly out of the room. Sam was walking stiffly, gingerly, but with some determination. 'Are you sure we can leave?'

That look again.

'Do you still have to work with him?' Sam asked, as they were passing the nurses' station.

'Who?'

'Michael. I don't know whether I want to see

him ever again or not. He's a total wanker.'

'Don't think about him now. Let's get you home, tucked up in bed. Rest, that's what you need. What you've been through, you're never going to be able to think clearly right now.'

'Will Zach be at home?'

'I don't know, darling.' Her phone in her Birkin was as heavy and useless as a brick — the lack of messages, the silence, for the past few hours. It wasn't only Zach. Frank should have been more forthcoming by now — not that she had tried him. What was going on with Sian? Celine's name then popped into her head for the first time in a while. That girl was so easy to forget. Could she know anything? She was under Sian's thumb, that was for sure.

Before Tatty knew it, they were nearing the exit, a surprisingly swift and zombie-free passage, Sam still walking with more strength than Tatty would have thought possible. Though she was a Goodwin after all. Took after her dad, all right, who'd never run out energy, determination. He was like a pneumatic drill. No, a wrecking ball.

Yet a swirl of names was continuing to make Tatty's head spin. The regulars: Sian, Simon, Graham Sands, Michael, Nathan. Others were churning around in there as well. Meek and mild Celine, the health and safety guy from the council, the fire investigator, with his cheap suit and silly clipboard. The fireman with his startling eyes.

'Are you all right, Mum?'

Tatty had paused, realising that Sam was supporting her, rather than the other way round.

210

'Sorry, darling.' She let go of Sam's arm, waiting for the floor to steady. 'I'm glad you're . . . ' She couldn't think what to say.

'What? Mum?'

'Young and fit.' That was it. Your father's daughter. Though she couldn't quite say that. People were coming into the hospital, bringing fresh sea air with them.

Once they were outside she paused again, breathed heavily. She was not old. Had been fit enough as well. All that pounding she'd accommodated — from Rich, and Nathan. He was the pneumatic drill. It'd kept her toned, if nothing else — which made her think. No wonder she was feeling out of shape.

'Are you all right, Mum?' Sam asked.

In the full glare of flat daylight, Sam could not have looked more pale. 'Me? Sweetheart, don't worry about me. It's you that we need to take care of.' Tatty took a much longer and closer look at her daughter. Realised she had left the bumf, as she'd called it, behind. 'We didn't bring the handouts they gave you. There might have been something important.'

'What do they know?'

'Quite a lot,' said Tatty.

'It was mostly head stuff.'

'And that isn't important?'

'Did you ever have an abortion?'

'Darling, you didn't have an abortion. You had a miscarriage and, what did they call it? An SMM.' That was it. Tatty even remembered what it stood for: Surgical Management of Miscarriage. She wasn't so old then. She didn't spell it out for Sam now. 'Under a local,' she added.

'Otherwise known as an MVA,' said Sam, faintly. 'Know what that stands for?'

Tatty was looking at the rows of cars. She couldn't remember where she'd left the Merc. Fuck it. She was shaking her head. 'Yeah, I did have an abortion once. Where's the bloody car?'

'When? Before Ben?'

'No.' She had an inkling it was over to their right. 'I think it's that way.' They had to get off the pavement and walk on the road because cars were now strewn all over the kerb, the verge. Tatty was gripping Sam's arm again, but she was leading Sam, supporting her. The fresh air had completely revitalised her. She'd never been great at locating her car in large, busy car parks. Perhaps because she'd never cared that much about it. There were far more important things to worry about than motors — only silly men worried about those. She looked up. Maybe the sun would come out later. Something so uncontrollably bright and explosive. Anything.

'Not before Ben?' Sam said loudly. 'When? Was I planned? Zach? Did you even want to have us, Mum?'

She stepped in front of Sam. Looked her straight in the eye, pouring all the love she had in her body. 'Oh yes, I wanted you more than ever. And Zach. The three of you, you made my life worth living. I got pregnant later, much later. That was an accident, and at my age? Your father never knew.'

24

'Look what's rolled up,' Frank said aloud, tossing his head, watching the shiny new Range Rover Sport pull into his driveway. He'd been about to get into his own Range Rover, for what should have been one of the very last times. He looked over his shoulder at his own stinking wreck. The thing was, he was loyal. Even to a great hunk of metal. Too loyal? Didn't like unnecessary waste either. The planet was having a hard enough time as it was. Maybe he was going soft in his old age.

'Yeah?' he said, as Zach pulled his own spanking beast to a stop by Frank's feet, and flung open the driver's door.

'Sian's in this up to her fucking neck — with Liam,' Zach said, planting his feet onto Frank's carefully raked shingle. Some swagger back.

'Why are you dobbing her in it?' Frank said, folding his arms. Fortunately, Zach had avoided tramping on a fledgling clump of sea holly he'd recently planted. 'Young love never dies.'

'Fuck you, Frank.'

'I was heading off on my morning rounds.'

'Yeah?' said Zach.

'Yeah,' said Frank. 'But seeing as you've bothered to come all the way out here to tell me something I already know — want a coffee?'

'I guess,' said Zach. 'How come you're so wised-up, then?'

Frank turned, headed to the side door of his house, which led into a boot room he used for potting, as the greenhouse was chock-a, and on into the pristine kitchen. He'd tidied away his breakfast things, as he always did, before giving the table and counters a once-over with a new J-cloth. He filled the kettle. Zach had followed him into the kitchen, but he was lingering by the door. Frank faced him. 'Rolly's place was a department store of stolen goods. Didn't see any evidence of manufacturing, but there was at least one key ingredient slap bang in the middle of the floor.'

'Sian's driven off in Liam's Beamer,' Zach said. 'Yeah, it was his car you saw outside. You were right.'

Frank filled the cafetiere, thinking of Sian's lipstick-red VW Up! still at the back of Goodwin House — so he presumed. And why Zach hadn't 'fessed up about Liam's Beamer sooner. 'Does she now know her dad's snuffed it?'

'Liam didn't know.'

'And she's still not answering her phone?'

'It's been going straight to voicemail. She's running scared, man.'

'She must be communicating with someone.'

'If I was to guess, I don't think she's gone far,' Zach said. 'She's a local. A day out shopping in Norwich unnerves her.'

'Family?'

'That family? Flexible concept.'

'Her mate Celine?'

'Celine's at home,' Zach said. 'I tried her.'

'So did I,' said Frank. 'Late last night, on my

way home from chips. Gave her a right fright.' He could still see her in her dressing gown, opening her front door, shaking. The dressing gown was pale pink and fluffy. She had matching slippers. He wasn't surprised she lived alone.

'Nothing giving?'

Frank shook his head. 'She doesn't know anything. She's not bright enough to lie with any conviction.' Which made Frank think that Sian was even more manipulative than he'd ever given her credit for. It was easy, picking on the weak, but it took much more nous playing the strong.

He glanced out of the kitchen window, at the wild plants being carefully cultivated. Maybe he'd move somewhere more isolated one day. Halvergate Marshes? Build a house. An eco house? However, he needed to be in control of the landscape, not swamped by it. Besides, he didn't want to draw unnecessary attention to himself. He was never any trouble to his neighbours here in Bradwell. Peaceful lot of retirees, a sprinkling of teachers as well; a few nurses.

'We don't need this distraction, Zach,' Frank said, reverting his attention to the counter. 'How do you feel about your mates running around behind your back?' The thing with Zach was, you couldn't tell him the obvious, he had to discover it for himself.

'What do you think?'

There was real hurt in Zach's voice. Frank turned his attention to stirring the coffee granules. Thought about getting the saucepan out, cooking up a full English. He'd kill for a

215

couple of slices of black pudding, three plump sausages, fried eggs, ketchup. He'd had a bowl of muesli for breakfast. His penance for having fish and chips at Ramsden's last night, with a side of scampi to go with the sliced white. Ice cream for dessert as well. He hated muesli, no better than bird seed, but had been persuaded by his doctor, who said it would help cut his cholesterol. He was meant to use some cholesterol-busting marge on his toast as well — made from a special plant extract. As much as Frank respected flora, if not fauna, there were limits.

He'd always been of the opinion that something a little more bullet-shaped would get him before his arteries furred up for good. But he was the other side of fifty now — fuck's sake. Like Simon. Who had once built his own house, hadn't he? Not so eco, with all the steel and shiny concrete, ablaze with electrical this and that. That man couldn't help drawing attention to himself. Loved the limelight. No wonder he'd hooked up with a wannabe reality TV star, who was now feeding the waders.

Nevertheless, Frank knew Simon hadn't returned to his castle. He was staying at the Pier View in Gorleston, Sands' gaff — so a big bird had not needed to tell him. There were birds everywhere, out for some crumbs. They hadn't been much use grassing up Rolly Andrews however. Maybe he needed to be more inventive with the fucking muesli.

'Is that coffee done, Frank?' Zach asked, stepping further into the room.

'Do you think Liam and Sian were using

216

Rolly's place to store gear? So much crap in there, it's not as if the old man would have noticed the odd carrier bag of pills, an extra box of cut.'

'Liam says he gets the pills from the Continent. They come in from Holland, ready-made. He didn't say where he's been keeping them. At his crib, I'd guess. It's a new venture for him. He's not in it big time. I'd have known. He's an amateur, man — always will be.'

'No one wants to be caught in possession, Zach. Not that amount. Liam's been seeing Sian, right?' Had Zach been wandering around with his eyes fucking shut?

'Yeah, I suppose,' said Zach.

'You suppose? Where's he now?'

'At home.'

'I wanted a word with him. You were meant to bring him to see me.'

'He's off his head. You wouldn't have got any sense.'

'This time of the fucking day? Have you spoken to your mother recently?' Frank watched Zach's cheeks flush. Poured the coffee. 'Sugar?'

'She's been ringing. I was busy — with Liam. I don't take sugar.'

'Healthy boy.' Tatty hadn't been ringing him, recently. He heaped a couple of teaspoons into his own coffee. Stirred. Took a sip. 'It's over here.' Pointed to Zach's coffee. Zach walked over, gingerly. Frank decided not to slap him on the back of his head as he reached for the coffee. He didn't want the kid to spill it. Besides, he'd bothered to drive over, even if he was bringing stale news. The boy had some sense, for a slow learner.

Frank knew he wouldn't be forgetting to teach Liam a very serious lesson one day soon, however. If you couldn't control the young, you were sunk. 'Drink up,' he said, having taken a large swallow, a smart new idea brewing. 'We need to be somewhere. You're coming with me.'

'Where're we going?'

Frank was then ushering Zach out of the side door, through the potting shed, and onto the crisp shingle. Sunrays were edging through the fuggy cloud, like neon curtains. They were falling on the bungalows across the street. 'Breakfast meeting,' he said, over his shoulder. If that's how Graham Sands did his business nowadays. 'Pull the door to, will you?'

'You're not locking it.'

'Never do,' said Frank. 'If people want to get in, a lock like that's not going to stop them.' Frank opened the driver's door of his vehicle, sniffing. Could he still smell death? 'Follow me, will you?'

'If you don't drive too fast.'

'Cheeky sod.' It wasn't the first time Zach had had a go at his driving style. He had his reasons for driving like an OAP — more than ever. Climbing in, Frank realised he couldn't be certain he knew what the retirement age for men was any more. It wasn't as if he had a private pension plan. He'd never expected anything from the state. You didn't retire from this life anyway.

Frank was about to tell Zach to ring his mum when he felt his phone start up. He closed the driver's door, settled into his seat, slowly pulled the phone from his pocket. 'Yeah,' he said, watching Zach reverse. The curtain of light had caught some wind, and the bungalows across the way shimmered. A smattering of gulls took flight from a near roof as he eased forward.

'Tatty?' What was she playing at now?

There was a sniff. A faint sob. A gasp for air.

'Tatty? You OK?' His pulse quickened — a million scenarios.

'I thought I was all right,' Tatty said, struggling to breathe, speak. 'We got home from the hospital and Sam's upstairs, and I'm in the kitchen, looking out of the window, and I don't know ... it's all going wrong. Poor Sam.'

'Hey, slow down.' Frank had stopped, his vehicle half on the road, half still in his drive. He could see Zach to his right, peering at him through the windscreen. He motioned that he was on the phone. 'What do you mean, hospital?'

'Where's Zach? He's not answering. I thought he might want to know. Be here for his sister.'

'He's with me. We were heading elsewhere. I'll bring him home right now.'

'Will you?'

'On my way.' He ended the call, having an idea what had gone on.

The breakfast meeting would have to wait. Wasn't as if Zach and he were expected anyway. Brunch? Whatever that meant. This was Great Yarmouth — full English, or fish and chips, no messing. The diet was playing havoc with his mind. He'd heard that people could hallucinate when starving to death.

219

25

Tatty checked on Sam, had a shower but was not in the mood to linger. Dressed double quick. Applied some foundation, a hint of mascara. Tried not to look at herself too hard and long in the mirror.

Michael's new phone was still going straight to voicemail. Sam said she hadn't been able to get a message to him on any other channel either. Tatty wasn't sure how hard she'd been trying. If Michael had any sense, he'd be on his way here — and on his own. Tatty had left a message for Ben, however. Cryptic. Now she stood in the hall, in a dry pool of daylight, watching the dust motes as if they were living organisms. She felt pathetic. To cry on the phone to Frank?

Shaking her head, she briefly shut her eyes, but still saw a million living things as she heard a large vehicle's suspension crunch as it rode up onto her property. She looked at her watch, her arm disturbing the motes, callously sweeping them away. Frank must have been pushing it, for him — his part of Bradwell to Gorleston in under eight minutes. At this time of the day? She was amazed at what she'd managed to get done in the time as well. The hours she used to spend getting ready. That was all she did, for years. And then she'd go shopping, so she had more of a dilemma the next day. What would her new blouse go with? Was it actually the right size, the right colour? The fabric seemed a little stiff, or flimsy, or too thick, for the price.

She heard another thump as another vehicle arrived — Zach, following. Good boy. She needed the company, family around her, her blood. Plus Frank, she supposed. He was almost family. She had to stop questioning his loyalty. Make clear she was giving him a pay rise, and other perks. Whatever he wanted.

Another sound followed that one. A third vehicle? She wasn't expecting this. Couldn't imagine how three vehicles would fit onto the front yard, as well as hers and Sam's. Her mind latching onto the most ridiculous things today — cars, clothes, birth control accidents with a lover — yea, she hadn't told Sam that part. Maybe one day. She backed away from the front door, rushed to the kitchen, looked through the wall of glass. She was panicking, her emotions shot. Though peering out onto the back garden didn't tell her anything. It was no looking glass. She heard people by the front door; voices raised, agitated. A key in the lock. Zach's?

She took a deep breath, thinking of her gun, upstairs in her bedroom. She needed to pull a trigger. Feel some power. Some sort of release. She walked back to the hall, past her temporary office, as the front door was flung open and Zach spilled in. Sea air followed. A lump of solid daylight. The dust motes scarpered.

'What's happened?' Zach said, stepping towards her. 'Frank was taking me off to some breakfast meeting, told me to follow him, and we end up here. What gives? Oh, and someone else

221

has pitched up too, Mum. It's like the fucking hippodrome out there.'

'Who?' said Tatty. Frank was still out the front. Talking, heatedly.

'Only fucking Simon.'

'Oh, Jesus, not now,' Tatty said. 'Your sister's not well. Where have you been? I've been trying you all night.'

'What's up with Sam?' He was heading for the stairs: long, youthful strides.

'Don't disturb her, Zach. She's sleeping.' Tatty hadn't used this voice for a few years. Must have reminded Zach of when he was a kid, misbehaving. He was the worst of them, by a golden mile.

He paused by the first step. Turned. 'What's happened? What's wrong with her?'

'She's lost the baby.'

'Right,' he said, quietly, slowing.

'The hospital were brilliant,' Tatty said brightly. 'Saw her immediately. She had a procedure.' Tatty couldn't read Zach's expression. He was doing something funny with his jaw. Angry voices were still going on outside.

'She's all right though?' he said.

'No, course not.' She couldn't summon any more brightness.

He exhaled. 'Did she even want the baby? It was an accident, right?'

'Zach, please, for God's sake, now's not the time to be talking like this. Don't use that word.' She looked over to the door. Saw Frank's bulk cutting out the daylight. Stopping Simon from entering, too, by the look of it. Her meltdown on

222

the phone to Frank was still troubling her, pressing on her brain like a tumour. For the first time in months she had an urgent craving for temazepam. One tiny pill. 'Don't go upstairs, Zach,' she said, using that voice again, wanting to rush up herself and delve into the bathroom cabinet, a distant shelf. But she knew there was nothing there. She'd ditched the pills months ago — with her old life.

'Whatever you do, Zach,' she said, 'damn you, don't go upsetting Sam any further by saying something stupid. She's resting. Think about it, if you haven't fried what's left of your senses on Candy Cane.'

'Whoa, steady on, the mother lode. What do you know about Candy Cane?'

She was not going down this route with him then and there — she'd hit a nerve, that was enough for now. 'This is about your sister. You'll never know how she might feel,' she said. 'You're the wrong sex.'

'And that's my fault, is it?'

Frank had stepped into the house. 'Tatty,' he said calmly, 'it's your call. Simon's out there saying he won't go away until he's had a word with you, in person. I can walk him across the road and push him over the cliff, if you want. Or, I guess, I could make you both a cuppa.'

Tatty looked at the door to her study. Thought what was behind it. A computer with virtually nothing on it. She looked up. Zach was staring at her. 'Go and tidy your room or something, Zach, will you? But leave your sister alone.' She returned her attention to Frank, who was still

223

manning the door. 'All right, let him in. Not sure my stomach's up to coffee.' She could still taste the last cup. 'I'd like you to listen in to whatever he has to say as well. I need you close, Frank.'

Frank had already turned away from her. 'All right, arsehole,' he was saying loudly, she presumed to Simon, 'you've got ten minutes.'

'Thanks, big boy,' came Simon's weasel voice.

Tatty watched Frank step aside, and Simon enter the house. It took her a moment or two to recognise him. He was wearing black jeans and smart brown leather trainers, usual gear, but he'd grown some designer stubble and had cropped and highlighted his hair. For a disguise? A pair of shades, gold aviators, were pushed up onto his head. Rich would have killed himself laughing.

He smiled. 'Hello, Tatty.'

She nodded. 'We'll go in here,' she said, pointing towards the study. She let both men enter before she stepped inside. It wasn't perhaps the best space in the world to hold a meeting. There was the over-stuffed office chair, and a small, two-seater couch. She sat on the office chair. Swivelled it round. Neither Frank nor Simon had taken the opportunity to rest their weary legs. She crossed hers determinedly, pleased she wasn't wearing a skirt. Frank remained by the door. There was no way Simon was leaving without Frank's say-so. 'Well?' she said.

Simon was looking at the couch, then looking at her. 'I'm the one who's waiting for the answer.'

'Yeah?' said Tatty.

'Only seems polite.'

'And you know all about manners.'

'I know about loyalty. Family.'

'Like fuck.' Tatty thought of the green Rolex box that used to be tucked away in a locked drawer of the desk. The small, loaded pistol that was kept inside. It was upstairs now, in its new hiding place.

'Did your doorman here not spell out the offer?' Simon was saying. 'When someone pops up to save your bacon, you could be a little more receptive. But you know what they say, let bygones be bygones.' He was over by the shelves, scanning the contents. 'Did Rich read all these books?'

There could only have been half a dozen. No cracked spines. She'd never opened one. 'Frank's told me what you want.'

'It's what I'm offering. A hundred mill. Back on the table.'

She didn't think Frank had mentioned a figure, that figure. *A hundred mill.* Why not? 'It's not enough.'

'It was last summer. What's changed?'

'Inflation.' She laughed. The pound was as weak as ever. The future no brighter, despite the recent election. More of that ugly, cold, grey old woman, like the North Sea in March. Yet prices were rising, fast. The country was sunk. 'I tell you what's changed — competition. We have a two hundred million pound deal in place.' There was no point hiding the figure, or telling him that that deal had collapsed in half. Simon wouldn't be in possession of such information for long. She looked at Frank. He was staying mum. She hadn't told him everything either.

Simon cleared his throat. 'Don't mind if I do,' he said, sitting. 'Oh, Tatty, where have you been?' He leant forward. 'I know where you've been,' he said excitedly, 'you've been led up the creek, without a fucking paddle.'

Tatty had a vague idea he was mixing his metaphors. She did read. Though not the sort of books that would ever have appealed to Rich. 'Still fiddling around with the under-aged, Simon?'

Frank was sucking in air loudly. He sounded like a faulty Dyson.

'I think it's best if we all keep our private lives private. Too many skeletons in the bedroom for all of us — and that includes you, Frank.'

Frank remained standing sentry, his expression unchanged. Tatty wondered exactly what Simon had on Frank. 'Who are your backers?' she asked Simon. 'Same tired old crew?'

Simon nodded. 'Experienced, is how I'd put it. Considered. Diligent. Brutally efficient. The deal's conditional on me being a part of it — no surprise. They know what they are getting with me. Trust, Tatty.'

'You and I both realise,' Tatty said, a flicker of opportunity stirring deep inside her, 'that a deal such as this involves setting up numerous investor vehicles, and one trading company at least, owned by a shell company, which in turn will be held by a network of trusts.' She glanced behind her at the blank computer screen, as if for more details. She didn't need a crib sheet. It was all in her head. She'd paid attention in the meetings with the company lawyer and accountant. Listened to what Ben and Sam had been saying these last few months as well, even if they thought she was talking hypotheticals.

'We'll have a project management operation, based in the UK,' she continued. 'It'll be as transparent as we're prepared to go. The appointing of the new architects and the building contractors will be handled by this arm. There'll be endless spin-offs from here.' She smiled.

'What are you trying to say?' Simon said, clearly not enjoying the hard padding of the small couch.

The air had grown still and heavy, while the room was shrinking. Tatty looked at the window, not sure when it had last been opened. Who knew where that security key was. 'We already own the land, as you know, through one of our property vehicles, based in Guernsey.'

'I thought you were using the British Virgin Islands,' Simon said.

'We've embarked upon a considerable restructuring of the core activities and trading vehicles, since you were last around,' Tatty said, catching Frank's eye. Some of what she was saying was true. He wasn't quite so expressionless. A smile was lurking not a million miles from his mouth. 'All part of the move.'

Simon cleared his throat, a couple of times. Finally removed the sunglasses from his head, held them tightly in his right hand. 'My name was on a lot of the business. You can't just wipe me away as if I never existed.'

'You ran off, having brutally dispatched your brother, and your wife — I think we can do what the fuck we want.'

'There're legal obstacles — no one told you that?'

'Relying on the law when you want to now, are you, Simon? I wouldn't bother, it's not pick and mix. Besides, we've had some fresh eyes on the old businesses. We've set up plenty of new products,' Tatty said. 'The casino project has a completely different framework now — and your name isn't on a fucking thing. You think I've been sitting around twiddling my thumbs these last nine, ten months?' Now confronted, she realised she had achieved a fair amount. 'I've a crack team in place helping me,' she said. But most of it was boringly legal.

'Sharma, Keene? A crack team? I don't think so.'

'There're plenty of other people I rely on as well. None you want to mess with.' She glanced at Frank once more.

'You can't even protect your buildings that do exist,' Simon shot back. 'Arson has to be the easiest form of intimidation. How are you going to manage anything in development?' He spat some air. 'Your crack team? Driving around in VW Up!s.' He laughed, and coughed, and laughed some more in a low-pitched cackle, like the call of a mating seal.

'What do you know about that car?'

'Company car, isn't it? Sian's? Just saying, you're not in control. I come here bearing gifts from our friends across the pond, find a once highly profitable business in chaos — people taking liberties all over the fucking place — and what do I get in return? A slap in the face? How are my friends going to react to this?'

Simon had stood, was towering over her in the tiny room. He wasn't a big man — but he was wiry and short-fused and capable of the most despicable things. His right hand appeared to be crushing his sunglasses. Frank stepped across, put his hand on Simon's shoulder, jerked him away, throwing him back to the couch.

'A hundred mill, Tatty, pounds not dollars. The American connections and guarantees to go with it — in this world? Don't chuck it away.' Simon rearranged his limbs — not as casually as he was trying to make it look.

'I don't intend to,' she said, the flicker of opportunity crystallising like a beautifully cut diamond in her mind. 'It's my land to be developed. The company's licence. My calls.' Why did she even need to tell him this?

'Ah,' Simon said, 'you might want to take another look at that licence, and the rest of it.' He coughed. 'You are aware of Graham Sands' new position in the council, aren't you?'

'We're aware,' said Frank — his first intervention.

'Nothing happens without his say so,' Simon said.

Frank caught Tatty's eye, rolled his. 'Call yourself a Goodwin?' Tatty said, shifting her stare to Simon. He didn't have Rich's eyes. There was no depth.

Simon stood again, a little unsteadily. 'You've put me in a very difficult position. My backers had set their hearts and minds on this project — they've stuck with it, with me, through thick and thin. They're not going to be happy. But fuck you.' He stood straighter. 'I have another channel for their cash. You think Graham Sands is going to sit on his large arse with all that say-so? He's expanding into the leisure industry like there's no tomorrow. Hotels, a shopping complex, a marina, and a casino. He's going to repurpose the outer harbour, not just some scrubby bit of wasteland. He's making connections with European cruise-liners. Punters will be pouring across the North Sea to our great, deregulated, finally independent island.'

Tatty was certain that that had been her idea. Rich's anyway. She was also thinking of the collusion between Simon and Sands over Rich's murder.

'Now,' Simon continued quickly, 'I've been holding off telling our American friends about it, thinking family first. But you don't give me a lot of options. Sorry.'

He smiled, his dark shallow eyes not reminding Tatty for a second of Rich, the intensity of Rich's gaze. He then suddenly reached out, his hand glancing her shoulder, and dropped his sunglasses onto the desk. They were crushed, the lenses cracked and popped from the frames.

'I'll be seeing you,' he said, stepping towards the door and Frank.

Frank put his foot out. Shifted the weight in

his body. There was no way Simon was getting out of there so casually, so disrespectfully. 'There is no money, is there?' she said. 'No Prime Poker cash on the table. You want your job back, your status.'

He was shaking his head. 'There's a hundred mill, in cash. No swaps or bitcoins — nothing stupid like that. It's up to us how we clean it for them — onshore or offshore, as the development progresses. Of course they get instant returns in the shape of management and consulting fees.'

'Management fees? I thought we were the management.'

'It's what it needs to look like on paper.'

'No overall stake?'

'They want a foothold here — yeah. That was always part of the package. Only thirty-three per cent, once they have all their initial investment back.'

'Once they have their hundred mill back?'

'Yeah.'

'We're giving away a third of our development, so we can clean some money for them? Fuck off.'

'Where else are you going to get that sort of money from? It's the margins we're after in any case. A hundred mill to play with?'

'This is pie in the cloudy sky,' Tatty said. 'Always was. Do these people even exist?'

Simon was shaking his head. 'You've never seen such an impressive business. I don't know why I'm telling you all this now anyway, seeing as it's destined for Sands.' He rubbed his hands. Tatty was not going to think about what else those hands might have rubbed recently. 'Sands,'

231

he continued gleefully, 'now that's a name that means something in Vegas.'

'You want me to see him out?' Frank said, glowering like a hippopotamus on heat.

'These people never go away,' Simon said, fast. 'Nasty old men.' He coughed and laughed at the same time.

'We don't need you, Simon,' she said, grappling for purchase in the thick air. 'We have our resources.'

'Not what I heard,' he said. 'What exactly did you lose in the fire, apart from your reputation? Took out your new office, didn't it? Maybe you were never meant to be at the helm. I'll be seeing you.'

'I still have a memory,' Tatty shouted, to Simon's back, finding that tone again, the one she'd always reserved for her kids, for Zach. 'It's all up here.' She tapped her head.

'Do you know how hard it is to meet these people? I spent years building their confidence.'

Frank had put his arm across the study door now. 'Let him go, Frank,' Tatty said.

'You sure?'

Tatty nodded, and Simon flung open the door to the hall and was out of the house in seconds, engine noise soon filling the silence. Frank had barely moved, yet air was beginning to circulate in the foul room. Simon must have left the front door open. 'He might be more useful to us alive, for a short while,' she said. 'And then we can have some fun getting rid of him for ever.'

She stood. 'Are you still in touch with that guy who was here doing the snooping for the Prime

Poker consortium, last autumn? The American?'

'Dennis?'

'Yeah.'

'No,' said Frank, too firmly.

'Something tells me you wouldn't mind getting in touch with him again.'

'You've got a plan, haven't you?'

'Yeah,' she said, walking out of the study, looking down at her clothes, wondering whether she was dressed for the great outdoors. More importantly, whether she could leave Zach to look after Sam.

'Want to share it?' said Frank.

'Hey,' said Tatty, looking up. A small woman had stepped into the house and was carefully closing the door. 'Nina?'

Nina turned, looked startled, then smiled slowly.

'This is Frank,' Tatty said, pointing to her huge associate. 'Have you ever met? Nina looks after the house.'

'Don't think we've had the pleasure,' said Frank, 'in all these years. Rich used to talk very fondly of you.'

'I miss him,' said Nina.

'Sam's not well,' Tatty said.

'I saw her car,' Nina said. 'I was hoping to see her.'

'The thing is,' she glanced at Frank, 'let's go into the kitchen and I'll explain. I'm so pleased you're here.'

'It is a Tuesday. I'm always here on a Tuesday.'

'Yes,' said Tatty. 'I need to go out for a few hours. Zach's here, but, well, you know what he's like.'

'It's not so blowy,' Nina said. 'Sun's forecast for later.'

Frank had strolled over to the front door. 'Frank,' Tatty said. 'Meet me by the Coastwatch tower, North Denes. You know what to bring.'

'It's some walk from there,' he said.

'It'll be good for you,' she said.

26

It was some walk, and it appeared they still weren't there. But as Nina had said, it wasn't so blowy. The wind turbines, seemingly only an arm's stretch away if you squinted, were basking in the sun like creatures from a future century. A supply ship was sat on the horizon, its bulbous helicopter deck looking like it was ready to gobble the turbines up. The beach in summer-time, sunshine anyway, always made Tatty light-headed.

She focused some more on the horizon, thinking not of the end of her world, but new beginnings. However, the longer she stared into the bright, watery stillness, the less she saw. It wasn't only Simon who needed a new pair of sunglasses. She removed hers for a second, looked at the smeary lenses. They hadn't had many outings this year.

She paused on a faint ridge of shingle, a tern perhaps a few steps ahead, twitchy. It then took fright, though not because of her. She glanced over her shoulder. The only thing huffing and puffing right now was Frank. He was more than some way behind her, catching up slowly. His face, even from this distance, was the wrong shade of puce, glimmering with sweat. Tatty looked the other way, sorry for him, seeking out more seabirds going about their business. Suddenly the foreshore was alive with the damn things, anxious for the next meal, or their nest. Were they nesting this time of the year? She didn't know.

She scanned further ahead, shamed by her lack of knowledge of the natural world. She should ask Frank, but she wouldn't. The vast shingle ridges were like fat veins of precious metal — silver and gold and platinum. The wide strips of pale sand were less liquid, and flatly reflecting the sun that was now beating down with brutal vigour.

To her left, inland, were scratchy dunes. Everywhere she looked she couldn't see a single soul. There was only her and Frank.

Her bag was weighing heavily on her shoulder, and she let it slip off, catching one of the handles with her left hand. The bag fell open and she delved inside, her heartbeat quickening. Removing the gun, she then let the bag drop to the ground. She spun round, aimed the Smith & Wesson snub straight at him. It felt solid in her hand. Purposeful. It wasn't the first time she'd aimed the thing at someone. But she'd never fired it.

She put her left hand on top of the back of her right hand, how she thought you were meant to, to steady your aim, and help counter the recall. She had thin arms, weak wrists.

'I hope that thing isn't fucking loaded,' Frank managed to shout breathlessly, slowing even further. He was wearing the wrong shoes for such a trek — black Oxfords today. The wrong jacket, some misshapen, bulky suede thing. An image immediately came to her of him as a little boy. Overweight, sunburned, in trunks too tight, and old-fashioned shoes and socks, wandering along the shore, all alone. No tears in his eyes, but a haunting determination.

She shifted her aim, the gun now pointing straight out to sea, and squeezed the trigger, gently. She felt it give a little, hit another buffer, and go tight. Was it faulty? Some knock-off Rich had procured for peanuts? The next time she exerted more pressure and the gun kicked back and a loud retort filled the empty beach, and rolled on out to sea. It was far louder than she had been expecting. 'Course it was loaded,' she said, her ears ringing.

The supply ship hadn't moved a centimetre, neither had the wind turbines. She couldn't see any terns, though. No gulls either. Before she knew it, Frank had his hand on her arm, was removing the gun from her hand.

'I hope no one fucking heard that,' he said. 'We could have walked further.'

'No you couldn't,' she said.

'Piss off,' Frank said.

'Hey,' she said. 'That's no way to talk to your boss.' She smiled.

'First thing to remember,' he said, 'is whether the gun is loaded or not. With one of these,' he held up the gun, so Tatty could see the chambers, clicked something, then rolled it, so she could see the bullets, and where a bullet was missing. 'It's simple. Holds six bullets.' He spun the chamber again. 'Now you've only got five bullets left.' He glanced over his shoulder, scanned the beach left and right.

'I've only got three targets,' she said, thinking hard, thinking anew. 'Maybe four.' What was she playing at?

'Yeah?' He was looking at her now. His cheeks calming.

'Michael doesn't trust us, Frank, even with a piddly hundred mill. Can't believe he's now threatening to turn up with a petty enforcer.'

'Not sure it's entirely his call. Of course, his crew don't trust us. But you don't want to start a war, not with that lot.'

'You don't think I've got enough ammunition?'

He laughed. 'Big investments are always about being accommodating.'

'I wouldn't mind having a few more bullets in any case.' She wasn't listening to him. She was in charge. She had the business brain. Frank was meant to do as he was told. 'No point having the damn thing if I can't use it,' she said. 'Can I have it back?' She held out her hand. 'You're meant to be giving me a lesson.'

'What do you think I'm doing? You need to think of this weapon as a deterrent,' he said, still gripping it tightly. 'Like a nuclear arsenal — for little people like us, this is the nuclear option. Got that? You don't want to let the thing off, without thinking first, very, very carefully.'

'Please, Frank, who do you take me for?'

'If you do,' he said, perhaps a touch embarrassed, 'it's the easiest gun on the block to use. They never jam. Did you feel the play on the trigger? Another safety measure. First trigger, as we call it, takes up the slack, exert more pressure, and bingo.'

'What's the range?'

'You don't want to think about distance — with this? It's a girl's gun. No further than across a room. Aim for the largest area of body mass. Always go for the chest. Unless you've got the thing pressed to some arsehole's head. But that would be very messy. You'd need a new mac.' He laughed. 'And a trip to the salon.'

'Here.' She reached for her weapon.

'Careful where you point it.'

She took the gun back. It wasn't feeling so solid or deadly. *A girl's gun?* 'You'd be pretty easy to knock off, Frank — the size of you. How come you're still alive?' She waved the gun towards him. Tried to look down the barrel. There wasn't enough of it to aim with much confidence, she decided.

'Because I always make sure I'm better prepared,' Frank said, pulling a gun from the inside pocket of his jacket. 'Besides, I'm on a diet — thinning down.' He laughed again.

Tatty wondered why he was in such a good mood all of a sudden. Because he was better prepared? Better informed? His gun was twice the size of hers, and didn't have some antiquated, revolving chamber, looking like it was out of a Western. His was matt black, and looked like the sort of thing you more commonly saw on telly. Modern, lethal, in Matt Damon's hands. 'What the fuck is that?'

'This,' he said, aiming not at her, but at a clump of marram to her right, 'is the Glock 19 those Lithuanians had the audacity to threaten me with last autumn.'

'Where's Michael's money coming from?' she asked, suddenly wanting information that mattered. New information. Information she should have been party to months ago.

'Good question. I'm still hoping Ben might be able to help us out there. But I'd suggest one of the Baltic nations, if not Russia itself. Amsterdam isn't all clogs and tulips.'

'Or weed and prostitutes,' Tatty muttered.

'A lot of such finance goes through the Dutch banks, often via Switzerland. The fund managers over there,' he was looking out to sea, 'are forever stopping by those coffee shops. Meeting the dodgiest fucking people.'

'And you're complaining?'

'They might not always be operating with the clearest of heads. Like our Zach.'

'What's that mean?'

'He's got himself well and truly mixed up with this Candy Cane business.'

Tatty exhaled a huge lungful of air. 'Yeah, I was gathering. I don't know, Frank, I guess his parents weren't the best examples he could've had. The other two are different. Zach's always been a worry. I don't know how to handle him. Too much leeway, I suppose. I should have been firmer. I didn't want him pissing off though. I wanted him near. At least we can keep an eye on him.'

'Can we? It seems he and his mate Liam have been attempting to shift some pills, which incidentally are also coming in from the Netherlands — so the kids are saying.'

'Like the pills Rolly Andrews had on him?'

'The same.'

'How?'

'That bit I'm still not sure about. Neither's Zach — and I believe him. It seems Rolly's place was being used to store all manner of gear — I shouldn't have been so surprised. I thought the old tyke had turned a corner. People never change that much — if I've learned anything over the last few days, it's that.' He looked seaward again. 'I don't think anything was being manufactured there, no evidence of that, but there was at least one interesting ingredient — a big box of cut. Could have fallen off the back of a lorry. What's really bothering me is the fact that Liam or Sian, or both of them, have been there. And at least one old codger is keeping an eye on the place. That caravan park is not the haven of peace and tranquillity it used to be. It's like it's been taken over. What happens when people get too old and muddled to keep control — the snakes move in.'

Tatty could feel the wrinkles on her forehead, like the ripple effect left in the sand after the tide has gone out. She needed to relax. Couldn't remember the last time she'd visited a spa. Or been on a date. 'Sian? My Sian?'

Frank nodded, eclipsing the sun. 'She's been having a thing with Liam, according to Zach, who's none too pleased about it.'

'What's it to do with him?'

Frank created some more shade. 'Young love moves in mysterious ways.'

'That little slut? Where's she now? Weren't you

241

meant to track her down, give her a grilling?'

'She's zoomed off, in Liam's Beamer.'

'And Celine knows nothing, I suppose.'

'No, nothing of any use. I paid her a visit last night. She was shuffling around her pad in a pair of pink fluffy slippers, listening to Beyoncé.'

'That is why she was employed. No point hurting her.'

'Don't worry,' said Frank. 'I'm not a monster.'

'As for Sian.' She whistled, the noise instantly lost in the great wilderness.

'We need to give her a chance to explain herself.' Frank was looking at his gun, doing something with the long cartridge, which then went back up into the bottom of the handle. There was a click. He then turned the piece over a couple of times in his large hand, carefully, lovingly. Men and their gadgets.

'She's running out of time,' Tatty said.

'We'll get to the bottom of it. Let's not forget her dad's just died. Some sensitivity is required.'

'From you? How you surprise me, Frank. Let's not forget the fact that she's been messing my son around. She needs a good slap.' She paused. Looked up at the bluest of blue skies. 'As does Zach.'

'Like I said, I'm not so sure he's done much wrong. He's back in the fold, I believe, in any case. Firmly under my wing.'

'Yeah? That's one of the things I pay you for.' Frank's raise, his bonus, was suddenly not looking so secure. 'Fuck's sake.' She could almost see the flash of anger inside her head, like a fork of lightning over a stormy sea. Where was her girl's gun? Dangling in her hand, uselessly. Though Frank wasn't so very far away, his massive chest. Except he was carrying a real weapon.

'I do what I can, Tat, you know that — calm down. I wouldn't let Zach get into any serious trouble.'

She half believed him. Still wasn't sure about him calling her Tat.

'Besides, he's showing some entrepreneurial spirit,' Frank continued, a smile creeping across his fat chops. 'That has to be applauded.'

'Let me look at your gun,' she said.

'This isn't a playground, Tatty.'

'No? You brought me here for some shooting lessons.'

'At your request.'

'Be good to know what I might be up against.'

'What's that supposed to mean?'

'Who else might be properly prepared.' She smiled, her anger abating, and looked down at her feet in the soft sand. At least she was wearing trainers. Suddenly she wanted to take them off, run free, free as a child. She'd been lonely and overweight as well. Her parents were not nice people. For a second she wondered about her sister. Whatever might have happened to her.

'You want to take another shot with your snub? Get the handle of that first?' Frank said.

She raised the Smith and Wesson once more. Aimed it at the clump of marram that Frank had focused his piece on. She then pulled the trigger hard and fast this time, riding straight through the slack and the second block. She was expecting the retort, the small recall, but not the dull thud as the bullet hit the low ridge, sending up a small spray of shingle and sand. The echo seemed to be contained as well.

'Good shot,' Frank said.

'You didn't know what I was aiming at.'

'You kept your arm nice and steady.'

'Now I've only got four bullets left,' she said. 'That was stupid.'

'We don't know the half of it, do we? What's your plan?'

'How many bullets does yours take?'

'This takes nineteen, why it's called a Glock 19 — get it?'

'Don't be cheeky.'

'It can take twenty if you put one up the spout as well.'

'Jargon.' She tutted.

'It takes different rounds. Yours is a point thirty-eight revolver — tried and tested since the nineteenth century — mine's a nine millimetre, semi-automatic, common as muck. Bullets look almost identical, but there's a slight difference in length and circumference. They're not inter-changeable.'

'You boys, and your particulars. What's more common, easier to get hold of?'

'None of them are easy — in this country. Probably the nine-millimetre rounds. It's the weapon the police use commonly, the army — across Europe, the world. There're more around, particularly coming in from Europe. Thirty-eights are all over the shop in the States.'

'Is anything made in this country any more?'

244

Tatty said, scanning the beach once more, then looking out to sea. The supply ship might have shifted a centimetre or two. 'We don't even manufacture our own Candy Cane.'

'Turkeys,' said Frank.

'You what?'

'We still rear turkeys, don't we? In Norfolk as well.'

'Never been a fan. Here, let me have a go with yours.' She was holding out her snub, wanting to get her hands on his Glock, a boy's toy. No, a man's lethal weapon — now that was a stupid film. 'I don't need to remind you who you work for again, do I?'

Smiling, he took her gun and handed over his. 'It's a semi-automatic,' he said. 'Completely different beast to yours. Some say yours is more accurate, but that's down to the shooter. Revolvers don't jam, but there's no getting away from the fact that nine millimetres carry more powerful rounds, and being semi-automatic, they're obviously quicker firing. Why they're the weapon of choice for the police and military.'

'And street dealers, who want to move up in the world,' Tatty said.

'And businessmen who don't like backing down,' Frank said, smiling at her.

'Business women,' Tatty said. She was surprised by how light the gun was — given that it was loaded with all those bullets — and comfortable in her hand. It didn't feel too big. She aimed it at the clump of marram again, finding that because it had a longer barrel, it was easier to sight a target. She clasped her right wrist with her left hand again, for support.

'You might want to put your left hand under your right wrist, not on top,' Frank said.

She didn't look at him. She was concentrating hard.

'There's no play on the trigger with this one,' Frank said. 'Squeeze and you're off. Squeeze again and you'll engage another round. Like I said, it's a semi-automatic. You can empty the magazine in less than three seconds — one thousand two hundred rounds per minute.'

'It's not World War Three, Frank.'

'But you need a better stance.'

She wasn't sure he was even listening to her. She wasn't sure she was listening to him any more.

'Move your feet apart. One foot in front of the other. And don't stand quite so tall.'

She'd never wanted to be any shorter, that was for sure.

'Crouch a little,' Frank was saying.

Was she sick of being told what to do for one morning. She was the person with the plan. She squeezed. Squeezed again. Nothing happened. 'It doesn't work.' She brought it closer, turned it over in her hand, as Frank had done. Thought better of looking down the barrel. Had no idea what was wrong with it.

'Here,' Frank said, 'give it to me.' He pocketed her snub, took the Glock, a broad smile on his sweaty face, all the fresh sea air in the world behind him. 'The safety's on. See this button — flick it clockwise. Always keep the safety on — with a semi-auto, you don't want this thing going off accidentally.'

'That's likely, is it?' She held out her hand, took the gun back. Flicked the switch. Aimed again.

'What's your plan, Tatty?'

She fired, tried to hang onto the recoil, and lower her aim, before firing again, and again. The three retorts were louder than her snub. The kick way more powerful. The damage to the small mound of marram didn't seem so obvious, however.

'Too high,' said Frank. 'Your first bullet glanced the top of that ridge. Fuck knows where the other two went.'

'What's the range?'

'Accurately — swings and roundabouts. But on paper, a nine millimetre goes further. With any purpose, across a garden, say.'

'Here's the plan,' she said, letting her right hand, still clasping the gun, fall to her side. She felt the weapon hit her thigh. Should she have put the safety on? 'We're now being offered a measly hundred mill from some Eastern European outfit, via Michael, but also a hundred mill from Prime Poker, via Simon. You think the people with the money care about their go-betweens? They want a safe investment opportunity — away from prying eyes. We can offer them that, better rates too for everyone if we cut out the middlemen. We don't want the wrong people getting ideas above their station. Middlemen have a habit, don't they?' They were always men.

She looked at him hard — his vast head framed by an even vaster natural world. People fucked everything up. They should leave it to the birds, the bees, the fish out there, the few codlings and herring, what was left of them. Crabs? Plenty of them. And seals. They'd come back with a vengeance, enjoying the barnacle-rich, underwater platforms the wind turbines sat on.

'Our power comes from being small. My husband knew that. You know that. We need to keep decisions tight. Outside backers have got to trust us. Proper, decisive action — that should put their minds at rest. Then they'd know exactly who they are dealing with.'

'Easy to see where two of your bullets could be headed then — Simon and Michael. But the third?' Frank said.

'You want Graham Sands with all that say-so getting in the way? I've never trusted him. Rich didn't. Unfinished business from the autumn, besides. What was he planning to do with that footage? Not go to the police with it, that's for sure.'

'Blackmail Simon?' said Frank. 'Some insurance policy?'

'Maybe.'

'Funnily enough, I was going to pop by his gaff this morning — crack his egg for him.'

'I've seen you crack a few,' said Tatty. 'You're too soft. Sands needs more than a warning, doesn't he? That council's only ever full of yes men.' Men again, she thought. 'They'll be scared of him, as they were of Rich. If he feels emboldened — who knows how far he'll go. Besides, we don't want Simon getting into his bed.'

'Too old for Simon, isn't he?'

'That might be funny, if it wasn't so sick.'

'Look, Simon's in there already, isn't he? Has been since last summer, at least. Like I said, I was going to pay Sands a visit.'

She turned towards the way they'd come. 'You keep saying you're going to do something, Frank, but you don't carry through. What's with you? Man or mouse?'

The Coastwatch station might have been a spec in the distance. Then again the shape might have been some sort of mirage, or reflection. The Tower complex perhaps, which once housed a restaurant on the viewing platform — she used to go there with Rich, when he was being nice. She'd have a Caesar salad, he'd have surf and turf, then wipe his hands on her bare legs under the table, as he reached for her knickers. The sand was shimmering. The marram fluttering. A breeze had appeared from nowhere. People had to be out on the beach somewhere not so far away — a day like this?

'I've been putting family matters first, Tatty.'

'Yeah?' Everyone seemed to be overstepping the mark, taking liberties, taking her for granted. 'Let's head back,' she said, a rage beginning to bloom once more, 'and get on with it.'

'Here's your piece,' mumbled Frank. He was holding out her snub. 'Hand me mine, will you?'

'I don't need a girl's gun, Frank. I'll hang onto this one, if you don't mind.' She bent down, picked up her Birkin. Dropped the Glock inside. Set off. Got so far. Looked over her shoulder. Frank hadn't budged, and was still holding the snub in his hand. 'What are you waiting for?'

She set off again, only for a second thinking, what if he shot me in the back? Girl down. Not yet. She had the best plan Frank would have heard all day. All decade. Besides, she had to be out of range already for such a silly little weapon.

27

Zach waited until he was certain Nina had left the house. Nevertheless, he still crept out of his bedroom, barefoot, silent, hesitant. He was surprised by how bright the landing was. He always kept the curtains shut in his room, blocking any glare from hitting his screens.

Sun was streaming through the long, landing window like it was lava, and onto the staid, beige carpet, thick as a shaggy dog. Of all the drab colours. But he'd always loved how it felt squishing between your toes, how it silenced your steps — the years he used to sneak in and out of his room.

He waded through the hot pool, a glance outside beaten back by the nuclear fusion going on only a hundred million miles away. He was no dunce. He tapped on Sam's door. Got no reply. Eased the door open. 'Sam?' he whispered.

There was a smell of stale air and fresh laundry. Some other cleaning product whiff. Nina must have given the room a proper going over. With Sam in situ?

'Sam?' His eyes were struggling with the changing light, his patchy mind racing.

She was there, and something pinged inside his chest. Her head was down on the pillow, the duvet mounded up to her chin. He padded round the bed, over more stupidly plush carpet, sat gently on the side she was facing, which was away from the door. Zach could tell she was trying to shut out the world, the universe. He didn't blame her. But her eyes were wide open, and he was her little brother.

'You're awake,' he said. 'How are you?'

'Where have you been?' Her voice was thin, and Zach didn't think Sam could have cleaned her teeth in a while.

'In my room,' he said. 'I looked in on you, hours ago. You were fast asleep.'

'Where's Mum?'

'No idea. She went off somewhere with Frank.'

'Frank was here?'

'Yeah.'

'Why?'

'Business?'

'Business? Fucking business. That's all they care about.'

'Life goes on,' Zach said, immediately regretting it.

'For some,' Sam sighed.

He'd asked for it. 'Look, I'm sorry,' he said, 'about the baby.' Man, he wasn't equipped to deal with this sort of shit. He reached out, was about to stroke her head, what was above the covers, though held back.

'It wasn't a baby, yet,' she said, strongly, raising her head. 'I don't want to hear that word again.'

'OK.'

'Fucking Michael,' she said. 'Fuck is he?'

'You want to see him?'

'Urrgh, no. What do you think? Like yesterday.'

'Didn't you say he was in Amsterdam?'

'He's meant to be coming back today. Could

have got on a plane sooner. He could have hired a fucking private jet. What time is it?'

'You do want to see him?'

'I don't know what the fuck I want.'

He stroked her head, her hair now, and she laid back down on the pillow. 'Everything will be all right, Sam. I'm here, Mum's here for you, Frank.'

'Frank? What's that mean? That he'll sort everything out, because Mum's not capable? Is that what you're saying? You think Frank can sort anything out because he's a big fat man with a shaven head?'

Zach shook his own, slight head slowly. Felt his thick, matted hair sway. He thought Frank was mostly bald as a coot, and didn't have to shave his head. 'That's not what I'm saying — why are you giving me a hard time? Mum's Mum, isn't she? She's new to all this. Still finding her feet.'

'No, Zach, she's not new to it. She's been living with it all her life. She just never had room to breathe, to be herself. She was tougher than we ever knew — all those years putting up with Dad and his shit.'

'I thought you loved Dad. You were his favourite.'

'You have to learn to stand on your own feet too, Zach. You're not always going to have people looking out for you.'

'We're still a family, Sis,' he said, looking around the dim, stinking room, as if a ghost might pop out of nowhere. 'That's the point. We look out for each other, don't we? Not sure I

253

want to stand on my own two feet, to be honest. It's good to be part of something. The right thing — anyhow.'

'Frank?' she laughed, weakly. 'What are you scared of — on your own?'

'Shouldn't you be resting?' he said. 'This conversation is way too heavy for any time.'

'I was. You disturbed me.'

'Sorry,' he said.

'Now I'm wide awake. So, what are you scared of?'

'I'm not scared of anything. Stuff's going on, that's all.'

'Could have fooled me.'

Somewhere in her exhausted, distressed state, Zach was pleased that Sam still sounded a tad like her normal self. He wasn't sure how tough he was any more, but she had guts. He supposed his mum did as well. Sam seemed to have changed her tune about their mum. Frank — well, it wasn't hard to see why his dad had trusted him within an inch. 'Nothing you need to worry about,' he said, desperate to get out of her room, the house. 'We're on top of it.'

'Michael?'

'He's not part of what I'm talking about.'

'Better not be, I guess. What time is it? I can't lift my head. My stomach's numb, but I've got a terrible pain right here.' She barely managed to tap her crown, the mushed-up hair.

'Can I get you anything? Something to drink? It's like lunchtime.' He presumed. He didn't have his phone on him. He never wore a watch. 'Are you hungry?'

254

'God, no. I want to die.'

'Don't say that.' He glanced about the darkened room again — there were no ghosts, so he trawled his own aching brain for something solid and uplifting to say. Liam and his nasty weed, it fucked your head for days. Nothing cheery came to mind, though something else did that he should have got off his chest yonks ago. 'I never finished what I was going to say about the fire.'

'What fire?'

'In the Smokehouse, on the weekend.'

'Oh that. God, those stupid investigators and everything. I'd forgotten.'

'Wish I could.'

'The stuff that's going on, right?'

'Yeah — sort of.'

'You sure Michael's nothing to do with this? Not sure I could take that right now.'

'Yeah, sure. But someone's to blame,' he said quietly, thoughtfully.

'I want to go back to sleep, Zach. Wake me up when he's here, will you?'

'He can't wake you up himself?'

'Maybe he won't want to disturb me, if he thinks I'm asleep. Don't be such a lazy fucking sod.'

'Sure.' Zach hadn't met Michael too many times. His mum was all over him. It was embarrassing. Frank seemed much less keen on him. Zach got to his feet, stepped around the bed. Stopped. 'I have to tell you something, Sam, about that night, the fire.'

'I don't care,' she said, hauling more duvet

over her head. 'Not interested. Leave me out of it.'

'But it's important.'

'Tell Mum.'

'I can't, it's too late. She won't understand.'

'Frank? Go away, Zach, please. I have had an operation.'

'I was there,' he said quickly, now he was by her bedroom door, and not at all sure why he did have to tell her. Was he thinking that if he spelled it out, what he knew, the missing bits would pop into place? Like ghosts, apparitions? His sister, in her state, was not going to judge him too harshly, was she? She had the legal brain. He needed her clear, smart thinking. Talking to Frank, Liam, hadn't helped. He couldn't be entirely straight with either. Last fucking time he tried to pull anything like this. He felt nine years old, sure enough — little lost boy, with his thumb stuffed into his mouth, sobbing silently.

'Where, for God's sake?' Sam was saying, muffled, and exasperated. 'You were where?'

'The Smokehouse, on Saturday night.'

'And?'

'I saw it on fire.' He knew he should leave her be. 'Flames were rising up into the sky,' he continued, 'like it was a movie. The wind, man. I couldn't think straight.'

'What were you on?' she said, like she didn't give a shit.

'Nothing heavy. We were trying to shift some gear, pills, this Candy Cane stuff — make a few bob. There are always a few scallywags out for a bite, Saturday night. I took a couple, we all did.

Then I lost the bag. Liam, I thought he'd nicked it. Everyone scattered, searching. We were at this rave, a warehouse or two away. A place we've used before. Cool space. Great guy on the decks — plays Amnesia in July. And then everything went fuzzy. I was out on the street looking, going up and down Main Cross, Suffling, Salmon, round to the power station, down to South Denes and back — you know what that part of town is like. Empty warehouses, derelict buildings, scrub behind all these chain-link fences. Which was when I noticed the flames, trying to get my bearings. The sky was lit up, like there was a massive party cooking, everyone sitting around the fire, warming hands, feet. You know those parties on the beach, a couple of years back, when we had a summer? Lazy, hazy days. Man, I loved those.'

Maybe it was three, four years ago, but there was a spell of warm weather early one July that Zach could still feel in his bones, when a gang of them got into beach parties up by the Hopton cliffs — night after night. No one ever complained. It was when he lost his virginity — on the fucking beach. A girl from Cliff Park, she was fifteen, like him. Sand in all the wrong places.

'I was so confused,' he continued. 'I didn't know where the time had gone. Where they'd gone — Liam, Sian, a couple of other dudes.'

He'd never closed the door to Sam's bedroom when he'd tip-toed in and he was aware of a noise coming up from downstairs. Aware of the silent irritation beaming out from Sam over on

257

the far side of the bed as well. There, it went again, the silly, battery-powered ding dong of the doorbell. Who'd ever ring that? Delivery people just thumped — as his dad used to, because he couldn't be bothered to get his key out and unlock the door himself. Thought their mum, all of them, should run around after him non-stop. Constantly be at his beck and call. Thank God his mum was more chilled — normally. The bell should have been ripped out years ago as it was.

'The door, Zach?' suddenly came Sam's voice, shrill as a gull. 'You expect me to get it?'

'I'm going — relax,' Zach said, leaving the room. He tore down the stairs, only remembering that it might not be Dominos when he was twisting the first lock, recovering his breath. A quick squint through the peephole told him there was nothing to worry about. But what the fuck was she doing here?

28

Frank had driven to the far end of the spit. Checked out the giant cranes and chunks of turbine, which were clogging the outer harbour. Where had they suddenly come from? It was like they had sprung up overnight. He thought Lowestoft was meant to be the new wind farm assembly and service base.

A fancy new marina seemed a much better proposition. He didn't want these hunks of machinery clogging up that idea, expensive as it would be. Yet they had two hundred mill coming their way, if Tatty's plan worked out. The world was their oyster — Yarmouth anyway.

He'd had to do a U-turn at the end of Beach Parade, still livid that the Port Authority had requisitioned that chunk of land, even if Rich had been part of the scheme. It was like the MoD was in charge with the amount of barbed-wire-topped fencing, not a bunch of overweight, middle-aged men, with impotency problems. The council needed a Goodwin back on the key committees. A Goodwin with a bright new agenda. Maybe Tatty would put herself forward one day.

Frank looked at his watch. Felt an accusing face over his shoulder. He didn't know where the day had gone, with so little achieved. Tatty was right. What had he carried through today, since the weekend, since the fire? It was some walk though — his doctor would be pleased. Tens of thousands of steps. Yet his next task required waiting, and that was exactly what he was doing. Waiting and watching.

The view through the windscreen had barely changed in decades. The river was endlessly shifting with the tides, but its banks, the quays, remained steadfastly stuck in time. Like him? Rich had been impatient, though he'd only got so far in the end — over the fucking quay edge that Frank was staring at right now.

Frank tried Dennis's number again, the last number he had for the graceful American. The call went straight to an anonymous voicemail. He decided he'd leave a message this time. 'Dennis? It's me, Frank. Remember?' Would he? 'Call me back, can you?' He recited his current number, presuming Dennis was still in the States, still working as the US casino consortium's investigator. It seemed pie in the sky, but what did they have without ambition? He admired Tatty's vision.

For the first time in a long while, Frank felt excited —   useful. He was more than a childminder for a spoilt brat.

He climbed out of the vehicle, walked across the rear parking lot of Goodwin House, his legs feeling the walk earlier. The VW Up! was still there, an opportunity presenting itself. Yet the keys must have been in one of Rolly Andrew's fetid pockets. He should have thought about that before. It wasn't too late. He'd be revisiting the caravan before long in any case.

He took another look over towards the back of

260

the Admiralty Steel lot, catching nothing but an absent work-force, and a flock of busy gulls. A service ship was moored on the far bend of Fish Wharf, where the old roll-on roll-off terminal used to be. It was a pristine white and blue. Some orange flare on the funnel. It appeared more than a touch out of place sat among the old warehouses. He'd noticed a few such vessels recently.

Rather than enter Goodwin House using Tatty's rear fire door trick, Frank walked round the corner of the old office block. Aware of his creeping shadow, he reached out and ran a hand along the concrete foundations. The building was a relic of the 1970s, when the town had gone bonkers for North Sea oil and gas. That was a decade or two after the herring industry had collapsed. Industry had never been stable in Yarmouth. Why it paid to take risks, to move with the times. He was beginning to think Tatty was a good deal smarter than her late husband. Less impatient, less impulsive, more canny.

He'd reached the front of the building, though he hung back, scanning South Denes, and the block across the way. Graham Sands' dark green Jag was in its usual place, inconsiderately slung across a corner of pavement. Frank patted his jacket, checking that he had the Smith & Wesson snub, the girl's gun, neatly concealed in the inside pocket. He knew he'd only need one bullet.

He looked at his watch again, wondering what Sands' evening plans would have been. Tea with the missus? A stroll on the beach with the dog?

He had some kids, didn't he? A skinny girl who was working at the Pier View Hotel, he remembered. His wife was rake-thin as well. Frank couldn't see her taking over his fledgling empire. There weren't many women like Tatty in the world.

The Jag was two years old, current XF model. The man didn't even have enough class to own an XJ. Nevertheless, Frank knew he wouldn't be able to break in, take a nap on the back seat, without the alarm going berserk. He'd have to wait. No, he'd have to hurry this up. He tapped at his phone, at the recent calls icon, found the number he wanted. Pressed.

'Ah, Mr Adams,' Sands said, after only two rings. 'I've been expecting your call.'

'Yeah?' said Frank, his mind twisting and stretching.

'Apologies are due first from you, matey,' Sands said.

'For what, matey?' Frank said.

'Hanging up on me the other day. Now, that's not a nice way to treat a friendly voice.'

'Graham, we might not always have seen eye to eye,' Frank said, deciding to change tack. 'Let bygones be bygones.' He felt slightly queasy. 'I had a word with Simon.'

'He was just here, as it happens,' Sands said. 'We thought you'd come round to our way of thinking. It's a man's world, Frank. You of all people should know that.'

'There are certain preconditions,' Frank said, now feeling completely nauseous.

'Wouldn't have expected anything else, from a

262

man like you. Let's have them, then.'

'Not on the blower, Graham. You know better than that, a man in your position.'

'Pop by my office. I'll be waiting.'

'I've got an aversion to offices,' said Frank. 'We can chat over a cuppa, nice and social like. Meet me at the old casino. They do sandwiches, scones, this time of day.' He'd stuck his head round corner of Goodwin House, saw across the way that no one was standing on the forecourt of Admiralty Steel. The giant doors were closed for once. No lurking fabricators. It was approaching knocking-off time — for a certain sort of business. Except Sands was still at work, plotting his takeover of Yarmouth. How many others were there? A secretary or two? Muscle? Where'd Simon gone?

'What do I want a fucking scone for?' said Sands. 'Not exactly neutral territory, is it?'

'It's nice and public,' said Frank. 'The only civilised place in town.'

'Yarmouth maybe, not Gorleston. You're not twisting my arm.'

'It could be joint territory,' Frank said. 'When were you last in? Be good to get your considered eye on the place. A boutique hotel, Tatty had thought. You've done wonders with the Pier View. You're a natural in the hospitality world, Graham.' Frank wondered how much of a natural he was, at lying. He'd spent most of his life at it.

'Quite the charmer, aren't you, matey — when you know what's good for you. All right, I'll meet you there.'

'Soon as,' said Frank. 'Or I might change my mind.'

'No you won't.' He laughed.

Sands had no idea what he was playing at. Frank had had enough of people laughing at him. A truck lumbered past, immediately followed by another, and another. With the ground still shaking, Frank darted across the road, crouched down by the rear, offside corner of Sands' Jag.

29

Old bones were not made for crouching; second time in a couple of days that Frank didn't need reminding. Thankfully Sands had finally beeped his car unlocked, his footsteps getting louder and clearer, some shortness of breath as well. Frank was spring-loaded for action, adrenalin defying his age and physique.

The second Sands opened the driver's door, and was easing into the seat, Frank opened the far rear door with his right hand, and slipped onto the back seat with the dexterity of a teenager.

'What the fuck?' said Sands, struggling to look over his shoulder, white anger spreading across his puce, pudgy face.

'Change of plan,' said Frank, pointing the snub, which was in his left hand, straight at Sands' temple. For a second he was almost pleased he was armed with the smaller, less powerful weapon. It was still going to make a right mess if he had to use it inside a car. 'What you need to know,' he said, 'is that I've got nothing to lose.'

'You don't need to tell me that,' hissed Sands.

'If I have to take you with me, I will.'

'Steady on, Frank.' Sands' shoulders relaxed. 'I don't know what's got up your arse lately, but you need to calm down, matey.'

'You need to start your engine, put your car into gear. Do exactly as I say.'

Sands exhaled, as if the world was suddenly a very heavy place. 'Is that thing even loaded?'

'There's only one way you'll find out,' said Frank. 'You want to try me?'

'You're an idiot, Frank. Why would you want to give up all this? We could have had such a productive partnership. The money and power I have at my fingertips. That doesn't come easily or quickly. I've spent years getting into this position.'

'I want you to head straight across town. Use Main Cross. Turn left onto South Beach, and then we'll have a nice tootle along the front. Plenty of time for a chat. Go on, pull out.' Frank hunkered down in the back as best he could, while pressing the pistol into the side of Sand's neck, above his stiff, white shirt collar. Hairs were sprouting, left, right and centre.

Sands did as he said and pulled out onto South Denes, devoid of trucks that moment. He took the quick left onto Main Cross, while Frank managed to ease his jacket off his shoulders and shrug it over his arm and the snub. With his free hand he covered his face as best he could. The Jag's windows were nicely tinted, nevertheless Frank didn't want any CCTV picking up his features too sharply. There were so few cameras in that part of South Denes. Vested interests had seen to that.

Besides, Main Cross Road had a way to go before anyone would think to film the place.

Sands drove, Frank thought. He did have plenty to lose. Seeing his garden mature. Watching Zach grow into a man; Sam get better and take control of her life. Ben to come back from London and play his part. He didn't want to lose sight of Tatty yet either. The bond he'd felt with Rich was one thing, with Tatty it was different, but no less powerful. He felt more of an equal. More necessary. There'd always be ups and downs, as with any relationship. Issues of trust. But his actions over the next few hours and days should more than convince her. While she had to convince him, of her trust, her commitment. Thank God he wasn't straight.

They were now passing the Lacons brewery on their left — that was going from strength to strength — and the Esso garage on the right. Sands stopped at the T-junction, where Main Cross met South Beach — the Golden Mile having come to an end some way before this end of town, leaving nothing sparkling or shiny, or very amusing, even in low afternoon sunlight.

The scrub across the way was idling in frustration. This was Goodwin Enterprises' land, still waiting for ground to be broken, the first cash instalments to arrive. Two hundred million pounds — a hundred from the Dutch venture capital concern, and a hundred from the Americans. Frank was struggling to believe that Tatty could pull it off. But with Sands out of the way, her life would be one hell of a lot easier.

'What are you waiting for?' Frank said, eyeing the glinting sea beyond the scrub. The road was clear.

'Fuck you, Frank.'

Frank shoved the spout hard into Sands' hairy purple neck. 'What did you ever do for this town? Drive.'

267

'I did my best to keep scum like you from taking control. I built a proper business, for one. Steel fabricating is not easy in any climate, but I made it work, as I'll make a success of my leisure interests. I'm a man who gets things done.'

Sands was gripping the leather-clad steering wheel so tightly his huge knuckles had gone white. The backs of his hands were spectacularly hairy. He clearly wasn't used to having a gun thrust into his neck.

'What did you and your crew ever do for the town — except spread fear and depravation, while filling your own pockets?' he continued.

'Oh, hark the good angel,' said Frank. 'Nothing could be further from the truth — matey.' Out of the rear passenger window he caught the skeletal orb at the top of the log flume, then an empty log coming over the top and beginning its clattering descent. 'When did Simon come running, tail between his legs?' Out of the other window was a stretch of near empty car park with the old naval hospital stoic in the distance. There had once been a plan to turn it into retirement accommodation. Bickering between the council and a clutch of half-baked developers got in the way. Goodwin Enterprises kept clear of that one, even if Rich had always said the old were ripe for ripping off.

'Where are we going?' Sands asked.

Traffic was slowing them down further — cars, a van, plus a horse and open carriage a short way further ahead, Frank could see. The horse seemed a hot and scruffy enough affair, with a great, shaggy mane. Frank felt sorry for it.

268

At least the carriage had people inside enjoying the weather — a large family with a ton of small kids, none sitting down properly. Where was the discipline? Why weren't they at school? Let them be, he told himself. They were having fun. People did.

He checked his coat was adequately covering his firearm, not that Sands appeared to be in any hurry to overtake.

'You want me to pull over?' Sands was saying as they crawled across a mini-roundabout, and neared the old casino on their left. 'Park up? Get that scone and jam.'

'Like I said, change of plan. Keep going.' Frank shoved the spout hard into the tensed flesh of Sands' neck once more. 'When did Simon make contact again?'

'I don't want to be part of some family tiff,' Sands said. 'You and me, we can keep out of it, can't we — if this is all about Tatty and Simon? We're not Goodwins — we don't have that curse hanging over our heads. I bet you come from a nice family, Frank.'

'No. No, I don't, Graham. Which is why none of this matters to me, anything like as much as it must matter to you. Do you want to see your wife again — your kids? How many kids do you have? Two, three? All grown up now, aren't they? Are you a close family, Graham? Enjoy the comforts of your Caister home, do you? Your dog?'

'Leave them out of it.'

'Strikes me you think nothing of interfering in family matters. Straight ahead, please.' Sands had slowed to a crawl by the next mini-roundabout, but the horse and carriage had taken another route and there was no traffic ahead.

'Where are we going?' Sands asked again.

Frank caught the neon glare of Britannia Pier, some lime green and dull pink plastic obstacles lined up by the entrance. A smattering of people. The sun didn't half brighten the place up, the English seaside when the sun was out — you couldn't beat it. But Frank's mood was as overcast as ever. 'Not so far now,' said Frank, nudging the spout into Sands' neck once more. He hadn't killed a man for some months. Hadn't shot anyone for years. 'When did Simon get in touch, Graham? You're running out of time.'

'OK, OK,' Sands said, his foot shaky on the accelerator.

The bowling greens were out on their right, lush and smooth, being readied for the new season. Frank couldn't believe people still played bowls, that there were enough pensioners around who remembered how. But he was an oldster now, wasn't he? Except he'd never played bowls. Though he had once seen someone drop one of the balls on a grass's knee, from a considerable height. He'd had no idea a kneecap could shatter in such a way.

'Two, three months ago,' Sands said. 'I got a call. He was in the States then.'

Frank was thinking: so Simon contacted Sands before he'd dared to get back in touch with Tatty, with himself. Yeah, course he had. 'Offering what exactly?'

'He wanted to see how the land was lying. What opportunities there might be for collaboration. I informed him of my new position on the council. That nothing could be developed without my say-so.'

'No council committee has that much power, and not over developments that have already been rubber-stamped. There's a legal framework, designed to circumnavigate abuses of power.' Frank couldn't believe he was being such an advocate of the laws of the land.

'You want to get snarled up in paperwork, expensive lawyers, court proceedings, yeah, there is a legal framework, Frank. Not the way we do business, though, is it?'

Frank couldn't have agreed more. 'Was Simon's idea always to ditch Tatty from any collaboration?' More evening traffic was slowing their passage on North Drive. The manicured greens and gardens giving way to the North Beach dunes and shingle ridges. The wind turbines were cresting the near horizon, spinning lazily. On the town side of the road the large Edwardian hotels and boarding houses had been replaced by detached and semi-detached villas. Now largely retirement homes.

Frank knew he would never end up in one. He realised he didn't like looking at the sea — why he lived a couple of miles inland, in Bradwell. He needed to see plants, flora. Leaves fluttering in the breeze. Not flat, wet sea. His arm ached like a dog. He sighed, still waiting for Sands' reply. 'Speak up, Sands, you're running out of time.'

'Simon doesn't think a bird's place is in the

boardroom,' Sands said.

'What do you think?'

Sands lifted his foot from the accelerator as the turning to Jellicoe Road approached. A bus shelter sat empty and exposed on the dune side of North Drive. 'Straight ahead,' said Frank.

'Tatty was never going to give him the light of day. He knew that. But we thought you'd like to come on board, Frank. I told you.' There was a falter to Sands' voice. 'You know the ins and outs. Where're we going? Caister's the other way.'

The Coastwatch lookout was approaching, and the North Drive dead end turning circle, where Zach and his mates would burn rubber. There was also the entrance to Rolly Andrews' caravan park. Sands slowed because he had to.

'What makes you think Simon has the cash, the money from the Americans, and isn't bullshitting you?' Frank said. 'Left here, Sands, if you don't mind. Drive past the lodge, and take the first path through the caravans. Frank tried to shrink further into the back seat. Now was not the time to be spotted.

'He put me in touch with them,' Sands said, as he slowed further and swung the Jag into the park. There was the sound of low-profile tyres hitting gravel. 'We've been in communication. They wanted to know what I could do for them. As head of regeneration, I didn't need to do too much explaining. As you'd know, Frank — you spent enough time eating out of Rich's pocket.'

'Leave him out of it,' Frank said.

'Have to say, Simon kept good company in the

272

States. These are some very important individuals. Exacting, but that's only to be expected. It'll be a pleasure doing business with them.'

'You won't be doing business with them,' Frank said. Sands attempted to turn his head. His face was dripping with sweat. Frank couldn't look at him, not in the eye, and peeped out of the rear windows instead. There was no sign of anyone washing windows or walking Jack Russells. But he had a feeling eyes were watching. Part of the drug cartel? The park wasn't what it used to be. He and Tatty needed to arrive at a strategy for it — a piece of land this large, in this position, couldn't fall into the wrong hands. He could see the sweat on the back of Sand's neck now, felt his own heart racing.

'Where now?' said Sands.

'Another hundred metres or so, straight on.' They were getting deeper into the park, where any sign of life was rapidly diminishing. The caravans were shrinking in size, yet growing rapidly in age.

'This where you come on holiday, is it, Frank? Bit deathly, isn't it?' Sands seemed to have regained some composure.

'Yeah, you could say that. See that big tree ahead, the caravan next to it? Pull over there.'

'Smart accommodation,' said Sands. He suddenly accelerated, sending Frank flying into the back of his seat, his arm, the arm with the gun in it, hit the roof of the car, the acre of hard beige velour.

'Fuck you doing?' Frank yelled, trying to regain some purchase on the seat, re-aim his weapon. Sands then slammed on the brakes as hard as he'd accelerated. As Frank was thrown into the back of the front passenger's seat, he felt the big Jag loose traction on the grass and skid into the busted chain-link fence that separated the caravan park from the racecourse. There was a dull clatter and a diesel belch as the Jag stalled.

Sands was opening his door and hauling himself out of the car with the sprightliness of not a teenager, but maybe someone in their thirties. Frank was seconds behind, fifty years of age and feeling it, before he'd managed to escape the rear of the saloon and begin a hot pursuit. In his suit, and city shoes Frank would normally have approved of, Sands tore across the open ground of a far corner of the racecourse.

In shoes with no more grip, Frank nevertheless started to make ground. The snub was in his right hand, but he knew he'd lose valuable time if he paused to take aim. Not that he wanted to fell Sands out in the open, and have to drag his body back to the caravan. Frank sucked in the largest lungful of air he'd ever taken in his life, and sprang forward with everything he had.

The moment must have coincided with Sands running out of steam, because he managed to take the steel-man's legs from under him, and was swiping him around the back of the head, hard, with the snub. For a second Frank glanced over his shoulder, hoping to see Howie, with all his muscle and technique, bounding up in support. But he was not in sight. No one else was either.

Frank was thankful for that. Also, that they

hadn't gone far from the caravan park. This part of the racecourse was not overlooked. The stands, half a dozen furlongs on, were empty. When was the next meet? Tomorrow, he dimly remembered from the faded billboard.

Sands was moaning. Struggling to catch his breath. 'You'll never get away with this,' he was trying to say.

'Up,' said Frank, getting to his own feet, and attempting to haul Sands up with him. Christ, he weighed a ton. 'Up,' he shouted again. Why shouldn't he waste Sands here? He put the gun to Sands' forehead.

Sands slowly got to his feet, reaching to brush the pistol away. 'What do you want from me?' he said.

'Move,' said Frank, getting behind him and pushing him, with the gun, back towards the caravan. The snout of the Jag was poking through the fence.

Sands was now fumbling in a jacket pocket. Retrieved a mobile, attempted to key in some numbers. 'Don't even think about it,' Frank said, snatching it from him, then dropping it back into Sands' pocket for him. 'Step on it,' he ordered.

Sands was stumbling, swaying, across the long, rutted grass on the perimeter of a racecourse that had seen headier days, while rubbing the back of his head. 'What are you going to do with me? Bullet in the back of the head? You're bigger than this, Frank. You think I'm the enemy?'

'Simon's the enemy. Anyone who facilitates him.' They were closing in on the bit of scrappy fence the Jag had torn down. 'Months, years, you've been plotting with him.' This was something of a guess, but Frank felt it in every gram of his tired and stretched body. Admiralty Steel had been the real thorn in Rich's side for years. 'When Rich went over the edge, who was watching, enjoying the spectacle? You filmed it all, happily enough. It was only one of your employees who had the good grace to share the evidence.'

'He's no longer an employee,' spat Sands, as he stumbled on.

'No,' said Frank. 'He's no longer alive either, is he?' The tall, straggly steelworker called Stuart, who'd given Tatty a copy of the crucial CCTV showing the moment of Rich's death, had disappeared back in the autumn. Frank had always presumed Sands was responsible.

'Information, in this world, makes you very powerful,' said Sands.

'Which is why you're going to give me the names and contact details of these Americans. Exactly who's in your pocket at the council I'll have as well, thank you very much.'

'Why don't you ask Simon?'

'Oh, we will. Let's hope the names, the numbers, corroborate.' He pushed Sands through the fence, Sands tripping on some rusty wiring, and shoved him past the Jag and towards the caravan. 'There's something else you can tell me. What'd you know about the fire at Smokehouse? Who'd you put up to do that? In fact, you don't need to tell me. I know.'

Little more than a mumble came out of Sands' gob.

276

Frank had left the door to the caravan unlocked and he caught the smell before he'd even opened it. It had been a warm, sunny day for a dead body and the remains of a turkey dinner to spend in an airless box.

'Christ,' said Sands, finding some strength, some voice. 'What the fuck's in there?'

'Your tea,' said Frank, glancing around the immediate vicinity. If Rolly Andrews had done one good and honest thing in his life it was to keep this part of the park down in the dumps, well away from the public gaze. 'And an old mate of yours.'

With one last almighty effort, Frank pushed Sands up the flimsy couple of steps with the pistol pressed against his crooked spine. There was no steel, no backbone to the man now. Frank would need some rope, some ties, he realised, if he wanted to keep Sands alive. That hadn't been his original intention. Man or mouse, what was he?

'We can cut Simon out,' Sands started saying hurriedly, not budging from the top step. 'I know how to get hold of the Americans. They'll listen to me. The fire was Simon's idea. Honest to God. 'Let's smoke them out of town,' was what he said.'

'Yeah? When exactly did he come up with that idea? Why'd he come rushing over to me and Tatty, wanting a deal? Not the way to go about it, is it, if he's destroying our property?'

'He's a bullshitter. The plan was, we wanted you on board. I guess he wanted to cut me out. Pin the blame for the fire onto me. It's not my style. Who'd I commission to do such a thing?'

'He's in there,' said Frank, pushing Sands forward. The man was built like a tanker.

'I rang you, Frank, Sunday morning, to tell you. It wasn't me. I want the town re-energised, renovated. Not fucking destroyed, whatever you may think. Simon was playing both of us — can't you see it? Setting us against each other, so nature could take its course. Don't fall for it, Frank.'

'Get inside, Sands. Your dinner's getting cold.'

30

Tatty hurried down the stairs, crossed the hall, hesitated. She looked at her watch. It was edging towards happy hour. Except it was anything but in her household. She was not sure which room, if any, she'd be made welcome in.

Go out for a walk on the beach, come home and the place was heaving. It was like when the kids were teenagers, and Rich was away on a business trip. For a second or two she felt tremendous nostalgia for those times. She hadn't always been such a dreadful mother, had she? The kids had never dared ask their friends over if they'd thought their dad might stomp in.

She stepped into the kitchen, holding her head high. 'You still here?' she said, glancing at the couple on the far side of the dining table. Her tone was only directed at one of them however. She'd showered, changed, but did not feel remotely freshened up, clean. It had been a wicked few days and worse was to come — before she could enjoy the fresh air and sudden summer. Knowing her kids were in the right place.

'Leave it out, Mum,' Zach said, surly as hell.

No she couldn't. 'You,' she said, looking straight at Sian this time, 'and I need a talk.'

'Now's not the time, Mum,' Zach said, using an unfamiliar, unwanted tone. He was his father's son when he wanted to be all right. Funny how they were all dredging up the old, ugly ways of communicating. She'd hoped, following Rich's death, they might have moved on.

'I'll take you home,' he said to Sian, quietly, and pushing his chair back, not calmly, and standing. 'Come on, let's go.'

Sian whimpered. Possibly for effect.

Tatty had arrived home to find Zach and Sian sitting in the kitchen — Sian weeping. Zach might have had his arm around her. They'd been sitting close enough. Sian had made it abundantly clear that she was in mourning, that Zach had told her about her dad — if she hadn't already known. Tatty had muttered her condolences and quickly disappeared upstairs, where more mourning was going on.

She was pleased to see that Sian had stopped weeping now, though her eyes were as red-rimmed as her mouth. Somehow in all the distress and while Tatty was upstairs the tiny PA must have found time to reapply her lipstick.

'Is that a good idea, for Sian to go home?' Tatty said. As angry as she was with Sian, she didn't think it would be too smart if she was allowed to disappear again. Not until she knew exactly what had gone on, what Zach had learned. He'd been the one who'd been burned. They all had, one way or another — and not just her property. She needed Frank to hear everything as well, once he'd finished his chores.

Sian hadn't stood, and was looking up at Zach. She hadn't said a word either. Another faint whimper might have escaped her extraordinary mouth.

'Look, I'm sorry,' Tatty said, 'about your dad.'

This was the second time she'd said this in about ten minutes.

'Mum,' said Zach, 'tell her it wasn't you, or Frank, will you?'

Tatty stepped across to the island, contemplated the huge coffee machine. Then looked over towards the massive fridge. She couldn't remember whether there was any white wine cooling inside. Or something sparkling. She knew she had plenty of work to get on with this evening and would need a clear head, but could really have done with a spritzer.

She turned towards the kids. 'Sit down, Zach, will you?' The sun had sunk too low for the backyard, but an orange tinge hung on.

'We're going, Mum,' he said, not sitting down. 'We're never going to get a straight answer out of you.'

'Oh, yes you are. Sian, love,' she lowered her tone, 'I don't know how much Zach's told you, but I found your dad. He'd died peacefully. Some sort of haemorrhage it looked like.'

'He hadn't been well,' Sian said. Her first words. She tapped her chest. Where her heart would be. Tatty supposed she had a rather flighty one.

'He'd been dead for a good while when I came across him.' She stared at Zach, but her youngest son was looking away. She needed a sign, some collusion here. He wasn't going to help her that minute, and she wasn't going to forget it in a hurry. Young love didn't half turn your mind to mush. There was Sam upstairs right now snuggling on her bed with the person who only a

281

few hours ago she'd professed to hate forever. It would make Tatty's life one hell of a lot easier if her daughter could stick to that line. While down here was Zach, the family's bright young hope. At least one of her kids had bothered to stick around. Though what for? To fall for a bitch with a big, lying mouth. It could have been sweet, she supposed.

Tatty didn't think she'd ever been so fickle. Her emotions going up and down like a yo-yo. She half wondered whether she'd ever loved anyone, apart from her children. She could see why she and Frank were going to get on famously. He wasn't the type to fall in love, though he'd perhaps loved Rich.

Tatty peered at Zach again. At Sian — oh, that blasted mouth of hers. Nothing else, however, was coming out of it. Not the obvious question. Tatty suddenly felt crushed by this enormous empty thing hanging in the kitchen. How could plain air be so heavy? Because it had to do with kids and their parents, the natural order of things, and untimely death. A world interrupted.

'Where's he now?' Sian finally said it. 'Can I see him?'

'Your father might have died peacefully, but he was in the wrong place, at the wrong time,' Tatty said. 'If you want to tell us what you know about that right now, the company would look very favourably on your severance.'

'Mum, I can't fucking believe you're saying that. Not now.'

'You ask her then. You're in this up to your eyeballs.' She turned. There was no point in hanging around with these two. She strode towards the door, thinking Sian was lucky to be alive.

'He didn't mean to harm anyone,' came Sian's weak local voice.

Tatty paused, swung round. 'What?'

'He wouldn't have meant to harm anyone, ever,' Sian said.

'What she's saying is, no one got hurt, did they?' Zach said.

Tatty sighed. 'Who was your father working for, Sian? He sets fire to my new office. Then whips across town, in your motor, with the full intention of setting fire to my old office. Now, there're many ways you can look at this, but none of them do your dad any favours. What was he trying to do? Bring my business down? Scupper a very significant investment? Then somewhere along the line he snaffles a bag of drugs. Was he dealing as well?' Tatty had found she'd somehow reached the fridge, and was opening one of the giant doors.

'No,' said Sian, shaking her tiny head. 'I don't know. He hadn't been himself for a few weeks. I don't know what he was up to. He wasn't dealing though.'

'Helping himself then, I reckon,' Tatty said. There were a couple of bottles of white wine in the fridge. Not much else. 'Clouds your judgement. Zach knows all about that, don't you, darling?' She didn't turn to face him, to accuse him. Instead she lifted one of the bottles out. It was a Sauvignon Blanc, delivered by Sainsbury's last week. She supposed someone would need to put in a new supermarket order, with the house this full. Sam wouldn't be up to it. Zach wasn't capable. She couldn't imagine Michael having much of a clue. Ben wasn't here. She'd have to do it. Tomorrow.

'He must have found the gear in the street,' Zach said.

'Because you dropped it?' Tatty said.

'Dad wasn't dealing,' Sian added. 'He didn't take drugs either.'

Something Frank had said sprung into Tatty's mind. 'So your dad helped himself to whatever he stumbled upon?'

'Where is he now?' Sian was welling up again. 'His body?'

'Too many coincidences for my liking,' Tatty said, still holding the bottle of wine.

'Where are the police?' Sian said, a sob escaping.

Tatty put the bottle back, time now pressing on her mind. 'Who was he working for, Sian? I don't believe for one second that your dad took it on himself to cause merry hell one Saturday night, Sunday morning.'

'Don't the police need to know?' Sian continued, tearfully, not answering Tatty's question, 'That my dad's dead?'

Tatty very nearly went back to the fridge for the wine, just managing to restrain herself. 'Your dad has been taken to a place of rest. The ashes will be released in due course. We don't involve the police in anything, if we can help it. I'm quite sure your father never did either. He'd understand. Zach knows the score.'

'This can't be happening,' Sian muttered, her head beginning to shake once more.

Tatty was horrified to see Zach had pulled the PA even closer to him. 'Oh yes,' she said, 'it's happening all right.'

'I don't understand,' Sian added.

'Think about where you came from, Sian. Are you telling me you're not surprised?' She thought Zach looked pathetic. Either that, or he was simply way out of his depth. He'd never had an emotionally stable upbringing, she supposed, poor boy. No proper girlfriends. Her fault largely, no doubt. She didn't want to hurt him, or see him hurt, but she couldn't have any weak links in her organisation. 'Where's Liam?' she asked. 'Isn't he part of your life, Sian? Your gang?'

'Not any more,' said Zach, confidently.

Sian flinched. 'He made me do stuff,' she said, 'that I didn't want to do.'

The way of the world, thought Tatty. She'd spent most of her life doing things she didn't want to do — until now perhaps. 'Frank'll take care of him,' she said.

'No he won't,' said Zach. 'I will. I have.'

Tatty smiled. 'Your dad,' she said, looking at Sian, 'who was he working for? Who told him to go and torch my new headquarters? That was very stupid of him. These things, Sian, aren't forgotten in a hurry. He was your dad. You're responsible for the mess he's left. It's how it works, from one generation to another.'

'Mum, please, leave her out of it. She doesn't know — no idea. We've talked.'

'She disappeared for a day or two, didn't she?' Tatty said. 'She conveniently stays at home Monday morning — with a migraine — when she was meant to meet me at Goodwin House, first thing.' Tatty was losing her patience. 'And then she scarpers.'

'She was scared, Mum. Of Liam,' Zach said. 'Stuff had gone on over the weekend. They'd had a falling out.'

'I did have a migraine,' Sian said.

'Liam,' said Tatty. 'It all comes back to him, does it?'

'All right,' said Zach, nodding. 'I'll explain — what I know. Liam got some stuff off Sian's dad, from time to time. Not drugs, nothing like that. Just stuff that came off the back of a lorry — you know what I mean.'

'How old are you, Zach?' Tatty asked.

'What's that meant to mean?' he said.

'What do you take me for?'

'My mother?'

'Don't be fucking cheeky. Liam was in partnership with your dad, Sian? Your dad would nick stuff, and Liam would sell it? Enterprising, in a minor way.'

'Not the drugs,' Sian said. 'They came from out of the country, Amsterdam. That was Liam's thing alone, he just used some of Dad's facilities.'

'What are you saying?' She suddenly looked guilty as hell to Tatty. In it right up to her neck. Families for you, generations. Either honest, or greedy and corrupt.

'Liam was dealing,' said Zach. 'Chemicals,

MDMA, E, nothing major.'

What could she say? *Grow up, and get involved with the real cash cow — cocaine. That's how your father first built his fortune.*

'He uses storage facilities at the caravan park, the lodge, now and then,' Zach said. 'Even I didn't know this until recently. It's not easy, getting a straight word out of Liam.'

'But you're going to put him straight?' Tatty asked. Zach used to be so fit and strong. Though never physically aggressive. She wondered who'd get to Liam first, Zach or Frank.

'Yeah,' he said. 'Course. Whatever Sian wants.'

Tatty sighed. Something was telling her that Zach would not be pursuing Liam with much intent. Wasn't sure there would be much to gain, except she couldn't have just anyone running around town, dealing drugs, stolen goods. Zach wouldn't look at her.

'The thing is, Mum — we don't know, honestly,' he said hesitantly, 'what Sian's dad was doing on Saturday night, the other end of town. No idea.'

'We do know what he was doing,' Tatty said, not exactly admiring the way Zach had changed the subject. 'Setting fire to my property.'

'We don't know who put him up to it,' Zach said. 'It wouldn't have been something he'd have dreamed up all on his own. No way.'

Sian was nodding her head in agreement.

'Sian,' Tatty said, 'it's your job to find out, being family and all. Come and tell me before someone else does. I expect you'll be wanting to help her, Zach.'

Zach shrugged his shoulders, stopped clasping Sian for dear life. 'Whatever.'

'He wasn't well,' Sian said, once more.

'That was clear,' Tatty said. 'He's bloody lucky he died the way he did, when he did. Had we got hold of him — '

'Mum,' sighed Zach. 'Give. Us. A. Fucking. Break.'

'Keep your voice down,' Tatty said. 'Sam's upstairs. Don't swear at me either. I'm getting sick of it.'

'He wasn't even meant to be in Yarmouth,' Sian said. 'I thought he was going to see some people in Lynn — that's what he told me. He's got old friends there. It's why he took my car.'

'You didn't think it was odd when I told you your car was at the back of Goodwin House, first thing Monday morning?' Tatty tried to read the look on Zach's face. It was like wading through *War and Peace*. Not that she'd ever read it.

'I had no idea what'd happened to him until Zach told me,' Sian said rapidly. 'It doesn't make sense. Not the fire. Nor why he was at Goodwin House.'

'Why did you leave town? In Liam's car, wasn't it? Where did you go?'

Sian's mouth frowned. No words came.

'Why did you come back?' Tatty added.

'She was scared, Mum,' Zach said, his voice tailing off. He was looking over Tatty's shoulder. His eyes were widening, while his mouth clamped shut.

The air in the kitchen had changed, Tatty realised. She turned. 'Creeping up on us, Michael?'

'Sam would like a chocolate, a hot chocolate,' Michael Jansen said precisely. 'I've come down to get it.'

'How kind of you,' Tatty said. He didn't look like he'd been comforting Sam on her bed. He was in a crisp white shirt, suit trousers, Chelsea boots. She doubted Michael would want to spill anything on his shirt. She wasn't going to help him make a hot chocolate. She couldn't remember Sam ever liking hot chocolate — Ben was the one who adored chocolate.

Tatty urgently needed to know what Sam now thought of Michael. Whether she wanted him hanging around or not. She was going to rush upstairs to ask her, while Michael was in the kitchen with a couple of other liars.

Walking out of the kitchen she wondered whether it was even Sam's choice. She couldn't have Michael turning up in Yarmouth with a flunky called Hans, who apparently was installing himself in the Pier View Hotel. Nice and nearby. For the foreseeable.

Not.

31

It was another evening unwilling to come quickly. Frank had got out of the caravan park fast and quiet enough, skirting the perimeter. Now he was on the pavement, as the seafront gathered purpose and solidity the further towards the Golden Mile he went, he slowed. There were no CCTV cameras the way he'd come. There were none until Euston Road and the old theatre.

He looked up at the sky, turning his head west. It wasn't the most comforting view in the world. That would be behind him. He checked his watch. It had been over fifteen minutes and still there was no sign of any emergency vehicles. Steadily moving forward, he dared to look over his shoulder.

The sky was darker and a sheen of cloud seemed to be drifting over the North Sea from the Netherlands. Everything drifted over from the Netherlands sooner or later, didn't it?

He found he'd stopped walking. His legs felt leaden. How many steps had he taken today? It would have to be approaching the thirty, forty thousand mark. He hadn't walked so far for years. He was still looking over his shoulder and he squinted, scanning the near horizon, the treeline, the roofs of the distant caravans. Where was the smoke? Smoke signals? He dimly remembered watching the odd Western when he

290

was a kid, in his first foster home. The breeze was stiffening. Gulls were squawking loudly nearby. Did they ever give it a break?

Then he saw a thin, dark plume, and he was overwhelmed by a wave of relief followed by a ripple of nausea. He squinted harder with his tired old eyes doing the best they could, wanting the trail to bloom and thicken. To beat out the message that he had not gone soft in his old age.

Frank didn't think Simon had been playing him and Tatty off against Sands — and even if he had it made no difference. Simon had been working with Sands, fair and square. For months, even years. Sure, he wanted to turn Frank — against Tatty, against Goodwin Enterprises, everything he'd worked for, for decades. He should have felt wanted. Instead he felt soiled, enraged. He'd never turn against the Goodwins.

The traffic had died and the calming sound of the sea flopping lazily onto the shore in the slowly gathering dusk was tickling Frank's small ears. For a man with such a big head he'd always been overly conscious of his minuscule ears. He presumed his hearing would start to go one day soon.

He could certainly hear everything clear enough right now, especially the stuff jamming the inside of his head. New and old voices. Sands' last gasps.

Frank was convinced Sands had known about Rolly Andrew's role, even though he'd denied it. There was no way he'd have thought to engage his services, even if he'd wanted the Smokehouse

291

torched, he'd pleaded. 'What do you take me for? A fucking idiot? Someone who'd hire a tramp like that?' Frank had shot him square in the chest, with the girly gun. Even Tatty couldn't have missed.

He was scanning the northern sky again, having lost the plume. *Come on, where are you?* Perhaps his eyesight was going. But he hadn't gone soft in his old age. A few swipes to the face with the Smith and Wesson had made the Admiralty Steel boss tell him that Simon had been enjoying all manner of room service, courtesy of the Pier View, and his own largess. Clever old Sands' information gathering. Blackmail was a powerful tool.

The sound of a highly revved, deeply powerful engine exploded into Frank's consciousness. Brake noise and wheels skidding across tarmac came next. Frank patted his pockets. Felt the snub deep inside his jacket. Looked up to see the huge chrome bonnet of a vehicle far more stupid than a yellow Rolls Royce. Its massive white shanks gleamed in the dusk. Its tinted windows showing an impenetrable blank.

To his left the wide pavement dropped off onto an ocean of greying marram grass. The sea beyond, a world of hard, flat water. Head that way and he'd have stuck out like an erect prick. On the other side of the road there was a stretch of private detached and semi-detached dwellings dating from an era when people retired quietly, before the first hotels and guest houses loomed with missed opportunity. Ahead was the long straight road further into town. Frank had nowhere to run, even if his legs had been up to it.

He waited for a window to be lowered. Abuse to be yelled. He waited some more. The dusk gathered close around him. Then the Hummer's engine cranked up, and the vehicle zoomed out, sounding like a tank on steroids. It travelled for some distance on the wrong side of the road before pulling over to the left-hand lane. Coming the other way, Frank could see, beyond the fading white glimmer of an Eastern European dream in an American dinosaur, were the flashing blue lights of the emergency services.

Frank did now drop off what amounted to an esplanade, and onto the unstable ground of a sand spit, that had nevertheless been there since before records began. He crouched in the marram by the damp wall, listening to the sirens getting louder, waiting for the emergency vehicles to pass. The tone told him it was the Fire Service, not the police, nor an ambulance.

Pulling his phone from his pocket, sandwiched between the deep shade of the wall and the encroaching night, a stiffening breeze coming in off the sea now, he noticed in all the excitement that people had been trying to reach him. He had a number of missed calls, some messages. A couple he wanted to attend to right away. The fire trucks shot by. There were two of them by the sound and shake of it. One would have been more than enough to douse a burning caravan.

A faulty gas canister, they might have been thinking racing forward. Or some kids up to no good. Wait until they got inside. Frank had not cut the pipe under the sink, anything as obvious as that. It wasn't necessary. He had used what was left of Rolly Andrews' accelerant. Splashed it liberally around the interior, over the bodies, chucking everything connected to Rolly Andrews onto the crowded bed, including the bag of pills. His stolen property could burn with him.

Frank had then lit a Chinese takeaway menu, dropped it on the bed. He waited until it was clear that the fire had taken, then let himself out, firmly closing the main door, before hearing the whumph of the gas canister catching as he was a couple of vacant caravans away. You would not want to be caught in a burning caravan.

The police wouldn't be far behind the fire service. Not when the bodies and the carcass of a turkey crown were discovered. Except he hoped that the charred scene laid out would be confusing enough for the brightest forensics officers. They'd eventually come to the conclusion that a drug deal had gone wrong, which was why Frank had thought it necessary to plug Rolly Andrews' body for good measure.

What Graham Sands, the council's new head honcho, was doing mixed up in such a scheme, with known lowlife, would take further investigation, and lead them all the way to Simon Goodwin. Who'd be found in possession of the weapon he'd used on Sands and Andrews — incriminating ballistics evidence all right. Except the snub, covered in prints and recently fired, would be with Simon's corpse — if all went to plan.

Frank looked over his shoulder, at the yawning

beach, feeling the gun in his pocket for now. He exhaled loudly, realising he must have been holding his breath. He did not like leaving bodies around, hoping investigators would come to the right conclusions, especially when there was a new jerk in charge of Serious and Organised: Kyle Neville — from terrorism, of all departments. But Britt Hayes was his superior, as Assistant Chief Constable. She'd pull rank, if he needed her to. Howie would see to that. That had always been the way.

So had burying bodies in the tidal mudflats of Breydon Water.

He stood, stepped away from the wall. Continued his walk into town, on the beach for the moment. The soft, uneven ground the heaviest of goings. He was shaking his head as he was walking, greatly troubled. This was a game he'd never played before. But the stakes had never been so high. It wasn't poker, more like chess. The moves that had to be made, all the while presuming the opponent's reading of the situation and tactics. Another sort of gamble. He stared at his screen again. Simon's murderer would have to appear to disappear — back to London, or Amsterdam. For good. That one was for Breydon Water.

The old boating lake was coming into view, concreted quietly out from the monotony of suburban North Drive. Further ahead, Britannia Pier was silhouetted against a lighter sky, as it strode brazenly across the sand, not quite reaching the sea now, except on spring tides.

A thought struck him. Now that the company

caravan was no longer, they should consider getting a boat. A craft that could tackle not only the inland waterways of the Yare and Bure, the Norfolk Broads, but something that could steam offshore. Play zigzag through the wind farms. Visit the seals on Scroby Sands. Properly weighted, bodies could be dropped over the side. All manner of hardware could be safely disposed of. Cleaner, more certain than any fire. Why had the Smokehouse not gone up with more conviction? Had Nathan Taylor actually done a good job, or Rolly Andrews a bad one?

He'd drive the boat, carefully. A Broom, or a Sunseeker, with a couple of Volvo Penta engines, powerful enough to power a small warship. They could get the boatyard back up and running.

Frank had his phone to his ear, continued walking while Dennis's soft American tones informed him that, yes, he was still in the land of the living. Happy to talk. Not on this number. He gave another. Frank smiled. The American had got back to him quick enough. Frank had to play the message a couple of times. Out on the beach the signal was always patchy.

In his free ear he heard a siren slowly getting louder. It seemed to be coming from the town-end of the spit. The police having been alerted to the full carnage in the caravan surely. Frank was now a good distance from the esplanade. An old man not walking his dog. Howie had thought about that carefully. A dog was a great disguise, even though Howie loved that animal with a passion that seemed to have deserted him with regards his fellow human beings — barring Britt and himself.

Frank cut through the iron girders footing the pier. It was suddenly much darker and the air felt cooler and there was a tang of fish and drains. Kids got up to all sorts under here, behind the pillars, in the thickest of shadows. However, there was no one else around at that moment, despite it being a fine, dry evening.

He thought he heard more sirens in the distance, as he checked his other messages. Tatty had rung, as had Zach. Terry from the club. As Frank stepped past the last row of rusty supports, his eyes glued to his screen, there was the faintest whoosh of air and the loudest bang on the side of his head. Falling to the ground, he knew he'd been hit by more than a fist.

32

Sam sat up with a start. She'd been having a dream that she was trapped under a ton of duvet, and it was so hot she could barely breathe, and water was coming from somewhere, like she was under a shower, or a waterfall, except it was boiling. No, she was on fire. Frantically, she began patting her arms, her chest. Her stomach, when the pain really hit her.

'Sis?' said someone, quietly. 'Sis?' It was Zach. She knew she had raised herself from horizontal, but she didn't know where she was. Zach was calling to her, rescuing her from the fire. I'm over here, she wanted to shout. No sound left her mouth as her eyes began to take in the dimness of her bedroom, the fact that she was not on fire. That she was at home, in bed. She felt her forehead. It was dripping with sweat. Her arms were soaked. She dreaded to think what state the sheets were in.

'Hey,' Zach was by her side now. 'You OK?'

'God, I've just been having a nightmare,' she sighed.

'Haven't we all,' said Zach. He remained standing.

'It was like I was in a fire.'

'Have you got a temperature?'

'It's so hot and stuffy in here. I've been in bed all day. Can't stand it any more. What time is it?'

'Bedtime,' said Zach, laughing.

'Where is everyone? Where's Michael?' She glanced over at her bedside table. Saw a cluster of glasses and mugs. Pill packets. Her phone, iPad. No flowers. Electric light was drifting in from the landing.

'He's gone out with Mum.'

'What?' She sat up further. A sinking feeling hit her stomach. Reality started to dawn. 'At this time?'

'Don't ask me why. They went for walk.'

'A walk — at this time?' The last thing Sam dimly remembered was speaking to her mum. Her mum had come up to tuck her in. Wanting to know whether she wanted a hot chocolate. Like she was her little girl once again. No, she didn't want a hot chocolate. She'd never liked hot chocolate. Didn't her mother remember that? She wanted — oh, she didn't know — a drink, a gin. Isn't that what she'd told her? No, him. She'd told Michael to fucking well go and get her a gin and tonic, if he couldn't be bothered to bring her flowers.

'I've rushed straight from the airport, my darling,' he'd said. 'Hans drove me here super-fast.' Whoever Hans was. 'Flowers were not the first thing on my mind. You were my priority — getting straight here. There are no florists at Norwich airport, no shops at all. This is not a civilised country.'

Despite being only half awake, feverish, Sam realised what was wrong with what he'd said. There were shops at Norwich airport. Not the most comprehensive maybe, but shops neverthe-less. Though she thought he was right about this country. It was not civilised. But was Holland? It wasn't all hippies and weed. There were plenty of nasty extremists there — white ones, the worst.

'Sam, did you hear what I said?'

Zach was shaking her shoulder. 'What?'

'I need to go out. Sian's here. I have to take her home.'

'Sian?'

'Yeah — Sian from work.'

'Why's she here?'

'Long story. But I need to take her home.'

'She can't drive?' Sam thought that that might be possible. She was so young looking. But didn't she have a company car? The local anaesthetic was still messing with her mind, her memory.

'She borrowed a car she needs to give back. I need to help her. Her dad's just died. She's in a state. I need to go with her.'

'OK, OK.' She was the one who was meant to be in a state, wasn't she? Her dad had died as well. He'd been murdered by his own brother.

'You'll be on your own for a bit. Will you be OK?'

'Yeah,' she said. 'Who do you take me for?' Mummy's little girl. She didn't say it. She'd never thought it. Her mother preferred the boys. The woman couldn't relate to women, girls, her own gender, well. Men were her thing. Except they weren't. She was more like a man — that was it. Cold and tough and steely. Dishonest. Though she wasn't all those things either, not all the time. She'd been brilliant about the miscarriage. Doing and saying exactly the right things. There was no way Sam would have managed without her. With only Michael around, for instance. Except he wasn't, was he, the bastard. He'd turned up too late, with no flowers. Not even any tulips. Who the fuck was Hans?

'All righty, dude-y Trudy,' Zach said, stupidly, heading for the bedroom door, taking a rank, fetid smell with him, or was that smell in the room? Coming from her? 'You want anything before I go?' Zach added, in the same silly, jaunty tone.

'Yeah, to start again.'

'Right. Got yer.' He left the room, shouting, 'You want me to bring you anything back?'

'A new boyfriend?'

Sam turned on the bedside light. What was Michael doing with her mum? Business. Bloody business. That was why he was here. Why he'd rushed here, with an associate. A minder? Not to see her, but to see what was going on in relation to his dodgy investment, to see how secure it was, given that someone had tried to raze the Smokehouse. He was a ridiculous control freak. Though he was not as in control as he thought he was. There was always someone higher up telling him what to do.

For a second she almost felt sorry for him. From the pit of her churning, drained, void of a stomach, she tried to dredge up feelings of love and loyalty. He had lost his child too. It wasn't a child. It was barely a foetus. No more than a broad bean. She had no feelings for Michael she realised, except hate.

She flung the duvet off her burning legs, swung her feet over the edge. Waited for the dizziness to abate, then edged herself off the bed. Her nightie was indeed soaked through. She removed it in a rage, kicking it across the floor as she walked through to the en suite. She took a towelling robe off the back of the door, and sat shivering on the toilet for some time, despite having wrapped herself in the robe, then returned to the bedroom.

She stepped over to the door, which Zach had left ajar. She popped her head out into the corridor. She could hear the sound of no one. They must have gone. Zach and his little girlfriend. Who'd have thought. But it was sweet, she supposed. He wasn't quite such the lad. More experienced than Ben when it came to lovers, flings. But as needy, she reckoned. As insecure.

She spent more time with her head stuck out in the corridor, determining that the house was empty. Her heartbeat was rising, because she had an idea of what she was going to do next.

Everyone was going about their business, at this ridiculous time of the night, except her, weren't they? Life went on. Business never stopped. The world continued to spin — as her head was. She was clinging onto the doorframe, she realised, her heart now thumping. She pushed herself off. Stepped back inside her room, closed the door behind her, and flicked on the main light.

There they were, Michael's things, at the foot of the bed, in their plush casings — acres of bridle leather and taut tan canvas. The longer she looked at them the more she realised that they were laughing at her, mocking her — the pristine state of them. How could someone so careful have been mugged? Why didn't they take this stupid bag, for instance?

She bent down, feeling her brain shift inside her head again, like it was sloshing around in there. This big, wet spongy thing that didn't know how to handle men, or life. Soppy, useless. Her mother's brain must have been made of granite or something. Marble perhaps, smooth and shiny. Though there were cracks.

Sam managed to lift his spanking new holdall — from one of those outfitters to toffs on Jermyn Street — onto the bed. It weighed a ton. She wasn't sure whether it was the bag itself, or the contents. Her stomach went into spasm — his fucking fault. She paused. Another pause in the endless cycle of indecision that had become her way. She needed to move on. Look more closely at her mum, how she'd handled her husband's death. Her father must have been such a bastard to her. Why did women still put up with this shit? Not any more.

Opening the chunky brass zip on the holdall was a full-time job. Peering inside was a disciplinary action — one she was more than willing to take for not just her own sanity, but for the sake of her future, the family.

Michael had never been surprising. She'd been a fool. The biggest fool in the world. She began pulling out the contents. His neatly folded white T-shirts from Sunspel. His white trunks, also from Sunspel — the Jermyn Street branch, because she'd been there with him once, when they were meant to be clothes shopping for her. A navy cotton sweater. A square black toiletries bag. His iPad.

His iPad? It hadn't been stolen, when he was mugged in Amsterdam. It was his iPad from before all right. She recognised the crack in the top left corner of the screen. A crack that drove him nuts, because the device was no longer perfect. She was surprised he hadn't bothered to change it earlier. But he hadn't and he'd had it all along. With his phone also she presumed. He had a ton of them as it was. Had he even been in Amsterdam? 'You wanker,' she said, turning it on. 'You fucking wanker.'

She fell forward on the bed, wanting something to press against the hollowness in her stomach, her head. There was no pain there now. Only emptiness, suppressed by paracetamol. That's all they'd given her to take home. Holding out the iPad as it sprung to life, she began racking her brain for a possible passcode. More expletives only came to her. One after the other.

'Sam.' The voice was loud and strong, right behind her.

Her heart, already pushed to breaking, skipped more than a beat. She struggled to pull in a breath as she slowly looked over her shoulder. 'You scared the shit out of me,' she said, feeling her eyes well up, and her bottom lip begin to wobble.

'What's up?'

Her eldest brother Ben stepped further into the room. He didn't come over to the bed, however, to give her a pat, a cuddle. He remained standing, awkwardly. She knew that stance intimately. 'What's up?' she said, as casually as she could. 'Long time no see.'

She rolled over onto her back, and tried to shuffle her body towards the headboard so she had some pillow to prop her weary brain on. She felt like a slug, as useless as. Did slugs have brains? Course not. Though how did they procreate? She was still clinging on to the iPad. Maybe Zach would be able to break into it later, and get to the bottom of Michael's disgusting dealings.

'I drove down as soon as I could after work,' Ben said. 'Traffic was shit leaving London. How are you?'

'Great,' she said. 'What do you think?'

'I'm sorry,' he said, looking away. 'Where is everyone?'

'Out.'

'I gathered that much.' He looked at his watch. He was always looking at his watch. 'It's getting late.'

'For round here,' she tried to laugh. Tears were still in her eyes. 'Mum's gone for a stroll with Michael apparently. To discuss business, I suppose.'

'He's here, in Gorleston?'

'He got here earlier this evening. Straight from Amsterdam — so he said.' She was no longer sure of anything, except Michael had to get out of her life for good. Her feelings might have been

305

all over the place, but that was one thing she was now certain of. She hated him, more than she'd ever hated anyone.

'Straight from Amsterdam? Right,' said Ben slowly. 'Not quite what I heard.'

'What do you mean?'

'Let's discuss it in the morning. You don't need to worry about anything unnecessarily. Not now. Zach — where's he?'

'You've just missed him,' Sam said, trying to get comfortable. She wasn't going to worry about Michael unnecessarily. She wasn't going to worry about Michael ever again. It was hard enough worrying about those you did love. 'Zach's been having a lover's tiff. You'll never guess with who.'

'Who?'

'Sian. Mum's PA.'

'He's been shagging Sian?'

'Seems so.'

'The dog.'

'Though some other mate of his is also involved.'

'With her? With them? A threesome?'

Sam wanted to laugh, but she couldn't. Her insides, hollow one minute, were now a jumble of knots, getting tighter. 'The three of them had a drug thing on the go, dealing MDMA, stuff called Candy Cane. There've hit a few snags.'

'Does Mum know? Frank?'

'Some of it.'

'So where's Zach now then?'

'Helping Sian get home safe and sound, he said.'

'Sweet.'

'Glad they've gone — all of them. They were making a right racket, shouting away in the kitchen. Oh, and Sian's dad's just died. He's caught up in all this.'

'The drugs?' Ben was shaking his head.

'You name it.'

'Oh boy.'

That was all he could say? *Oh boy.* Ben was wearing unflattering jeans and a blue shirt, tucked in at the waist. No belt. Brown suede shoes. He might have put on some weight since she last saw him. He'd had another bad haircut. And he was meant to have a girlfriend? He was no womaniser. No crook, either. She doubted he'd ever be that, however hard her mother tried to drag him in.

'Can I get you anything? You don't look well.'

'What do you expect?'

'Sorry.'

'No,' she said, 'I don't want anything. Nothing you can provide right now.' Frank was the person she needed to see about a weapon. Hiring an assassin. Oh, for God's sake, what was she thinking?

'How long ago did Mum and Michael go out?' Ben was looking at his watch again. Yet he was rarely punctual.

'I don't know, I've been snoozing on and off. Hard to get any peace and quiet round here.'

'You need to rest,' Ben said, distracted. 'I'll leave you to it.'

'Why are you here?' she asked, watching him reverse towards the door.

'To see you. See if I can help. Zach told me to get my arse down here ASAP. With the fire and everything. So here I am. Oh, I brought you some chocolates. Charbonnel et Walker. They're downstairs. Fancy one?'

Why did everyone suddenly think she liked chocolate? Because she was a woman? 'What have you found out — about Michael, his business? I do need to know.'

'In good time, Sam. When you're feeling better. Best if I speak to Mum, first. It's business stuff. She can deal with it.'

'Don't fob me off.'

'Is Frank around? It's dark out. How long have they been gone?'

'Oh, for God's sake, she's a grown woman. She can handle herself. Besides, Michael's far too precious to ever get his hands dirty.'

'It's his associates I'm more worried about right now.'

33

Someone hadn't done that to Frank in a very long while. It tickled. The tongue was warm and moist, slathering the exposed side of his head, his left ear.

He was becoming more aware of the panting that went with the licking. The excruciating pain on the other side of his head, which was pressed into something that was damp and not completely soft. He was lying on his stomach, and it wasn't just his head that hurt. There was a throbbing ache around his waist, his kidneys. The fuckers must have kicked him when he was down. His spine felt bruised. His eyelids took an age to open. When they did, one at least, all he saw was black.

'Hey, get off.' He felt behind him. At least he could still use his arm. The back of his hand had touched something warm and shorthaired.

'Baz,' came a not too distant shout. Frank was aware of the sea. Waves breaking on an empty shoreline not a million miles away. He was so tired, yet in too much pain to sleep. His mind was rattling. *Baz?* He tried to turn his head, tasting sand. His eye was beginning to see faint lights. Were they out to sea? Along the front?

'Baz,' came the female shout again, much nearer. But the dog did not run off and remained by his prone side, licking him and snuffling. Leaning protectively against him in that way Boxers did.

'Jesus,' the female voice said, up close.

Frank felt a hand shoving his shoulder gently, and a splash of mobile phone light bathing his battered face.

'Frank? Are you OK? What are you doing here?'

'Britt?' said Frank, mildly amazed he could speak.

'What happened?'

'Some cunt clonked me on the head.'

'I thought you'd had one too many,' she said. 'And were sleeping it off.'

'No you didn't.' The dog had not stopped leaning against him. Frank was enjoying the warmth, the affection. 'What time is it?'

'It's gone ten.'

'Shit. I must have been out for a while.'

'Can you sit up? Stand?'

'No idea. My head's throbbing like a marine diesel.'

'Should I get an ambulance?'

'No, Britt. Not my style.'

'You're going to have terrible concussion if you haven't broken anything.' She was kneeling by his side. He could smell her breath.

'Have you been eating chips?' Using his hands, he tried to push his head, the upper half of his body, off the sand and sit up. He felt like he was on the waltzer, his least favourite ride. Thought he was going to puke.

Britt helped him to sit up, thoughtfully hung onto his shoulder in case he crashed straight back down. Both of his eyes seemed to be working now, though he could see no further than the pool of light Britt's phone was making. Baz had settled himself in the sand close by.

'What the hell happened?' Britt said again.

'What are you doing here?'

'Taking Baz for a walk.' She sat down next to him, using her body as a prop to keep him from toppling, while the waves continued to flop onto the shore, and the moon pulled and pushed the tide.

'Isn't that Howie's job?' Frank's head was clearing quickly. A massive headache was brewing nicely, but something was connecting up there. Blood was flowing. Tiny electrical currents were forming, in a brain that was heavily protected by thick bone. Bone toughened and honed by decades of use cracking others' skulls.

'He's running around town for you, I thought. Look, the new Serious and Organised chief, Kyle Neville, the guy I was telling you about on the blower, is here already, directing operations up at the caravan park. The remains of two bodies have been discovered. Nothing to do with you, I'm sure.'

'And you're out walking the hound?'

'It's Neville's operation.'

'But you're the new Assistant Chief Constable, aren't you?' His memory was still there. He felt himself smile weakly.

'I'm not going to step on his toes just yet.'

'You're here anyway, on the ground.'

'My boyfriend lives here. I'm taking my dog for a walk. We'd just started out.'

Howie's digs were this end of town, the last Frank knew. Though he also knew not to probe

311

too deeply, where Howie and Britt's relationship was concerned. More perplexing was the fact that this was the second time in a couple of days that Howie or Britt had practically stumbled upon him in a time of need. Were they looking out for him, or looking into him? Frank shook his weapon of a head. 'And Howie's where?'

'I thought you'd know,' Britt said. 'But he'll be all right. He can look after himself.'

'I thought I could.'

'You'll live, I reckon,' she said, getting to her feet. 'You can tell me what you've got Howie involved with, if you're worried.'

Frank shook his head some more. 'You know how he is, he got himself involved. Stolen turkeys, handbags. MDMA coming in from Holland. Arsonists coming out of retirement and taking orders from the wrong people. Corrupt council chiefs land-grabbing. A few family disagreements. Nothing out of the ordinary.'

'Howie can't help himself,' she muttered. 'He can't let that life go.'

'Which is why you love him,' Frank said, wondering whether he could get up. 'Here, give us a hand.' He held out his right hand, pushed off with his left.

'Fuck's sake, Frank, when are you going on a diet?'

'I'm on a diet,' he said, getting to his feet. He shook some feeling into his limbs. Began brushing the sand off his clothes. Patted again the front of his jacket. 'Shit, the bastards have taken my piece.' He patted some more. 'My wallet, my phone, my keys as well — they've

312

cleaned me out.' He didn't care about his wallet especially. Or the phone, which he should have jettisoned long ago — he had the numbers that mattered backed up in a safe place. Or his keys. If someone wanted to save him the trouble of ditching the motor, then fine by him — he had a spare set somewhere not too safe as well. But the shooter? He'd had such elaborate plans for that — too elaborate perhaps. Served him right.

'Oh, Frank, don't tell me you wandered down the beach with a recently used murder weapon.'

'Wouldn't have dreamed of it.' He avoided her eye, furious with himself. 'Where would I have got that from?' The last time he'd had concussion he was garbling bollocks for days apparently. He tapped his skull, the wrong side. 'Ouch. Don't know what I'm saying. Can't possibly be held responsible.' Had they cracked the bone? He let his hand travel further over the bald surface. Discovered a lump the size of a mango. It was still swelling. No external bleeding though.

'This isn't going to be an easy one to deal with, Frank.' She switched off the torch on her phone. Baz got to his feet.

'Who said anything about anyone being shot?'

'There've been reports of people hearing what they thought were gunshots going off all damn day. What is it with this town? You can't keep running around doing whatever the fuck you want.'

'Why not? You lot are on a skeleton staff, aren't you? All doubling up. Cuts all over the shop. No more budget for community support officers, etcetera. Who's meant to protect us?' He

313

supposed he was smirking to himself.

'Try explaining that to the forensics, when they find God knows what.'

'I don't have to. That's your job — to keep me, Howie, those you love, out of the frame.' He wasn't sure whether he was still smirking, or pleading. Pushing his luck.

'It costs. That's the deal. You know that. We're all out on a limb.'

Frank supposed he'd never been sure whether Britt was another bent copper, or someone who was far more twisted. 'Let's get out of here,' he said, stepping towards a less sheltered bit of the night. He looked back. Neither Britt nor Baz had moved. 'Coming?'

'What did I just say?' Britt said, walking towards him. 'Here, take my hand. You're staggering around like an old drunk.'

Frank didn't take hold of Britt's hand, but grabbed her arm, tightly. They set off, slowly. She seemed to be in sports gear: trainers, leggings, a light, tight kagoule; all made for speed. He was holding her back like there was no tomorrow. 'Rolly Andrews had resorted to his old ways — not sure he'd ever left them behind,' he said. 'You might want to get your new chap to set the sniffers on his digs. Has to be a complete health hazard.'

'I do talk to Howie, Frank. I need more than that. Besides, Kyle Neville is his own man.'

They took a swerve inland across drier sand. The hard line of the esplanade shaping up not so far away. Frank thought he might be able to make it to the concrete world. 'A small-time drug operation seemed to be working out of there as well. There's a box of cut at least.' He wasn't going to dump Zach's friend Liam in it just yet. He wouldn't have been trained in loyalty, the vow of silence — too young, too stupid. Frank had yet to tackle him, give him a chance. He was Zach's mate. 'Not sure how much the old pikey knew about it.'

'Language, Frank. Hate crimes are part of my new remit — remember? Are you really OK?'

'What's still bothering me,' Frank continued, regaining his footing, and hold on Britt's arm, 'is why Rolly Andrews had his dirty fingers in so many pies. The guy'd retired years ago. He obviously didn't mastermind the attack on Goodwin Enterprises' property. Not sure the obvious arseholes tell all the story. I'm missing something. I need more time.'

'I've leant on those my end to back off. Let you decide,' she said. 'Electrics, if that'd make your life simpler. I know how you like to do it when you're seeking revenge. Though don't forget domestic's in my new remit too. And not some stupid turf war, Frank, please.'

'Simon would have needed help,' Frank said.

'He didn't get it from Sands?'

'Sands? What's he got to do with it?' Playing the innocent had never been Frank's thing. He was no actor.

'I always hated the bastard.' She whistled. 'We all want a cleaned-up town. A pleasant place to live, to take your dog for a walk. You and me, we're not institutional people. We do things differently, but we get them done, don't we?'

'I don't get it. Howie's wanted you to leave the force for years. Be truer to yourself.'

'Howie doesn't know what's good for him. Do you? Who whacked you on the head?'

They'd reached the esplanade wall, but Frank couldn't see any steps up. A rain shelter loomed. Behind, the Marina Leisure Centre sat like a big block of curtailed dreams. It was the ugliest building on the front, taking up pride of place. There was a building that needed razing, if ever there was one. He yawned, feeling the mango, doubting he'd be able to climb up, and stroll along the promenade with any panache right now, even if the front had warranted it. That was for the future. 'Petty thieves?' he said. 'Chancers? Where are the fucking steps?'

'I don't think so.'

'No, neither do I.'

'There're some steps, over there.' She was leading him along the beach now.

Sand might have been in his shoes, but it felt like lead. He was exhausted. For a second he wished he hadn't chucked the bag of Candy Cane into the burning caravan. He needed an uplift, if not a stair-lift. 'I don't like impersonators, any more than I like imposters,' Frank said. 'Graham Sands thought he was the new Richard Goodwin. That he could run Yarmouth his way. Except he went about it on the cheap, by pulling in Simon.'

'Simon didn't approach him?'

'Does it matter now?'

'Depends who else Simon Goodwin might be talking to.'

They'd reached the steps, and Frank found he was going up first. Even Baz was hanging back. Except there was no rail. He took one small step at a time, wobbled, thought he might fall backwards. Saw stars. Felt Britt pushing him from behind. Her hands were on his arse, the poor dear.

After a decade or two they were on the promenade, Frank gazing left and right. There were people across the parade, dotted under neon advertising the arcades, chip shops, boozers. Some youths. A couple of old geezers. No sign of flashing lights, emergency services. Tuesday night, Great Yarmouth, an average scene.

'The guys who went for you,' said Britt, attaching a lead to Baz's collar, 'why didn't they finish you off?'

'Lack of experience?' said Frank. 'I had an altercation a little earlier with a glittering white chariot. It blocked my path as I was walking into town, but then pissed off soon enough. Nothing was said. No one even stuck their head out of the window.'

'The Hummer? Those Lithuanians? They're cleverer than you might think,' said Britt. 'We haven't been able to pin enough on them yet. Don't have a handle at all on their ambitions. Maybe Neville will do a better job than me. Or you could always take them out. Come to think of it, why haven't you?'

'Wannabes like that, motoring around town making a racket, takes the heat off those of us doing the real work.' He smiled. Shaky light from

317

a string of streetlamps was falling on them. Britt's eyes were dark and penetrating. She'd had a smart new haircut, he noticed. A bob. It suited her eyes, which were as sharp. 'Besides, the way this country is going I won't have to. They'll be sent home soon enough, won't they?'

'Don't you believe it. If anyone needs to go home right now it's you, Frank. Get some kip. Can I give you a lift?'

He had no money on him, no phone, no keys, no gun. His legs had done a couple of marathons. A large, squashy, overripe fruit was hanging off the side of his head. What was on his clothes, his skin, under his nails, could be read by a child, let alone a forensic scientist. Yet he didn't want to go home, get cleaned up, have a nap. He had to find Simon. Tatty might need him. 'I'm OK,' he said, 'I'll walk.'

'No you bloody won't. I'm taking you home, even if I have to kidnap you.'

They'd reached the road. It was wide and empty, except for a few parked cars. He paused. A thought came to him. 'You, you and Howie, haven't been following me, have you?'

'We look after you best we can,' said Britt. 'Always have.' She smiled, cuttingly, tugged on the lead. Baz tugged back. But she was stronger. 'My car's this way.'

'Did Howie tell you about Michael Jansen?' he asked, rooted to the spot like an old oak tree. 'Dutch chap, who fancies himself.'

'As I said, we look after you best we can.'

'You'll know all about who he represents then?'

Britt might have nodded.

'We need that investment,' said Frank. 'What he represents. Though not him, or any low-level sidekick he might have turned up with. He's another middleman, like Simon, who's got ideas way above his station.'

'That's what happens with big organisations.'

'You said it.' Frank looked up at the night sky, at the dirty smear of light pollution hovering over the town. 'He won't be hanging around for long. If he hasn't gone already.'

'Most people don't,' she said. 'Not here.'

'That's not true,' Frank said. 'Some of us love it.' He looked at her, not sure what he was really seeing.

'And Simon Goodwin?' she said. 'The American money he was bringing back?'

'You know everything, don't you?'

She didn't say anything, so Frank helped the conversation along, perhaps beginning to realise the extent of his support network, 'We don't need him squirming back in, that's for sure. With his record?'

'Are you getting along well with Mrs Goodwin?'

'Swimmingly,' said Frank. 'She's smart. She wants the American cash and what Jansen's offering, the European money. My job is to make sure there're no twats in the way, and that it's nice and safe when it gets here.'

'Two pots,' said Britt. 'Ambitious. I like strong women.'

'So you know,' said Frank, 'it's for the good of the town.'

'For the good of the town,' she repeated softly. 'What's in store for Simon Goodwin?'

'He was to be found dead, in possession,' Frank smiled, 'of the snub used to kill Sands, and Andrews,' he added.

'Murder suicide?'

'No. He came across a more ruthless assailant. A guy who likes his clobber. Crockett and Jones Chelsea boots, shirts from Turnbull and Asser, Glock 19 — you name it.'

'Jansen?'

Frank nodded. Then thought better of it — feeling the mango having descended as far as his ear. Low-hanging fruit.

'Who then disappeared? Except, that plan's gone to pot, because the shooter's now in the wrong hands.'

'Maybe not.'

'You're still coming with me,' she said, 'right now.'

34

Ships were sitting out to sea, three, four of them. Their navigation lights, faint reds and whites, were twinkling soulfully. For a desperate moment, Tatty thought she'd like to be on one, sailing away into the night, with a handsome firefighter by her side — before she did anything she might regret for the rest of her life. But the doubt, the yearning, only lasted a moment. Sailing away was for another time, when she'd procured her super yacht, with its helipad and any number of plush cabins — for family, and friends, and lovers, whoever they might be. Captain of the high seas, master of the universe.

Nearer to land, to Tatty's left, as she faced the big unknown, were the lights atop the wind turbines. Hundreds of them perhaps. She knew they were static, but like the ships' navigation lights they were also twinkling. Lights in the dark. They seemed so alive, electric.

She turned the other way, which took in the sweep of Gorleston beach, the gentle clifftop, the houses straddling Marine Parade, Michael standing with his back to the railing, at the very end of Gorleston Pier. There were no amusements on this pier. It was purely functional. Except, strictly speaking, it wasn't even that any more.

Behind her, a short distance away, was the Coastwatch lookout. Once upon a time this used to be the harbour master's lair, manned day and night. Port traffic was now controlled by the Harbour Office, over on South Beach Parade, who reported to Humber. Radar continually swept the area, but no one sat around with a pair of binoculars. This Coastwatch station shut at 8 p.m. in the summer, 7 p.m. in the winter — for years Rich bemoaned its redundancy. When he was a kid his dad used to take him to see the harbour master, an old guy with a beard of course, who could be bought for tuppence to turn a blind eye. No electronic surveillance then.

The only CCTV there was now was on the other side of the structure, angled straight onto the entrance, to deter burglars, vandals, disaffected youths. Zach and his mates, once upon a time, Tatty thought. Ben had never been so disruptive. Sam had been more subtly transgressive — her father's daughter — drinking and smoking and sleeping with boys from the earliest of ages, but trying to keep quiet about it. Tatty thought she'd got all that out of her system, especially sleeping with the wrong sort of boy. Taking no care to protect herself. But who was she to talk?

The sea swirled angrily, invisibly, around the foot of the pier. She had no idea what the tide was doing right now. Going out, she hoped. The breeze had strengthened, or maybe it was where she was standing, out on a limb. It was always blowy here. She looked at her watch, for effect. Her bag was weighing down her other arm. 'I want you out of here, Michael,' she said. 'In fact, I never want to see you again.'

'Lovely evening like this,' Michael said, 'we're not making the most of it.' He kept looking back towards Gorleston Pavilion, where once stars performed badly. 'You're a good-looking woman. How about it? I come from a family of strong women. In Holland we have progressive attitudes to things like sex, relationships.'

'And drugs,' Tatty said to the wind. 'Laundering money for Russians, Albanians, Lithuanians. Drug dealers, arms dealers, people traffickers.'

'You of all people have a problem with that? The hypocrisy of the British. No wonder your country's sunk.'

'You were keen enough to pump a load of cash in. The thing is, you weren't exactly honest about where it was coming from or who actually controlled it. Or your cut — were you?'

Michael flicked his head upwards, mouthed a sigh. 'No one's honest in this world.'

'A secure fund with very considerable assets from a group of private, high net worth individuals spread across Europe — isn't that what you said?'

'And?'

'Who's in charge? Who really calls the shots? I'd like some names, contact details, now.'

'You and your lawyers have seen all the paperwork you're going to see,' said Michael. 'Besides, you don't want to meet these people. They're not very nice.'

'So you keep saying. They're not very reliable either, are they? They think they can dictate the terms, and cut the investment in half, without having the balls to tell me in person? Fuck them.

You think I'm nice?'

'You're lucky a hundred mill is still on the table.'

'Lucky?' The sea continued to swirl below them. 'Lucky?' Tatty repeated. 'Frank and I don't like middlemen. They always screw things up. I doubt your bosses are pleased with you either. Sending a minder to keep an eye on you? You can't even be trusted to look after the deal yourself.'

'It's not me he's keeping an eye on, it's you. Shame he's not as appreciative of older women as me. Where is Frank, by the way?' He pushed himself off the railings. Came one step towards her, with more confidence than he had any right to.

Tatty took one step back. The lights out to sea stopped twinkling. She had no idea where Frank was. She hadn't been able to raise him on the phone for hours. 'He's working,' she said. 'Frank's always working. Cutting down more middlemen,' she added. She hoped he hadn't been caught out, hurt.

'Frank's not a middleman, then?' Michael asked, looking over her shoulder again and back down the pier.

She wasn't going to follow his gaze. He was watching out for someone, waiting to be rescued. She almost smiled. She wanted them to hurry up, she wanted that witness. It was only a short stroll from Graham Sands' Pier View Hotel.

Would his skinny wife keep it going? Was it possible that Sands could have been talking to Michael Jansen all along as well? 'No,' she said.

'Frank's my partner, he's not a middleman.' She needed to promote him, officially.

'Tatty, you and me — we have such a future together. Look at you, you are a beautiful woman.'

'Any more compliments you want to pay me?' Michael was a beautiful man. There was no doubting that. Immaculately attired and accessorised as well. His mind, though, was as ugly as any she'd ever encountered. His will, pathetic. Was he trying to flirt with her — her daughter's boyfriend, the man who was very nearly the father of her first grandchild? 'I said I never want to see you again. Get out of our lives. Walk away, Michael. Disappear. Now.'

'You want to throw away a hundred million pounds? I'm not giving you the names, the details of the people I work for. You'll never know. If you want this deal to go ahead, you need me.'

There was a hint of desperation in his voice. More so than a Dutch accent. Whether two hundred mill or a hundred mill, the people whose cash it was would not take kindly to being rebuffed, however much they might have been fucking everyone around. That was their prerogative. Their allegiance was not to the runner.

Tatty did glance over her shoulder now, catching the thin trail of lights dipping along the pier, the streetlights of the old fishermen's cottages surrounding the Victorian lighthouse, the Irish pub, the lights on Marine Parade; the Pier View Hotel not so much bright and sparkling as glaring and defeated. Maybe Goodwin Enterprises would finally be able to acquire it. They could revisit the idea of a boat shuttle between that bit of the Yare and the super casino. It wouldn't be such a bad idea to take over Gorleston Pavilion, and the Ocean Rooms, as well. Revamp this corner of Gorleston, now the beach was back. Shame you couldn't order the weather to behave.

Tatty was facing him again. He hadn't come any closer. She hadn't backed any further away. The sea continued to churn. 'My husband had a certain reputation, that went way beyond these shores. You and your backers, did you really think that because he was no longer around, you could do what you want? Pick at the pieces? In our business there's only one thing that people respect. You know what that is, Michael?'

He suddenly smiled, knowing and cocky. Laughter in the dark. She could've smashed his head in with a clog for what he'd done to Sam. 'Strength,' she said. 'Your associates, wherever they are in the world, are impressed by one thing and one thing only: strength. Without strength there is no money.' Tatty felt she could give a lecture on the topic, surprised again with what she knew, what she'd picked up in her hasty rise to the top.

'Ah,' said Michael brightly, stepping to the side. 'There you are.'

Tatty spun round. An arm's length away was a giant of a man. He wasn't so wide, but he towered over her. She thought of the lighthouse, Gorleston lighthouse, that had withstood storms and floods, lightning strikes and civic cuts, yet it remained standing, triumphant, even if it was

326

now also technically redundant. This was such a man, though with youth on his side. He didn't look any older than Zach. He didn't look redundant.

Enough light was dripping off the Coastwatch station for Tatty to make out the man's smile. He probably whitened his teeth. 'Who the fuck are you?' Tatty said, knowing exactly who he was.

'Tatty, meet Hans. Hans, meet Tatty,' Michael said smugly.

Hans nodded.

His hair was not fair but the colour of wet sand. You wouldn't want to run your fingers through it, she decided, even if she'd been able to reach. He had a scar, she noticed, in the mild glare of an old halogen. It crept out from his temple, and still looked livid. It must have been some gash. He wasn't quite so neat and innocent looking, despite the stupidly white teeth. He was fucking terrifying. She edged away from him, towards the railings.

'Are you not going to say hello?' Michael said, looking at her. The smile still lurking on his handsome face.

'Hans,' said Tatty, 'where are you from?'

He pointed at his chest with both hands. The same spot Tatty would have aimed for. But she had other plans for Hans. 'Yeah, you,' she said.

'Amsterdam?' he said, in a thick accent that was not Dutch. Slavic was lurking in the vowels. It was so predictable.

'Good,' she said, 'because I want you to do something for me.'

He pointed at his chest again. What a chest.

His lips curled downwards. She would not have wanted to kiss him.

'Yeah, you,' she said, allowing her bag in the crook of her arm to slide down so her left hand grabbed the handle. One of the handles. It was not fastened, and she knew it was hanging open a fraction, not that she was looking at it. She was smiling and concentrating on Michael, fully aware of exactly where Hans was. He hadn't moved. The sea continued to swirl around the end of the pier. A thumping crash was followed by a long sucking sound. No ships were entering or leaving port. It didn't operate twenty-four hours a day.

She took a deep breath, tasting the salt, always somehow more pungent at night. Fresh sea air that floated in with the moon. She shifted her head as far as she dared, to the left and the right. 'Hans,' she said, 'I want you to go back to Amsterdam, or wherever it really is that you've come from. Have a word with the people who sent you here.' There was no movement across the harbour mouth, no vehicles, let alone people that she could see, on what was now Port Authority land, the entrance to the outer harbour complex. There were lights showing razor-wire-topped fencing. Some tufts of dunes.

He nodded, doing that thing with his un-kissable lips, 'Yeah, to say what?' he said.

He was not a young man of many words, she felt.

'You know I only ever got together with Sam because of you,' Michael piped up, perhaps sensing she meant business. 'I dream about you,

Tatty. I want to be with you, to put my arms around you.'

He was not being serious. She heard the cool smirk in his voice. She found she'd retrieved the Glock from her bag, and was holding it with some professionalism. That trip out onto the beach had done wonders for her confidence. How many bullets did this thing hold? A damn sight more than the girly gun. Was the safety off?

'What the fuck is this?' Hans said. He looked at Michael, as if to say, she's your problem.

Tatty swung the Glock his way, which gave her another opportunity to look behind him, and back down the pier. There was nothing but fresh sea air blowing over the tired concrete and rusty railings, and the thicker, wooden barriers running down the left-hand side of the pier. She needed to get them on the north side of the pier, where the railings were less substantial and where the drop led to the mouth of the harbour and the fastest currents.

'Michael,' Hans shouted, 'what's she doing?'

Tatty thought she'd give Hans a taste of his own medicine and say not a lot.

Michael seemed to have lost his voice as well.

'What is this?' Hans said, panicked. 'Some psycho bitch pulls a gun on me?'

Tatty aimed the Glock at Hans's head. 'What did you call me?'

He stepped back. Held up his hands, splaying his huge fingers. Shook his head in submission.

'Michael,' Tatty said calmly, shifting her aim, 'walk over to that bit of railing for me, will you?'

'You want me to unlock the keys to this fund

329

for you, then think again,' he said, not budging.

'You know what, I'm not sure that'll be necessary after all. I've got Hans here to help me. He'll do as a messenger. Michael, over there, please.'

'Sam said power would go to your head,' Michael said. 'That you've a history of mental instability, and spent the last couple of decades on one drug or another. Antidepressants, sleeping pills. You useless, weak, pampered woman. Sam said I should be very careful going into business with you. You know nothing, you've never done anything.'

'Over there, Michael. That's right.' Michael was edging closer to the railings. He was not quite where she wanted him, but there was only so much waving of a gun she was prepared to do. It was heavy.

'She said you were a shit mother,' Michael continued. 'That you've only ever cared about yourself, having an easy life. Forcing your husband to look elsewhere. She warned me.'

Tatty had a feeling that Sam might have said a few things to Michael that were unkind, unwarranted. She wasn't sure she'd ever confront her about it, however. She'd just have to try triply hard to make amends. 'I thought you dreamed about me, Michael. That you wanted to put your arms around me.'

'Yeah, and throttle you. You mad cow.'

Tatty fired, aiming a little above his head. He ducked. The retort immediately sunk into the North Sea. She swung round. Hans had lurched her way, then thought better of it. 'Hans, you

330

don't think I'm serious?'

Michael was hurrying tentatively away from her, hugging the railings. He kept looking over the side into the drink. It was where every rotten bastard deserved to die.

'Another step, Michael, and it'll be your last.' He took another step, then another, before he began scrabbling over the railings. Aiming for his upper body, she pulled the trigger, feeling the gun urging her to take more. Another couple of shots slipped out of the barrel. She didn't hear the splash, Michael's body falling into the river, because of the retort ringing in her ears. She didn't bother looking over the side. It was a sheer drop.

There was a lifebuoy further down the pier. Neither she nor Hans made any attempt to go for it. Hans was not moving and stood there in the dark, staring at her. She pointed the gun at him once more. 'Go back to Amsterdam, Hans. Tell whoever sent you here that I'm happy to do business direct.'

He remained staring at her. Fortunately, a mild June evening did not bring out the hordes. She'd noticed a couple of cars running along Riverside Road. One made it to Quay Road and parked up, the other was going the other way, past Nathan's new apartment block. 'Go on,' she said to Hans, 'off you trot.' Despite the cool night air she could feel sweat on her forehead. Her pulse was going crazy.

Hans began stepping away. Stopped. Looked back at her. 'We come from London,' he said. 'Not Amsterdam.'

'Same message,' she spat. 'I'm in charge, and open for business. But on my terms. Tell them that.'

He turned and increased his pace, so he was practically sprinting by the time he'd reached the pavilion. He did not look back again. She hoped he wouldn't look back until he got to London. Then she wanted him to tell his bosses exactly what he'd seen. If they were as nasty as Michael Jansen had suggested, they'd respect her, her strength. They wouldn't think twice about pumping in the hundred mill — she fucking hoped.

Another vehicle was coming along Riverside Road, towards the pier, at speed. There were no flashing lights. However, with all her strength Tatty flung the Glock into the Yare, knowing that they would never be able to dredge that part of the river, while the salt water would soon remove any trace of her from the weapon. Besides, Frank still had the other piece, should they need it.

Pulling her mac tighter around her, she dipped her head and walked towards Quay Road. It wasn't until she left the pier that she remembered her car was at home. She and Michael had strolled here along the upper esplanade — Michael having arrived in Gorleston with Hans in a rental. Hans had dropped Michael off at the house, and driven back to the Pier View. Hans had the car, which, if he had any sense, he'd already be in, motoring south.

Tatty paused by the pavilion. She was too full of adrenalin to go straight home and tuck herself up in bed. She wasn't sure she'd be able to face

Sam yet either. She still didn't have the fireman's number — she really had to get on to Frank about it — otherwise she might well have rung him up. However, there was someone a short way up Riverside Road who'd be more than willing to provide her with an alibi. He could put his arms around her for old time's sake, she supposed, and call her beautiful. She needed someone to hold her right now, stop her from shaking.

She was more than certain that Nathan would kick his cheap Mancunian floozy straight out of his bed — if she was still hanging around, inappropriately attired. She was in for one hell of a slap if she didn't jump to it. Nathan too.

35

Zach slipped off the bed. Stepped to the kitchen area, his bare feet sticking to the floor. Poured himself a glass of water. Drained it. Looked down at his todger. Morning glory. He glanced over to the bed, which was not a million miles away. It was a tiny flat for a tiny bird. Sian was out for the count. There was a splat of dark hair on the pillow. No sign of her face, her mouth — where monstrous fibs came from. She was a great kisser though. Never thought he'd enjoy kissing so much. Didn't think he should wake her up. Shame.

He pulled on his jeans with some difficulty; his T-shirt. Opened the blind above the sink. It was overcast. A flat grey mid-week June day. The summer having disappeared as quickly as it had arrived. What could be worse? Except he felt surprisingly sunny.

He found his phone in his pocket. Noticed it was nudging eight. No sign of anyone calling or texting him back. No one else was trying to reach him either. That made a change. Not that it was so welcome right now. Where the fuck was Frank? He had some priceless information for him. He knew who'd been leaning on Sian's dad — getting him to commit arson. Sian had been too afraid to say in front of his mum. Zach didn't blame her. He also knew who'd been leaning on Sian, wanting her to suck his knob. Families for you. Fucked you up. Sam used to say something like that with more of a rhyme, when she was going through her poetic days.

'Trudy dudey,' he said aloud, his version of poetry, tapping the screen, then putting the device to his ear. It went straight to voicemail again. He tried another number for a different jerk. Unfinished business, deep betrayal, not that he'd ever raise the tosser at this time. The call was answered, straight off. Surprising.

'Yo.'

Zach struggled to gather his thoughts. 'Sian told me about your frigging Dutch contact,' he gabbled. This was another thing Sian had let on, post-coital. When her mouth had been finally free to blurt.

'Big deal,' Liam said.

'Yeah, well — they're not fucking Dutch, are they? I can't believe you're bowing and scraping to those scum.'

'The work ethic, man, of the Lithuanians. Why wouldn't you let them do all the hard graft, while we reap the profits and have the fun? They're not going to be around forever. Another year and they'll be kicked out anyway by May and her storm troopers.'

'You lied to me, Liam.' A buzzing was ringing in Zach's other ear. Like an old-fashioned alarm clock. He glanced over at Sian. She hadn't moved. No wonder. She must have exhausted herself.

'No, mate, I took on the burden of being party to compromising information. Kept you out of the loop on purpose — with your connections?

335

We've been through this.'

'You didn't say you were getting the Cane off the Lithuanians.'

'So what?'

'So they're the fucking low-rent enemy, man.'

'Exactly — you'd have gone dodo and called in your fancy boy Frank — before you did, snitch. You should be grateful — spoilt little shit.'

'Those scum, Liam? You're no better, are you? You want to watch out for Frank — he's after you as it is. Man, will he whip your arse.' The ringing had been replaced by thumping.

'Yeah, I can see him doing that. That's his thing. The peachier the arse, the better.'

Liam wasn't sounding like Liam. He'd picked up some balls from somewhere. Gone hardcore. He was on something new. People had been mentioning this gear called Blue Rock. Where Viagra met crack — that was the tag.

'What's going on?' It was Sian's voice, thick with sleep, and annoyance.

For the briefest of seconds, Zach had a terrible thought of waking up to that every morning. The nagging, the petty complaints. He was way not ready to settle down. 'I'm on the phone,' he said firmly, holding the device away from his mouth. Imagine having a kid with her.

'Someone's at the door,' Sian said, shifting under the covers.

'Fuck,' said Zach, realising what the ringing and banging were. It was like he was on the opposite to Liam, some heavy dope.

'You going to open it then?' Sian said.

'I haven't finished with you,' Zach said into

the phone, before tapping an end to Liam.

Sian lived in a flat on the ground floor of a drab yellow-brick block, off Nottingham Way, built in a time when there was little money or taste. In the 1970s, Zach presumed. He hadn't been here too many times. Never in daylight. The front door was an arm's stretch away. He glanced again at Sian. She'd burrowed her face back into the pillow. He wondered whether she dyed her hair. It was remarkably black. She waxed her pubes, like every bird he'd ever been with, so that was no indicator. He supposed they had pubes in the 1970s. Would fit with the general lack of style, care and attention. In fact he knew they did. He'd seen enough vintage porn. Amazed they ever had sex then.

'Answer it, for God's sake,' came another muffled squawk from Sian.

He was dawdling, while shitting his pants. He pulled open the door. 'Yeah?' he said, tensing, taking a second or two to compute who was standing there smirking like an idiot. 'The fuck?'

'Yo,' Liam said.

'But I was just speaking to you,' Zach said.

Liam held up his mobile. It was in his left hand. He shook it like a rattle.

Zach was the idiot. 'You could have said.' He could have punched his mate in the face.

'That I was around the corner? No guessing where I'd find you,' Liam said, a heaviness to the tone.

'What are you doing here, with the sparrows? The earliest you ever get up is teatime.' He should have known it was weird when Liam answered his phone.

'Man, the night is long, the morning is early.'

They hadn't moved from the doorway. Zach didn't feel like letting Liam in any further. It was complicated, knowing Liam used to occupy this space — the man about the house. 'How come you're here? Have you been waiting outside, peeping?'

'Who'd you take me for? A perv? Man, I've been so busy. The town's erupting. Would have been here earlier. I was on my way over when you called — coincidence. Where's Sian?' He was trying to look past Zach. 'She in the sack?'

'What do you want?' Zach noticed Liam was clutching something in his other hand. He was holding it down by his side, not making much effort to hide it. It was black, no shine.

'We need to iron out a few things.'

Zach was trying to look past Liam, his turn, and through the dull grey air, out onto the street. A big blob of white caught his eye. A flash of chrome grille. It was parked up across the street. 'That what I think it is?' he said.

Liam nodded, creepily.

'Don't tell me that's your ride?'

'Had to get over here somehow, mate. Sian's still got my wagon, hasn't she.' Liam slammed Zach in the chest, pushing him back into the flat.

Zach lost his footing, his body twisting from the impact and stumbled over Sian's coffee table. There was a minor crash.

Sian screamed.

Zach had cracked his shin on the corner of the glass top, the pain was piercing, and it took him a moment to get his bearings, decide his next move. It wasn't up to him, however. Liam was standing over him, pointing a gun at his head.

'Motherfucker,' Liam said, putting on a gravelly voice. Sian screamed again. He turned to her, waving the piece. 'Shut it,' he said, 'or we're all going to get it.'

'Man,' said Zach, rubbing his shin, 'where'd you snaffle that?' It looked very familiar.

'They want you and her out of the way for good,' he said, stepping backwards so he could sweep the room with ease. Take them both out just like that. Pop, pop.

'You fucking what?' said Zach. He was sitting up, contemplating diving for Liam's legs. His best mate wasn't going to shoot him, or Sian. But he wasn't his best mate, was he? He was a lying, disloyal cunt, who'd been sent to pop them. Did he even know how to use such a weapon? The world had twirled a long way out of kilter.

'This isn't personal,' Liam added. 'I want you to know that.'

As if it ever was, Zach thought. So what if he'd nicked his bird. Liam had never shown that much interest in her. In anything, apart from getting off his head — until now. But he was off his head — on some toxic shit from the Balkans, or wherever Lithuania was. The joke was wearing thin.

His eyes flickered over to Sian, back to Zach. 'I never cared that you two started getting together. Honest. She's riddled, Zach, if you haven't found out already. Not that it matters now.'

'What?' said Sian. She was covering herself

with the duvet. Zach knew she didn't have a stitch on. 'Get out, Liam, fuck's sake. Arsehole.'

'After everything I've done for you? Lending you my car, bringing you into a little dope-dealing business? Not to mention a lucrative line in frozen turkeys, handbags, you name it. Nice.'

'I helped you, you wanker,' Sian said, switching her terrified gaze to Zach. 'Me and my dad — most of the stuff was his. You were meant to find a market for it. Bollocksed that up, didn't you? Where's all the cash? I only took your car because you wanted me to offload the rest of the Candy Cane you were too scared to deal yourself.'

'We wouldn't have needed to make the money so fast if your dad hadn't helped himself to what wasn't his — the dirty pikey.'

'Fuck you,' said Sian, gathering more duvet around her.

'Liam,' said Zach, still sitting on the floor, 'put that thing down, will you? What's your fucking problem?' He couldn't take him seriously; he never had. Now he was under orders from the Lithuanians? 'We're mates, aren't we? Business partners?' Sian hadn't told him why she'd taken off in Liam's Beamer. He hadn't known there'd been any more gear. News to him that everyone had decided that Rolly Andrews had lifted Saturday night's bag of cane, and that he hadn't just lost it. He was struggling with the duplicity, and the pain in his leg.

'No, not business partners. Not any more. This is coming to an end,' Liam said. 'The police are all over the caravan park — the lodge, all that end of town. There was a fire in one of the caravans. A couple of bodies have been found.'

'Which caravan?' said Sian.

'Yeah, I wonder,' said Liam, like he knew damn well.

'What's that mean?' Zach said, getting to his feet. His jeans were sticking to his shin. He must have cut his leg.

'Ask her.'

A blush, which had started somewhere near her rack, swiftly crept up Sian's neck and began flowering her cheeks. 'Sian?' said Zach.

She shook her head. Her mouth, raw and unpainted, drooped and quivered. No coherent words came.

'Where your old man used to fuck his birds and store his weapons, Euros and fake passports,' said Liam. 'The company caravan it was known as, by him. Everyone else thought of it as Richard Goodwin's knocking shop.'

'How the fuck do you know this?' Zach shouted.

'Ask her,' he said, waving the gun in Sian's direction. 'She showed me — bounced around on the flimsy bed and all. I wasn't the only one she took there either.'

Zach looked at Sian. How could someone so small be so devious?

'Dad told me about it,' she said, quickly, crawling off the bed, while hanging onto the duvet.

'Think about it Zach,' Liam said. 'It was your old man's escape clause. The minute the authorities closed in, he'd have pissed off. Not

341

much of a family man, was he?' Liam said. 'How's that make you feel?'

Zach looked at Sian again. She was standing now, in the small space between her bed and a chest of drawers, while hanging onto the duvet, her modesty, as best she could with one hand. None of the drawers were closed properly and there was a mountain of stuff on the top.

'Frank knew all about it, too,' Liam said, clocking her movements. 'Didn't he tell you? We left him a present last time we were there — a local delicacy.'

Zach didn't answer, but was increasingly aware of Sian. She was about to do something, probably very stupid. 'Put that thing down, man,' he said to Liam, 'it's making me nervous.'

'Life's short and fucked up,' Liam said, not putting the gun down. 'I don't want to blow you two away. It's like I've got no option, man. They're going to kill me if I don't.'

Zach laughed. 'Let's ring Frank. He'll sort it out.' If he'd answer his blinking phone.

Dropping the duvet, Sian pounced on Liam. There was something in her hand, a glint, and she was swinging this towards Liam's head with a ferocity and suddenness that made Zach think of a medium-sized cat, a puma or something, that he might have seen when he was taken to the Africa Alive safari park at Kessingland as a kid. It would have been a school trip because his mum never took him to anything like that.

There was a grapple, Sian was an animal all right. It was all happening so fast Zach didn't see

342

the exact moment the glint connected with Liam's neck, but blood immediately began spurting across the room, as far as the bedhead, and up the wall behind it, right to the ceiling. A thick, vivid fountain. It was the most extraordinary thing Zach had ever seen.

He managed to drag his attention back to Liam, catching the deepening panic on his oldest mate's face; the demon whites of his eyes. Sian was clutching a pair of black-handled scissors in her right hand, the blades thin and coming to a bloodied point. Her pale skin and face, her naked body, was already splattered with blood, like she was being spray-painted.

She was looking at Zach. There was shock and an icy stillness on her face. She couldn't believe what she'd done. Then she was being blown backwards onto the bed and the room was filled with the deep, sharp crack of a gun going off. There was an instant smell of cordite as Liam fell to the floor, the pistol in his hand, blood still pumping from the wound in his neck, maybe with a touch less vigour. The lights going out in his fluttering eyes.

He did know how to fire it. The last stupid thing he ever did.

Sian had collapsed on the bed. Her eyes were also wide open. Unblinking. Unseeing. She was not moving. There was a terrible mess in the middle of her chest. Zach couldn't look at it. Had Liam hit her in the heart? Taken her straight out? There was so much blood Zach had no idea whose was whose, but no blood seemed to be pumping out of Sian's tiny frame.

Her heart hadn't been so small, had it? He wanted to think of the good things about her.

Holy fuck.

36

A supply ship was heading out to sea. It was new and bright against the flat sky, the still rushing water, the slump of warehouses and vacant lots across the river in Southtown. Frank followed it as it left a plume of thick diesel, slowly passing Fish Wharf, and on round the gentle bend of the Yare. He wasn't going to think about how much he'd like to be on it. Anything that'd give him a lift.

A minicab had dropped him at the front of Goodwin House, and his stiff, sore legs and back meant that it had taken him an age to get to the rear parking lot. Like the old man he was. Christ, he needed a Zimmer. No, a mobility scooter — plenty of outlets for them in this neck of the woods. The choice he'd have. Perhaps he'd be eligible to get a disability allowance, help him with the cost. He couldn't even laugh at his own joke, his sides hurt too much.

Gathering his strength, he'd spent a further stretch of time taking in the view. A gulp of air, and he turned away from the river, clocking the back of Admiralty Steel. No worker was in sight taking a fag break, despite it having gone eight. He supposed they had foremen, a structure that would see the operation continue even after their boss's demise was made public. Watching Sands' operations unravel was going to be fun.

The VW Up! was sitting, tantalisingly, next to

his stinking Range Rover. He'd have happily driven off in the minuscule lump of red tin, but he only had his spare keys with him — plus a new burner, a wad of cash, and a headache the size of Norfolk. He climbed into his Range Rover painfully, powered it up, U-turned, knowing he had even less time to get rid of the stinking vehicle, persuade Tatty of his bonus, his raise, that he needed a Lexus — if not a spanking new invalid carriage. He didn't even try to laugh again.

Over the edge of the quay right here was not where the beast was going. There were plenty of deep, isolated dykes the other side of Breydon Water, towards Halvergate. It wouldn't need to remain unnoticed for ever. The brackish water would do its job. He'd drive out there later today, get young Zach to pick him up.

First he had an urgent date with another old codger, who'd be enjoying his last meal of juice and muesli in the Pier View Hotel. Frank couldn't see Simon enjoying a full English. He should have popped along last night, that was the plan. But Britt had frogmarched him home, and then sent Howie to keep sentry. By the time Frank crawled out of bed in the morning, there was no sign of either of them. Friends for you.

Traffic was moving in both directions. Frank pulled out after an articulated lorry, it's flatbed carrying the trunk of a turbine. It was going at some pace, for such a load. Making sure he kept to the speed limit, Frank followed the turbine, like a relic from a lost civilisation, as it made its way along South Denes, Southgates and into

South Quay. By the new cobbles of the recently restored historic quarter, Frank swerved over to the kerb, mounted it, slammed on his brakes. Wheezed with the pain. Opened the passenger window. 'Zach, fuck you doing? Get in.'

The boy'd been on foot, head down, skulking and filthy.

Seeing it was Frank, he got in fast enough. Conscious of stopping where he shouldn't, Frank immediately re-joined the traffic as it funnelled towards the Haven Bridge. It was rush hour, and the traffic thickened, slowing them to a crawl.

Frank glanced over. Zach was shrinking in the seat. He had blood on his jeans, his T-shirt. He hadn't said anything. He was as pale as a frosty morning.

'Fuck's going on?' Frank said.

'They'd gone,' he said. 'I watched them drive off. They didn't even come in.'

'Who?'

'The Lithuanians.'

'The guys who thrash around in the Hummer?

'Anyone else drive a white Hummer that you know?'

'Calm down, Zach.'

'They're dead.'

'Who?'

Zach was shaking his head. His eyes were red and glistening. The kid had been bawling hard. 'What the fuck's this traffic doing?' he said. 'You've got to get me away. I'm in so much shit, man. They're going to lock me up for life.'

The lights switched and they were rolling over

the Haven Bridge. The water underneath was a dull grey, metallic compared to the dirty white, unreflecting sky. Wind was patching the surface. Plenty of gulls were picking at what they could. An ambulance was coming the other way, lights flashing, siren blaring. There was another one not so far behind it. 'Who's dead? Who've you taken out?' No police, yet.

'Not me, man.'

'You're covered in blood.'

'I was there, but I didn't do anything.'

They were by the giant Matalan. Frank indicated left, carefully took Southtown Road. He wanted the street to swallow them up. It was like he was stuck in a dream, a nightmare, one of those ones where you're being chased but there's always something stopping you from getting away. As a kid he had the weirdest dream. It continued to haunt him. He was in a corridor, long and institutional, all on his own. He was trying to make it to the outside, where the grass was green, the sky blue, the air fresh. Except the corridor was filling with plasters, hundreds, thousands of giant, floating plasters. All shapes and sizes, for every type of wound. He would wake before he was suffocated to death. He never got out of the building.

'It's OK, Zach. I'm here for you,' he said. The boy's shoulders were shaking. He'd started blubbing again. 'Where's your car?'

'I don't know. Home?' he snuffled. 'Yeah, at home. I took Sian to her place in Liam's Beamer last night. She'd borrowed it. She wasn't up to driving. I took her home in it. Was going to then

348

drop it off at Liam's, get a cab back, but one thing led to another. Oh, fuck.' He collapsed into sobs again.

'You need a holiday,' Frank said. 'Get yourself out to Ibiza. I have to do a couple of things this morning then I'll take you straight to Stansted. Go home, pack your clothes, get your passport, and you're out of here. When you return, I want you to do as I say — stick to the hacking.'

He'd call on Howie to help him ditch the car, once he got back to Yarmouth. Get him to give him a hand with what other cleaning up needed to be done as well.

'They're dead,' Zach mumbled.

'Who, son?' Frank knew his brain wasn't fully up to speed. Half of it felt like it had fallen out of his skull and was hanging to the side of his head in a big sack of leathery old skin. They were approaching the Beccles Road and Malthouse Lane junction. Frank took Malthouse, and then the quieter route down to the river, wanting to avoid the High Street.

'Sian, and Liam,' said Zach.

'Fuck, no way.'

'Yeah — it's true.'

'I'm sorry. They're too young. How'd they die?' Rolly Andrews, then his daughter — a family gone. He hadn't seen that coming. Rolly was a fool, his daughter as well. Sian's position would no longer have been tenable. Yet she'd had some spark. Zach'd fallen for her, plenty of others too, by all accounts. What a waste. He blinked as the river came into view again, gleaming like mercury under the dull sky.

'I was at Sian's and Liam turns up first thing. He was wired, man. Gabbling away. Then he pulls a gun on us.'

'Bit smaller than my hand?' Frank said, taking his left hand off the wheel and making it into the shape of a gun. 'With a barrel?'

'Looked like Mum's.'

'You knew about that?'

'Who do you take me for?'

'She'd parted company with it a while ago,' said Frank. 'Must have got into the wrong hands.'

'No kidding,' said Zach. 'Liam had been driving around with the Hummer lot. He'd been doing the Candy Cane business with them all along, so it turns out. He'd told me the stuff was coming from Amsterdam, but it wasn't, man. They were behind it.'

Frank didn't know why they hadn't finished him off under the pier, why he was still alive. Had they been disturbed? And then out of the blue, Baz and Britt Hayes come to his rescue. He needed a fully functioning head to deal with that. Not the further distraction of police, ambulance and lifeboat activity ahead. They were congregated in the large public car park by the lifeboat station on Riverside Road. The inshore, orange inflatable launch was being readied. Personnel were gearing up.

As Frank slowed the vehicle his heart began pounding. An image of him and Tatty, as kids, sprung into his damaged head. They were the same sort of age. He was holding her hand and they were running down the corridor, fast as they could, aiming for the fresh air, the blue skies, but the air was filling with adhesive bandages. He felt for his phone, then remembered it was a new burner. No one had this number.

'Put your foot down,' Zach shouted, 'fuck's sake.'

A community support officer was standing by the entrance to the car park. Frank did put his foot down, but on the brake. He lowered Zach's window. Zach was practically in the foot well, trying to get out of view. 'What's going on?' Frank shouted across to the woman. He didn't recognise her. She didn't recognise him.

'It's an exercise, sir,' she said, not quite smiling. 'Nothing to worry about. The helicopter will be over shortly, and they'll be launching the main lifeboat soon. If you'd like to watch, we're suggesting people use the parking up by the lighthouse. This car park will be out of use to the public all morning.'

'Cheers,' said Frank brightly, pressing the button to raise the window, then doing what Zach had wanted him to do and accelerate. 'How'd they die?'

Zach struggled to sit up properly. 'This vehicle, man, it stinks.'

'It's for the knackers' yard,' said Frank, 'whether its legs still work or not. Long overdue, son.'

'What have you been ferrying around?'

'You haven't answered my question.'

'Liam was going to shoot us — he'd been sent in by the Lithuanians.'

351

'They're not all Lithuanians,' said Frank. 'Don't do that country down. Most of those guys come from no further than Essex. One from Liverpool.' Britt had been more than forthcoming, driving him home last night. Information she'd come by as Assistant Chief Constable, she'd said. He didn't understand why she hadn't known this as head of Serious and Organised. He owed her a call already, he supposed. Anything to get this amount of heat deflected.

'Wherever they're from, they'd done something to Liam. Brainwashed him — I don't know. He was going to shoot us, Frank. Sian went for him, with like hairdressing scissors. Sharp as hell pointy things. Got him in the neck and she must have hit an artery because blood started spurting everywhere — never seen anything like it — which was when Liam shot her. She died — oh man — like immediately. Then Liam must have run out of blood. This is the honest fucking truth. Fuck, man. I didn't kill anyone, and the two of them are lying there dead. Blood dripping from the walls. Fucking messed-up world.' His voice cracked, his shoulders went again.

Frank drove past the lighthouse, went with the road as it skirted the foot of the pier, and straight into an empty parking slot by the new steakhouse on the lower esplanade. The shutters were down. It had yet to open for the day. Not a breakfast place. Frank cut the motor. 'Did you touch anything?' he asked. 'The gun, the scissors?' He knew the kid's prints, DNA, must have been all over the place in any case.

'No, no way. I ran out of there. I didn't care whether the flat was being watched. I had to get out of there. The blood, Sian, Liam. Both dead. I was panicking. But when I got to the street the Hummer was gone. Like they were always going to split, having set Liam up, or something — maybe they wanted the cops to catch him, and get rid of all of us. Total annihilation. I can't fucking believe it.'

'You got out,' Frank said. 'There'll be no point denying you were in the flat at some point — if the cops ask. Let's hope it looks like how you described it.'

'I'm not lying. I never lie to you.'

'I can get this dealt with,' Frank said. 'Easier if you didn't touch the gun, the scissors.' He wasn't convinced he could get it dealt with. But he knew Britt Hayes would be able to work it so a certain story emerged. She outranked this new guy Neville. Be good if Zach was out of the country for a bit, nevertheless. He needed to calm down.

'Where're you going?'

Frank had opened the driver's door, was taking his time climbing out. 'Wait here, will you, I won't be long.'

'Where're you going?' he repeated.

'To check up on your uncle. He's staying in the Pier View. I want to surprise him.'

'That's where he wanted Sian to meet him,' Zach said. 'She said she never — but I don't know.'

Frank was out on the pavement, finally, catching his breath, letting the pain subside. 'You what?'

353

'She got a text from him last night. She never let me see it — deleted it before I got near enough to read it all. She went bright red, man. She said it was to do with his and Sands' deal to buy the caravan park, and they couldn't get hold of her dad.'

'They were buying the caravan park?'

'For a shedload. Sian reckoned it was so her dad would do whatever they wanted him to do in the meantime. They made him torch the Smokehouse. Which is why he didn't do such a good job. He didn't want that place destroyed. Nor Goodwin House.'

'He was an old man,' Frank muttered. 'Took the easy way out, did he?' Frank hadn't contemplated suicide as the factor behind Rolly Andrew's death. They'd never know. Rich should have bought the caravan park years ago — but Rolly Andrews wouldn't sell it. Why now, because he knew he was ill, and wanted to leave something for Sian? Sweet in a way.

'Sands and Simon wanted to fuck up Mum's casino deal, so they could have free rein. I've been trying to ring you.'

'I've got a new phone.' First person he'd rung on it this morning had been Dennis, calling him back, wanting to tell him about the new financing arrangements, that Tatty was spearheading a major new link-up, East meets West. The fact Simon was history. The American hadn't answered. Frank put it down to the time difference. Simon wasn't history yet either. Unless Tatty had got to him first. She'd promised him that Simon was his. 'I know how much Rich

354

meant to you. Now's the time for your revenge,' she'd said out on the dunes, 'make the most if it.' She insisted she was to tackle Michael Jansen, because he'd hurt her child, and demeaned her business, her authority. 'I'm going to prove to him who I really am,' she'd said. Frank hadn't doubted that's exactly what she'd do. He couldn't now doubt who he was once more either.

'Wait up,' Zach said, opening his door. 'I'm coming with you.'

'Not a good idea,' said Frank. 'You've seen enough blood for one day.' If he had to use his bare hands, he would.

37

Tatty let herself in, quietly crossed the hall to the kitchen, feeling like a naughty schoolkid. Not a mother.

The house was still, perfectly quiet. Looking at the coffee machine, and back to the glass wall out onto the tidy garden, all she could think of was flat white. 'Flat white,' she said aloud, as if to drive home the point. It wasn't what she needed. That was a short, strong espresso. She'd showered, for a solid thirty minutes, at Nathan's, but she was tired. She couldn't have had more than a couple of hours' sleep. Nathan couldn't have been more excited to see her.

His floozy had bolted back to Manchester apparently, straight after her last unannounced visit. Embarrassed, he wasn't going to tell her. It'd been a mistake seeing him. It was always a mistake. This time she couldn't stop looking out of the window, at the dark current flowing metres away. The sex hadn't been distracting. It had been boring. She hadn't felt safe. He wasn't the man she wanted to be with then.

She put her bag on the dining table. She should have parted with it. For some reason, she couldn't. Nostalgia for a time when she was pampered and didn't have to call the shots? For a man that maybe she had loved once, despite everything? It had been tough enough leaving her mac at Nathan's. She hoped it was easily replaceable, like him. She supposed she should ditch all her clothes in case there were traces of cordite or whatever it was. She didn't feel like a naughty schoolkid. She felt like a squalid murderer. The cold flat light of day.

She stepped over to the coffee machine, listening out for signs of life. She would have come back earlier had she not known that Ben was here, able to keep an eye on Sam. He'd texted. A rare occurrence, cherished all the more because of that. She began arming the coffee machine. Then stopped. Her hands were shaking. She hadn't told Nathan about Michael of course. He hadn't said anything, as he'd driven her home, but he'd also noticed the commotion by the RNLI building, the emergency services gathering in that car park.

How long did she have before they pieced it together, and there was a knock at the door? Could they add it up? Where the fuck was Frank? His phone was going straight to voicemail.

Coffee was not what she wanted after all. Bottle, that was what. She left the kitchen, ran upstairs. Barged straight into Sam's room. Took one stride in. Froze.

The room was light, the curtains drawn back. Sam was dressed, sitting on the end of the bed. She barely looked up at Tatty. By her feet were her bags. Neatly packed. Next to them were Michael's. Not packed. The contents were spread across the room.

Tatty walked over to the bed. Sat gently next to her. 'Didn't you hear me downstairs? What are you doing?'

Sam wouldn't look at her. 'Going.'

'Where?'

'Where do you think? Home.'

'This is your home.'

'London,' she said. 'That's my home.'

'How are you feeling? Your stomach?'

'Where have you been? Where's Michael?'

Tatty breathed out. 'I've been with Nathan. I should have let you know.' She paused, waiting for Sam to say something. She didn't. 'I knew Ben was here — thought you'd be OK.'

'Nathan?'

'The architect.'

'I know who he is.'

'I'm a single woman,' Tatty said. 'I can see who I want. It was a mistake anyway, if you must know. There's someone else I've got my eye on.' She didn't know why she was telling Sam this. 'A fireman.'

'For God's sake, Mum, how old are you? What's happened to Michael? You went off with him last night. You don't return until breakfast time, and there's no sign of him. It's like he's disappeared again — twice in a fucking week. I hate him anyway, but he could have rung. His new phone's going straight to voicemail, and the old one.' She sniffed. 'Where is he?'

Tatty put her arm around Sam. Her hands were no longer shaking. She hugged her. 'I don't know,' she said. It wasn't a total lie. She didn't know where his body might have washed to, whether anyone had seen anything. Where the lifeboat people might find him, one day. 'He was here with this guy Hans — or that's what he called himself. Muscle, from London. I don't think Michael had come straight from Amsterdam.'

'He wasn't mugged there — that's for sure. The lying wanker. His iPad was in his bag.'

'We can get Zach to break into it, that might tell us something,' Tatty said brightly. She was thinking of the fund, Michael's contacts, if Hans wasn't to do his job and pass on the message to the real bosses.

'Maybe Michael can himself,' Sam said, looking at her now, unblinking. 'When he turns up.'

'Yes,' Tatty said, standing. She got to the bedroom door before she turned and faced Sam, who was still looking at her. They had the same eyes, cold and clear. The same heart?

'He's not coming back, is he?' Sam said. 'You've done something.'

'I don't know what will happen, to me, the business right now, but you'll be all right from now on. I'll not stand for anyone messing you around — or me and the business.'

'I'm an adult. I can look after myself, thanks.'

'We all need one another, from time to time — you, me, Zach, Ben.'

'And Frank, yeah?' The sarcasm was still there.

'Don't go back to London. Please stay.'

'Why? Give me one good reason?'

'Because I love you.' She closed the door behind her, wanting Sam to think about that. Knowing she couldn't say any more to her right now.

38

'When did you sneak down here?' Tatty said, walking into the kitchen. Ben was at the coffee machine.

'I've just got up,' Ben said.

'Late for you.' She smiled. She was clutching her phone in her right hand, her trigger finger wrapped around it.

'Sea air,' he said. 'I heard you talking to Sam. Didn't want to interrupt.'

He didn't come towards her to give her hug, which was not unusual. Metres apart, she stood on the hard stone kitchen floor still feeling dirty and soiled. Would she ever not?

'Are you OK, Mum? Busy night?'

'I was telling Sam, I was at Nathan's. Big mistake,' she repeated. 'How's your love life?' She smiled again. 'Give us a hug, darling.' She walked over, put her arms around him. 'I haven't seen you for ages. Thanks for coming.' He did put his arms around her, pulled her in tight, kissed the top of her head, let go too quickly and stood back.

'Coffee?'

'Yeah, thanks.' What did she smell of now? Guilt? Fear? She wasn't going to lose her children, or her freedom. She walked round to the other side of the kitchen island, rested against the edge. For a second she thought she might faint. She let go of her phone, pushed it away, across the marble top. No word from Frank. She needed to

360

get a grip on reality. 'Your sister's going to be OK, I think. She's better off without Michael anyway. We all are.'

'What's that mean?' Ben said.

'We need to bypass him. Go straight to the people behind his fund. They don't want to deal with intermediaries — weak links like that.'

Ben was making the second coffee, with some expertise. 'Is now the time to be talking about this? With Sam upstairs? She's about to go back to London.' He kept his focus on the machine.

'I hope she doesn't,' said Tatty, reaching for her coffee, short, black and strong, exactly how she wanted it. Before taking a sip, she glanced over her shoulder, catching the overcast day, which was at least falling drily on the garden. Windows would be in short supply in prison. Any glimpse of the outside world would be something, she supposed. She wasn't going to prison. 'She shouldn't be driving, not today. She needs to rest, stay in bed.'

'I've offered to take her.'

'You've just got here.'

'If she wants to go.' He paused, cleared his throat. 'I'm not so sure it's particularly safe round here.'

'It's getting safer by the minute — believe me.' She took a sip of coffee now. 'Your text? You implied you had information.'

'Not sure it'll be anything new to you.'

'Try me.'

'Michael's fund — well, we can all guess where the money comes from.' He took a sip of his coffee.

361

'I'm not worried about that,' said Tatty. 'Cash is cash.'

'Sure,' said Ben, 'as long as you can handle those people should something go wrong.'

'If something goes wrong, something goes wrong. We'll deal with it.'

He took another sip of coffee, draining the small cup. 'More?' he asked.

Tatty hadn't finished hers. Her stomach was not settled. 'I'm OK.'

'Michael's reputation's shit,' Ben said, fixing the machine to go again. 'And I mean within his crowd. His outfit isn't even registered with the FSA — don't know who's monitoring it, if anyone.'

'Suits us,' said Tatty.

'What I heard was, he was given a shaking down the other day — in London. He'd been taking liberties with his percentages, apparently. Getting greedy. They've given him a minder, along with a final warning.'

'Where do you get your information from?' It was all tallying nicely.

'I did some digging. Had some luck, I guess. Not everyone I work with is on the straight and narrow — Dad got me the job, don't forget. I haven't pushed such a line before. Oh, and another thing, he's not Dutch. He's from Belgium. His real name's Alexander Jacobs. He's lucky to be alive, by all accounts.'

'Ben, don't take Sam back to London. I can look after her here best.' Maybe she hadn't needed to shoot Michael. He'd have been taken care of sooner rather than later. It was the message she wanted to get across, however. She

362

believed she'd achieved that. At what cost?

'It's up to her.'

'What about you? You've only been here five minutes.'

'I came for Sam. And Zach. Where's he?'

'Not sure. Try and persuade Sam to stay for me, will you, please?'

'You want everything your way, don't you?'

'The moments when we're all together are rare enough nowadays. Let's make the most of them.'

'Under these circumstances?'

Tatty drank the rest of her coffee in one, not because she felt like it, but because she wanted Ben to make her another. Anything to stop him from leaving already.

'That a car I hear?' Ben said.

She'd heard the thump of a heavy car ride up onto the forecourt as well. She took a large breath, as if she were about to duck under the waves. Not that she'd ever dream of swimming in the North Sea, summer or not. Maybe she should take a short holiday, a week or so in Ibiza, splash around in the pool, if not the Med. Get Sam to come as well. It'd be a good place for her to recuperate, forget things. They could all go. Leave Frank to hold the fort. Assuming he'd carried out all his assignments.

'I'll get it,' said Ben, leaving the kitchen.

If they all flew happily away this summer, for a proper family holiday, she made a pact with herself, crossing her fingers tight, she'd never shoot anyone again. She'd get Frank to do it. He knew about guns.

She heard the door opening and voices out in

the echoing hall. Loud and anxious, though not unfriendly. Familiar too. She didn't leave the kitchen to go and greet them. She stayed by the stone island in case she needed to reach out for something solid to hang onto.

She remained standing there in the kitchen on her own for far too long. Finally, Frank appeared. 'Jesus, what's happened to your head?'

'Wasn't looking where I was going,' he said. His face, the bits that currently worked, seemed full of questions for her. His eyes were practically begging for answers.

She could have done with a few as well. Except Ben appeared, with Sam. 'Hey, darling,' she said to her daughter. Sam smiled. A proper smile. Tatty watched her walk over to the table and sit slowly. She was as white as the cloud tumbling down onto the garden.

'We need breakfast,' Ben said.

'You're not going?'

'Not if there're any eggs. I'm going to make Sam an omelette.'

Tatty was surprised. She didn't know that Ben could cook. She wanted to meet this alleged girlfriend of his. She hoped he cooked for her.

'Zach's gone straight upstairs,' Ben said. 'He's in a mess. Blood all over his clothes.'

Tatty looked at Frank. Frank raised one eyebrow. The other eyebrow was lost in the bruise.

'He's not hurt,' said Frank.

'You and me, let's go into the study for a chat,' she said, walking round the counter, wanting to get him out of the kids' earshot.

'Sure,' said Frank, following her out of the room.

'Who's scribbled on the cover of my *Vogue?*' Sam shouted behind them.

In the study, Frank sunk onto the sofa like a vast lump of wet clay. Tatty hadn't said he could sit down. Mildly affronted, she took the desk chair, which was already swung round so it faced the room. She hated this chair, hated this room. She couldn't work in here or from home, she suddenly knew. It wasn't the place for business. She'd get the Smokehouse patched up as quickly as possible.

'Zach's fine,' Frank said, 'he's had a shock, that's all. Witnessed stuff no one wants to see. A thorough scrub, fresh clothes, he'll live. Might be good if he got away for a week or so. Took a holiday.'

'I've been thinking, it might be good if I took all the kids to Ibiza. Lovely time of year there. You wouldn't mind staying put, keeping an eye on things, would you?'

'No problem,' he said. 'I've got no wish to go anywhere. There's plenty to catch up on in my garden as it is.' He smiled.

Tatty could have leant over and hugged him. Instead, she looked at her hands. 'Where the fuck've you been? Who clonked you? Have you done what you said you were going to do? What's Zach seen?' She was shaking her head with the enormity of it all.

'Sands is out of the way. There's been a complication, though. The snub ended up in the wrong hands, courtesy of the guys who drive around in that fucking white bronco.'

'Where's the gun now? Don't tell me Zach's part of this.'

Frank scratched his forehead, the small bit that wasn't livid. 'I'm not happy they smashed me on the head, but they didn't kill me. They might have let someone else go as well.'

'Zach?'

'Liam and Sian weren't so lucky,' he said. 'According to Zach, and I believe him, they went for each other. You don't want to know any more details than that.'

'This time I think you're right — I don't. What about the police?'

'They'll be all over Yarmouth for weeks. Not sure how much they'll link up, the way they operate. There's a new guy, so who knows.'

'You've still got a contact though?'

'She'll do what she can. We don't want them connecting Rolly Andrews with the fire at the Smokehouse. We need those fire investigators to confirm it was an electrical fault.'

'They'll do that,' said Tatty. 'I've got their names. We can always get Nathan to put up his hand as well. Get him to accept negligence or something — that he'd hired dodgy contractors. Pay him for the trouble. He's short of cash, and it's not as if it'd land him in the nick.' Frank looked at her as if to say, you're above that — mucking around with grey-haired architects. She knew, all right. 'It was Rolly Andrews who lit the fuse for sure, was it?'

'Yeah. Sands, and Simon, bribed him with the offer of buying the caravan park.'

'Rich could never buy that bloody park for love nor money.'

'Rolly was ill. Thought he'd do what he could for his daughter. Leave her a little nest egg. Imagine having a parent who'd do that for you? Sweet.'

'Shit,' said Tatty.

'Zach's pretty cut up about her.'

'He hasn't had many successful relationships.' She looked at Frank now, as if to say, Have you?

He looked down at his feet — a pair of black brogues. 'She's dead, Tatty. Be good for you all to get away, relax, sit by the pool. I'll keep you informed if the heat rises.'

'And if it does? What are we meant to do, sail away to South America?'

He smiled. Said nothing. What could he say?

'There're too many loose ends, Frank. The Hummer lot for starters?' She didn't mention what she'd seen down by the lifeboat station. The RNLI readying for action. Maybe she'd imagined it.

'They'll want what those gangs always want — territory.'

'And we're going to give it to them?'

'We can open a dialogue,' Frank said. 'There're places in Yarmouth we don't need to control. I'd be more than happy to give them some streets — in exchange.'

'Not sure how that'll go down with our backers, both sets?'

'Dialogue, Tatty.'

'Since when have you become United Nations?'

'Always worth trying to have a conversation, to begin with.'

She wanted an enforcer not a bloody diplomat. 'Don't go soft on me, Frank. I know you've had a bump on the head.' The room was already airless.

'Want to tell me about Michael?' he said.

Did he doubt her strength, determination, resolve? She did. She needed so much more practise at this. But she'd made that pact. 'Like Sands, he's out of the way. As long as he doesn't resurface too soon.'

Frank nodded, a chunk of admiration on his face. 'The right message will be sent back?'

'Hope so, if Hans knows what's good for him.'

'They're doing a lifeboat drill this morning. The inshore and offshore boats, the helicopter. Let's hope they don't spot anything too soon.'

Tatty laughed, nervously. 'A drill? Really?' She sighed.

'Yeah, an exercise. That's what they said. You want to go and watch it?'

'Fuck off.' She still wasn't going to tell him she'd been down there this morning, and had seen as much. Then he would have known she'd spent the night with Nathan. She didn't want him thinking she was that weak, anybody's. She wanted him to give her the fireman's number. *A drill?* She was so relieved, for half a second. 'Want to tell me about Simon?'

Frank sighed. Leaned forward. Put his elbows on his knees. 'He's gone. The hotel wasn't sure when he left. He didn't check out, but took his stuff. His car.'

'You were meant to get to him last night, to stop this happening. Shit.'

'I was unconscious for a large part of it. He must have found out about Sands.'

'Simon's got away — again?' Tatty's voice was raising.

'The only place he can go is off the face of this earth. My American friend is on standby if he gets that far. Where's my gun? I need it back.'

'It's in the Yare. You'll have to get yourself a new one. One that's clean.'

'None of them are clean.'

'I can't fucking believe this.' Tatty stood.

'I'll get him next time,' Frank said, also standing. 'I need to ring a mate. He'll be helping me with some transportation later. I said I'd drive Zach to Stansted first. Do you all want a lift?'

'Fuck's sake, Frank. How am I meant to run a business with you? You fail to do the most important bloody thing.'

'You don't run a business with me. I work for you — there's a big difference.'

'I've been thinking,' she hadn't, not for long, but it suddenly seemed to make sense, if she wasn't going to be carted away for swabbing and questioning, 'that you do need to run the business with me.' Something deep inside her was fluttering, because she realised she wanted it, she needed it, so much. She'd never felt like this in a business situation before. She was still new to the corporate world, and knew she couldn't do it on her own. Even if he had failed to extinguish Simon — not entirely Frank's fault. He'd been unconscious. The poor man did have a terrible bruise on his head. Perhaps she'd gone soft. Always had been. 'The kids don't seem ready to step up,' she added.

'I get a new company car? That Lexus?'

'Of course.'

'Shares?'

'I'm happy to split my share with you. What do I need all that money for?' She didn't need a super yacht with a helipad. She already had a villa in the sun. 'I'm not greedy. The kids' share will always be theirs.' A new fella, with sparkling blue eyes, now that was a different matter. They were out in the hall. 'I guess I need to get organised if we're going away — tell Sam and Ben.' She headed for the kitchen.

'Tatty, you know what?' He'd got his phone out. One she didn't recognise. He was looking quizzically at the screen. Appeared he wasn't familiar with it either. 'I'd only leave those shares to you and your kids anyway. Let's forget the paperwork.'

'I'm not sure I'd have had it written down anyway,' she said over her shoulder. 'There is something I'd like written down, however. The telephone number of a certain fireman.'

'Competition in the boardroom already,' Frank chuckled behind her.

It hadn't occurred to Tatty that the fireman might have been gay. If he knew Frank, moonlighted as a bouncer for his club? Fuck's sake. But that didn't mean for sure.

There was thick smoke in the kitchen, a dirty contrail at head height; the smell of burnt eggs, butter, toast. Sam and Ben were at the table. They were eating. 'We do have an extractor fan,' Tatty said, furious, though not with her kids. 'Turn it on next time.'

She retreated into the hall. Frank was on the phone. To whom? She'd check on Zach, before presenting Sam and Ben with the holiday plans. She might check her bikini situation while she was upstairs as well. It had been a while. Maybe she'd meet someone on the beach.

We do hope that you have enjoyed reading this large print book.

Did you know that all of our titles are available for purchase?

We publish a wide range of high quality large print books including:
Romances, Mysteries, Classics General Fiction Non Fiction and Westerns

Special interest titles available in large print are:
The Little Oxford Dictionary Music Book Song Book Hymn Book Service Book

Also available from us courtesy of Oxford University Press:
Young Readers' Dictionary (large print edition) Young Readers' Thesaurus (large print edition)

For further information or a free brochure, please contact us at:
Ulverscroft Large Print Books Ltd., The Green, Bradgate Road, Anstey, Leicester, LE7 7FU, England. Tel: (00 44) 0116 236 4325
Fax: (00 44) 0116 234 0205

HARBOUR STREET

Ann Cleeves

As thick snow blankets Newcastle, boisterous crowds of Christmas revellers jostle onto the Metro. And Margaret Krukowski — sitting quietly in the middle of the busy train — is viciously murdered, though nobody sees the stabbing take place. Margaret's murderer is seemingly invisible; her killing motiveless. As DI Vera Stanhope arrives at the scene, she feels a familiar buzz of anticipation, sensing that this will be a complex and unusual case. When a second woman is murdered just days later, Vera knows that the key to this new killing will be found in Margaret's past. What was troubling this reserved, elegant lady so much before she died? Vera can feel in her bones that there's a link between the killings — one that she must discover before another life is lost . . .

THE LATE SHOW

Michael Connelly

Detective Renee Ballard, once one of the department's young hotshots, now works 'The Late Show', the graveyard shift at the LAPD. It's a thankless job keeping strange hours in a twilight world of tragedy and violence, handing over her investigations as the sun rises, never getting closure. Some nights are worse than others. And tonight is the worst yet. Two cases: a brutal assault, and a multiple murder with no suspect. Ballard knows it is always darkest before dawn. But what she doesn't know is how deep her dual investigation will take her into the dark heart of her city, her department, and her past . . .

THE BIRDWATCHER

William Shaw

Police Sergeant William South has a reason for not wanting to be on the murder investigation: he is a murderer himself. But the victim was his only friend; like him, a passionate birdwatcher. South and his new partner find the body, violently beaten, forced inside a wooden chest. Only rage could kill a man like this; South knows it. Soon — too soon — they find a suspect: Donnie Fraser, a drifter from Northern Ireland. His presence in Kent disturbs William, because he knew him as a boy. If the past is catching up with him, South wants to meet it head on. For even as he desperately investigates the connections, he knows there is no crime, however duplicitous or cruel, that can compare to the great lie of his childhood.

THE VISITORS

Catherine Burns

Marion Zetland lives with her domineering older brother, John, in a decaying Georgian townhouse on the edge of a northern seaside resort. A timid spinster in her fifties who still sleeps with teddy bears, Marion does her best to shut out the shocking secret that John keeps in the cellar. Until, suddenly, John has a heart attack, and Marion is forced to go down to the cellar herself and face the gruesome truth that her brother has kept hidden. As questions are asked and secrets unravel, maybe John isn't the only one with a dark side . . .

PERSONS UNKNOWN

Susie Steiner

As dusk falls, a young man staggers through a park, far from home, bleeding from a stab wound. He dies where he falls, cradled by a stranger, a woman's name on his lips in his last seconds of life. DI Manon Bradshaw can't help but take an interest — these days she only handles cold cases, but the man died just yards from the police station where she works. She's horrified to discover that both the victim and prime suspect are more closely linked to her than she could have imagined. And as the Cambridgeshire police close ranks against her, she is forced to contemplate the unthinkable. How well does she know her loved ones, and are they capable of murder?